Alexander McCall Smith is the author of over sixty books on a wide array of subjects. For many years he was Professor of Medical Law at the University of Edinburgh and served on national and international bioethics bodies. Then in 1999 he achieved global recognition for his award-winning series The No.1 Ladies' Detective Agency, and thereafter has devoted his time to the writing of fiction, including the 44 Scotland Street series and the Isabel Dalhousie novels. His books have been translated into forty-five languages. He lives in Edinburgh with his wife, Elizabeth, a doctor.

Praise for Alexander McCall Smith and the Corduroy Mansions series

'Other novelists can only eye with envy Alexander McCall Smith's apparently inexhaustible ability to conjure up characters and incidents, devise conversations, and mix comedy with moral reflections on the way we live now'
Allan Massie, *Scotsman*

'Bags of warmth and wisdom and easy, accomplished writing that begs for a comfy chair and a supersize cocoa'
The Times

'Seriousness is always sugar-dusted with Alexander McCall Smith's delight in the ridiculous and his perfectly paced humour'
Helen Brown, *Daily Telegraph*

'When it comes to the light touch, no one beats Alexander McCall Smith'
James Naughtie, *Financial Times*

'The best scenes, as in all McCall Smith's work, feature nothing more earth-shattering than conversation: little tête-à-têtes in which normally shy people open their hearts to each other'
David Robson, *Sunday Telegraph*

'Told with warmth, wit and intelligence, it's a page-turner with many happy endings. Perfect'
Daily Express

ALEXANDER McCALL SMITH

THE DOG WHO CAME IN FROM THE COLD

A CORDUROY MANSIONS NOVEL

ABACUS

First published in Great Britain in 2010 by Polygon, an imprint of Birlinn Ltd
This paperback edition published in 2011 by Abacus
Reprinted 2011

A CIP catalogue record for this book
is available from the British Library.

ISBN 978-0-349-12321-9

Typeset by Palimpsest Book Production Limited,
Falkirk, Stirlingshire
Printed and bound in Great Britain by
Clays Ltd, St Ives plc

Abacus
An imprint of
Little, Brown Book Group
100 Victoria Embankment
London EC4Y 0DY

An Hachette UK Company
www.hachette.co.uk

www.littlebrown.co.uk

This book is for Michael Holman

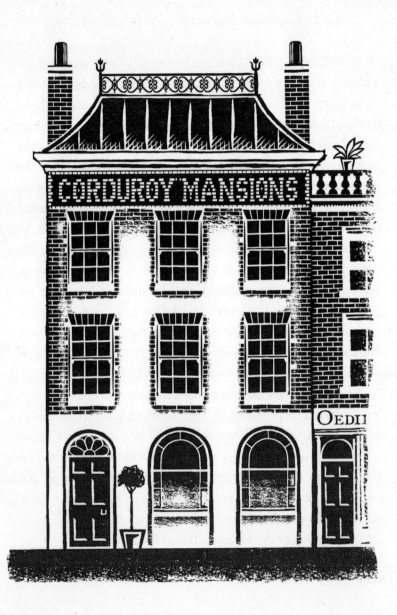

1. *What Our Furniture Says About Us*

William French, wine merchant, Master of Wine (failed), some-where in his early fifties (hardly noticeably, particularly in the right light), loyal subscriber to *Rural Living* (although he lived quite happily in central London), long-time supporter of several good causes (he was a kind man at heart, with a strong sense of fairness), widower, dog-owner, and much else besides; the same William French looked about his flat in Corduroy Mansions, as anybody might survey his or her flat in a moment of self-assessment, of stocktaking.

There was a lot wrong with it, he decided, just as he felt there was a lot that was not quite right with his life in general. Sorting out one's flat, though, is often easier than sorting out oneself, and there is a great deal to be said for first getting one's flat in order before attempting the same thing with one's life. Perhaps there was an adage for this – a pithy Latin expres-sion akin to *mens sana in corpore sano*. Which made him think . . . Everybody knew that particular expression, of course; every-body, that is, except William's twenty-eight-year-old son, Eddie, who had once rendered it within his father's hearing as 'men's saunas lead to a healthy body'. William had been about to laugh at this ingenious translation, redolent, as it was, of the cod Latin he had found so achingly funny as a twelve-year-old boy: *Caesar adsum iam forte, Pompey ad erat. Pompey sic in omnibus, Caesar sic in at.* Caesar had some jam for tea, Pompey had a rat . . . and so on. But then he realised that Eddie was serious.

The discovery that Eddie had no knowledge of Latin had depressed him. He knew that the overwhelming majority of people had no Latin and did not feel the lack of it. The problem with Eddie, though, was that not only did he not have Latin, he had virtually nothing else either: no mathematics worthy of the name, no geography beyond a knowledge of the location of various London pubs, no knowledge of biology or any of the other natural sciences, no grasp of history. When it came to making an inventory of what Eddie knew, there was really very little to list.

He put his son out of his mind and returned to thinking about the proposition *mens sana in corpore sano*. Was there an equivalent, he wondered, to express the connection between an ordered flat and an ordered life? *Vita ordinata in domo ordinata*? It sounded all right, he felt – indeed, it sounded rather impressive – but he found himself feeling a little bit unsure about the Latin. *Domus* was feminine, was it not? But was it not one of those fourth declension nouns where there was an alternative ablative form – *domu* rather than *domo*? William was not certain, and so he put that out of his mind too.

He walked slowly about his flat, moving from room to room, thinking of what would be necessary to *reform* it completely. Starting in the drawing room, he looked at the large oriental carpet that dominated the centre of the room. It was said that some such carpets gained in value as the years went past, but he could not see this happening to his red Baluch carpet, which was beginning to look distinctly tattered at the edges. Then there was the furniture, and here there was no doubt that the chairs, if once they had been fashionable, no longer were. If there was furniture that spoke of its decade, then these chairs positively shouted the seventies, a period in which it was generally agreed design lost its way. It would all, he thought, have to be got rid of and replaced with the sort of furniture that he saw advertised in the weekend magazines of the newspapers. *Timeless elegance* was the claim made on behalf of such furniture, and timeless elegance, William considered, was exactly what he needed.

He would give his own furniture to one of those organisations that collect it and pass it on to people who have no furniture of their own and no money to buy any. The thought of this process gave him a feeling of warmth. He could just imagine somebody in a less favoured part of London waiting with anticipation as a completely free consignment of surplus furniture – in this case William's – was unloaded. He pictured a person who had previously sat on the floor now sitting comfortably on this Corduroy Mansions armchair, not noticing the large stain on the cushion of which Eddie had denied all knowledge, though it was definitely his responsibility. It was a most unpleasant stain, that one, and William had never enquired as to exactly what it was. Yet he had noticed that Marcia, when she had lived with him, had studiously avoided ever sitting on that chair. And who could blame her?

Our furniture, he reflected, says so much about us, and our tastes – perhaps more than we like to acknowledge. We may not like a piece of furniture now, but the awkward fact remains that we *once* were a person who liked it. And unlike clothes, which are jettisoned with passing fashion, furniture has a habit of staying with us, reminding us of tasteless stages of our lives. William looked at his settee; he had bought it at a furniture shop off the Tottenham Court Road – he remembered that much – but he would never buy something like that now. And certainly not in that colour. Did they still make mauve furniture? he wondered.

He moved on to the kitchen. William liked his kitchen, and often sat there on summer evenings, looking out of the window over the roof-tops behind Corduroy Mansions, watching the sun sink over west London. Sometimes, if conditions were right, the dying sun would touch the edge of the clouds with gold, making for a striking contrast with the sky beyond, as sharply delineated as in a Maxfield Parrish painting. He would sit there and think about nothing in particular, vaguely grateful for the display that nature was providing but also conscious of the fact that there was not enough beauty in his life and that it would be nice to have more.

Now, surveying his kitchen from the doorway, he saw not the outside vista but the inside – the cork floor that needed replacing, the scratched surfaces that surely fostered an ecosystem in which whole legions, entire divisions of *Pseudomonas* were encamped. Best not to think about *that*, nor about the bacteria which undoubtedly romped around the faithful body of his dog, Freddie de la Hay, who was sitting on the kitchen floor, looking up at his master in mute adoration, and wondering, perhaps, what the problem was.

2. *Chinese Submarines*

Freddie de la Hay was a Pimlico Terrier, an unusual breed obtained through the judicious crossing of an Airedale with a Border Collie, and perhaps just a touch of something else about which the breeders themselves were now hazy. There were very few Pimlico Terriers in Pimlico itself, although William had once seen an advertisement in a local shop window for a meeting of the Pimlico Terrier Owners' Club. He had thought for a moment that this was a meeting he should attend, but then stopped and asked himself why. What was the point of a group of dog-owners getting together? What made them think that they would have anything in common, or indeed anything to talk about, apart from Pimlico Terriers of course, a topic of conversation that surely would be rapidly exhausted. It was the same with motorcyclists – why did motorcyclists insist on congregating and travelling in large, leather-clad packs? Did it actually have anything to do with being a motor-cyclist, or was it just because they were all a particular type of person who could then talk about the things they felt they had in common? Identity, of course, was a complex matter – he knew as much, and so did Freddie de la Hay, who always liked to encounter other dogs and explore their identities when William took him for walks.

'He likes to see his friends,' Marcia had once remarked when accompanying William and Freddie on an evening walk through the immediate neighbourhood of Corduroy Mansions. 'He likes to be reminded that other dogs exist. Makes him feel less lonely.'

5

'Possibly,' said William. 'I suppose he does *identify*.'

'Of course he does,' said Marcia. 'He knows which side he's on.'

William thought that this was doubtful, if not plainly wrong; dogs were *not* on the side of other dogs, at least not when it came to a choice between another dog and their owner. In such circumstances they always chose their owner, because he or she led the pack to which they belonged. That was just how dogs saw it. Very few dogs would ever join a strange dog in an attack on his owner, other than in the fog of battle, the special circumstances of a dog fight; they just would not. It might be different if the dogs were members of the same pack; that might involve confusion which could lead to a dog turning on his owner, but otherwise it would never occur.

Marcia said things that were, quite simply, wrong, even though she said them, as then, with an air of calm authority. It was a difficult issue between the two friends, and William found himself torn between benignly ignoring her solecisms and misinterpretations, or correcting them, which could lead to an edgy debate and a slight air of offence on Marcia's part.

It happened quite often, particularly in those months when Marcia had stayed with William at Corduroy Mansions, following her successful campaign to encourage Eddie to move out. Usually it began with a general observation from Marcia about something she had read in the papers or heard from one of her clients. This observation would be made in such a way as to invite approving comment from William, often with the phrase 'I'm sure you will agree' added at the end.

There had been an egregious example only a few weeks

earlier, when Marcia had called in on her way back from a catering engagement. She had been sitting in the kitchen drinking a small glass of Amontillado that William had poured for her, when she had suddenly said: 'You know the Chinese kidnapped an Australian Prime Minister once. You know that, don't you?'

William looked at her over the rim of his glass. 'That chap? The one who drowned?' He had heard this nonsense before, not from Marcia, but from a book he had picked up and read while waiting his turn at the hairdressers. It was a well-thumbed paperback called *Things They Don't Want You to Know*, and it had included this story.

'He didn't drown,' snapped Marcia. 'He was called Harold Holt, and he didn't drown.'

William pursed his lips. 'Oh. Well . . .'

'He was picked up by a Chinese submarine,' continued Marcia. 'It was waiting offshore because they knew he was going swimming. They got him.'

William shook his head. 'I doubt it,' he said. 'Why would they do a thing like that?'

Marcia looked mysterious. 'They think in centuries,' she said. 'As you know.'

William stared at her. This was one of the reasons why it would be impossible to have Marcia as anything more than a friend. It was not that she was always irrational – she was not – but there were times when he found it difficult to fathom how she thought. For his part, he was used to reaching a conclusion on the basis of what he knew to be true from the evidence of his senses. Marcia seemed to go about it in a very different way. She leaped to conclusions, and then tried to construct a basis for her position after the fact. And she would often also resort to the most extraordinary non sequiturs, as she did with this reference to the Chinese thinking in centuries. That was their diplomacy, was it not – they took the long view – but he did not see the relevance of this to the alleged kidnapping of an Australian Prime Minister.

No, he could not become romantically involved with Marcia because he could not bring himself to admire her mind – and that, for William, was a very important part of romance. For some men, the old saw that they never made passes at women in glasses might be true, but it was not true for William. He liked women in glasses because it was suggestive of intelligence, which he found a very attractive quality. Of course glasses were really nothing to do with intellect – he knew that – but relations between people were often affected by vague, subliminal associations, and somewhere in William's mind there was an equiparation of eyewear and sexual attraction.

And why not? A dimple was only an indentation in the flesh, but how powerful could that minor imperfection be. A well-placed gluteal mass could tip the balance from indifference to ardent, urgent attraction. What indiscretions, what acts of human folly, have been triggered by such little things; how weak men were, and women too perhaps – but not quite as much.

William looked at Freddie. 'Freddie, old chap,' he said. 'I really must do something about getting myself a lady friend. You know how it is, don't you?'

Freddie looked up at William, listening attentively. He had

a very limited vocabulary, a small number of words that he recognised, and he was straining to pick up one of these. Just one. *Walk* or *biscuit* would do very well; but now he could make out no such profoundly welcome sounds, and he resigned himself to staring at his master, ready for what was coming next, whatever it was.

It was the doorbell.

3. *A Middle-class Woman Comes to the Door*

When William opened the door, it was to find a woman standing before him – an attractive woman in her forties, wearing a navy-blue trouser suit and, most significantly, a pair of elegant gold-rimmed glasses. He had seen her before some-where – he was sure of it – but he could not place her now. Was she collecting for the lifeboats perhaps? Or for the Heart Foundation? Was she something to do with the Neighbourhood Watch? He tried hard to remember, but could not.

The woman smiled. 'I'm sorry to disturb you,' she said. 'I meant to phone you first, but I lost your number.'

So she knew him. 'Not at all,' he reassured her, gesturing for her to enter. 'This is quite convenient. I was doing nothing.' Actually, he thought, I was doing something. I was thinking about my life and how I need to meet a woman, and lo and behold . . . But that could not be said, of course; like most of our thoughts, William reflected, which can be thought but not said.

The visitor stretched out a hand. 'Angelica Brockelbank.'

William shook her hand. It was soft to the touch. 'Of course.' Angelica Brockelbank?

'Would you like tea?' he blurted out. Tea was so convenient. Not only was it an appropriate and immediate response to any crisis – 'Sit down and I'll put the kettle on' – but it was also a tool for social stalling. Tea would allow this encounter to proceed to the next stage, which William hoped would be the stage of discovering who Angelica Brockelbank was.

But then it came back. Angelica Brockelbank – of course! She had run the bookshop next to William's first wine shop in Notting Hill, a good fifteen years ago. They had seen a certain amount of one another and then, when William had moved to larger premises they had lost touch. She had been beautiful then, but William had been married at the time – as had she – and had admired her from a respectable distance. He wondered now whether she was still married, and whether there might just be a chance . . . He hardly dared think about it.

'It's wonderful to see you again, Angelica,' he said with renewed confidence. 'After all those years. How's the book-shop doing?'

Angelica, who had sensed that William was having trouble placing her, looked relieved. 'That's very much in the past, I'm afraid. Actually, I closed it fairly soon after you moved. It didn't make much, you know, and I decided to get a job. Something with a salary.'

'Understandable,' said William. 'Business is all very well, but . . .'

'Yes. A salary is a salary.'

He led her into the kitchen and filled the kettle with water.

'And your husband?' He had only met her husband a few times and could not remember his name. Rick?

'Dick and I are divorced,' said Angelica. 'Utterly amicably. And we're still very good friends.'

'It's so much better that way,' said William. 'It's ghastly when people fight. And they so often do, don't they?'

Angelica nodded. 'We just decided that we were friends but not lovers. It was as simple as that. He remarried – a German doctor, a radiologist, who's charming – and it's worked out very well for everybody.' She paused. 'You would have thought that a radiologist would see through him, but there we are. And you? I was sorry to hear . . .'

'Yes,' said William. 'It was very sudden. Poor Maggie.'

He wondered how she had heard about it. He was not aware of their having any mutual friends, but London was a village in spite of its size – people could humanise even the largest of cities.

'And your son?' Angelica asked.

'Eddie.'

'Yes, of course.'

She waited for him to answer. 'Eddie's fine,' he said. 'He stayed here until about six months ago. He was one of those offspring who find the parental home so comfortable that they're disinclined to leave.'

Angelica nodded sympathetically. 'I gather that it happens.'

'Eddie found somebody,' William went on. 'A rather nice woman, in fact. They're together. She has a place in the Windward Islands and they spend half the year there.'

'What a dream,' said Angelica. 'Six months in the Windward Islands. How very fortunate.'

William nodded. Eddie did not deserve his good fortune, he felt; if Fate was going to allocate either of them a place in the Windward Islands, surely it should be to him, rather than to Eddie? But he knew that this was not the way Fate operated; she handed out her benefits according to a scheme that was beyond the comprehension of mere mortals. Perhaps the Greeks, he decided, had had a better understanding of the world in predicating the existence of entirely arbitrary, capricious gods; such gods would take no account of hard work or public service when allocating places in the Windward Islands.

William switched on the kettle and took two cups out of the cupboard above the sink. 'And you?' he asked. 'What are you up to these days?'

He hoped that the answer to the question might reveal the reason for this unexpected – though welcome – call. She could hardly just have dropped in, particularly after fifteen years; people rarely did that in London – not any more.

'I'm working for the government,' said Angelica. 'After I closed the bookshop, I answered an advertisement in the papers. A job in information processing.'

William wondered what information processing was. The trouble with job descriptions like that was that they frequently disguised something much more mundane. There used to be clerks, until they were abolished and became ... what had clerks become? Perhaps they had disappeared altogether.

'It was at GCHQ,' Angelica continued. 'You must know the place.'

William did. Government Communications Headquarters was a vast building outside Cheltenham, a place that bristled with aerials, even if mainly metaphorical ones, and hummed with electronic activity. So information processing in ordinary English was eavesdropping.

'How interesting,' he said. 'Monitoring radio traffic.'

Angelica smiled. 'Yes. Or the equivalent. I hadn't intended to get into that line of things, but it was a regular job and I wanted to get out of London for a while. And I found I really enjoyed it.'

William agreed that it must be interesting. But what qualifications, he wondered, did Angelica have for the job? Or was a job at GCHQ like a place in the Windward Islands – allocated with no regard to desert?

'They took me because of my degree in Russian,' Angelica said. 'I don't know if you were aware that I studied Russian at university.'

William was not.

'Well, I did,' said Angelica. 'I went to St Andrews. Russian was quite a popular subject in those days. I didn't use it very much, of course – not when I was running the bookshop. But then it came in very handy when I went to GCHQ.'

'It would,' said William, picturing Angelica at a desk, in headphones, in front of a crystal radio, a frown of concentration on her brow.

'And then I was transferred,' Angelica continued. 'Back to London. To MI6.'

William thought that he had misheard her. 'MI6?'

'Yes,' said Angelica calmly. 'Intelligence work. But of a different sort.'

4. *The Dangers of* Boeuf Stroganoff

For a few moments after Angelica's revelation, William said nothing. He had read of MI6, of course, and had passed its building near Vauxhall Bridge on numerous occasions. For an organisation whose business was secrets, the building seemed hardly appropriate, being, as it was, quite open-looking, and apparently not at all suitable for shady work of the sort that MI6 – and presumably Angelica herself – engaged in.

He knew, as everybody did, that it was MI6 headquarters and had speculated on what went on within. He had seen people going in and out of the front door – quite openly – and they had seemed to him to be no different from the people who went in and out of any building in the City, for example. And perhaps their jobs were not all that different from the jobs of any others among the legions of civil servants who worked in London. They attended meetings, no doubt, wrote memos, and strove, he imagined, to meet targets. At the end of the day they probably went home in much the same mood as everybody else, leaving behind the cares of the office. He wondered if they had a clear-desk policy, as other organisations had, whereby there would be no papers left un-filed by the time work finished at five o'clock. He thought that they probably did; the sort of papers these people dealt with certainly could not be left lying about for the prying eyes of cleaners who might have been recruited by *the other side*. And it would be very easy, he reckoned, to recruit a cleaner; their weakness was *tea*, and they could doubtless be tempted by a large cup of Darjeeling . . .

He smiled at Angelica. 'Well, I must say that I'm somewhat surprised. I've never met anybody who actually works there.'

Angelica returned his smile. There was nothing guarded about her manner; she seemed completely open and unembarrassed. 'I know that it takes many people by surprise, but it's essentially an ordinary job. I don't really think about it, you know.'

'A daily grind like everything else?'

Angelica thought for a moment. 'To an extent. A lot of what I do is pretty mundane, but there are times when things . . . well, when things hot up.'

William was intrigued. Did Angelica ever find herself in danger? He decided to ask her outright, and she shook her head. 'I've never been in physical danger myself – as far as I know. But some of my colleagues have.'

William wanted to know more. 'I suppose you can't say too much,' he said. 'But can you give me an idea of what happened to these colleagues of yours?'

For a few moments Angelica appeared to be weighing the merits of saying more. 'I have to be careful,' she said. 'We're not meant to talk about our work, but . . .'

'I'm very discreet,' said William, putting a finger to his lips. 'I really am.'

The tea was now ready, and William poured a cup for Angelica.

'You may recall a recent very unfortunate case of poisoning,' Angelica said, as she took a sip of her tea. 'A Russian who had got on the wrong side of somebody powerful found that his drink contained a very nasty slow-acting poison. The poor man died.'

William remembered reading about this in the papers. 'There was a row over extradition, wasn't there?'

Angelica nodded. 'HMG was livid. And we didn't like it at the office. We don't like these people fighting their wars on British soil.'

'Of course not.'

'Well,' Angelica went on, 'although that case got into the papers, there was nothing about another attempted poisoning that took place. One of our people was having dinner with a contact in a restaurant. The waiter brought them their main courses, but he had mixed up who had ordered what. Our man was given the *boeuf stroganoff* instead of the pan-fried salmon. So he swapped the plates around and his contact – a completely innocent member of a foreign embassy – took a couple of fork-fuls of the *boeuf stroganoff* and became violently ill. It had been intended for our man, of course.'

William grimaced. 'Just like the Pope.'

'The Pope?'

'Yes,' said William. 'John Paul the First – the one who lasted thirty-three days, or whatever it was. He was entertaining some grandee of an Eastern Rite church – one of their patriarchs, or whatever – and his visitor took one sip of his coffee and keeled over.'

Angelica looked dubious. 'In the Vatican?'

'In the Vatican,' said William. 'And then, of course, the Pope himself succumbed later on. No autopsy. No normal procedures. Just popped into his red slippers and buried. It was very odd, if you ask me.'

Angelica smiled. 'You have to be wary of these conspiracy theories,' she said. 'Most untoward events have a very simple, rational explanation. The Pope's visitor probably had a heart attack – it was probably nothing to do with the coffee. And John Paul the First himself was certainly not murdered. We know that for a fact.'

William raised an eyebrow. 'How can you be so sure?'

'Because we have our man in the Vatican,' said Angelica. 'We had a very full report from him, and he indicated that all those rumours were groundless.'

William could not conceal his surprise. 'You have your man in the Vatican? A spy?'

Angelica shrugged. 'Of course we do. He's a highly placed cleric. A monsignor. He works in the Holy Office.'

'And he spies for you?'

Angelica held up a hand. 'Steady on. I wouldn't call it spying. He reports, that's all.'

'But what possible interest do you have in Vatican affairs? They're hardly a threat to our security.'

It was Angelica's turn to raise an eyebrow. 'You think not? You should study history, William. The Vatican has been meddling in the affairs of other sovereign states for centuries. They have a very clear idea of what's in their interests and how to achieve it. And why not? If you look at it from their point of view, why not attempt to ensure that things work out in the way they want? Everybody else does precisely that.'

William was at a loss as to what to say. He was astonished by the disclosure that Angelica had made, but there was something else that was also puzzling him: why was she telling him all this, and, more than that, why had she come to see him in the first place? This, he thought, was not a purely social call.

He glanced at her tea cup, which was empty. 'More?'

She slid her tea cup towards him. 'You may be wondering—'

He cut her short. 'I certainly am.'

She watched as he poured the tea into her cup. 'Well, I'd expect you to wonder why I've come to see you and also why I'm speaking about my work – which is meant to be confidential.'

He nodded. 'I am.'

'You know that we've been watching you?'

William gasped. Had he been *under suspicion*?

Angelica was quick to reassure him. 'No, we don't have anything on you. We call it a friendly watch. Perfectly friendly.'

'Then what . . . ?'

'We want to ask a favour,' Angelica said. 'You can say no, and we'll leave it right there. But if you say yes . . . well, HMG would be terrifically grateful.' She paused, watching him closely. 'What did JFK say to his people at his inauguration? "Ask not what your country can do for you, but what you can do for your country." He said that, didn't he?'

'I believe so,' said William. His mouth was dry, and he found himself thinking, somewhat uncomfortably, of *boeuf stroganoff*.

5. A Nice Boy

While William was engaged in his curious, ultimately rather alarming conversation with Angelica, in the flat directly below his in Corduroy Mansions Caroline was making a series of telephone calls, the last of which was to her friend James.

Caroline and James had known one another for not much more than a year, but each felt as if the other was an old friend. They had met on the first day of the course on which they were both enrolled at Sotheby's Art Institute – a one-year Master's course in art history designed specifically for those with their sights on a career in the fine art auction rooms or in a gallery. There were twenty-three people on the course that year, every one of them paying, or rather having paid on their behalf, the seventeen thousand pounds in fees that the course commanded. In Caroline's case this cost was borne by her father, a reasonably well-off land agent in Cheltenham. He had grumbled about it, but had eventually come to share his wife's view that the chances of Caroline's meeting what she described, with no trace of irony, as *a nice boy* were substantially increased by her being involved in the world of expensive auctions. Little did he know.

James met the fees for the course himself, dipping into a legacy left him by an aunt. The legacy was enough to pay the fees and keep him for that year and perhaps a year or two beyond. 'And then it's work,' he said. 'Reality catches up with one, you know – sooner or later.'

For Caroline, reality had taken the form of a job with Tim Something, the photographer. He had offered to take her on as his assistant at a salary that seemed extremely generous. She had accepted the offer, and had recently completed her first week in her new job. James, who had settled for a six-week unpaid internship in one of the auction houses, was now anxiously awaiting the firm's decision on whether he would be allowed to stay on. The Old Master's department had a vacancy, but was reluctant to commit just yet. James suspected that the job was being kept in reserve for somebody else, and was feeling pessimistic.

'They'll never take me,' he had complained to Caroline. 'I'm not nearly grand enough.'

Caroline had sought to reassure him. 'Nonsense,' she said. 'It's not like that any more. Nobody cares about things like that – not these days.'

'But they do,' protested James. 'If you look at the people who work there, they're tremendously grand. They really are. They're all called Michael de Whatsit, or the Honourable This or That, and so on. I'd be the only ordinary person.'

'Rubbish,' said Caroline. 'You're not ordinary. You're really unusual.'

There was an awkward silence.

'I mean, you're really extraordinary,' Caroline blurted out. 'Extraordinary. That's what I mean. You're really extraordinary.'

James looked at her balefully. 'Really? Why do you think I'm extraordinary?'

Caroline looked up at the ceiling. This conversation had taken place in a favourite coffee bar of theirs on Long Acre, and she knew the ceiling well, having frequently stared at it when writing – or planning to write – her final essay of the course, on Alessandro Bonvicino and the Brescia school. Now she noticed how the light coming through the window reflected off the surface of the mirror on the opposite wall, throwing hazy liquid shapes on the ceiling.

'You just are, James,' she said. 'And you should be pleased. Too many people are plain ordinary. You aren't.'

'But why?' asked James again. 'Why am I extraordinary?'

Caroline began to look annoyed. 'It's very difficult to explain,' she said. 'But since you insist, I suppose it's because you're bright. You're much brighter than most people. And you've got good aesthetic judgement – most people have appalling taste, as you well know. And you're funny. You make me laugh.'

James continued to look reproachful. 'But what if I just want to be ordinary? What if I want to be . . . to be like other blokes?'

Caroline watched him carefully. They were on difficult ground now, and she was determined not to say anything tactless. James was not like other blokes – she knew that – but it was not a subject she wished to explore. She was convinced that he was interested in women and simply had not fully reconciled himself to it.

'You're sensitive,' she said. 'It's a great advantage to be sensitive. Most men are . . . well, they're just insensitive. But you aren't. You *feel* things, James.'

James thought about this. 'But what if I don't want to feel things?'

Caroline shook her head. 'That's not an option,' she said. 'You can't decide to be insensitive. You can't *unknow* things.'

'What do you mean *unknow*?'

Caroline thought it perfectly obvious. 'You can't put the genie back in the bottle. Once you have knowledge – whatever knowledge it may be – you can't go back to a state of innocent ignorance. It's like any attempt to return to childhood – we can't.'

'Pity,' said James.

'Maybe. But the point is this: you are a very sensitive, sympathetic man. That makes you extraordinary. And there's nothing you can do to change the fact of your sensitivity – it's who you are, James.'

That conversation had left James feeling vaguely dissatisfied. What Caroline had said about him was complimentary, indeed flattering, but he was not sure that he *wanted* to be a sensitive, sympathetic man. He wanted to be able to identify with the ordinary men he saw every day travelling on the tube or chatting to one another outside the pub – men who seemed to enjoy an easy camaraderie, who appeared not in the least troubled by what other people thought about them. He wanted to stop thinking about other people's feelings. He wanted to stop being so vulnerable to hurt.

But he would not be able to do it without Caroline's help, and he had decided that the only way of securing it was to formalise the relationship between them. He would ask her to be his girl-friend – that was what he would do. He would simply ask her.

When James raised the topic, Caroline was ill-prepared for it, but quickly concealed her surprise.

She reached out and took his hand. 'Is that what you really want, James? Are you sure?'

He was sure. Lowering his voice, he said, 'Yes, I'm sure. I want us to be lovers.' *Lovers* – it was such a luscious, dangerous word, and he could hardly believe that he had used it.

Caroline looked at him. 'Have you got a sore throat?' she asked.

James shook his head. 'Oh, Caroline,' he said, his voice returning to its normal pitch. 'I really do love you, you know. You're everything to me.'

Caroline looked at him in disbelief. She was *not* everything to him, she knew that. What about art? What about the paintings of Nicolas Poussin? What about a whole lot of other things? And yet it was only a figure of speech, of course, and she knew that too.

6. *All Those Germs*

The issue for Caroline was not just a simple choice between Man A and Man B, a choice with which some women might very much have liked to be faced; her choice went beyond that to embrace a third possibility, namely: *neither*.

'I just don't know what to do,' she confided in her mother when she returned to Cheltenham for a weekend with her parents. 'There are these two men, you see, and I really don't know which one to choose. But maybe I shouldn't choose either.'

Caroline's mother had always felt rather irritated by her daughter's indecision in these matters. Her philosophy was uncomplicated: find a man, satisfy yourself as to his suitability, and solvency of course, and then, if everything was in order, proceed with all dispatch to tie him down. It was a clear programme, and one which many of Jane Austen's heroines would have recognised as being highly practical, and indeed the only thing to do.

The option of choosing to remain by oneself was not one which her mother's friends would have entertained at all seriously; for most of them there had never been any question but that one should get married if one possibly could. They appreciated, of course, that life did not always work out as one wished, but single women, they felt, were single for a *reason*. This could be demographic, as when there were simply not enough young men to go round, or it could be a concomitant other misfortune, of looks, perhaps, or attitude. Some women, it had to be accepted, were just too mousy to attract a flicker of interest from men, even from men who were themselves on the shelf, or virtually there – men with pebble-lensed spectacles and sloping shoulders; slightly seedy army officers of questionable tastes; dusty accountants with possessive mothers. Such men were hopeless, it was generally accepted, although there were always women – noble women – who looked beyond these drawbacks, took these men on, and thought of England when necessary. Did such women, Caroline wondered, sometimes utter *in medio rerum* the word *England*? It would be cause for disappointment for the men, she imagined; but better, of course, than the uttering of the name of another man, a known cause of matrimonial discord.

Her mother's generation had simply not understood that women might choose to remain by themselves because they thought the single life better. Of course in their day it was not better – at least not for women, whose career choices were still so unfairly limited by the dominance of men. Caroline, however, belonged to a generation for which there were all sorts of interesting jobs available to women, and indeed many of these jobs were now increasingly a female preserve. Medicine, for instance, was a fallen citadel – so much so that soon the majority of doctors would be women. The law was a harder nut to crack, but cracked it would duly be, as would the worlds of finance, aviation, broadcasting, and so on. Soon there would be no place for men in any of these callings, although there would always be secretarial positions, of course.

So deciding that she did not *need* a man was a real option. And yet, and yet ... The problem was that in spite of the persuasive voices claiming that men were not necessary, she still had the feeling that men were *really rather nice*, and that by and large most women were happier if they had a man to come home to, or a man to come home to them. It sounded tremendously old-fashioned, but it was true. Her mother, naturally, would have been unsurprised by this proposition, but for Caroline it ran counter to the received wisdom to which she had been exposed ever since she first started her studies at university; a received wisdom which stressed independence and liberation from the shackles of heterosexual domesticity. Caroline found herself reaching a conclusion that was the polar opposite of all that: most women needed men, and most men needed women.

If she fell within the majority – and she thought she did – then it precluded the single state – the third option she had identified – and meant that she came back to the choice between A (James) and B (Tim Something, the photographer). Tim Something was very attractive – suave, and handsome – of course, but in James's favour there was, first and foremost, the fact that he was easy company. Like an old pair of sandals or a battered straw hat, or even a comfortable domestic cat. None of these analogies would have flattered him, and yet Caroline thought that they were undoubtedly apt.

She and James could talk together for hours about the most mundane of subjects; and if conversation failed they could contentedly sit in silence in each other's company. They could telephone one another – as they often did – even if there was really nothing to say beyond a comment on the state of the weather. James had once telephoned Caroline to tell her that it was raining, and she, on looking out of the window, had confirmed that indeed it was true. To have such a pointless conversation with another and nevertheless feel that it was worthwhile showed a level of communication and empathy quite strong enough to sustain years and years of being together. Caroline knew it, and realised that James would be an easy and reassuring partner.

And yet there remained one misgiving, and it was a major one: James had rarely touched her, and when he had done so it had been in a gentle and slightly detached way – the lightest of touches to the elbow, for example, or to the forearm, both of which parts of the anatomy have their uses, but were not, she felt, exactly erogenous.

Nor had James ever kissed her, except lightly on the cheek,

in greeting or farewell, and he had always kept his lips firmly together when bestowing these chaste kisses.

'Your kisses are very light,' she had playfully remarked after one such exchange. 'And they're always on the cheek.'

James had looked at her in surprise. 'But where else would one kiss?'

She stared at him. 'Well, sometimes people kiss one another on the lips,' she said. 'Haven't you seen that? In films?'

James frowned. 'Of course. But I've always regarded that as being a little bit . . . well, a little bit unhygienic. Like taking communion from the common chalice. All those germs swimming around in the communion wine. Same thing with mouths.'

Caroline sighed. 'We all have germs, James,' she said. 'And it does no harm to *share* them from time to time – especially with people you really like.'

'Oh,' said James. 'To boost one's immune system?'

7. *Tic-tac and Other Matters*

Caroline's conversation with James about kissing had unsettled her. It was not that James had in any way implied that her mouth, more than anybody else's mouth, was particularly hospitable to germs – he was far too kind to make any such suggestion. What worried her, rather, was the fact that her friend was anxious about germs in general. Such people, she knew, could become more and more obsessed with cleanliness and end up thinking of little else. She did not think that it would be easy to live with somebody who spent his time nervously applying hand sanitiser, or rushing off to wash his hands several times an hour. It was nice to know that one's boyfriend was clean, and took the occasional shower, but not *that* clean.

A week or so after this osculatory discussion, Caroline was travelling on the tube with James when she noticed him take a little plastic bottle out of his pocket, flip open the top and apply a small amount of clear gel to his hands. This he proceeded to rub in, all the while talking to Caroline about some article he had been reading on gestures in Renaissance painting.

'It's very strange, you know, Caroline,' he said. 'There isn't a single dictionary available on the meaning of gestures in painting. Can you believe it?'

Caroline saw the gel glisten and then disappear as James rubbed his hands together. 'What about Hall's Dictionary?' she asked. Did the gel dry the skin? she wondered. It probably did; but back to gestures. 'I thought that Hall told you what all those things meant.'

James shook his head. 'No. Hall is all right for basic symbolism. What hedgehogs represent, and so forth.'

Caroline momentarily forgot about the gel. 'What do hedgehogs mean?'

'Gluttony,' said James. 'I think.'

Caroline felt that this was rather unfair. Hedgehogs were no greedier, surely, than any other animal. She would have defended hedgehogs, but she was not in the mood for the sort of earnest discussion that might follow. James knew so much, it seemed to her, far more than she did. And he thought about things that would never cross her mind – such as the meaning of gestures. Why had she not thought about that before?

'As you know,' James went on, looking doubtfully at Caroline (he *knows* I don't know, she thought; he's just being nice), 'as you know, there are certain accepted gestures in art. Affirmation, for example, is shown by an arm which is lifted to face the spectator, the back of the hand facing outwards. Like this.' James demonstrated, and Caroline saw a woman on the other side of the carriage watching him intently. Perhaps she knows, she thought; perhaps she's an art historian who understands these things. But what were the odds of three art historians being in one carriage of a London Underground train at the same time? Very long.

'And then there's shame,' James continued. 'Shame is signified by the placing of the fingers over the eyes. *Comme ça.*'

Caroline was not surprised by the representation of shame; it might have been a Renaissance gesture, but it was also the gesture of those convicted of contemporary crimes, those unfortunates led from the court who shielded their eyes with their fingers in exactly the same way. *Schadenfreude*, she remembered; we love the shame of others – nothing makes the mob happier than the sight of somebody humiliated. She had read an article somewhere about its effects: how we enjoyed our feeling of moral superiority; how readily we exploded into moral outrage over the misdeeds of public people caught out. And all the time we ignored – or were unaware of – the glaring fact that such people were the way they were because we were the way *we* were. A rotten society produces rotten public figures.

As their train rattled on to its destination, James continued with his observations on the language of gesture. 'Of course there are all sorts of sign language,' he went on. 'Auctioneers, merchants, bookies. Have you seen tic-tac being used?'

Caroline had not.

James smiled. 'It's the sign language used by bookies,' he said. 'They signal across the track. They show the odds that way.' He paused, and then reached up and put a hand on either side of his nose. 'That's odds of five to two,' he explained.

Caroline raised an eyebrow. 'Why don't they use mobile phones?'

James sighed. 'They do these days,' he said. 'It's so sad. It's another language that's biting the dust. But at least there are the monks.'

'The monks?'

'Monastic sign language,' said James. 'People like Cistercians, who discourage unnecessary talking. Do you know that they have an elaborate system of communicating without speech?'

'Why?' It struck Caroline as odd that one would eschew one form of communication only to resort to another: what did it matter how one communicated if the end result was the same – the message was conveyed?

James shrugged. 'It's to do with rejecting the noise and distraction of the world,' he said. 'I think they've got a point. There's so much *noise*, Caroline.' He gave her an intense look as he uttered the word *noise*, as if to suggest, she thought, that she was the source of more than her fair share of this din.

If James had intended to blame Caroline for the shattering of the peace, he did not pursue the accusation. There was more to be said, it transpired, on monastic sign language.

'I once saw a whole book on the subject,' he said. 'It had pictures of monks making gestures with their hands. So, do you know how to do *soul*?' He paused, but only momentarily; of course Caroline could not be expected to know something like that, it was *monks'* business. 'You put your hand above your head – like this – and then you look upwards.'

'I think it's ridiculous,' said Caroline. 'It's all male silliness – like those ridiculous signs that Masons have. The handshakes and so on.'

James narrowed his eyes. 'How do you know about that?' he asked.

Caroline glanced across the carriage as she prepared to answer. A man seated opposite her – a man wearing a pinstripe suit – was staring at her with interest, as if awaiting her answer. Suddenly she felt inhibited.

The man leaned forward. One did not talk to strangers in such circumstances, but he seemed indifferent to this; she sensed danger. 'Nothing ridiculous about the Masons,' he said, his voice barely raised above the clatter of the train. 'You should remember that, my dear!'

8. Tibetan Hats

They emerged into the light through the Charing Cross Road exit of Leicester Square Station.

'Obviously a Mason,' said James. 'Spooky.'

'They've got that big hall near here,' said Caroline.

'Freemasons' Hall. Great Queen Street. Perhaps he was on his way there.'

James smiled. 'For a ceremony of some sort, do you think?'

Caroline was not sure. 'Should we have asked him?'

James did not think this a good idea. 'You can't ask members of a secret society what they're up to,' he said. 'It spoils their fun. And it's rude, too. It's like laughing at Black Rod or the Garter King of Arms when they're all dressed up for one of those occasions of theirs.'

They made their way round the corner into Cecil Court. This was a shopping expedition of the curious variety that James and Caroline enjoyed undertaking in each other's company – an expedition in search of something small and obscure. They never shopped together for the functional or the necessary, for sweaters or shoes or the like; it was hardly any fun going with somebody into a shop on Oxford Street or Regent Street. In fact, nor was it any fun going into such a shop *without* somebody.

James had to collect something from a book-dealer in Cecil Court, an out-of-print monograph on the sense of imminent event in the works of Nicolas Poussin – not something one could readily buy on Oxford Street, given its lamentable decline. For her part, Caroline planned to pick up a Tibetan wool hat from a stall in Covent Garden Market. She had seen the hat a few weeks earlier and had vacillated, a fatal thing to do when confronted with shopping temptation. Since then, she had regretted her failure to make the purchase.

'Fifteen pounds,' she said to James. 'That's all it was. I should have bought it.'

'Fifteen pounds is not much for a hat these days. Tibetan, you say?'

'In concept,' said Caroline. 'I think they're actually made in Bermondsey.'

'By Tibetans?'

Caroline did not think so. 'The woman who sells them was knitting one when I was at her stall. She was Irish, I think. Or she certainly sounded it.'

'She might have had a bit of Tibetan in her,' said James. 'One never knows, and perhaps one should give the benefit of the doubt in such a case.'

'Does it matter?'

James shook his head. 'Of course not. Hats don't have to come from where they claim. Look at panamas. They come from Ecuador.' He slowed down to peer into the window of a secondhand bookshop. 'You know, I saw the Dalai Lama once.'

Caroline was interested. 'Where?'

'Outside Foyles,' replied James. 'He had been signing copies of a book he wrote. And he came out of the shop as I was walking along the pavement. He had some people with him who sort of ushered him into a car, and off they went up towards Tottenham Court Road. Floated off, really. It was very . . .' he seemed to be searching for the right word. 'It was very spiritual.'

'How strange. In the middle of London, with all the traffic and so on.'

James agreed. 'Exactly. What struck me was the sense of peace that he radiated – it was a sort of *glow*. You know how some people *glow*.'

'No.'

'Well, they do. They glow because they're full of inner peace and resolution.' He turned away from the bookshop window and looked directly at Caroline. 'Most of us don't really know what we want in this life, do we? We spend our time rushing around from here to there, and then back again. We have a very strong sense of forward motion. The Dalai Lama wasn't like that – or at least he wasn't when I saw him in Charing Cross Road.'

They continued to walk down Cecil Court. 'You know that they *find* him?' said James.

'Who?'

'The Dalai Lama,' he said. 'They find a new Dalai Lama as a child. He's the reincarnation, you see, of the last one. They look for signs.' He paused. 'We could do that with the Archbishop of Canterbury, don't you think? We could find the reincarnated Archbishop of Canterbury as a small boy and bring him up in his new role.'

Caroline laughed. 'He'd have a terrible time at school,' she said. 'Imagine how he'd be teased by the other kids. And it would be difficult for the teachers too. "Stop talking and get on with your work, please, Archbishop of Canterbury." It wouldn't be easy.'

'They'd call him Your Grace,' said James. 'That's what you call the Archbishop of Canterbury. Teachers would know that sort of thing.' He paused for a moment. 'Or maybe not . . .'

They reached a small bookshop with a display of modern first editions in the window. 'This is the place,' James said. 'Tindley and Chapman. It's a great place. They've got all sorts of stuff.'

They went in. Mr Tindley was at his desk, paging through

a book. He looked up and smiled at them. 'Poussin?'

'Yes,' said James.

Mr Tindley half turned and extracted a small pamphlet from the shelf behind him. 'It's in quite good condition,' he said, handing the pamphlet to James.

James looked at the price. 'Seventeen pounds?'

Mr Tindley nodded. 'It's quite rare.'

James reached into his pocket and extracted a twenty pound note. Mr Tindley took the note and gave the change. They went out.

Caroline noticed that after he had slipped the pamphlet into a pocket, James put the three pound coins into his wallet. Then he reached into another pocket and took out the bottle of sterilising gel.

'Money's really dirty,' he said as they began to cross St Martin's Lane.

She watched as he poured a small quantity of gel onto the palm of his right hand.

'Dirty in what sense?' she asked. 'Corrupting? Or because it represents exploitation of others?'

James looked at her in surprise. 'Of course not,' he said. 'Nothing political. I meant because it's often covered in germs. It's handled by so many people, you see.'

Caroline said nothing for a few moments, but once they were safely across the street she turned to James and touched him lightly on the forearm. 'Listen, James,' she said. 'Aren't you being just a little bit too fussy about germs? I mean, there are germs all over the place. We're covered in them.'

James gave a shudder. 'Speak for yourself,' he said.

9. The Use of the Subjunctive

While Caroline and James made their way to Covent Garden Market, not far away, in their offices in a discreet square in the heart of Soho, the Ragg Porter Literary Agency was about to have its quarterly review meeting. There were three principals in the firm, two of whom, Barbara Ragg and Rupert Porter, had taken over the business from their respective fathers. Gregory Ragg and Fatty Porter had collaborated amicably for over thirty years, and had blithely assumed that their offspring would do the same. The hope that Barbara and Rupert would work together was not misplaced, but that their relationship should mirror that of their fathers proved to be a wish too far; for although they made a success of the agency, Barbara and Rupert would never have described each other as friends.

The main reason for the coolness between them was an historical one rather than any fundamental incompatibility of temperament. And like the old enmity between Ecuador and Peru, or between Chile and Argentina, the ill-feeling between Barbara and Rupert was based on a territorial dispute. In the case of Ecuador and Peru, the argument had been about ownership of part of the Amazonian Basin; in the case of Barbara and Rupert, the *casus belli* was the ownership of the Notting Hill flat Fatty Porter had sold years ago to Gregory Ragg. According to Rupert, this sale had only gone through because Fatty believed that Gregory wanted the flat for himself; but in the end, after living there for only a year or so, Gregory had retired to the country and passed the flat to his daughter. Had Fatty known that this would happen, Rupert maintained, he would never have sold the flat in the first place, and he – Rupert – would now be comfortably ensconced in it. As it was, Barbara lived in it and enjoyed the advantages of its substantial drawing room, which was very much larger than that which Rupert and his wife had in their own, markedly inferior flat.

The disagreement between Ecuador and Peru had resulted in a state of armed tension between the two countries. Every so often, in the *war season* as it became known, when the weather allowed for good flying, this would flare up into an exchange of actual hostilities, during which the Ecuadorians would shoot down a few Peruvian MiG fighters, and vice versa. Eventually better sense prevailed and the issue was resolved by the World Court – largely in favour of Peru, a decision that did not meet with wide support in Ecuador. (It is still possible to engage the taxi drivers of Quito in discussion of this matter, making the Ecuadorian capital one of the few cities in the world where taxi drivers are prepared to discuss the jurisprudence of the World Court. London taxi drivers, although opinionated in some areas, are not known for the strength of their views on the decisions of the Hague court.)

There had never been open hostilities between Barbara and Rupert, who restricted themselves to the occasional slightly needling remark – just enough to keep the matter alive but not sufficient to lead to actual conflict. There was one such exchange that morning, as Rupert came into the meeting room at the Ragg Porter Agency to find Barbara flicking through an unsolicited manuscript, a look of amusement on her face.

'I see you're enjoying that,' Rupert observed. 'I took a manuscript home last night and left it there, I'm afraid. There's so much clutter in my study in the flat, you see – not quite enough room. The manuscript disappeared under a pile of papers.'

Barbara picked up the inference immediately. What Rupert was saying here was that her flat – to which he did not think her entitled – was much roomier; had he lived in the flat to which he was morally entitled (hers) he would not mislay manuscripts.

So she looked up and replied: 'You really should think about moving some time, Rupert. I hear that this is a good time to buy. There are quite a few for sale signs in our street, you know. Not that I would ever think of moving myself.'

Rupert, of course, understood perfectly what this meant, which was: You should forget the past and stop moaning about things that happened a long time ago. You should find a larger flat because I'm never going to move out of the flat that you think is yours, so just forget it and shut up. So there.

Rupert pursed his lips. The subject would not be discussed further now, and possibly not again that entire week, but it would not be dropped. Oh no. When one was as certain of the rectitude of one's cause as he was it would take more than a cheap salvo about moving and for sale signs to take the subject off the agenda altogether. But for now there was business to be done.

He sat down. The directors usually spent half an hour or so talking about agency affairs before the firm's three other agents, who were not on the board, joined the meeting. This gave them an opportunity to catch up on who was doing what, and also to exchange odd bits of publishing gossip that might be useful in negotiations on their clients' behalf.

'Your man, Great . . . What's his name again?' said Rupert.

'Greatorex. Errol Greatorex.'

'Yes, him. Where are we? Has he delivered the final manuscript yet?'

Barbara tossed aside the manuscript she had been reading. It would never do. 'Unpublishable,' she said, and added quickly, 'This one, not Greatorex's. This is by a man who set out to sail from Southampton to Istanbul in a small yacht barely the size of a bathtub.'

Rupert smiled. 'And?'

'It all went terribly well, as far as I can make out. There were no storms, no incidents with larger vessels, and the Turks were terribly good to him when he arrived. It makes for dull literature when the Turks are kind to one. We can't have books like that.'

'But what about Greatorex?'

Barbara sighed. 'He's in London at the moment,' she said. 'He says that he's still putting the finishing touches to the manuscript. He promised me that it would be ready soon, but I'm having great difficulty in getting it out of him.'

Rupert sighed. There had been a lot of talk – *hype* even – about the launch of Errol Greatorex's *Autobiography of a Yeti*, a story dictated to the author by a yeti who worked as a schoolteacher in a remote Himalayan village. But they had been waiting for some time now, and he was beginning to wonder whether the author would ever deliver.

'Are you sure that he's genuine?' Rupert asked. 'The whole thing seems a little bit . . . How should I put it? Dubious.'

'Oh, I think he's the real thing,' Barbara assured him. 'I had

39

lunch with him the other day, when he came back from Tibet. He gave me a lovely Tibetan knitted hat. He picked it up in Lhasa.'

'Generous of him,' said Rupert. 'It's nice when you meet an author who isn't selfish – rare though it unfortunately be.'

Barbara was impressed. 'I love your subjunctives,' she said.

And she was sincere in her praise. She *did* love a man who used the subjunctive mood, as Hugh had done that very morning when he kissed her goodbye at the door of the flat. 'Were I to search for twenty years,' he had said, 'I would never find somebody as lovely as you.'

It made her feel warm just to think of it. A beautiful subjunctive, as warm, as loving as a caress.

10. How Dim Can You Get?

It was not only Barbara Ragg's remark about the subjunctive that made Rupert wonder about her; there were other things he had noticed, little things, perhaps, but which taken together indicated that something was afoot. She was engaged, of course, and he asked himself whether the mere fact of engagement could make a person dreamy and distracted. He tried to remember what he had felt when he had become engaged himself, but found it difficult even to recall when that was, and in what circumstances, let alone how he felt at the time.

Of course Rupert knew that Barbara's private life was none of his business, and he would never have dreamed of prying, but if her state of mind was affecting her work, then that was a different matter altogether. And there had been signs of it. A few days previously, Barbara had written to an author and told him that not only had his manuscript been accepted for publication by a well-known publisher but that a sizeable advance had been negotiated. This must have been good news for the author in question, who had not been published before and whose work, although worthy, was on the very margins of what was commercially viable.

Her discovery two days later that she had written to the wrong author could hardly have been comfortable. The manuscript that had been offered for was by a quite different author – one who was widely published already and would barely have noticed yet another publisher's advance.

'La Ragg,' Rupert had said to his wife that evening, 'made an absolutely colossal blunder. Colossal. She told somebody that his novel had been accepted for publication when it hadn't. She got the wrong author. Stupid cow.'

Gloria Porter smiled. 'How dim can you get?'

'Not much dimmer,' said Rupert. 'And you know what? The story gets better.'

'Difficult to imagine,' said his wife. 'Tell all.' She liked to hear stories of Barbara Ragg's ineptitude; she, too, had come round to resenting Barbara's enjoyment of the flat that surely had been meant for her Rupert, and ergo for her. She had tried to get Rupert to stop going on about the issue, but eventually decided that it would be simpler to join in his campaign. So now she found a curious satisfaction in his diatribes against Barbara and indeed came up with her own contributions to the feud. Well, it was all very well having the larger drawing room, she pointed out, but how could one possibly benefit from it when one's life was such a mess in other respects? Barbara's affair with the odious Oedipus Snark, for instance. It was as if the Recording Angel was *punishing* her for occupying a flat that was not, by rights, hers.

Rupert was enjoying himself. 'I went into her office to get something or other, and there was la Ragg sitting at her desk, white as a sheet. Drained. So I said, "What ails thee, dear Ragg?" or something to that effect, and she looked up and said, "I fear that I've made a small mistake."'

'Small mistake!' expostulated Gloria. 'La Ragg certainly believes in understatement.'

'Indeed,' went on Rupert. 'She told me about sending the letter to the wrong author. So I said, "How could you do that, Barbara?" And my question, I assure you, was an apposite one. I just didn't see how one could possibly write to one author in the belief that he's another.'

Gloria shook her head in disbelief. This was such fun. 'Absolutely,' she said. 'And her answer?'

'Answer came there none,' said Rupert. 'At least to begin with. For some time she said nothing at all, and then she opened her bovine mouth and said something about the two authors having very similar names. "In what respect?" enquire I. "Oh, they're both Welsh," la Ragg responds. I ask you! Both Welsh! So Neil Kinnock is Welsh and . . .' He waved his hand about airily, trying to think of another name. 'And that other chap's Welsh, but would we confuse the two of them, just because they come from . . .'

'Wales,' said Gloria. 'There are loads of Welsh people. Loads of them. I don't see how one can confuse people on the grounds of their nationality. I just don't.'

Rupert rolled his eyes upwards. 'Well, she did. But wait – here's the denouement. She then told me that this poor chap – the one who thought that his book had been sold – had gone out and spent the advance.'

Gloria was very pleased to hear this; the story was getting better and better, just as Rupert had promised. She enjoyed her husband's stories of office affairs – stories in which he came out rather well, as was to be expected, but Barbara Ragg and various other members of staff were shown to have fairly major failings, again, as one might expect. 'No!' she exclaimed.

Rupert nodded with satisfaction. 'Apparently he went out and bought a new car. Cleaned out his bank account in the expectation that he would soon be getting the money for the book.'

'Poor man,' said Gloria. 'But I suppose he'll be able to take it back.'

Rupert beamed. 'Not so fast. Apparently he spent the entire day driving up and down Wales and clocked up an awful mileage. You can't take a new car back if you've put several hundred miles on it. It's not a new car any more. The value drops very quickly and dramatically the moment you drive out of the showroom, and even more so when you put a few miles on the thingometer.'

'Odometer,' said Gloria.

Rupert raised a finger. There was even more to come. 'La Ragg then says to me, and I quote verbatim – *ipse dixit* – she says, "I do hope that the agency will refund him the difference between what he paid and what the garage gives him when he takes the car back. In fact, I hope you don't mind – I've written him a letter to that effect."'

Gloria's eyes glinted. 'Outrageous!' she said.

Rupert reassured her. 'Oh, I nipped that in the bud all right,' he said. 'I told her that I *did* mind and that if she chose to rectify this mistake it was to be from her drawings on the firm and *not* from anywhere else. Those who make mistakes should pay for them, I said. And not with other people's money.'

'That taught her, no doubt,' said Gloria.

'She sulked,' said Rupert. 'She's a terrible sulker, is la Ragg. Went all moody. You know how women get from time to time.'

Gloria looked at him sternly. '*Some* women,' she corrected him. 'Not all.'

'Of course,' said Rupert. 'Of course, *mon chou*. That's what I meant.'

11. Caroline Meets Berthea

Caroline put down the receiver. She had finished the telephone call she had been making to James, and had ended by blowing a kiss down the line. When, she asked herself, did I last do something like that? As a teenager, perhaps, when she had enjoyed those long conversations with her first boyfriend, Will Brown, and had found it so hard to hang up, although they really had so little to say to one another beyond half-whispered declarations of undying love. And then Will Brown had gone to university in Cardiff and broken his promise to phone her every day. So much for men, she thought; they promise things and then don't deliver. It was ever thus.

James was different. He always did what he said he was going to do, even if it made him just a tiny bit predictable. No matter. They had arranged to meet later that evening, when James would come round to the flat. They would cook a simple meal and watch a film together, making it the sort of evening that both she and James preferred. James had offered to cook if Caroline would go and buy Arborio rice – he had a special risotto recipe that he wanted to try – as well as a carton of crème fraiche and a punnet of raspberries. He would bring Parmesan cheese and asparagus for the risotto, and a bottle of wine that some friends had given him for looking after their cat while they went to Norwich for the weekend.

Caroline decided to go out to the shops immediately. None of her flatmates was in, and so she double-locked the door behind her and made her way out into the street. A short walk later, as she turned the corner onto Ebury Street, she found herself faced with a woman who had dropped her shopping bag and was bending down to recover a scattering of Brussels sprouts from the pavement. The woman looked up at her apologetically.

'I'm very sorry,' she said. 'I'm sure that you didn't expect to find your way blocked by Brussels sprouts, of all things.'

Caroline laughed, and bent down to help her retrieve the last of the vegetables. The woman looked vaguely familiar; obviously Caroline had seen her in the area before, but had not met her. There were plenty of people like that; they were the neighbours – in a loose sense – but one had no idea who they were.

'London pavements are perhaps not as clean as they ought be,' the woman remarked. 'But boiling will get rid of most things, I'd have thought.'

'Of course it will,' said Caroline. She sounded very authoritative, she realised, although she had no reason to profess expertise in the matter. 'My boyfriend wouldn't approve, though.'

She had not called James her boyfriend before, but it came quite naturally. And it was true: James would be appalled by the idea of eating Brussels sprouts that had been on the pavement. She could just hear him: 'They should be put down, Caroline, not eaten!'

The woman straightened up. She seemed interested in Caroline's remark. 'Oh really? He'd disapprove? Why's that?'

Caroline felt disloyal talking about James in this way but she could hardly leave the matter up in the air now. 'He worries a bit about germs,' she said. 'In fact he worries a lot about them.'

The woman tucked the last of the Brussels sprouts back into her shopping bag. 'I've seen you before, I think,' she said. 'We haven't met, of course, but we've seen one another, haven't we?'

'I live back there,' Caroline said, nodding in the direction of Corduroy Mansions.

The woman extended a hand. 'I'm Berthea Snark. I think I'm just behind you. You know the little mews?'

'Of course. I sometimes walk past those houses and think how nice they are. I've often wondered what they're like inside.'

Berthea Snark smiled. 'They're very comfortable. *Gemütlich*, even.' She paused. 'But why don't you come in for a cup of tea? I was going to put the kettle on when I got back. You could satisfy your curiosity – mine is a typical mews house.'

Caroline hesitated. One did not accept invitations from complete strangers, and yet surely that rule did not apply to invitations from middle-aged women whose bags contained nothing more sinister than Brussels sprouts. No, this was not a 'Have some Madeira, my dear' invitation; this was one neighbour inviting another in for a cup of tea after she had helped her pick up dropped Brussels sprouts. What could be more innocent than that?

Caroline accepted, and began to retrace her steps with Berthea Snark.

'Tell me about your boyfriend,' Berthea said as they walked along. 'Does he worry about germs all the time?'

Caroline laughed. 'Of course not. In fact, I think I may have given you the wrong impression. He uses hand steriliser, you see, and is worried about handling coins, but I wouldn't say he's obsessed.'

Berthea raised an eyebrow. 'Some degree of concern about germs is quite natural,' she said. 'But, if you'll forgive my saying so, your young man seems to be rather too concerned.' She hesitated for a moment before continuing. 'You see, perhaps I should explain. I'm a psychotherapist. I'm professionally interested in these matters.'

Caroline attempted to make light of the situation. 'I assure you, James is quite normal.' Is he? she asked herself. Is he really?

They were now at the entrance to the mews, and Berthea

Snark was pointing to a red-painted door halfway along the row of houses. 'My place,' she said. 'Let's talk further once we're inside. You can tell me all about your James.' Then she added, 'And his fears.'

Caroline frowned. Perhaps she should not have accepted this invitation after all. Hansel and Gretel, she thought.

12. The Wound in the Psyche

'A cup of tea?' asked Berthea Snark. 'Or would you prefer coffee?'

Caroline chose tea, explaining that she could not drink coffee in the afternoon or early evening. 'It's the wrong taste,' she said.

'I couldn't agree more,' said Berthea. 'Coffee is possible between seven-thirty in the morning and eleven-twenty. And then again after eight-thirty at night.'

Caroline laughed. 'That's very precise,' she said.

'I'm not entirely serious,' said Berthea. 'And I'm quite happy to bend the rules I set for myself. But we do need some rules in our lives, you know. As a psychotherapist, I can assure you that we need rituals and rules to anchor ourselves.' She paused. They were standing in the entrance hall to her mews house and she now directed Caroline along the small corridor, which led to a room at the back. 'You know, we did ourselves a great deal of damage in the sixties and seventies. Which was before you were born, of course, but will be affecting your world every bit as much as anybody else's.'

Caroline looked about her. They were in a comfortable sitting room, neatly furnished in a surprisingly contemporary style, with one wall entirely taken up by shelves. A row of CDs, stacked two deep, occupied one of the shelves, the rest being filled with books.

'What did we do?' she asked.

Berthea gestured to a chair. 'Please sit down. What did we do? Well, I suppose I should have said something was *done to us*. We, in the sense of the mass of the people, the men and the women in the street, so to speak, didn't do it. It was done by people who considered themselves opinion-formers. Social change tends to come from the moulders and manipulators of opinion, does it not? So people who may be dismissed as theorists are actually immensely important. Mrs Thatcher made the great mistake of thinking that the academic talking heads did not count. They did.'

Caroline raised an eyebrow. Was this woman *mad*? Was she one of those people who had some grand theory that they would thrust upon anybody they met, even somebody who had helped them retrieve their Brussels sprouts from the pavement? She waited for Berthea to go on.

'There was a body of opinion in this country that set out to remodel the fabric of our society,' Berthea continued. 'They weakened the common sense of the people; they intimidated them. They decried that which people – ordinary people – actually believed in. They spoke in the language of liberation, but what did they liberate people to? To a new servitude – a servitude of shallowness and impermanence, of loneliness and alienation.

49

'They destroyed the familiar – they preached against it, ridiculed it. And in doing this they weakened the notion of order in people's lives. People used to have a sense of what their lives meant because they belonged to things, and observed certain rules. You belonged to a union, or a church for that matter, which gave you a sense of who you were. It made you proud of your craft or your trade, or of being Catholic or Church of England or whatever. It gave structure. You also knew where you came from – you had a body of which you were a member. You shared a culture.'

Berthea continued to talk as she moved into the little kitchen off the sitting room. Caroline watched her as she filled the kettle and plugged it in. This woman *was* mad. She would drink her tea, then look pointedly at her watch and make her excuses.

'Half my professional time,' said Berthea over her shoulder, 'is spent trying to help people who simply don't have any purpose in their lives. They come to me because they are unhappy – they think that therapy will help. But what are they trying to heal? The wound in their psyche or the wound in society? They're actually perfectly all right in themselves – it's society that has done the damage because it's the one that's sick.'

Berthea came back into the sitting room carrying a tray on which there stood a teapot and two mugs. She sat the tray down on a side table and poured for both of them.

'These observations,' she said, 'make me sound rather like some unreconstructed Marxist – saying that society's to blame for everything. I'm not a Marxist, but I can't help noting the insights that many Marxists have offered in that respect. I think they're right, you know. They're right in their analysis of how the human self is largely defined by social and economic factors. Of course it is. And they're right when they insist that recalcitrant social problems – crime, for instance – have a social foundation. I would go further: I'd say that a very great deal of personal unhappiness stems from those roots.'

Caroline sipped at her tea. It had an unfamiliar flavour.

'Malawian Lost Tea,' said Berthea. 'A little discovery of mine. Do you like it?'

Caroline nodded.

'I give tea to my patients,' said Berthea. 'I find that it calms them. But it's also a little ritual, isn't it? The pouring and the serving, the sharing. And that's what these poor people who come to me need so desperately: a sense of belonging. And what's better for inducing a sense of belonging than shared ritual?'

Caroline was about to say something but Berthea was now in full flow. 'Eating together,' she went on. 'That's one of the oldest, most basic rituals. If we eat together we join one another in an experience that declares and reinforces our shared humanity. If you eat with another you are, for the duration of the meal, joined with that person. The proud cannot be proud when they are eating with others because all are on an equal footing – creatures in need of sustenance. And yet what are we doing to mealtimes? Destroying them. Do schools teach children to eat together? They do not. Snatch a meal from a cafeteria, eat in isolation, huddled over a tray. Where's the bonding in that?'

To her surprise, Caroline found herself agreeing. Her attitude towards her hostess was changing rapidly; the suspicion she had felt earlier was being replaced by a feeling that here was a woman who was really rather wise. And this made her ask herself whether she belonged? And if she belonged, what did she belong to? To Cheltenham? To the world of her parents? She had sought to distance herself from all that – from the world of the haute bourgeoisie, with its preoccupation with possessions and class – but had she found anything to replace it? Berthea had mentioned rituals, and her parents had plenty of those, with their Sunday lunches and golf club dinners (they certainly ate together) and bridge evenings, and all the rest. Were they happy as a result? In a moment of sudden understanding, Caroline realised that they were. Her parents were perfectly happy.

The realisation struck her as depressing – ineffably depressing. For if they were happy, then it must mean they had something right. And if they had it right, then she had it wrong.

13. I Do Not Want to Be My Mother

'Now how on earth did we get onto that subject?' asked Berthea Snark. 'I thought we were going to talk about your boyfriend.'

'It was rather interesting,' said Caroline. 'What you said made me think about my parents.'

Berthea put down her mug and signalled for Caroline to pass hers for topping up.

'I'm not surprised,' she said. 'Most people think about their parents rather often. Every day, in fact. We find ourselves doing something the way our parents did it, or using an expression they used. It's alarming, because we think that we're turning into our mother or our father. But we aren't really. We show some of their traits, perhaps, but we don't turn into them. Not unless we have a very passive personality. Such people become their parents because they've nothing else to be.'

'I do *not* want to be my mother,' said Caroline.

'Of course you don't,' said Berthea. 'But the fact that you say it with such conviction indicates that perhaps you need to change the way you view your mother. You need to accept her.'

Caroline said nothing. Berthea Snark did not know her mother; if she did, she would understand.

'Acceptance is so important,' said Berthea. 'Acceptance comes first, then liking. Accept yourself, and then you'll end up liking yourself. Not that I'm suggesting that you do not like yourself – I'm sure you do.'

Caroline felt emboldened. 'Do *you* like everybody?'

The question seemed to take Berthea by surprise, but she soon recovered. 'Me? Well, no, I don't think I do.'

'Who don't you like, then? Your mother?'

Berthea shook her head. 'Oh no, I admired my mother deeply. She was the most selfless of women. She did educational work in the East End – years of it – at a time when such things were encouraged. There were university missions – they thought of themselves as missionaries. Nowadays we'd find that very condescending. No, my mother was a good person.' She paused. 'It's my son I don't like.'

Caroline gave a start. Mothers did not say such things. Mothers loved their sons. They had to.

'But let's not talk about me,' said Berthea quickly. 'Your boyfriend – what's his name?'

'James.'

Berthea had fixed her with a gaze that Caroline found quite disconcerting. Perhaps it was time for her to look at her watch.

'James is such a *solid* name,' said Berthea. 'Is he a solid type?'

It was as much as Caroline could do not to laugh. 'I wouldn't call him solid,' she said. 'More artistic. He's interested in fine art. We did a course together.'

'Then it sounds as if you have common interests,' said Berthea. 'That's always a good sign. But you said that he's worried about germs.'

'Yes.'

Berthea looked thoughtful. 'I don't know why I'm discussing this with you,' she said. 'As a psychotherapist, one is not meant to enter into attempts at diagnosing at one remove. Even if asked to do so – which you haven't really done, have you? You haven't asked me.'

Caroline hesitated. Did she want to know more about James, or should she leave matters where they were?

'I can see that you're undecided,' said Berthea. 'So let's leave it at that.'

'Oh, no,' Caroline blurted out. 'Please tell me.' She had not intended to offer Berthea encouragement, but now she seemed to have made up her mind anyway.

Berthea sat back in her chair. 'There's something called OCD,' she said. 'Obsessive–compulsive disorder. It's possible that your boyfriend has that. Probably a very mild form of it.'

Caroline said nothing. She had read about OCD in a magazine not long before. There had been an article about a woman who had been unable to stop cleaning her house. She never went out; she just scrubbed and vacuumed and dusted, finishing one part of the house and then immediately starting all over again.

'Of course, it's astonishingly common,' Berthea went on. 'You shouldn't imagine that your boyfriend is all that unusual. So many of us have some degree of OCD – you and me included.'

Caroline smiled. Berthea was obviously trying to make her feel better.

'You don't think I'm serious?' asked Berthea.

'Well, if you could see my room,' said Caroline, 'you wouldn't accuse me of being an obsessive–compulsive.' Her room was not tidy; it was, in fact, the untidiest room in the flat, and she could not remember the last time she vacuumed it. Last month? The month before?

Berthea was amused by the suggestion that a diagnosis could be an accusation. 'We don't stand *accused* of conditions,' she pointed out. 'Conditions are things that happen to us. And tidiness and neatness are not the sole criteria. OCD has many facets. Intrusive thoughts, for example.'

Caroline frowned. 'Thoughts that . . .'

'That you don't want to think,' supplied Berthea.

'Such as?'

'Doing something terrible. Imagining the worst of yourself.'

Caroline looked down at the floor. What if she were to jump to her feet and accuse Berthea of being an interfering busybody? What if she swore at her – foully – turning the air in this mews house vividly blue with scatological invective? Or she could even reach forward and slap Berthea in the face – quite hard – without saying anything but by this gesture making it very clear that she did not approve of being corralled inappropriately into this community of obsessive–compulsive hand-washers and vacuumers.

Berthea was watching her. 'Would I be right in saying that some – how should I put it – impermissible, but rather delicious temptations have just run through your mind? Those are intrusive thoughts, you see. I believe that you might just have demonstrated the phenomenon to yourself.'

Caroline did not reply.

'But don't worry about it,' said Berthea. 'To be mildly obsessive–compulsive is an indication of a certain sort of achieving personality. Creative people – people who have the urge to excel – commonly fall into this category. And if we didn't have them, then we would be a terribly dull society, don't you think?'

Caroline was not sure what to think; obsessive–compulsiveness had seemed to her to be a pejorative label but perhaps it was really a compliment. One interesting fact was emerging from this discussion: that she and James might have more in common than she had imagined. She felt rather consoled by this; perhaps they could be obsessive-compulsive together, in a companionable way, sharing bottles of hand steriliser, or, if they wished to avoid possible cross-infection – and what obsessive–compulsive would not wish to avoid *that* – having his and hers bottles, carefully set out on the dressing table, lined up, of course, so that the edges of the bottles were in a perfect straight line.

After this unplanned meeting with Berthea, Caroline set out again on her trip to the shops. She had a great deal to mull over, and when she returned to the flat she found that there was even more to wonder about. There was a note, slipped under the door, addressed to her. *I am having a little gathering tonight*, she read, *just a few people who belong to a society of which I'm a member. Would you care to join us downstairs? Tea and sandwiches. 6.30, for about an hour.* And it was signed, *Basil (Wickramsinghe)*.

14. *Basil Wickramsinghe Throws a Little Party*

Shortly after Caroline returned home from her unsettling cup of tea with Berthea Snark, a thin, rather dowdy-looking woman somewhere in her mid-thirties made her way to the front door of Corduroy Mansions, peered at the list of flats and their corresponding bells, and rang one. Within the building the bell sounded in the flat on the ground floor.

Basil Wickramsinghe, accountant and High Anglican, moved to his window and discreetly peered out. By craning his neck and standing far enough back he could just see who was calling upon him. There were some callers he did not like to receive and whose ringing would be ignored – local politicians soliciting votes being at the head of that list, just above so-called market researchers. Or his distant cousin, Anthony, an ear, nose and throat surgeon, with whom he had very little in common and who invariably outstayed his welcome. Today, however, he was expecting visitors – quite a number of them – and he could see that this was the advance guard in the shape of Gillian Winterspoon, who was coming early to help him with the sandwiches.

Gillian Winterspoon was the sort of woman who in the language of marriage banns would be called 'a spinster of this parish'. She had met Basil during an advanced professional training weekend at the Great Danes Hotel near Maidstone; a weekend during which they had both wrestled with the intricacies of the latest taxation regulations affecting non-residents. It was exotic stuff as far as they both were concerned; neither had any involvement with the heady world of non-resident taxation – or non-taxation, as Basil so wittily called it during the tea break after the first session – but both needed the credit that attendance on the course brought and which the Institute of Chartered Accountants quite rightly required of its members lest any of them become cobwebby.

'I'd call all this the non-taxation of non-residents,' quipped Basil, 'leading to non-revenue.'

Gillian Winterspoon, who had found herself standing next to him at the tea break, nervously scanning the assembled accountants to see if any of them might conceivably talk to her, had seized upon this remark with delight.

'That's terribly funny,' she said. 'You're right. No taxation with non-representation. Perhaps we should all throw our tea into the Medway.'

Basil smiled at her. He appreciated both the compliment to his humour and the reference to the Boston Tea Party. He introduced himself, and she reciprocated. Each was relieved to find a friend in this room of others who appeared to know one another so well.

At the end of the weekend they were sitting next to one another at every session. Gillian was delighted to have found a man who appeared to enjoy her company – not a reaction she had encountered in many men, alas – and for his part, Basil found her mild manner undemanding. He was nervous of women and did not have a great deal of confidence in that sphere, especially when he found himself with high-powered woman accountants power-dressed in brisk business suits. Gillian gave rise to none of these anxieties.

They had found, too, an important common interest. Both attended a High Anglican church – in Basil's case a local church in Pimlico, fortunately extremely high in its liturgical attitudes; in hers, one near her home on the fringes of Maida Vale. So it was no surprise that at the end of the conference on the taxation (non-taxation) of non-residents, Basil invited Gillian to attend a future meeting of the James I and VI Society (incorporating the Charles I Appreciation League). And it was equally unsurprising that Gillian accepted this invitation with alacrity and pleasure.

Within a few months Gillian had been elected to the committee of the Society, in the role of secretary, while Basil was chairman. This rapid rise to office suited her very well as it gave her a pretext for frequently contacting Basil, ostensibly in connection with the society's business, but in reality because she was deeply in love with him and could think only of him. In her thoughts she addressed him as The Blessed Basil, an ecclesiastical status to which he was not, strictly speaking, entitled, but which she felt fully justified in conferring upon him. For he was blessed, she thought; he was kind, considerate, courteous and handsome. It was true that blessedness, and indeed saintliness, had nothing to do with looks, but she felt that somehow they *helped*. There were very plain saints, of course, but somehow they seemed less – how should she put it – less *spiritually exciting* than handsome saints.

St Sebastian was a case in point. He was always depicted as a young man of great physical beauty, clad only in a conveniently placed loincloth. He was extremely spiritual, thought Gillian; much more so than dear St Francis, who was somewhat homely – exactly the sort of saint whom a grateful animal might lick in appreciation.

Gillian had been incensed when a cousin of hers, a rather cynical woman who enjoyed making iconoclastic remarks, had suggested that many of the pictures of St Sebastian's martyrdom were thinly disguised exercises in homoerotic art.

'I'm sure he didn't wear quite as seductive a loincloth in real life,' this cousin had said. 'Saints rarely did, you know.'

Gillian had bristled in her indignation. How did this woman know about saints' underpants? It was ridiculous. 'The point of the loincloth,' she observed, 'was to show the arrows with which poor St Sebastian was pierced. That's the whole point of the pictures. They remind us of his suffering in a very vivid way. If he were wearing clothes we wouldn't see the arrows piercing his flesh.'

The cousin smirked. 'But what evidence do we have that he was so . . . so lithely muscular? In real life, that is?'

'I'm not going to discuss this with you any further,' said Gillian.

Later, she had mentioned the disagreement to Basil, who had listened intently to her, and then sighed. 'People don't understand,' he said. 'And of those who do not understand, there are some who do not understand because they *will* not understand.'

Gillian agreed with this wholeheartedly. 'But at least we understand,' she said. 'That is understood, I think.'

'Of course it is,' said Basil.

Oh, if only *you* understood what I feel, Blessed Basil, Gillian thought. But she suspected that he did not; or, rather, would not. In that respect he was like those people who he said did not understand because they did not want to understand.

That is my burden, she thought. And it's the burden of so many women. Men simply will not *see*. And we have to wait in the wings for them to make up their mind, to decide whether they like us enough to confer the benefit of commitment upon us. Why do we put up with it? Why don't we spell out to them that we're fed up with waiting, that we're not going to tolerate their detachment any more, that it's going to be us, women, who are going to decide in future.

She sighed. That was not the way the world was – or certainly not for people like her.

15. The Sudoku Remedy

James arrived at Corduroy Mansions earlier than he had anticipated. He had allowed himself more time than he needed to travel from his flat in Clerkenwell and had fifteen minutes in hand by the time he found himself outside Corduroy Mansions. Dee answered when he pressed the doorbell and buzzed him into the entrance. He noticed that something was going on in the ground-floor flat – a party, by the sound of it – but he did not linger and bounded up the stairs to Caroline's flat. James was pleased that Dee was in; he liked her and had not seen her for a few weeks. Dee gave him news of the latest health food products, and occasional free samples too. Last time he saw her, she had given him a one-month course of a brain-power-enhancing supplement, ginkgo biloba, and he had taken it conscientiously until the bottle was empty, without any noticeable result. 'Of course, you don't really need this,' she had said to him. 'There are lots of people I know who could do with a course of ginkgo. You're really not one. Here's some garlic as well.'

Dee opened the door to him when he reached the landing. As he came in, she bent forwards to give him a kiss. James winced.

'I'm not going to bite,' said Dee.

James was embarrassed. 'I know that.'

'Then why not let me give you a little kiss? Caroline won't be jealous.'

James blushed. 'I don't normally kiss,' he said. 'It's not just you. I don't like all this kissing that goes on. Why not just shake hands?'

Dee laughed. 'I won't kiss you if you don't want me to,' she said. 'Anyway, come in.'

She took him into the kitchen, where she had been sitting at the table tackling a newspaper sudoku. James noticed that the puzzle was marked *extremely easy*.

'If you took ginkgo-what's-its-name you'd be able to do difficult sudokus,' he said. 'In fact, why don't you sell ginkgo in little bottles marked Sudoku Remedy?'

Dee stared at him. 'That's a rather good idea,' she said.

'I wasn't serious,' said James. 'Just a joke.'

'No,' said Dee quickly. 'It's not a joke, James – it's a really good idea. That's exactly what they've done with echinacea, isn't it?'

James was not sure what they had done with echinacea.

'They sell it as protection from infection while you're travelling,' Dee explained. 'Then they sell it as a protection against flu. And so on. It's the same basic stuff, of course – it simply boosts your immune system. But you can package it in a hundred different ways.'

'Well,' said James. 'I didn't know about that. But will people who do sudokus want help? If they did, then surely they could just put the figures into their computers and the computers would come up with the solution.'

Dee shook her head. 'That's not the way they think,' she said. 'People who do puzzles want to solve them themselves.'

James was not so sure. 'So what about those gadgets that help with crosswords? You put in a couple of letters and it comes up with the solution for you.'

'No self-respecting crossword person uses one of those,' said

Dee. 'But every self-respecting crossword person would be quite happy to take something to help get their mind in gear. A cup of coffee, for instance. That would not be cheating. Neither would some ginkgo.' She paused. 'And we could market a Crossword Remedy too.'

James smiled. 'You'd get very rich,' he said. He looked at his watch. 'Where's Caroline?'

'She's gone to a party,' Dee replied. 'Or I think that's what she said. Something about a drinks party. I wasn't paying much attention.'

'But she's meant to be having dinner with me,' said James. 'We made a date over the phone.'

Dee shrugged. 'Well, maybe she's forgotten. I did that once, you know. Maybe she needs to take some ginkgo.'

'It's not funny. I'm cooking dinner for her. Here. And she's gone to a party.'

Dee's instinct was to protect her flatmate. 'Maybe I got it wrong,' she said. 'I wasn't really listening.'

'Well, she's not here, is she?' said James. 'She's stood me up.'

'Oh come on, James. Anybody can get dates mixed up. I remember once—'

James interrupted her. 'Something that's arranged a week or two ahead, yes, you can forget about that sort of thing if you don't put it in your diary. But not the same day.'

'Oh. Well,' said Dee.

James looked at his watch again. 'It's really inconsiderate. I was going to cook something and then we were going to watch a DVD together.' He paused. 'Are you doing anything, Dee?'

Dee thought quickly. She would love to have dinner with James. She had nothing in the fridge except a small piece of cheddar and a tub of yoghurt. Anything would be better than that.

'Not really. Why?'

'I'll take you out to dinner,' said James. 'We could go to the Poule au Pot.'

'The Poule au Pot!' She had walked past the restaurant many times but of course she had never been able to go inside. Dee was permanently hard-up, and a meal out, even in a much more modest restaurant, was a rare treat for her.

'Yes,' said James. 'Let's go and see if they can take us. If they can't, I know somewhere else. There's a really nice Greek restaurant ten minutes away. Would that suit you?'

Anything would suit Dee, who felt only a slight pang of doubt as she went into her room to change. It's her fault, she thought. She takes James for granted – anybody can tell. If he belonged to me, I wouldn't do that. I'd spoil him. I'd do everything for him. I'd make him really happy.

They left the flat and walked the short distance to the restaurant. It was not a busy night, as it happened, and a table was quickly found. They sat down, and James ordered a bottle of wine. Then, while waiting for their starters to appear, James said, 'I'm really cross with Caroline, you know.'

Dee looked around her at the room. She was basking in the pleasure of being out for dinner, in an expensive restaurant, with somebody as good-looking and as generally *nice* as James. She turned her gaze to him.

'I don't blame you,' she said quietly. 'Poor you.'

16. England Expects William to Do His Duty

When William awoke the following morning, he did so with the realisation that this was a significant day. But it was one of those realisations, only too common, when the actual reason for the day's significance fails to come immediately to mind. So might a politician, on the morning of his inauguration into high office, awake with a feeling that something was about to happen, but, in that curious stage between drowsiness and full wakefulness, not remember what lay ahead; or so might a prisoner, facing release after long years of incarceration, forget that the front door to freedom would open for him within hours. Yes, something important was due to happen, but what was it? It took a moment or two for him to remember: today was the day that he was due to meet his contact, following the instructions he had received.

Ever since the surprise visit from Angelica Brockelbank, former bookshop owner and now employee of MI6, William had been puzzling over the implications of what she had said. Although she had not been reticent in admitting that she worked in intelligence, and had been direct in her suggestion that MI6 wanted William to do something for them, she had been coy about saying exactly what it was.

'We can't talk too openly here,' she had said, glancing about her at William's kitchen, as if to imply that their conversation might be overheard.

William had been tempted to laugh. 'What do you mean by that?' he asked. 'Are you suggesting my flat's bugged?'

Angelica looked at him with complete seriousness; she had

not been joking – not at all. 'You'd be astonished,' she said. 'If I were to give you a list – even a highly abbreviated one – of the places in this city that are bugged, you'd be utterly astonished.'

William looked at her with amusement. These cloak and dagger people, he thought – too much imagination. On the other hand, there had been those journalists who had hacked into the telephones of prominent people. How dare they? They did not even have the excuse of protecting national security – which Angelica and her people could at least advance; they had been motivated by pure salacious interest or, in some cases, a desire to humiliate and embarrass public figures.

'But people's private houses . . .' William began.

Angelica smiled. 'An Englishman's home is his castle? Not any more, William, not under our current masters. Remember that these are the people who want to keep a record of every mobile phone call, every single email you send, no matter how banal. The authorities want to know about it. They really do.'

It seemed to William that Angelica was getting into her stride. What he was hearing was so unexpected, so out of the ordinary, that he sat meekly and listened.

'And here's another thing,' she went on. 'The census. You may have noticed that there is pressure to ask people to disclose their sexual orientation in the census questionnaire. Yes, people would be asked whether they are gay or straight or whatever. What a cheek! What people are is their own business and nothing to do with the state or social researchers or anybody else really. Nothing. Sex is a private matter and adults should be allowed to do what they like without having

67

the government breathing down their necks. And the same goes for religious beliefs. People are entitled to their private conscience, if that is what they wish.'

William shook his head. He resented people asking him what party he would vote for, and he knew that there were people for whom that question would be only the beginning. It surprised him, though, that this was coming from Angelica. Surely the whole point of having spies – if that was what she was – was to obtain information about other people. Did a spy who believed in privacy make sense? Were there *libertarian* spies?

'This country used to be free,' he said. 'We used to be able to speak and think as we liked. We used to be entitled to a private life.'

Angelica nodded. 'I'm inclined to agree with you. I went into this job, you know, because I felt that I would be helping to protect freedom. Freedom of speech, freedom from arbitrary arrest and intimidation, freedom to walk about the place without being obliged to give an account of yourself to some officious gendarme. I really believed that.'

'And now?'

She looked William in the eye. 'I still believe that. I still think that the work we do is meant to protect our society from people who would impose their will on us. From ideologues who use violence to intimidate others. Who would impose tyranny of one sort or another on us. I still believe that . . .' She faltered. 'Except, I think that while we're trying to protect freedom, there are plenty of people who are busy destroying it. And they're not doing it with threats or bombs, they're

68

doing it through regulations and legislation and a hundred little restrictions on freedom of thought and speech. Each of these may be small, but their cumulative effect is a massive erosion of freedom. Death by a thousand cuts. They're hooked on getting as much control over us as they can. They're thoroughly illiberal. They really are.'

William listened. He agreed with her; what she said seemed very reasonable. And yet she had made this absurd, almost paranoid suggestion that they could not talk openly in his flat.

'I can assure you that there's nobody listening in to what is said in this place,' he said. 'Corduroy Mansions isn't bugged.'

'That may be so,' said Angelica. 'But the point is this: we have to have strict rules about when we can talk with our contacts. We like to control the time and place. It's a procedural issue.'

'So when do you want to see me?'

Angelica took a piece of paper out of her handbag. 'The details are here,' she said, handing it to him.

William glanced at the paper. 'Written in invisible ink?' he asked. 'Do I have to iron it to get the ink to appear? That's what we did when we were in the scouts. We wrote in lemon juice, if I remember correctly, and an iron would bring out the writing.'

Angelica laughed. 'No, this is perfectly legible. But I'd appreciate it if you'd make a mental note of what is written there, and then burn it.'

William let out a hoot of laughter. 'You're not serious, Angelica!'

Angelica nodded. 'Deadly serious,' she said. 'And tell me,

since you mentioned the scouts, when you were in the move-ment did you make a promise? Did you promise to do your duty?'

William remembered standing in a circle and raising his arm in the scout salute. He remembered the words of the scout promise, dredged up now from the deep recesses of memory; it was so long ago, and the world was so different then. It was before sorrow and failure and the sense of things getting thinner.

'I suppose I did,' he said. 'I wonder if modern scouts promise to do their duty?'

'I have no idea,' said Angelica. 'But do remember what you promised. A promise is a promise, isn't it?'

William stared at his visitor in silence. He wondered if this was the way they recruited people these days, and if so, whether anybody responded to such tactics. Nobody believed in anything any more, as far as he could make out, and promises appeared to mean nothing. And if that was the case, then why was he so readily agreeing to meet these people?

The reason came to him suddenly. He loved his country. He loved it because it might be a bit frayed round the edges but still it was filled with good-natured, tolerant people; with eccentrics and enthusiasts; with people who really did drink warm beer and ride bicycles (well, some of them did, although the cyclists now were mounted on racing bikes and drank high-energy drinks from aluminium flasks rather than warm beer – but they were still loveable).

So he agreed to do what they wanted him to do and to meet them where they said they wanted him to meet them.

'Remember to bring your dog,' said Angelica. 'Don't forget to bring Freddie de la Hay.'

William nodded his agreement. But then the thought struck him forcibly: how did they know Freddie's name? He had not mentioned it to Angelica, and yet she knew. Was it the business of these people to find out *everything* – even the name of one's dog?

17. An Icelandic Poet

Marcia looked at William in frank disbelief. 'What?' she asked. 'Could you tell me again what you've just told me?'

Marcia, who was William's old friend, former flatmate – for a very brief time – and general confidante, had called in at Corduroy Mansions the same day he had received the visit from Angelica. Marcia was a caterer, and she owned a small company that specialised in cooking for events. In the days when boardroom lunches were more common she had concentrated on those, but now, with companies being encouraged to be slender in every sense, she had been obliged to diversify. Catering for weddings and funerals was now the staple of her business but she had also developed a profitable line in providing canapés for diplomatic cocktail parties and political receptions.

That day she had prepared a small finger-lunch for the Icelandic ambassador in honour of a visiting Icelandic poet, Sigurlin Valdis Antonsdóttir. The ambassador's assistant had asked for several varieties of northern fish to feature on the menu, to mark the fact that the guest of honour was the author of *Cold Waves*, a highly regarded saga of migrating cod, which had won Iceland's premier literary prize and had recently been translated into Finnish. Marcia had risen to the challenge and served herring rolls, cod roe, and a great deal of smoked salmon. Some of it had been left uneaten and was not wanted by the embassy, so Marcia dropped round to deliver it to William. He always welcomed the surplus snacks that Marcia brought him, and indeed had once remarked that he could live almost entirely off the scraps from her table. This pleased Marcia. She had been brought up by her very domesticated mother to believe that of all the satisfactions open to women, feeding men was ultimately the most profound. She knew that this was, quite simply, wrong, but the beliefs instilled in childhood and youth are hard to dislodge, and Marcia had eventually stopped fighting the convictions that lay deep within her.

'I know I'm pathetic,' she once said to a friend. 'I know I should be all independent and self-sufficient and so on, but that's just not *me*. I want to feed men. I just love putting large plates of food in front of them. I love it.' She paused. 'Does that mean there's something wrong with me?'

Her friend looked at her pityingly. 'Yes,' she said. 'It makes you inauthentic, Marcia.'

Marcia winced. 'Does it really?'

The friend nodded. 'Yes, it does. You have to live for yourself, you know. You have to do things that fulfil you, not others. Women are not there to look after men.'

Marcia thought about this. 'But who'll look after them if we don't?' she asked.

Her friend rolled her eyes. 'Marcia, dear . . .'

Marcia tried another approach. 'But what if you're fulfilled by doing things for other people? Why can't I feel fulfilled by making food for other people . . .' She corrected herself. It was not the feeding of people that gave her pleasure, it was the feeding of *men*. 'Making food for men, that is.'

The friend's frustration showed itself. 'That's really sad,' she said. 'It's sad because you don't know that you're being used by a system – the old, deep-rooted system of male domination. Of course men want us to feed them. Who wouldn't?' She looked at Marcia, as if to challenge her to contradict this. But Marcia just listened, and so the friend continued, 'Most men, you see, don't grow up; they're fed by their mothers when they're little boys and they realise how satisfactory that is. And being fed by somebody else *is* really very comfortable. So they manipulate women into carrying on doing it for the rest of their lives.'

'But if women want . . .'

'No, Marcia, that's not going to work. Women *think* they want to make food for men, but that's false consciousness. You know what that is? No? Well, I'll explain it to you some other time. The point is that women are made to think that they like doing things, but they don't really. They want to do their own things, things for themselves.'

The conversation had ended at that point, and Marcia had gone about her business, which was feeding people. Her friend might have been right but she felt that there was not much she could do about the state of inauthenticity that her friend had diagnosed. And now that she came to think of it, perhaps

73

it was quite pleasant to be inauthentic, and if one was happy in one's inauthenticity, why should one try to change it? It was an interesting question, but there were canapés to be prepared and that was a more immediate task than the rectification of false consciousness.

Now, as she removed the cover from a dish of rolled herring, she felt a warm glow of satisfaction at William's obvious pleasure.

'My absolute favourite!' he exclaimed, picking up one of the strips of herring on its cocktail-stick skewer.

Marcia smiled. 'Well, I'm glad. The Icelandic poet turned up her nose at these. And yet her poems are all about cod and herring, apparently.'

'Perhaps she couldn't bring herself to eat the subject of her poems,' suggested William, reaching for another. 'Poor woman. It would be like Wordsworth eating daffodils. One just can't.'

William went on to tell Marcia about Angelica's visit and the assignation that he had the next day. Marcia put down the plate of herring and listened intently.

'This is ridiculous,' she said, when he had described the incredible conversation for the second time. 'I take it you won't be going.'

William shook his head. 'No. I mean, yes, I am going.'

Marcia stared at him incredulously. 'But this is a lot of nonsense, William. You can't get involved in these ridiculous schoolboy games. Get a grip, for heaven's sake!'

William looked away. He did not like Marcia telling him what to do, and he felt that this really was none of her business. But she was a difficult person to argue with and he had to admit that it was a rather absurd situation.

'But I told them I'd come,' he said. 'They're expecting me.'

'Then stand them up,' she retorted.

He looked at her reproachfully. Marcia might have been a friend but there were times when he realised that there lay between them a gulf of difference in attitudes to things both large and small. One of these was their attitude to obligation: if William said that he was going to do something, he did it. Marcia, although not unreliable, was more flexible. That was the difference between them.

Marcia stared back at William. She knew what he was thinking, which would be something to do with doing what one said one was going to do; she could read him so very easily.

'Don't go, William,' she said quietly. 'You're going to regret it if you do.'

18. Freddie de la Hay Goes to the Park

Marcia had put it bluntly. 'Listen William,' she said, 'You haven't crossed the . . . the Nile yet.'

'Rubicon, Marcia,' corrected William. 'One crosses the Rubicon.' He paused. 'And then, if one is *really* into mixing metaphors, one burns one's boats.'

'Rubicon, Nile – whatever,' said Marcia breezily. 'The point is you've crossed nothing yet. So you can still get out of this. Don't go. Just don't go.'

But he had ignored her advice, and found himself taking a delicious, almost perverse pleasure in doing so. The problem with Marcia, he thought, is that she thinks she's my *mother*.

For some men, of course, that would be a positive recommendation, the many men whose deepest ambition is to find their mother in another woman; but for William exactly the opposite was true. His mother had sought to run his life for him, and he had engaged wholeheartedly in both a conscious and subconscious cutting of apron strings. So any suggestions from Marcia were viewed through the very strong anti-maternal filter developed over time. This filter had led William to become a wine merchant precisely because his mother had been a teetotaller; it had prompted him to apply – unsuccessfully – to the University of Cambridge because his mother had set her heart on his going to Oxford; and it had resulted in his living in Pimlico because his mother had once expressed an antipathy for that part of London.

The trip from which Marcia sought to dissuade him was hardly a dangerous one. William was no Mungo Park, setting off into uncharted regions of the upper Senegal Basin; Mungo Park's mother, he imagined, was probably dead-set against her son wandering off to Africa like that – as, no doubt, was Mrs Livingstone. But if they had advised their sons not to go, then they had been ignored. And likewise William would take no notice of Marcia's advice, even though he was only proposing to take a taxi to Birdcage Walk, stroll across the road into St James's Park, and then along a footpath in the direction of the Mall. At the point where the path skirted the ornamental lake, he was told, he would come across a bench facing a copper beech tree, and that was where he was to sit until he was approached.

He left the flat with Freddie de la Hay half an hour before

he was due to be in the park. As always, Freddie was delighted at the prospect of a walk and sniffed the air appreciatively as they set off from Corduroy Mansions.

'They were very insistent that you should come along, Freddie,' William explained. 'That's why you're here.'

Freddie de la Hay glanced up at his owner. He was aware that a remark had been addressed to him, but of course he had no idea what it was. He was a well-mannered dog, though, and he wagged his tail in that friendly way dogs have of encouraging their owners. Freddie de la Hay valued William highly, not simply because he was his master, but because Freddie was what the Americans refer to as a *pre-owned* dog, and as such he had a distant memory of somebody else who had not been as kind as William; who had made him eat carrots and use a seatbelt when he travelled in the car; who had forbidden him to chase cats and squirrels, lecturing him sharply if he set off in the pursuit of either. It had been a world of unfreedom, a world from which all joy and canine exuberance had been excluded, and he did not want to return to that dark and cold place. William was to be valued for that – for rescuing him from bondage, from durance vile.

They caught a taxi in Ebury Street. The traffic was light, and in just a few minutes William and Freddie completed the short journey to Birdcage Walk. As they alighted from the taxi, Freddie sniffed again, raising his muzzle and taking in the air, which to a dog's sensitive nose was very different from the air in Pimlico. He gave a low growl of anticipation; he could already smell the squirrels and, rich and tantalising, the lingering scent of an urban fox. Deep inside him, the dog's heart leaped with joy; it was only St James's Park, but Freddie might have had the whole Serengeti at his feet, or the rolling fields of the Quorn, so great was his sense of anticipation.

William looked about him. It was mid-morning on a Saturday, and such people as were out and about in the street were in casual attire, rather than in the uniform of the civil servants who abounded in those parts during the week. A small group of visitors sporting rucksacks emblazoned with the Australian flag passed him on the pavement. One of them bent down to pat Freddie on the back.

'Nice dog, mate.'

William smiled 'Yes, he is. Thank you.'

'What's his name?'

'Freddie de . . .' William stopped himself in time. He had been about to give Freddie's full name, but he realised how odd it would sound, particularly to an Australian. The Australians were always – mistakenly – accusing the English of stuffiness, and he could just imagine the reaction that the name Freddie de la Hay would provoke when the story was told back home.

'Even the dogs in London have got surnames,' the traveller would report. 'We met one with an incredibly posh moniker. Freddie de la Hay. Would you believe it? No, I swear we did. We really did.'

'Good on yer, Freddie,' said the visitor, and moved on.

They made their way into the park itself. William was experiencing a curious sense of anticipation – not an unpleasant sensation – but mixed with foreboding. He had not felt like that for a long time, and now he tried to remember what it reminded him of. It was elusive. It had been something like this before he sat examinations at school, but on reflection he decided that it was different. And he had felt rather like this when, as a boy of sixteen, he had been taken up in a glider by a friend of his father's; it had seemed such a flimsy machine, spun gossamer in the currents of air, and he had closed his eyes in sheer terror. But again the sensation he felt now was a bit different; it was more a state of astonishment that he, William French, wine dealer and quinquagenarian (just), should be doing something quite as foolhardy as this.

19. Pericolo di Morte

He found the bench without any trouble. It had not occurred to him that anybody might be sitting on it already, and for a few moments he wondered whether she could be his contact – the woman sitting at the far end, dispensing breadcrumbs to a small flock of pigeons on the ground before her. His eye moved from the woman to the pigeons; they had a dishevelled air to them and he began to look at them, and the woman, with disapproval. These pigeons had become *dependent*; they were the unintended casualties of her kindness.

William found himself wanting to warn her of the consequences of her misplaced generosity. 'They'll lose the ability to fend for themselves,' he might say. 'They could even forget how to fly.' But he stopped himself; it was none of his business, and it made him sound like some curmudgeonly opponent of welfare schemes, which he was not. And yet these birds were obviously *lazy* – and opportunistic too, in their greedy devouring of this woman's largesse. What bird, though, would not take advantage of free food? And what bird actually seeks out a life of hard work? The half-remembered line came back to him: Consider the birds of the air, they neither sow nor reap nor gather into barns . . .

The birds had been settling into an untroubled feast but they were soon rudely dispersed by Freddie de la Hay. Freddie, who had been gazing at tree trunks in the hope of seeing a squirrel, suddenly noticed the pigeons and uttered a challenging bark. The birds took to the wing in a flutter and squawk, surprising their benefactress, who clasped one hand to her hat and the other to the bag of breadcrumbs. She glowered first at Freddie de la Hay and then at William, before rising to her feet and moving off. That at least solves that, thought William as he took her place on the bench; *she* is definitely not MI6.

Ensconced on the bench, William spread himself in a way calculated to discourage any other passerby or feeder of pigeons to join him. He had brought with him a copy of a newspaper, and he now opened it and began to read, while Freddie, rapidly reconciled to the conclusion that this would not be an overly energetic walk, sat down at William's feet to await developments.

Twenty minutes passed, and William began to regret arriving so early. Not only was it rather boring sitting on the bench with nobody to talk to, but he decided that it was also rather embarrassing. As people walked past him – and the park was by no means empty – they glanced at him, sometimes with looks that struck him as being almost pitying. And then there were others whose glances seemed more enquiring, and these disturbed him. Was this bench a meeting point for people who came to the park for . . .? Surely not; surely not in St James's Park, so close to the centre of government and Churchill's war rooms and all the rest of it? And yet he had read those odd, salacious reports in the newspapers of goings-on in the royal parks. If one wanted to meet a guardsman, for example, to discuss defence policy or whatever, presumably one came and sat about on benches exactly like this. Or did one lurk in bushes and go 'psst' when likely-looking persons walked past? William was not naive, but there were certain parts of the city's life, perhaps, of which he might be innocent.

And then something happened. William was looking at his watch and wondering whether to call the whole thing off when he became aware that a man was approaching the bench. Out of the corner of his eye he saw that the man, who was somewhere in his forties, was wearing a lightweight grey suit and had a newspaper tucked under his arm. The man drew near and then, without hesitation, sat down. The newspaper was unfolded and he began to read.

William glanced at the paper. So *that's* what they read, he thought.

'Bad business,' muttered the man.

William half turned to face his companion.

'No,' whispered the man. 'Just look straight ahead.'

William stared at the surface of the lake. A duck, sitting on the bank, decided to launch itself with a little plop.

'Yes, it's a very bad business,' the newcomer continued.

'What is?' asked William, out of the corner of his mouth.

'This business with the politician,' said the man. 'Frightful.'

William said nothing. The situation, he thought, was becoming increasingly ridiculous.

'My name's Sebastian, by the way,' said the man, turning a page of the newspaper. 'Sebastian . . .' He paused, lowering the newspaper and looking out over the lake. 'Sebastian Duck.'

'I see,' said William.

'And I take it that this is Freddie de la Hay?'

William nodded.

'Good,' said Sebastian, folding up his paper. 'Now, let's go for a walk. Normal pace. Not too fast. As if we're enjoying the sunshine. All right?'

They set off, with Freddie trotting contentedly beside William.

'Angelica says that you've accepted our offer,' said Sebastian. 'C's very grateful.'

William frowned. 'C?'

'Yes, C himself. He had a word with the head of section, and they've both very pleased that you're on board. C hopes to meet you quite soon, and wonders whether you could meet him for lunch at the Garrick some day. But he's off to Singapore in a day or two and has rather a hectic month ahead of him.'

'He must be pretty busy,' said William.

Sebastian nodded. 'We're understaffed. Everybody thought that the end of the Cold War would mean a considerable reduction in our workload. Hah! For a year or two, maybe, and lots of chaps took early retirement. Then lo and behold, the other side merely changes its colours and a lot of extremists

82

of one sort or another pop up under our noses. So it's business as usual, and when we take a roll call we discover we're three hundred people short.'

'I don't know how you cope,' said William.

Sebastian shrugged. 'With difficulty. Here's me working on a Saturday – just for instance. My wife wanted us to go down to Sussex to see her mother, but we had to beg off because I had to meet you. Not that it's your fault, of course – it's the rota. The rota's a mess.'

William thought for a moment; he felt he should at least try to say something. 'Can't C do something about it?'

Sebastian considered the suggestion. 'He could, I suppose, but I don't think that he should have to concern himself with that sort of stuff. No, the answer's to recruit more staff. But try telling that to the establishment people. A flat refusal is what you get. Public spending restraints and so on.'

'Everybody's feeling the pain,' said William. 'My own margins are down a lot.'

Sebastian turned to him. 'You're in the booze trade, aren't you?'

'Yes.'

'I was wondering if you could recommend a not-too-expensive bubbly for an occasion? It's my mother-in-law's sixty-fifth coming up, and we need to get something that will keep about forty people – no, maybe a few more – happy. Somebody suggested cava, but frankly I'm not too keen.'

William smiled. The absurdity of what was happening was now complete. 'New Zealand produces a number of very good champagne-style wines,' he said. 'They're more expensive than cava, but well worth the extra.' He was on the point of saying something more, but his companion seemed suddenly to have lost interest.

'You do realise that all this is potentially fairly dangerous,' Sebastian said.

William stopped walking. 'Dangerous? For me?'

Sebastian shook his head. 'No, not for you.' He pointed down at Freddie de la Hay. 'Dangerous for him. As our friends in the Italian secret service are rather fond of saying, *pericolo di morte.*'

20. *The Open Society and Its Enemies*

'Look,' said William. 'I agreed to meet you because Angelica asked me and I . . . well, I suppose I felt it was my duty.'

William didn't want to continue walking, but Sebastian Duck, although he inclined his head sympathetically, took hold of his arm and pressed him onwards. 'Just make it look natural. Two colleagues taking a stroll during a quiet hour out of the office.'

'It's Saturday,' William pointed out. 'And one of us has a dog. Not very credible, if you don't mind my saying so.'

Sebastian smiled. 'Office dog,' he said. 'Quite a few places have them these days, I'm told. Helps staff to bond, I believe.'

William said nothing.

'However,' Sebastian continued, 'I fully understand your concerns. It probably seems a bit strange to you, meeting me in the park and all this cloak and dagger stuff . . .'

'Precisely,' said William emphatically. 'Ridiculous, if you ask me.'

Sebastian was silent for a moment. Then, when he answered, there was a note of steely seriousness in his voice. 'Oh, you think so? You think this is all play-acting? Well, let me tell you something: this isn't a game. Kipling talked about the Great Game – remember? *Kim*? You ever read that? Well, it isn't a game any more, I can assure you. You know the stakes?'

William shook his head. 'I know nothing about intelligence work,' he said. 'Which makes me wonder what on earth I'm doing here.'

'You're helping us,' said Sebastian. 'And I can assure you, we're extremely grateful.'

'Well—'

Sebastian cut him short. 'The reason I mentioned the stakes is that many people just don't know what we're up against. We're an open society, Mr French. And any open society is in one sense extremely weak – vulnerable, indeed. We have great strengths and resilience because we're open, but there are numerous people willing to take advantage. People who abuse our hospitality. People who hate us for one reason or another. And then there are people who use this city as a playground for battles which are really nothing to do with us, but which can be fought by proxy on our streets.

'I suspect that you understand all that. What you may not know, though, is that every one of us involved in this work is a potential target. You may think that I'm being unnecessarily furtive, but I assure you I'm not. Over the last three years I've lost two people I've worked with closely. One drowned in

Ireland. Where was his lifejacket? He had it on when he went out in his boat, but he wasn't wearing it when they fished him out of the water. Another died of food poisoning. Very sudden. Where had he had his last meal? In a restaurant that had opened up at the end of his street the previous month and closed two days after his demise. And where was the proprietor? Nobody knew. One of the staff said that he had heard him addressed by three different names. Interesting.

'So if you think I'm being too careful, let me tell you, I am not. Let me also reveal to you that the woman who was sitting on the bench when you arrived is known to us. She was arrested by the police five minutes after she left the bench – charges of littering – just to get her out of the park and prevent her from witnessing our meeting. Yes. You may well be surprised. And you'd be surprised to know who she works for. Which I can't tell you, I'm afraid.'

Sebastian paused now and looked at William. 'So, does that put a different complexion on the matter?'

William nodded. He was beginning to feel miserable; the farce had turned to dark drama within the space of a few minutes. He had no doubt about the seriousness of these people, but what he did not know was what they wanted of him. Sebastian had said nothing about that.

But the explanation soon came. 'Look, William – you don't mind if I call you William, do you? Look, I can't tell you absolutely everything, but I can give you the broad outlines. We – that is, my section – are currently involved in watching a group of Russians who have taken a year's lease on a flat near Notting Hill Gate. These people are simply not who they claim to be. They have form, as we put it – lots of form. We suspect that they're in this country to buy sensitive commercial and military information. I can't really say much more than that.'

William shrugged. 'I suppose I don't really need to know.' He was keen *not* to know, in fact; some information, he thought, was best left well alone.

But Sebastian had more to tell him. 'We've obtained the flat next door to them and put one of our people in it. A woman. Often women are less the objects of suspicion than men. As far as they're concerned she's just the neighbour – a harmless, middle-aged woman, who likes dogs.' He paused. 'Which is what the head Russian likes too. He's called Anatoly and he's talked to our woman on a number of occasions. He told her that he had a dog until about eight months ago, when it died. He said it was a Pimlico Terrier.' He stopped, and looked at William. 'He said that he could never bring himself to have another breed. It would have to be a Pimlico Terrier. And yet there were so few of them around . . .'

William held his breath. He glanced down at Freddie de la Hay, who was, of course, a Pimlico Terrier. Freddie gazed back up at him with mild curiosity. He had given up on the hope of finding a squirrel and was now vaguely thinking of going home, where he might be given something to eat.

'You will no doubt see where this is going,' said Sebastian.

William was not sure. 'Well, Freddie's—'

Sebastian did not let him finish. 'Exactly,' he said. 'So our woman said that as it happened she was just about to get a Pimlico Terrier, although she was worried about having to put him in kennels when she went off to Swansea to visit her sister, who was not very well.'

Sebastian watched William's expression as the story unfolded. By now, he thought, it would be obvious what MI6 had in mind, and he was sure that William would pick it up.

He was right. William gasped.

'Yes,' said Sebastian. 'Exactly.'

'Exactly what?'

Sebastian smiled. 'Well, I assumed that you had worked out what we had in mind, which is to borrow Freddie de la Hay for a while – a couple of months perhaps.'

'And?'

'And get the Russian to look after him for a few days now and then.'

'And put a transmitter on his collar?'

Sebastian inclined his head, as if to bestow praise. 'Exactly,' he said.

William grimaced. It was *very* annoying when somebody said *exactly* all the time. When he was fourteen there had been a boy at school who had said *d'accord* to virtually everything anybody said to him. Eventually, William had punched him, quite hard, breaking his nose in the process, which was something he had regretted down the years, and still did. He knew that one should not punch people who annoyed one, although there was a case for it at times, a seemingly irresistible case. He wanted to punch this man, this enigmatic Sebastian Duck – if that was his real name – but he knew that he could not. *Wine Merchant Punches Duck in Royal Park* . . . that was how his son, Eddie, with his annoying habit of talking in headlines, would put it. No, he could never do it. *Wine Merchant Shows Restraint in Meeting with Spy*. So he simply said, 'Oh, well,' and Sebastian Duck, interpreting this as agreement, nodded and said, 'Exactly.'

But there was no agreement – at least not yet. 'I'll need time to think about it,' William said. 'Can you give me a telephone number? I'll get back to you.'

Sebastian Duck nodded, and took a card out of his pocket with a telephone number printed on it. 'Here,' he said. 'Don't pass it on, though.'

Oh really, thought William. You people are ridiculous. He grunted.

'Exactly,' said Duck. 'I'm pleased you understand.'

21. Recycled Sandwiches

After his meeting with Sebastian Duck, William walked all the way back to Corduroy Mansions. He wanted to give Freddie the exercise – even though only a small part of the walk would be through the park – and he wanted, too, some time to think. William had always found that walking encouraged thought. Unlike the unfortunate American president who, waspish critics said, found it difficult to walk and chew gum at the same time, William could walk and think very effectively. He did not chew gum, of course, and indeed chewing gum was one of his pet hates. 'People look so bovine when they chew gum,' he had said to Marcia once. 'Like cows chewing the cud.'

'Oh, I don't know,' said Marcia. 'If people enjoy it, then why shouldn't they do it?'

Marcia was fundamentally libertarian at heart. She might not have described herself as a Benthamite, but that was what she was, and she would have enthusiastically endorsed Bentham's view that the only things that should be prohibited are those things that harm others.

'Because it's disgusting,' said William. 'As I said, it makes people look bovine.'

'But if that's what they want to do,' said Marcia, 'why shouldn't they? If I want to look bovine, then surely I'm entitled to do so. It's not as if I'm harming anybody by chewing gum. It's not that—'

'But it *is* harmful,' William interjected. 'It makes a terrible mess. That's why Lee Kwan Yew objected to it. That and failing to flush the lavatory. That's an offence too in Singapore.'

Marcia looked astonished. 'Your own loo?'

'No,' said William. 'Just public ones. And why not prohibit it? It harms people.'

Marcia shook her head. 'Hardly. Offends them, maybe. Doesn't really harm them.'

William was not going to let Marcia get away with that. 'But it does harm them. Public health. Same with spitting. Spitting should be illegal because it spreads disease, and that harms other people – it harms us all.' He paused. 'And anyway, I still think chewing gum is awful. It's on a par with eating with one's mouth open in public. It's just . . .' He tailed off; he and Marcia would never agree over some matters – rather a lot of matters, in fact – and that was one of the reasons why it was not to be . . . There could be no romantic attachment to somebody who might at any moment take out a stick of chewing gum and start to chew like a cow.

But their difference of opinion on that matter did not prevent him from deciding, as he walked back across the park, that he would discuss the meeting with Marcia when he saw her that evening. She had told him that she would drop in on her way back from a catering engagement for the Romanian embassy.

'They're having a cocktail party,' she had explained. 'But it'll be over by seven – poor dears, they can only rise to two canapés per guest and one and a half glasses of wine. But I'll throw in a few bottles free, just to give them a slightly better party. And some free sandwiches, which will be only *slightly* second-hand – leftovers from a lunchtime reception for a firm of solicitors. They never eat very much – they're far too *driven* – and there are bound to be bags of sandwiches left over that can be diverted to the poor old Romanians.'

'Quite right,' said William. 'One would not want to waste sandwiches. Particularly in these straitened times.'

Marcia nodded in agreement. 'And very few sandwiches *are* wasted,' she said. 'Did you know the Prime Minister passes on his extra sandwiches to the Chancellor of the Exchequer for use at his receptions? Did you know that? That's why you never get any egg mayonnaise sandwiches at the Chancellor's parties – because the egg sandwiches always go before the cucumber and the cheese ones. It always happens that way.'

William smiled at the thought. It was the cascade system – the same system that allocated older rolling stock to less prosperous railway regions. It was exactly the same, it seemed, with sand-wiches.

Marcia was smiling too. 'I'm not sure if I should tell you this,' she said, 'but I heard the most wonderful story. It's been going round catering circles for the last few weeks, but every-body who tells it to you asks you to keep it under your hat.'

'Then you shouldn't tell me,' said William firmly.

'Oh, I don't know,' said Marcia. 'I know how discreet you are, William. You won't pass it on.'

William said nothing; he was wondering what sensitive stories there could possibly be about sandwiches.

Marcia lowered her voice to a whisper. 'There are plenty of receptions in the House of Commons, you know. Members of Parliament are always giving parties in honour of this, that and the next thing. The Commons Antarctic Treaty Group, the Joint Committee on South American Relations and so on. Every evening without fail.'

William made a gesture, the gesture of one who knows that things are going on, but knows too that he is never invited. The parties of others – or those that one doesn't attend – are always so self-indulgent. For most of us, the knowledge that somebody, somewhere, is enjoying himself more than we are is strangely disturbing. A common human response is to disap-prove, and to try to stop the enjoyment; that has been the well-established response of the prude in all ages. William was not like that, but he did feel the occasional pang at the thought that London was full of parties and yet when he contemplated his own social diary, it was virtually empty. Very occasionally he received an invitation to dinner somewhere, and there were always the occasions when Marcia dropped in. And of course there was his club – the Savile – where the conversation sparkled at the members' table, but the members all seemed so much better informed than he was, and he felt too shy to push himself forward in conversations where he was at a disadvantage.

'Well,' continued Marcia, 'I heard from a catering friend that MPs have developed a racket in wine. There's a group of them who call themselves the Parliamentary Committee on Sustainable Receptions and go round at the end of these occasions, pour all the dregs from the glasses into large containers and *then rebottle it*. Yes! They pour it back into bottles and re-cork the bottles. Then, when it comes to the next reception, they serve the dregs and take the full, untouched bottles for themselves.'

William was appalled. 'I thought we'd heard the end of all that,' he said. 'What if the *Telegraph* got hold of this?'

Marcia shook her head. 'This story will never end up in the *Telegraph*.'

'But that's dreadful!' William exploded. 'And it's not just because I'm a wine dealer. Think of all the bits and pieces – the crumbs, the lipstick . . . It's disgusting. It's . . . it's beyond belief.'

'Precisely,' said Marcia. 'And do you know something? They're all members of one party.'

William frowned. An all-party scandal was one thing, a single party scandal quite another. 'Which one?'

Marcia waved a hand in the air. 'Oh, I can't remember, I'm afraid. They all seem so alike these days.'

22. Codes and Things

Of course William knew what Marcia would say about his meeting with MI6; she had already said it. He owed these people nothing; they had no right to make any demands of him. They were playing games, these espionage people – that's what they did, and there was no difference, no difference at all between what they did and what boys, mere boys, did when they played in the playground. William knew that, didn't he? He had been a boy, hadn't he? (Absurdly distant prospect.) It was ridiculous, all this cloak and dagger business in the middle of London *in broad daylight!*

But as he walked back to Corduroy Mansions, he tried to put Marcia's voice out of his mind. You are not my mother, he muttered. And Marcia, or the idea of Marcia, looked askance at him, as if to disclaim any such notion. 'Why on earth should you imagine that I think of myself as your mother?' He shook his head; it was too complex even to begin to explain, but every son knew instinctively what the problem with mother was. It was mother who *fussed*; who told you what you could or could not do; it was mother who was always there . . . providing love, and security, and solace; who was prepared to stand up for you whatever you did. He sighed. That was the problem: mother provided all that, but at the same time a boy wanted to be free of his mother, wanted to go out into the world and do things on his own account, to lead his own life. Mother and freedom, then, stood in contradiction to one another.

'I'm sorry, Marcia,' he said to himself. 'I'm very sorry, but this is something that I'm going to decide myself.'

The virtual Marcia smiled in a rather self-satisfied way. 'Then why ask me in the first place?'

'Because I need to talk to somebody. And I like talking to you.'

'Some consolation! You like talking to me, but you don't want to listen to my advice, do you?'

This internal conversation might have continued for some time, had William not been distracted by Freddie de la Hay, who, having picked up the scent of a squirrel, was straining at his lead. William checked Freddie, and as he did so he came to his decision. He would say yes. He would telephone Sebastian Duck immediately and tell him that he was prepared to go along with what had been suggested and lend Freddie de la Hay to them.

He reached into his pocket and took out the card that Duck had given him. He scrutinised it for a moment, as if the number itself might reveal something. It was one of those very easily remembered mobile numbers, unlike one's own: a sequence of 123 and 666 at the end – 666, whose number was *that*? The Devil's, of course. William laughed. What nonsense! He would be imagining the smell of sulphur next.

William dialled, and Sebastian Duck answered immediately. 'Duck,' he said.

'It's William French.'

'Of course. Well, I enjoyed our meeting. Such a nice day. And you're still in the park, making the most of it.'

'Yes. I thought that my dog might enjoy ...' William stopped. How did Duck know that he was still in the park? The question presented itself, but was quickly dismissed;

Duck and his colleagues might be paranoid, but he would not be.

'I've given the matter a bit of thought,' said William. 'And the answer is yes. I'll do what you people want.'

Sebastian Duck's pleasure showed in his voice. 'Well, that's very good indeed. Thank you. Should we make the arrangements right now?'

William asked what there was to arrange. Did he have to sign something? The Official Secrets Act, if that was what they still called it?

'No, nothing so formal. A waiver form – that's all. Standard procedure.'

'All right.'

'Then we'll take him right now, if you don't mind. And I might add that he'll be terribly well looked after. We use the Met's dog-handler people. One of them will be specially assigned to this case. They're very experienced.'

William looked about him. 'Right now? Not when I get back to the flat?'

'No. Here and now. In the park, if you don't mind. One of our people is not far from you, you see. She'll take Freddie.' Duck paused. 'Or F as we'll call him for the purposes of this operation.'

William spun round. A short distance away there was a young couple, obviously immersed in one another, walking arm in arm; another man with a dog, walking in the opposite direction; a teenager carrying a skateboard under his arm; and . . . He became aware of a woman approaching him along the path.

96

'Somebody's coming,' said William. 'Is this . . .'

'That's her,' said Duck. 'When she comes up to you, she'll engage you in conversation. She'll say, "Nice weather," and you'll say, "Of course, but it could change." Got that?'

William wanted to laugh out loud. This was a comedy, and a weak one at that. Would his next set of instructions be tucked away in a hollow tree, he wondered.

The woman, who was somewhere in her late thirties, was attractive, and she smiled brightly at William as she reached him on the path. 'Nice day, Mr French.'

William found himself momentarily confused by the deviation from the agreed code. Did it matter? And what had he been meant to say? *Could change*?

'Yes,' he said. 'I mean, nice weather. Er.'

The woman's smile broadened. 'Oh, don't worry about all that. Ducky is a little . . . how shall we put it? Melodramatic. He's read too many John le Carré novels, I think. This is Freddie?'

She bent down and stroked Freddie gently behind the head. The dog looked up at her with undisguised affection.

'He loves that,' said William.

'Don't we all?' she said, as she stood up.

William looked into her eyes. For a moment he entertained a wild, impossible hope: that this pretty, vivacious woman might be just the person he was looking for. There had been stranger meetings, after all; people who met their life partners in lifts or in the queue for tickets to the Tutankhamun exhibit, or on jury service in a murder trial. There was no end to the strangeness of the circumstances in which we encounter those whom we love and who love us, so why should he not meet somebody like this in a place like this, on an errand as absurd and ridiculous as this? Why not?

23. Dee Lies to Caroline

Saturday was Caroline's day for a long lie-in, but not that Saturday. She had not slept well the previous night, having gone to bed in a state of intense anger. Never let the sun set on your wrath – that was the motto in one of those preachy needlework samplers that her mother liked so much. Dignified with an ornate Victorian frame, it had hung in her room at home until, at the age of sixteen, she had hidden it in a cupboard and denied all knowledge of its whereabouts. Well, on Friday night, she had certainly forgotten the adage, or at least left it mentally sequestered in its cupboard, as she switched out her light in a state of unambiguous wrath, all of it directed against James.

How could he have forgotten their arrangement to have dinner together? It was not as if it had been made weeks, or even days, earlier; it had been concluded a few hours before it was due to take place. One did not forget obligations as freshly minted as that; one simply did not.

What had happened? Had he simply decided that he had something better to do? James would never behave with such discourtesy, and yet, when she tried to telephone him, she found that his mobile phone was turned off. The only time he did that, she knew, was when he did not want to hear from her. It had happened once or twice before, after a minor row or misunderstanding, and he had even admitted it.

'I can't bear conflict, Caroline,' he explained. 'I simply can't. There are some people, you know, who *like* to fight with others – I'm not one of them. I'm really not.'

'But you can't just turn off your phone,' she said. 'That's running away.'

'I'd never run away from you,' he said soothingly.

'You'd simply turn me off?'

He smiled. 'Not you! But I must admit there are some people who really *need* an on–off switch. I can think of at least three. Maybe even more.'

The fact, then, that he had not answered his phone on Friday night pointed to only one conclusion – he had been avoiding her because he knew that he was standing her up. And even if the phone was off because the battery had run down, or he had simply forgotten, still he stood accused of thoughtlessness at the very least.

Unless something had happened. It was this thought that, more than anything else, ruined her sleep. There were many dangers in London. A traffic accident, for example – James was so unworldly and she had often had to grab his arm to prevent him from walking out into the traffic expecting it to stop. There was that, of course. She imagined herself standing in the police station while the police ran through a list of traffic incidents involving pedestrians. 'An art historian, you say, Miss? Well, we did have a young man knocked down near the Courtauld ...'

And there were other dangers. People simply disappeared

in London. One moment they are on their way to a meeting with a friend and the next they are nowhere to be seen. What happened to these people, she wondered. They were abducted, she had read, but where to? And how did their abductors keep them once they had them? It would be difficult, surely, to imprison somebody in central London; there simply wasn't the space.

James had no enemies – or none Caroline knew of. He had not even written a critical review. It would be understandable if he had written something scathing about an installation artist, for instance; such a critic might suddenly find himself put into a tank of formaldehyde or something like that by the artist's supporters. But James had never had anything published, not even a review.

Anger turned to anxiety, and then back to anger as yet another possibility suggested itself. James might have gone off with somebody else: while Caroline was waiting for him in Corduroy Mansions, he might have been in some entirely other part of London *cavorting* with somebody else. She tried to imagine James cavorting; she tried to imagine *anybody* cavorting. It was difficult. And if James had already expressed an antipathy to kissing for fear of germs, then surely he would be highly unlikely to *cavort*. Cavorting, even if it was difficult to picture, was surely even more likely to pose a risk of contamination by germs. For a moment she pictured James in the arms of another woman, preparing to cavort ... She put the thought out of her mind, only to have it replaced by a still more unsettling one. What if James had decided to go off for dinner with one of those rather foppish young men who hung about the auction houses? There was one who she was quite convinced was interested in James; she had seen him looking at him, in that way. James had said, 'Oh, him, he's not at all my type,' and laughed, but now the exchange came back to her in a most unsettling way.

She decided to get out of bed and make herself a reviving cup of coffee. She would not phone James, she thought; she would wait for him to phone her. And then she would be cool – no matter what effort it cost her. She could even pretend to have forgotten the engagement herself, which would be very satisfactory revenge – if he phoned to apologise and she asked him what he was talking about.

She went into the kitchen. Dee, who drank green tea first thing in the morning, was standing by the window, nursing a mug in her hands.

'Go out last night?' asked Caroline.

Dee looked out of the window. 'Yes.'

'Party?'

Dee shook her head. 'No, nothing special. Just went out for a meal.'

Caroline thought that rather unlike Dee, who was perpetually moneyless. 'Special occasion? By yourself?'

'Yes,' said Dee. 'Just me. Private treat.'

24. Berthea Reflects on Oedipus

Berthea Snark, psychotherapist and mother of Oedipus Snark MP, had settled herself into her seat on the train, and was now waiting patiently for it to pull out of Paddington station. It was a Saturday morning, and the station was halfway between the busyness of a weekday – when driven hordes of commuters poured into London from Oxfordshire and beyond – and the relative somnolence of a Sunday. On Saturday morning there were people travelling to see friends for the weekend, grown-up children returning to parents in the country for much-missed home cooking and laundry services, and tourists in search of an England that had once existed but now survived only in the imagination – an England of quiet villages and cricket greens and tiny, silent pubs.

Berthea Snark was on the train because she was going to visit her brother, Terence Moongrove, in his poorly maintained Queen Anne house on the edge of Cheltenham. She made this trip four or five times a year, and although her main motive for these journeys was concern for Terence, for whom she felt a considerable degree of responsibility, she also went because she enjoyed getting out of London. Her visits were usually for four or five days – quite long enough to feel the benefit of being in the country but not long enough to make her forget that she lived in London.

Sometimes, of course, they were longer; recently she had spent several weeks looking after Terence following his near-death experience. This had happened when Terence, a mechanical innocent of the first water, had attempted to recharge the battery of his Morris Traveller by connecting it directly to the mains. Not only had Terence stopped breathing for a few moments after this incident, but the battery, and the Morris itself, had stopped functioning altogether. This had resulted in Terence acquiring a second-hand Porsche from Monty, the son of his neighbour, Alfie Bismarck. Berthea had her misgivings about the acquisition of the Porsche, as she had about everything that Terence did. Her brother had always been a dreamer, and a lesser sister would have lost patience well before this, perhaps, with a brother who went on about sacred dance and the writings of the Bulgarian mystic, Peter Deunov. But Berthea was a tolerant sister – up to a point – and, of course, a psychotherapist, and she understood that no amount of dissuasion on her part would ever divert Terence from his mystical preoccupations and his alternative lifestyle. All that she could do, really, was to protect him from the more obvious dangers inherent in such an approach to life. And always, in the background, she could hope that one day he might meet somebody who would take him off her hands. Not that this was at all likely, given Terence's unprepossessing appearance – which included a propensity to cardigans and yellow slippers – and, more importantly, his utter inability to understand the way women – or indeed anybody else – thought.

But as she settled herself into her first-class seat – a luxury justified, she felt, by the ability it gave her to work during the journey – Berthea was thinking not so much of her brother Terence but of her son, Oedipus Snark, a well-known Liberal Democrat MP and *boulevardier*, as one newspaper had sarcastically described him. Berthea cut out all newspaper references to Oedipus, including this one, which appeared in a particularly waspish diary column. She did this not as most fond mothers did, pasting the cuttings into bulging scrapbooks; she preserved these items as material for her project and, possibly, as *evidence*.

Berthea's project was the writing of an unauthorised biography of her son. This was admittedly an unusual activity for a mother, but, as the commissioning publisher had acknowledged, a mother was surely better placed than most to write a warts-and-all biography of a son.

'Not that many do,' mused the publisher. 'Loyalty, I suppose . . .'

If Berthea felt reproached by this mention of loyalty, she had not shown it. She felt no compunction in writing her son's biography because, after a great deal of soul-searching, she had decided that he simply had to be stopped. Now, normally one would not have to say of a Liberal Democrat MP that he or she had to be stopped. It was unnecessary, as few Liberal Democrat MPs, alas, needed to be stopped. This was not their fault – such MPs were usually principled, hard-working and effective; the problem was that the party to which they belonged – admirable though it might be – regrettably seemed unlikely to be in a position to form a government. So the stopping of a Lib Dem MP seemed uncalled for, whereas the MPs of other parties could be really dangerous in that they could well find themselves with hands on the levers of power. Some of them – the most egregiously selfish or unscrupulous – had to be stopped for the public good, lest they find themselves in power.

Oedipus Snark, his mother believed, was only in the Liberal Democratic Party because the other two main parties had rejected him. Not many people knew this, of course, but she, being his mother, had seen the correspondence he had carelessly left lying about in the days when he still occupied a room in her mews house behind Corduroy Mansions. There were letters from party secretaries, politely phrased but clear in their message that he was not what they were looking for as a prospective candidate. The Liberal Democratic Party, however, in its profound decency, had allowed him in and then, as a result of the vagaries of the selection process, he had found himself selected as a candidate for a London constituency. And that could have been as far as he got, had it not been for the fact that both the main party candidates for that particular constituency had simultaneously been involved in serious scandals. They went down, and Oedipus Snark, then only thirty-one and one of the youngest parliamentary candidates, went up.

Berthea Snark might have left it at that, but there was still a danger that Oedipus might find himself near power, this by his own admission. 'Mother,' he had said, 'I know you think that I won't get anywhere politically, but may I let you into a little secret? They want me to cross the floor, to join up with *them*. And you know what mother? I'm going to do it when the time is ripe, and in return . . . Guess what? A cabinet post! Not a junior minister – a real, six-cylinder, eighty-four-horsepower ministerial post! What do you think of that, mother?'

Berthea said nothing. But what she thought was this: what if people knew about you? What then? And then, as a delicious – but guilty – afterthought, she muttered to herself, Creep!

25. *Cars and Auras*

When Berthea's train drew into Cheltenham station, Terence

Moongrove was waiting to meet her. He had arrived at the station half an hour earlier, allowing, as usual, a generous amount of time to park the car. This had taken him less time than anticipated, however, because he found the Porsche much more manoeuvrable than the Morris Traveller. It was not just the steering that seemed different; it was the response of other drivers, who generally seemed to get out of the way when they saw Terence in the high-powered German sports car.

'It's a very funny thing, Mr Marchbanks,' he said to his long-suffering *garagiste*. 'When I drive this new car you got me, I find I get *looks* from other drivers. Admiring looks, I think. Do you think that Monty Bismarck got the same thing when he drove this car?'

Mr Marchbanks raised an eyebrow. 'Looks? Well, I don't know – you'd have to ask Monty about that, I suspect. But I do know that some people judge others by their cars.'

Terence found this very strange. 'What a peculiar thing to do,' he said. 'What really counts is the spirit, Mr Marchbanks. Or a person's aura. That's the really important thing to look out for.' He paused, weighing up an idea that had come to him. 'Do you think that cars have auras, Mr Marchbanks?'

Mr Marchbanks was used to strange questions from Terence Moongrove. He sighed. 'Could be. Mind you, I'm not sure what an aura is. Cars certainly have emissions. Is an aura anything to do with that?'

Terence thought for a moment. 'The concepts are not altogether unrelated. An aura is a sort of emission – an emission of light. And I suppose that inanimate objects can have waves associated with them. Water has a memory, after all.'

Mr Marchbanks stared at Terence. 'Water has a memory, you say?'

Terence was now on firm ground; he knew about these things. 'Yes, it does! Jolly surprising, but it does. They've done amazing experiments, Mr Marchbanks. There's a professor called Beneviste. He's the one who discovered that water could remember things that happened to it – stuff you put into it. It remembers it all and reacts to the same stuff when it next has it put into it. Amazing.'

Mr Marchbanks moved the top set of his false teeth out over his lower lip; it was a little mannerism of his that manifested itself when he was puzzled. 'Well, I'll be damned,' he muttered.

'Indeed you will be,' Terence went on. 'Of course there are bags of people – bags of them – who were ready to throw cold water on this idea . . .'

'Cold water,' said Mr Marchbanks. He wondered whether the water would remember being thrown.

'Yes. People with closed minds – people who aren't prepared to accept any new ideas that don't match their view of how things are. There are plenty of people like that, Mr Marchbanks.'

The mechanic looked thoughtful. 'So are you suggesting that cars have memories?'

'They might have,' said Terence. 'I wouldn't state it as a fact – not categorically. But think of it – if inanimate objects can absorb vibrations, waves, energy, call it what you will, then it explains a lot, doesn't it? Hauntings, for instance. Energy is absorbed by stones and then released. It explains why places have an atmosphere.'

Mr Marchbank was interested. 'Yes, places do have an atmosphere, don't they? My mother-in-law's house, for instance. I've always said that there's something rum about that place. My wife doesn't agree, but I always pick up a very negative feeling when I go there.'

Terence nodded encouragingly. 'There you are, you see. Something negative has gone into the bricks and mortar. You're just picking it up, Mr Marchbanks.'

'But I'm not sure about cars. Houses are one thing, but cars . . .'

Terence made a gesture of acceptance. 'I didn't say that cars necessarily have that ability, but they could do. My Porsche, for instance. I must admit I get a sort of . . . vibration when I drive it. I feel somehow . . . a bit . . . well, a bit younger.' He blushed. 'A bit amorous even! Not that I would say that to anybody else, of course, but you're a mechanic . . .'

Mr Marchbanks was wide-eyed. 'Amorous, Mr Moongrove? Well, bless me! They say that these cars do help a bit in that department.'

'I always control myself,' said Terence quickly. 'I'm sure that the Highway Code has something to say about amorousness and cars.' He paused, composing himself after the admission. 'But I do find that people look at me with what I'm tempted to describe as respect. Very strange.'

And now this respect had meant that a car that had been thinking of claiming his parking spot near the station yielded when the driver saw him coming. Terence slipped into the parking place and, with time on his hands, walked into the station to buy a newspaper before Berthea arrived. So spent, the time passed quickly and there she was, his sister, carrying her weekend bag and waving to him from the end of the platform. Dear Berthy, he thought. So many things change in the world, but she always looks the same: same funny old jumper and odd-looking skirt; same old weekend bag, a holdall that she had had for ages and ages and which Uncle Edgar bought to take to Madeira.

And Berthea, for her part, looking down the platform, saw her brother walking towards her and thought: Dear Terence! What a disaster area he is! That defeated old cardigan and those shoes with the Velcro fastenings. And his ghastly glasses. Oh dear! He must be the only Porsche driver in the world – in the whole world – who wears shoes with Velcro fastenings. What a distinction to have in this life.

'Berthy!' exclaimed Terence, looking at his watch. 'Your train's arrived on the dot – on the absolute dot. Just as Mussolini promised it would. Only he wasn't talking about England, was he? And he made such a beastly mess of Italy, didn't he?'

Berthea leaned forward and kissed him lightly on his left cheek. 'I have stopped noticing when trains arrive or do not arrive,' she said. 'My life is quite full enough without that to exercise me.'

'Time is relative,' said Terence, reaching to take her holdall from her. 'It's a tyranny we invent for ourselves.'

'Mmm,' said Berthea.

'And anyway,' said Terence, 'Like you, I find myself far too busy to think about time.'

Berthea threw him a sideways glance. Her brother, as far as she knew, had absolutely nothing to do – apart from his ridiculous sacred dancing and the occasional meetings of the various lunatic societies to which he belonged. How could he possibly be busy?

They made their way to the car. 'I've got a nice surprise for you,' said Terence as he opened the passenger door for her.

'I've already seen this car,' said Berthea. 'And I must say—'

He cut her short. 'No, not the car. It's nothing to do with the car. It's a surprise for you at the house.'

'Oh.'

'Yes. I've got some people staying there. Roger and Claire. They're terribly nice people. You'll like them, I know it. They're writing a book together, and they're staying with me while they do it.' He laughed modestly. 'I suppose that makes me a sort of patron of literature. Like those people who had salons. Madame de Staël, and people like that.'

Berthea said nothing. She was not going to like Roger and Claire – she knew it.

'Their book is very important,' said Terence. 'It's going to change the way we think about so much.'

Berthea looked out of the window. 'How long is it going to take for them to write this *magnum opus*?' she asked.

'Four years,' said Terence. Then he added. 'That's for volume one, of course.' He paused. 'And, listen, Berthy, it's very unkind of you to call it a magnum opus in that sarcastic tone. Naughty, naughty! I've read about salons, you know, and there was a very strict etiquette, which included not saying anything nasty about the books of those present. Which in this case means Rog and Claire.'

Berthea sighed. Madame de Staël. Rog and Claire. Five minutes in my brother's company and I'm already wading in a morass of intellectual treacle.

26. Pantoufles

But the conversation soon moved on, as it always did with Terence. *Flight of ideas*, thought Berthea – but not quite. It was true that Terence could talk at great length – and frequently did – but there was usually a reasonable connection between the topics he rambled on about. A true example of flight of ideas would go from this to that at the bat of an eyelid, and that would, of course, be indicative of bipolar disorder or attention deficit disorder, or even schizophrenia. No, Terence was afflicted with none of those things – Berthea's trained eye could spot that well enough. His problem, she thought, was more one of magical thinking. He had spoken to her – as well as to Mr Marchbanks – about the memory of water, and that was a good example of the problem. He *wanted* the world to be otherwise than it really was; he wanted to see causality and connection where none really existed. He wanted to believe that pure thought could change the world.

She paused. Who doesn't? she asked herself. As children we try to create the world along the lines we want it to be. We wish an imagined world into existence through play – castles and kingdoms, fairies and elves, imaginary friends – but at some point we have to let go of it. Santa Claus dies; for all of us a personally felt demise that brings down one of the great pillars of that self-created world. From then on, although reality asserts itself for most of us, for some the memory of that power to create, the memory of that universe of the imagining, persists. It is this that tempts us still to believe that the world actually functions in ways other than those that we understand through our senses. How sad, she thought, and she was reminded of those patients of hers who were stuck in some earlier stage of their development, for example the City trader who sat in her consulting room once a month and repetitively recited, in loving, nostalgic detail, the events of his eighth year, when the world was innocent and fresh and he was happy. And then wept – not every session, but often enough – for everything that he had lost. Slowly she was leading him to an understanding of why he mourned, laying bare his unhappiness.

Or how about the woman who would talk only of her mother, and of what her mother had thought about things. Everything triggered a maternal memory; Berthea had given her a cup of tea, and she had launched into a long description of the china her mother had once possessed but which had been broken by the removal men. *Removal men*, Berthea had written in her notes, and underlined the words. Removal men were such a powerful metaphor for brutal change, for dispossession, for the shattering of the security of the domestic universe. They came and put our life into boxes and took it away. *Boxes*, wrote Berthea, and underlined that too.

She glanced at Terence, beside her at the wheel of his Porsche. Then she looked at the speedometer. Twenty-eight miles per hour, and they were out of the speed limit zone, as

Terence's house was just into the country on the very fringes of Cheltenham. Poor Terence, with his magical thinking, and his Porsche . . .

'I do like this little car of yours, Terence,' said Berthea. 'But you must miss that old Morris of yours.'

'Morris is gone,' said Terence firmly. 'Mr Marchbanks took him away.'

Berthea smiled. Morris is gone. The title of a novel, perhaps. Or a song, like that haunting one she had heard the other day, 'Tortoise Regrets Hare'. Terence regrets Morris. Morris gone.

'Yes, maybe he's gone,' Berthea said. 'But don't you miss familiar objects, once they break or are replaced or whatever? I do. I had to throw out an old pair of slippers the other day. You know, those sheepskin ones – I used to bring them down here for the weekend and pad about your house in them. Frightfully comfortable.'

Terence nodded. '*Pantoufles*,' he said. 'I called them your *pantoufles*.'

'So you did. Such a good name for them. The French are often better at naming things than we are, don't you think? We come up with such prosaic names.'

Terence was silent for a moment. 'Where do you think they are now? Do you think that they might have been picked up by some old tramp, who's wearing him in his . . . wherever tramps live, and feeling rather proud of them? Do you think?'

'I doubt it,' said Berthea. 'But it's possible. And it's rather nice to think that our things have an afterlife, as it were.'

'Yes,' said Terence. 'I got this cardigan from a charity shop, would you believe? It belonged to somebody else, you know.

Some other chap. Then it belonged to me, and I've had it for eight years now.'

'So I've noticed,' said Berthea. 'Have you thought of getting . . .'

'No,' said Terence firmly. 'I don't need new things yet, Berthy. These outer things are of no real significance, you know. What counts is the spiritual state. Peter Deunov . . .'

But there was no time for Deunov, as they had reached the driveway of Terence's house, and Berthea, anxious to avoid further explorations of the Bulgarian mystic, was commenting on the profusion of rhododendrons at the garden's entrance. 'Such thick foliage,' she said. 'I've always loved rhododendrons. I remember when those went in, you know. We were very small, so they've lasted an awful long time.'

'Like us,' said Terence. 'We've lasted a long time, haven't we, Berthy? And we've—' He did not finish. A figure had stepped out from behind one of the rhododendron bushes, causing Terence to brake sharply. Berthea, who had been gazing at the bushes, gave a start.

'Who . . .'

Terence answered her question. 'Rog,' he said. 'He loves walking about the garden. He says that the energy of the plants is conducive to his creative processes. He spends a lot of time in the garden.'

The man who had appeared so suddenly was staring at Berthea through the window of the Porsche. He was a tall man, dressed in white – as many of Terence's friends seemed permanently to be. His face was craggy, with high cheekbones – a slightly patrician face, the face of a boarding-school headmaster, or a senior army officer. This was not what she had expected. A Rog, Berthea had thought – shuddering at the abbreviation – ought to have a weak face, the face of one who did not quite know what was going on and was writing a book about it. This Rog, she decided, knew exactly what he was about.

She looked away, unwilling to meet the scrutinising gaze of the stranger. But then she turned back, and held the man's gaze. *Charlatan*, she thought.

27. Dee is Exposed as a Liar

Caroline almost put the phone down. (Metaphorically, of course: mobile telephones have spoiled *that* gesture. What could one do – throw the phone to the floor? The abrupt movement of the thumb onto the End Call button lacked the dramatic force of the slamming down of the receiver.) But she resisted the temptation and did not push the button; she listened coldly to the voice at the other end. James.

It was the morning afterwards – as it so often seems to be. 'Caroline? It's me.'

Silence ensued.

'Caroline?'

And then, faintly, like the sound of ice creaking at the edge of an ice-field, and as cold, 'Yes. What do you want?'

Now the silence came from the other end of the line, from James. Caroline swallowed hard. 'James, are you there?'

'Yes, I'm here. It's you I was wondering about. Is there something wrong with your phone?'

She closed her eyes. 'Wrong with my phone? Wrong with my phone? It's you who's wrong . . .' She was almost incoherent. 'Last night. You said that you were coming round and . . . I waited and then . . .' She stopped herself; she sounded like a parody of the wronged woman, and that was not what she wanted. She wanted to appear composed and distant, indifferent to James's failure to keep to their arrangement. Dinner? What dinner? Oh, you were coming round – sorry, I'd forgotten. No, I didn't really notice . . .

'Hold on,' James stuttered. 'Just hold on, Caroline. *You* were the one who didn't turn up. Yes, you.'

'*Me!*' Caroline half screamed. 'Me?'

'Yes, you. I came to the flat. And where were you? You'd forgotten.' He paused. 'Thank you for thinking me so *interesting* that you can't even be bothered to remember that we were having dinner together. And I was going to make that new risotto that I'd read about in the Ottolenghi book. And you weren't even . . .'

'I wasn't . . .' She paused. She had gone to the party downstairs and perhaps she had been a little late – but no more than fifteen minutes. Well, half an hour perhaps. But then James should have waited. She felt herself calming down. Perhaps this had been a mere misunderstanding. 'Look, I was downstairs. I came right up but maybe I was a little later than I had intended. I can see how maybe you felt that—'

'I did,' snapped James. 'I did feel that.'

Caroline was now ready to apologise. 'I'm sorry, James,' she said. 'You must have felt that I had forgotten all about it. I can see why. I'm really sorry.'

James was relieved. He had never had a full-blown fight with Caroline before and he had no desire to do so. He took a deep breath. 'I'm glad that it was just a silly mistake. I'm really glad. Shall we have dinner tonight? I'll cook.'

She accepted with alacrity; there was no further need to be distant. 'What time?'

They agreed a time, and he said, 'I'll write that down in my diary. Large letters!'

She laughed. 'I'll put a note on the fridge. That always works. By the way, what did you do last night? Did you go home and think of what you were going to say to me?'

James hesitated before he gave his reply. 'No, I went out for dinner. On the spur of the moment. Nothing planned.'

'Where?'

'The Poule au Pot.'

She was surprised. They had walked past the restaurant together many times, but James had always said that it was too expensive for them. 'When we're rich,' he would say.

'The Poule au Pot,' exclaimed Caroline. 'Did somebody else pay?'

'No, I paid. Me.'

Caroline's tone changed as a note of suspicion crept into her voice. 'Just by yourself? You treated yourself?'

James was truthful. 'I went with Dee.'

Caroline needed a few moments to take this in. Dee? Her flatmate. 'Dee?' she asked. 'Her?'

James defended himself. 'Well, she was there. She had nothing to do, and I was there, and she said that . . . Or maybe I said that I would take her—'

'You said?' Caroline interjected. 'You invited her?'

'Possibly.'

'Liar,' said Caroline.

'What?' James protested. 'Me? A liar?'

'No. Her. Dee. She said, you see, that she went out to dinner by herself. And all the time she went with you. You.'

James said nothing. Why would Dee have lied to Caroline about what was an entirely innocent dinner outing? Unless, of course, it was not altogether innocent in her mind? No, surely not. Not her. He liked Dee, but he could never contemplate being attracted to her in any romantic sense. Did Caroline really think that he could be interested in *Dee*? With all her vitamins and echinacea and acai berries? The problem, of course, was an intellectual one. He and Caroline could discuss things at the same level – or they were at least interested in the same things. With Dee it was different: easy company though she might be, talking to her was like talking to somebody who did not quite share one's world and its references, as happens, sometimes, in one of those casual conversations when one realises that there is simply insufficient common ground to get beyond banalities. Dee was not stupid – far from it – she just *saw* things differently. And she had never even seen a Poussin, and indeed when he had mentioned Poussin – over dinner at the Poule au Pot – she had thought that he was talking about a recipe for chicken. How could Caroline imagine that he and Dee could become involved with each other? It was unthinkable.

But he did not have time to make that clear. 'I'm going to talk to her,' said Caroline abruptly. 'I'll see you some time. Goodbye.'

James was about to protest against the finality of this, but Caroline had rung off. He dialled her number several times but on each occasion he was told that she was unavailable; she had switched the phone off. He sighed. Caroline was his first proper girlfriend. He had heard, of course, from his contemporaries how difficult women could be, and had smiled at their descriptions of moody, capricious behaviour. *Not for me*, he had told himself, and yet here he was encountering it, and feeling every bit as perplexed and at a loss as his friends felt. Would it be simpler to bring things to an end with Caroline? James did not *need* her, when it came down to it. Or did he? I do, he thought. I can't bear being shut out emotionally, I can't bear it.

I need you, Caroline, he muttered. But how can I *show* it?

28. *Barbara Regrets Giving her Key to Rupert*

If relations between James and Caroline were not all that they might have been, then the same was certainly not true of relations between Barbara Ragg and Hugh Macpherson, the young man whom she had picked up in Rye. And she had picked him up, in the most literal sense, because he had asked her in the car park of the Mermaid Inn whether she would be able to drive him back to London. On the way back there had been a terrible incident when the scarf Hugh was wearing had become entangled in a wheel of her small open-top sports car, threatening to bring about an Isadora Duncan moment. That had been averted – fortunately – and they had continued their journey to London where, quite suddenly and, Barbara thought, miraculously, they had fallen in love. It was as simple as that.

Now they were engaged, and if people like Rupert Porter were sniggering about it behind her back – and she knew that he was doing this – then let them; it would make no difference to the happiness she was experiencing. There was a history there, she reminded herself. Her father, Gregory, had worked for many years with Rupert's father, Fatty Porter, and they had been friends as well as business partners. But, as with any close partnership, there had been occasional stresses in the arrangement, and Barbara had not forgotten the discussion her father had had with her shortly before his death. He had been confined to his bed, and was weakening.

'I know that you and Rupert will keep the business going,' he said. 'And that makes me very happy. It's a wonderful thing, you know, for a parent to feel assured that something he or she started is being carried on by the family. It's difficult to describe the feeling exactly, but it's something like the conferment of immortality. Yes, that's what it's like: it's like being given a small measure of immortality . . .

'Rupert's a nice enough young man,' Gregory went on. 'But I do hope you won't end up marrying him.'

Barbara had laughed. 'I give you my word I won't do that.'

Her father smiled. 'Good. I don't think it would work, frankly.'

'It certainly wouldn't,' agreed Barbara. 'And I've never seen him . . . in that way. So don't worry.'

Gregory rested for a moment. Speaking was becoming difficult and he was trying to conserve his strength. 'The problem is that as much as I get on with Fatty, and as much as we are close friends, there's a side to him that I just don't trust. It's difficult to put your finger on it, but I get the feeling that at the end of the day, Fatty might just let you down. He'd always do the thing that was in his best interests.' He paused. 'Do you know what I mean? Looking after number one?'

Barbara nodded. 'Yes. But then, don't all of us do that? Don't we all look after number one when it comes down to it?'

'I'm not sure about that,' said Gregory. 'I suppose there's a sense in which we are all our number one priority, but there are plenty of people who actually do seem to think of others first. Or at least spend more time on others than they do on themselves.' He hesitated. 'Did I say plenty?'

'You did.'

'Well, maybe not plenty. Some, rather. Some people are strikingly altruistic.'

'And Fatty's not one of those?'

Gregory grinned. 'Heavens, no. Nor will his son be. Watch him. Because . . . Well, you know my views on heredity. It shows. It always shows. If you want to know what somebody is going to be like, look at the parents. There's your answer.'

And now, sitting in her office, tidying up on the last afternoon before she was due to begin a ten-day holiday with Hugh – their first holiday together – Barbara remembered this warning from her father. She had heeded his advice, of course, and over the years she had seen little instances of Rupert's selfishness that had confirmed her father's judgement of him. But now she wondered whether she had done something that flew in the face of the paternal warning. I have, she thought; and it's too late to undo it.

Rupert had come into her office that morning to discuss a rather difficult client who was proposing to change agencies. He was torn; on the one hand it would simplify life if this demanding client were to make his unreasonable demands on another agency altogether, but . . .

'On the other hand,' said Barbara, 'if he goes then he may eventually take another five or six people with him. We know for a fact that he's very friendly with Molly and Pete . . .'

'And George,' added Rupert. 'He and George are very close. And if George went that would be a big blow.'

'Precisely.'

'So I try to persuade him to stay?'

'Yes,' said Barbara. 'Definitely.'

They had agreed on a strategy of persuasion and then Rupert had raised the issue of Barbara's impending holiday. 'Lucky you. I'm stuck in town for another two months.'

She thought, he's trying to make me feel guilty. He always does. She smiled up at him from her desk; Rupert never sat down when he talked to her – he liked the advantage of extra height.

'I'm looking forward to it immensely. We're going to Scotland.'

'We?' asked Rupert, and then, quickly, 'Of course, you and Hugh. Of course. How nice.'

Then Barbara had mentioned her boiler. 'It's rather awkward, though. I've got somebody coming to install a new central heating system in the flat. They insist on doing it next week, but I don't want to hand over the keys to people I don't know. I was hoping to get a friend to supervise – to let them in and see that everything was in order. But I haven't yet . . .' She stopped herself, realising what was coming next.

'But let us help,' said Rupert effusively. 'We're just round the corner, as you know, and since Gloria went freelance she's very flexible. Miss Flexibility herself, in fact. She could pop in and supervise things.'

'I don't want to . . .'

'Look, it's not the slightest imposition. Gloria would love to help. Just give me a key and all will be fixed.'

Barbara knew that she should have resisted, but it was too late. She could hardly refuse this offer without appearing churlish and distrusting, and yet even as she handed over the spare set of keys she understood what a profound mistake it was. Rupert had wanted her flat for years, and felt that he had a moral claim to it. And here she was handing over her keys to him when it might have been better to prevaricate, or make an excuse. Could anything be more foolish? Or weak?

After he had left the room, she looked down at her desk and took a deep breath. It was absurd to worry unnecessarily; there was nothing that Rupert could do. After all, one couldn't steal a flat – could one?

29. Rupert Scorns the Yeti Project

Barbara made a conscious effort to stop thinking about Rupert and his wheedling ways. She had only another three hours in the office before she could leave for the next ten days, putting all thoughts of Rupert and the Ragg Porter Literary Agency out of her mind. These ten days would be spent in the company of Hugh Macpherson, her fiancé, in the wilds of Argyll, staying on his father's farm. It was a blissful thought, and Barbara allowed her mind to dwell on the delights that lay ahead. She would have Hugh all to herself; her companion, her plaything. She felt a frisson of anticipatory pleasure as she allowed herself to imagine moments of intimacy together; Hugh was attentive, the ideal lover, and made Oedipus Snark, with his hurried, insensitive ways, seem like a bad dream. Oedipus had not really *felt* anything for her, she now realised; he had stayed with her for several years simply because his vanity required that he have a partner. He had not loved her, and if she had persuaded herself that she loved him, then it was no more than wishful thinking and self-delusion.

She closed her eyes, allowing herself one final image of Hugh lying beside her, with the window open to the Highlands sky that in the summer was light even at eleven at night, and the scent of the sea loch that Hugh had explained lay just a short distance from the house; and she pictured herself getting up and looking down at Hugh, still asleep, and then crossing to the window and seeing the deer going down to the machair, that strip of grass between the sea and the land proper. She imagined all that, and then opened her eyes again and frowned, and began to dictate the final few letters that she had to give to her secretary before she left for this idyll with Hugh. She glanced at her watch: it was three o'clock. In seven hours they would be boarding the Fort William sleeper for the trip north; just seven short hours.

There was a letter to Errol Greatorex, the amanuensis who claimed to have written the autobiography of a yeti. Rupert had initially been scathing about this project, and was still somewhat dubious about Greatorex's credentials. 'Firstly,' he had said on one occasion, in that insufferably pedantic voice that he used when he wanted to explain what he thought was very obvious. 'Firstly, the very existence of yetis is doubtful. It's all very well producing photographs of giant footprints, but if these creatures existed, then surely we would have found skeletons, at the very least. Unless they're immortal, of course. There's always that possibility, I suppose. If they're like Zeus et al and the Himalayas are like Mount Olympus, then I suppose that we wouldn't find skeletons, would we, they having no mortal coil to cast off – *d'accord*?'

He drew breath. 'Secondly, if abominable snowmen do exist, then it would be very unlikely that they would have the gift of speech, being some sort of sub-*homo sapiens* primate. So how could this yeti have conveyed his experiences to your friend, Mr Greatorex? Somewhat unlikely, I would have thought. Correct me if I'm wrong, of course. *Cela va sans dire*.

'You have to be careful, Barbara. Literary frauds are always lurking in the undergrowth. Grey Owl – look at him. Ojibway Indian – I ask you! Archie Belaney from Sussex, in actual fact. And how did his publishers and agents feel, I wonder? And that book, *My Uncle Joe*, about Stalin, by his nephew, except he wasn't Stalin's nephew at all. We're on well-worn ground here, Barbara, and I don't think that Ragg Porter should end up with egg all over its face.'

She had resisted Rupert's opposition to the project, and

encouraged Errol Greatorex to produce a manuscript. So far four chapters had been written and had been submitted in a neat folder marked *Yeti's Life Story, Confidential.* She had taken these home one evening and had pored over them, so transfixed by the story that her soup had boiled over and burned, unnoticed.

'My earliest memory,' wrote the yeti, 'is of being taken by my uncle to a place just outside one of the high villages in a remote part of the country. There was a monastery outside this village, a square stone building with a commanding view of the valley below. I had never been in a proper building before – we lived in small shelters, tents of a sort, that we disguised with snow. They were comfortable enough, but the sight of this monastery with its darkened windows and its high parapets made a great impression on my five-year-old self.

'I wanted to go into the monastery, but my uncle, with the natural shyness of our people, refused. "They will not understand," he said. "That is part of their world, not ours."

'I heard the monks chanting within, and the sound seemed to me to be beautiful beyond imagining. Yetis do not have any music of their own – they have small singing bowls that they sometimes use to produce a single note, but I hesitate to call it music. Hearing the chants of the monks filled me with excitement. It seemed to me that I was being addressed, personally and directly, and that if I did not respond this mournful, moving sound would disappear from the face of the earth.

'My uncle, however, told me to be quiet, and so I said nothing, but crouched there with him, watching the monks going about their tasks, tending their struggling vegetables in the patches of raked earth they had prepared in front of the monastery.

'I had no idea that, six years later, I was to return here and be given the chance of an education. I had no idea, too, that some of the monks whom I had watched with such curiosity would come to mean so much to me. At that point they were just men in saffron robes, clutching hoes, scratching at the thin soil of the mountainside, behind them the prayer flags fluttering in the wind: blue, green, yellow, red – colours that had until then been no part of our world, which knew only the white of the snow and the pale, singing blue of the sky above.'

30. The Sleeper Train

'That's our sleeper train,' said Hugh, pointing along the platform. 'See it?'

Barbara Ragg nodded, momentarily distracted by the sight of a group of staggering football fans being searched by a contingent of transport police before they were allowed on the platform. The search was being conducted in good spirits, it seemed, even though it was proving productive. At the side of the concourse was steadily growing a motley pile of bottles and cans, taken off the fans by the police. Barbara did not want to stare, but found it difficult to tear her gaze away. For a moment she was consumed with shame; where else in western Europe could such sights be seen? Where else was public drunkenness so manifest? On the streets and in the cafés of France?

She thought not; such places always had a light, civilised air, even if the statistics showed that the French consumed vast lakes of wine. But they drank it with food, while engaged in pleasant conversation, not like this. Nor, she imagined, did they have mobs of drunken young women, screeching hen parties, tottering in high heels and short skirts from bar to bar, fuelled by sweetened vodka concoctions. And in Germany? The Germans got drunk at beer festivals, in large tents, to the strains of oompah music – again, all very different from this. And yet if you said anything about it to anybody, they merely shrugged, or smiled at you as if to imply that you were some sort of killjoy.

Hugh did not appear to have noticed. Perhaps, being Scottish, he was inured to such sights. 'I like sleepers,' he said, as they made their way down the platform. 'Do you?'

'I don't really think very much about them,' she said.

Hugh quoted Norman McCaig. 'There's a Scottish poet,' he said. 'He wrote a poem about the Edinburgh to London sleeper. He said something about not liking being carried sideways through the night. That's such a powerful image, isn't it? Being carried sideways through the night.'

Barbara agreed. 'Sometimes,' she said, 'when I look up and see an aeroplane overhead I think of all the people in it. All those people being carried in the sitting position through the air. If you just took the outer skin of metal away, imagine what it would look like. Rows of people shooting through the air.'

Hugh smiled. 'Yes, very odd. I think I probably prefer being carried sideways through the night to being carried through the air like that. One is less of a hostage to fortune when one is only a few feet off the ground, don't you think, rather than, what is it, four miles above it?'

'Five, I think.'

'Give me a train any time.'

Trains were normally of little interest to Barbara, except as a means of getting from place to place, but this one was different. At first, it seemed to her that it had no windows, that it was that curious thing, a *sealed train*, of the sort in which Lenin travelled from Switzerland to Russia; then she saw that there were windows, but they were rendered opaque by drawn blinds.

'I can hardly remember when I last took a sleeper train,' she said. 'As a teenager I did some travelling on the continent. We were in a *wagon-lit*, I think.' It was a hazy recollection: a vague memory of sounds; of being rocked through the night on the way down to Italy; the slightly acrid smell of sleeper carriages, a smell redolent of batteries and stuffiness, and slightly sour milk.

'I want to go on the Orient Express one day,' said Hugh as they neared their carriage. 'To Istanbul. I've always wanted to. It's such a romantic idea, isn't it?'

'I suppose so,' said Barbara.

'Shall we do it?' asked Hugh. 'Should I book?'

She laughed. 'Perhaps.' He had started to say *we* now, quite frequently, and she was still getting used to it. It touched her. Oedipus Snark had never said *we*; her life with him had never been a shared one. With Oedipus, it was always *I*.

They boarded the train. A woman with a clipboard, a diminutive woman with a strong Glaswegian accent, showed them to their compartments, two single-bed cabins with a communicating door between. For a moment Barbara felt a twinge of disappointment, but then asked herself what she had expected. Sleepers did not have double bunks, of course, because that was not the point of a sleeper. You were meant to sleep when on a sleeper – as the name suggested.

The woman took their order for morning tea, which would be served, she said, just before they drew in to Glasgow. Then it would be on to Fort William, where they would arrive shortly before ten. Then, with a smile, she left them.

Barbara put her case on the rack and went to raise the window blind. As she did so, she caught sight of her blurred reflection in the blank glass of the window. I am on a train with my *fiancé*, she thought. I am going to Scotland. I am with the most beautiful man I have ever met – yes, he really is that – and it is I, Barbara Ragg, who has him. He is mine. Mine.

It was an unexpected thought, and it made her reflect on how she had come to be where she was. She felt that what had happened to her was not deserved, but had happened at random and quite unexpectedly. She felt a sense of wonder over it; it had not been in her script; it was not meant to be like this. And that, of course, made her situation seem all the more precious, all the more vulnerable.

She turned round. Hugh was standing behind her.

'My darling, beautiful, wonderful Barbie,' he whispered.

The first part of this was fine; the latter not quite. He had never called her Barbie before.

She made light of it. She smiled. 'Barbie™?'

He put his arms around her. 'Barbie. Well, it's short for Barbara, isn't it?'

'Yes. But ... But do you know who Barbie™ is?'

Hugh looked puzzled. He planted a kiss on her brow. He was wearing some sort of cologne; there was the scent of sandalwood. 'No.'

'She's a doll.'

Hugh smiled. 'I knew somebody who called his girlfriend "doll". She seemed to like it. She was one of those blondes, you know, not a great intellectual. Doll seemed to suit her.'

The train gave a sudden shudder.

'We're on our way,' said Hugh. Then he whispered, 'To be in love *and* to be on the sleeper. Bliss.'

Barbara closed her eyes. 'Oh, Hugh ...' And then she thought: Barbie. Few mistakes were genuinely without meaning – Professor Freud had told us that, and the lesson still stood. So was Barbie *Barbie* or another Barbie? Or even her? Or was she *Barbie*? It was enough to confuse even a semiotician.

'I have a surprise for you,' said Hugh.

31. The Cool Kindliness of Sheets

The surprise that Hugh had for Barbara was revealed shortly after the sleeper train slipped out of Euston, rocking through the somnolent suburbs of London, headed for Scotland and the Great Glen. The surprise was a demonstration – nothing more than that – of a special way of keeping the interconnecting door between their two compartments open during the journey. This was done by attaching one end of a leather belt to a coat hook in one compartment and the other end to a second coat hook in the other.

Barbara watched, and if her smile seemed rueful, it was. What had she expected? When a devastatingly handsome man, one whom one can – with complete pride – call one's fiancé, says that he has a surprise in store, what is one *entitled* to expect? A present of some sort, perhaps? Something one would never buy oneself – an item of jewellery, a brooch, a set of earrings. Or, more imaginatively, and perhaps even more romantically, a concealed miniature picnic basket, produced and opened to reveal a tiny pack of delicate sandwiches – translucent cucumber slices on slivers of bread – a half-bottle of champagne, kept chilled in a tight-fitting ice-filled life-vest, and flecked quails' eggs, as neat and beautiful as the tiny birds that had laid them. Such a picnic could be eaten in the half-light of the sleeper compartment, the two of them perched companionably on the one bunk, like two children enjoying a midnight feast in the far-fetched pages of some schooldays story. One would not expect merely this, a mundane way of keeping a door from opening and closing with the movement of the train.

'Now we'll be able to talk,' said Hugh, pointing at his vaguely Heath Robinson arrangement.

She looked down, a look tinged with regret. 'Of course.'

'Talking in the darkness is very special,' said Hugh. 'You hear your words going out into the night, almost like a prayer – because you can't see the person you're addressing them to.'

He took off his jacket. She saw that a button was missing

132

from his shirt; there was a glimpse of brown beneath. He was one of these people who did not need the sun to look tanned. He took off his shoes. There was a hole in one of his socks exposing the tip of a toe; it made her smile. He looked so vulnerable.

'What's funny?'

She pointed to his holed sock. 'Your poor toe.'

He wiggled the toe. 'This little piggy,' he said, 'went . . .'

'If you do that,' she said, 'you'll enlarge the hole.'

Hugh finished the line – the pig's destination should not remain unclear – 'Went to market. What do you think that means? All those nursery rhymes have a hidden meaning, you know. Often quite sinister.'

'They can be dreadful,' agreed Barbara. 'They're full of violence and cruelty.' She paused. 'Why do you think we feel the need to scare our children?'

Hugh thought for a moment. He wiggled his exposed toe again. 'Bettelheim?' he asked.

'Oh. *The Uses of* . . .' The uses of something.

'Of enchantment. *The Uses of Enchantment.*'

'Of course.'

Hugh bent down and started to remove a sock. She watched him; the simple act of getting undressed in a confined space brought home the intimacy of the relationship into which she had entered. This was not occasional, which had been the nature of her relationship with Oedipus, and the boyfriend who, some years previously, had preceded him. It was quotidian, diurnal–nocturnal. She averted her eyes lest he see her *looking upon him*, as biblical language would have it; one would not want to be found *looking upon* another.

He took off the other sock. 'Bettelheim said that violence in fairy stories and the like has a very important function. It enables us to experience it as children, and to deal with it. If you look something in the face, then you are no longer frightened of it.'

He turned away from her and switched out the main light in the compartment. The bunk reading-light, though, was still on, giving out a low, reassuring glow. The train rocked, and he had to reach out to steady himself by holding onto Barbara's shoulder; she was already seated on the edge of the bed. Once steadied, he sat down.

'I'm very glad that you're coming to Scotland,' he said.

She said that she was glad too. But she hardly knew Scotland, she added; it seemed very far away, particularly places with names like Fort William. 'It makes it sound like a distant outpost.'

'It is.'

'But a fort. Were the locals *so* unfriendly?'

'At one time, yes. Remember that it was in the heart of Jacobite territory. It was occupied. Our culture was suppressed. Our national dress interdicted.'

He shifted round and lay back on the bunk, his shirt riding up over the flat of his stomach.

'"How many miles to Babylon?"' he recited. '"Three score and ten. Can I get there by candlelight? Yes, and back again."'

Barbara turned and lay beside him on the bunk; there was not enough room, and had the train stopped suddenly she would undoubtedly have fallen off.

'I should get to my bunk,' Hugh said. 'There really isn't enough room for two.'

She wanted him to stay, but it was impractical. 'I wish you could stay,' she said. 'Then we could lie here, carried sideways through the night, just as that poet didn't like. What was his name?'

'Norman MacCaig.'

'Yes, like him.'

'Unlike him. We'd like it.'

She sat up in order to allow him to get off the bunk. As she watched him move past her and cross to the narrow doorway into his own compartment, she felt a sudden pang of sorrow. It was a premonition of loss, she decided; she would lose him, this beautiful stranger. For that was what he was to her still, a stranger who had come into her life, a gift from somewhere else altogether. What if he died? People did, even the young; people died.

Barbara prepared herself for bed, and then slipped between the sheets. Trains were scruffy places usually, but the sleepers had clean, beautifully ironed sheets, slightly rough to the touch as good linen and cotton can be. Rupert Brooke wrote of the 'rough male kiss of blankets'; and what did he say of sheets? 'The cool kindliness of sheets, that soon smooth away trouble.' That was it.

She reached up and turned out her reading-light. Through the interconnecting door she saw that Hugh had done the same. She felt safe; the morbid thoughts of a few moments earlier, when she had imagined that she might lose him, had dissipated. She was safe.

He was saying something, muttering, and it suddenly occurred to Barbara that it was a prayer. It occurred to her, too, that she had never actually asked him whether he believed in God. Who asked such a question of a lover, even of a fiancé, these days?

She strained to hear the words. It was in fact not a prayer, but a poem.

Travelling northwards through the night
Heading to a Scotland
Of forbidding mountains, and poetry,
And sea; home to me, of course,
But to one whom I love
A place of unknown and unpronounceable names;
May the rain that will surely greet us
Be gentle; may the sky over Ardnamurchan
Allow a glimpse of islands, of Coll, perhaps,
Or Tiree; may she encounter kindness
And the things that kindness brings;
My wishes for her, now, the one I love,
As we travel northwards through the night.

Barbara lay in complete silence. She could have slipped out of bed and embraced Hugh, hugged him, showered him with kisses of gratitude. But she did not do this, because she was awed by the moment. 'My wishes for her, now, the one I love.' That's me, she thought. That's me.

32. A Homeopathic Joke

Dee had discovered from experience that opening the Pimlico Vitamin and Supplement Agency on a Sunday brought particularly good results. She had made this lucrative discovery a couple of years earlier when she had gone into the shop on a rather dreary Sunday to do a stocktaking and had inadvertently turned the *Closed* sign to *Open*. This had resulted in a stream of customers, most of whom spent considerably more than the average. The average spend of her customers on weekdays was £6.38; on that Sunday it reached £18.76. A subsequent trial Sunday opening had resulted in an even higher spend of £23.43. That clinched matters, and from then on the Vitamin and Supplement Agency opened its doors at eleven on a Sunday morning and remained open until five in the afternoon.

She had tried to work out why Sunday should be so successful. It was not the case for every business – a nearby commercial neighbour who ran a small card shop sold practically nothing on a Sunday, and spent her Sundays tackling the more difficult weekend crosswords. Another trader at the end of the street, who ran a dress shop for thirty-somethings, did a certain amount of business round about eleven in the morning, only to have these purchases almost invariably returned by five o'clock the same afternoon. The owner was puzzled, until the realisation dawned: her customers were buying the dresses purely in order to wear them to Sunday brunches and lunches at friends' houses before returning them for specious reasons later in the afternoon. It was a radical solution to the complaint of having nothing to wear, or at least nothing that one's friends had not seen several times before. Fashion for free, as one offender so honestly put it; one can, after all, be honest about dishonesty.

'We have become a thoroughly unscrupulous nation,' said the shopkeeper to Dee one day.

'Have we?' asked Dee.

'Oh yes. There's been a survey, you know. And they – the scientists or whatever – found that fewer than half the men asked about this phenomenon of pretending to buy a dress thought that it was dishonest.'

'And women?' asked Dee.

'I remember the figure exactly. Eighty-eight-point-five per cent thought it was dishonest.'

'Well, there you are,' said Dee. 'It shows that we aren't all bad.'

The other woman disagreed. 'Not at all. The fact that eighty-eight-point-five per cent of women thought it was a dishonest thing to do wouldn't necessarily stop them doing it. They all do it – or most of them – even if they think it's dishonest. They *just don't care.*'

Dee sighed. She would never do it herself, but she suspected that the shopkeeper was right, most people now would do this sort of thing without hesitation. Look at the way people treat insurance companies, she thought; look at the way they think nothing of claiming for things that they haven't lost. *Fiddler nation*, she thought.

It was all very interesting, if depressing, but it did not address the issue of why Sunday should be such a good day for selling vitamins. The answer, she suspected, had to do with what some people got up to on Saturdays. If people behaved in a virtuous way on a Sunday – and Dee was firm in her conviction that the buying and taking of vitamins was an entirely virtuous activity – it was possible that they were compensating for having behaved in a vicious way on the Saturday night. And to a large extent, people did. They drank too much; they ate to excess; they stayed up too late. With the result that on Sunday, if they walked past a vitamin shop, their consciences pricked them like a thorn.

Now, sitting at the till of her shop, reading the latest copy of *Anti-oxidant News*, she kept half an eye on a couple of customers huddled at the back of the shop in the flower remedies section. In general, her customers did not steal; on Sundays at least, they were clean-living types, with consciences as clear as their lower intestines (or that was the case for those who underwent regular colonic irrigation, anyway). No, she need not worry too much about shoplifting.

But there was something that did worry her. She was reading a report in *Anti-oxidant News* to the effect that a new study purported to show that homeopathic remedies achieved no better results than placebos. This worried Dee. Principally, she doubted it were true; everything in her rebelled against the thought that mere evidence-based medicine should seek to debunk an entire section of her shop, for that, indeed, was what she had: half a wall of homeopathic remedies, designed to deal with a wide range of those ills to which the mortal flesh was heir.

She read on. 'The authors of this so-called study' – that was fighting talk, thought Dee, with approval – 'argue that the very small dilutions of the active ingredient cannot possibly have an effect on the human body. They forget succussing, of course. So many critics of homeopathy forget about succussing.'

'Exactly,' muttered Dee. 'Succussing changes everything.'

'There is ample proof,' continued the article, 'that the act of striking the container of the dilution ten times or more on a firm surface makes all the difference to the molecular properties of the water. So why do these allegedly dispassionate scientists ignore something as significant as that?'

Why indeed, thought Dee. Because they don't want to find out the truth? Because they don't *want* homeopathy to work? Talk about homeophobia!

Succussing: it was a most peculiar thing, but she was convinced of its efficacy. Only last night, a friend had given her a gin and tonic as a treat, and Dee had found herself succussing the glass against the arm of her chair. The drink had been delicious, and she was sure that it had been much more potent as a result of the succussing. Perhaps that was why James Bond called for his martini to be shaken, not stirred. It was for homeopathic reasons.

She was reflecting on the so-called study, her outrage growing, when she saw a tall man in his early thirties enter the shop. Many of her customers she already knew, but not this one; she was sure she would have noticed him before now.

He came to the cash desk. 'You telephoned me,' he said. 'Richard Eadeston.'

She looked at him blankly. 'Did I?' And then she remembered. Of course she had. This was Richard Eadeston, the man who described himself as a venture capitalist. She looked at him with renewed interest. So this was what a venture capitalist looked like. Rather dishy. An *adventure* capitalist, perhaps!

'Can I make you a cup of tea?' she offered. 'Peppermint? Ginger? Mixed fruit?'

'I rather like peppermint,' he said. 'It's so refreshing. Thank you.'

'10x dilution?' said Dee, and then laughed. 'Just a little homeopathic joke. Nothing serious.'

33. Further Examination

'Delicious,' said Richard Eadeston, savouring his peppermint tea. 'So delicate.'

'And it helps you concentrate,' said Dee. 'You could take it when juggling figures, or whatever it is that you do.'

'Indeed.'

He looked at her over the rim of his teacup. She was not in the usual mould of his clients but she had an interesting face, he thought. Plucky. A risk-taker – in a rather fuzzy Age of Aquarius way, of course. There had been lots of girls like her when he had been an undergraduate at the University of Sussex. It was something to do with the air down there – Brighton and Glastonbury and places like that attracted these people.

'You weren't at Sussex, were you?' he asked. 'At university there, I mean.'

Dee showed her surprise. 'Yes, I was, as it happens. How did . . .?'

'Oh, I just wondered,' said Richard. 'There's a Sussex look. I was there too, you know.'

They sized one another up wordlessly, discreetly computing ages. Yes, they might have been contemporaries.

He broke the silence. 'Remember that pub? What was it called again?'

'The Shaggy Dump?'

'That's the one! I wonder if it's still there.'

Dee nodded. 'Yes. I went down to see somebody there last month. A friend who lives in Kemp Town. And there was the Shaggy Dump – unchanged. That chap with the ring in his nose, remember him? He's still running it. He had all those kids, each with a ring in the nose as well. I saw one or two of them too. It was just like the old days.'

Richard laughed, and thought, and now I'm a venture capitalist.

'What did you do at uni?' he asked.

'Anthropology and Turkish,' said Dee.

He was not sure what to say. So he smiled, and said, 'Cool.' *Awesome* would perhaps have been a shade too strong.

'And you?'

He had done business studies, although he usually called it economics; now he renamed it development studies.

Dee gestured towards the loaded shelves. 'As you can see, now I'm involved in vitamins,' she said.

'And you've had an idea, too. Which is why you phoned me, I assume.'

She nodded. 'You must get some real crackpots.'

'Oh, we do. Lots of them. Probably nine calls in ten are

from nutters of one sort or another. But we take them seriously. That's why we call ourselves Alternative Vision Capital.'

'Some of them are good ideas then?' She pointed to the teapot. 'More peppermint?'

'Yes, please.' He passed her his cup. 'Yes, we get some very interesting ideas. And we don't turn up our noses just because somebody doesn't look as if they're straight out of the business pages.'

Dee smiled. 'Like me?'

'Well, you're not . . . Yes, like you. Why not? Look at Richard Branson. When he started that record shop or whatever it was he could hardly have looked less like the stereotypical capitalist, could he? The beard and the casual clothes and so on. And look what he's achieved.' He paused, holding out his hands in an all-embracing gesture. 'We're open to ideas. Any ideas.'

Dee nodded. They were seated behind the cash desk and a customer now approached bearing a small bottle of pills. Dee indicated to Richard that she would be a moment attending to the customer. Afterwards he asked, 'What did she buy?'

'Just magnesium,' she said.

'Magnesium? Do we need magnesium?'

Dee's eyes widened. 'Do we need magnesium? Boy, do we need magnesium! Did you know that there are over three hundred – yes, three hundred – bodily chemical reactions that require magnesium?'

Richard shrugged. 'I didn't. But I don't take magnesium pills and I'm still—'

Dee cut him short. 'You get it in your diet. Or should do.'

143

She looked at him in a way that suggested she was assessing his magnesium levels. 'Do you eat many nuts?' she asked. 'Or whole grains?'

Richard shook his head. 'Not really.' He patted his stomach. 'Nuts are fattening, aren't they? I love those big fat ones – macadamias. They're seriously good. But eat too many of those and you begin to look like a macadamia nut yourself – you know, big and fat and round.'

Dee's answer came quickly. 'There are other nuts. Almonds, for example. Pine nuts are full of magnesium too.' She paused. 'You've probably got a magnesium deficiency, you know. Do you get tired?'

'I suppose so. Who doesn't?'

She did not register his question. 'And do you suffer from sleeplessness? Wake up at odd times?'

He nodded. He had not slept well the previous night. There had been a barking dog somewhere down the road; a magnesium-deficient dog, probably.

'I'll give you a magnesium supplement,' she said. 'Try it for a few weeks and you'll see the difference.'

He thanked her. 'But I think we should talk about your proposition. You said that you had a new product you want to develop.' He took out a notebook. 'Tell me about it.'

Dee looked at him doubtfully. 'You wouldn't . . . take the idea, would you? I'm sorry to sound distrustful, but obviously . . .'

He held up a hand. 'No, don't apologise. Not for natural caution. Of course you have to be careful. Intellectual property gets stolen every day. You come up with a good idea and the next minute it's in production somewhere else. And it's not your name on the packet.'

'Oh.'

'Yes. But I assure you, you're safe with us. We'd never do something like that.'

There was a silence, another one of those periods of unspoken mutual assessment that occur when we weigh up another person and choose between trust or natural, self-protective suspicion. What do I know about him? thought Dee. The University of Sussex – a shared background there. The Shaggy Dump – a shared pub. What else? He enjoyed peppermint tea and he likely had a magnesium deficiency. That was all the information she had.

She made her decision. 'There's a substance called ginkgo biloba,' she said. 'We sell a lot of it, particularly to people who are worried about memory loss or failing brain power.'

'Who isn't?' he asked.

'Exactly. And I think that it helps. I really do.'

'And?'

Dee reached for a small bottle from a display on the counter. 'See this?' she asked. 'This is echinacea. It's a very common, popular remedy for toning up the immune system. But here it's being sold as a pill to protect you from germs on aircraft. You take one before you board. People love it. We all know that we're breathing the same air as a hundred other passengers when we're on a flight. So we take a pill. And I happen to believe it works.'

Richard was watching her closely. She noticed that he had a slight tic in his right eye. It twitched slightly, almost imperceptibly. 'I see where you're going,' he said quietly. 'And I like it. So what are you wanting to sell this ginkgo stuff as?'

'A sudoku remedy,' said Dee. 'Improve your sudoku performance with a pill.'

Richard sat back in his chair. He was beaming.

34. *Among the* Rosbifs

'Well, I'm very sorry to say it, Rupert, but that meal was not terribly good.'

Rupert Porter looked at his wife, reproachfully at first, but then he too shook his head in disapproval. 'You're right, Gloria,' he agreed. 'It was ghastly. And on your birthday, too! I'm so sorry, my dear.'

Gloria reached out across the table and took his hand. 'Don't even think about it, darling. It's not your fault. The important thing is that you took me out to dinner.'

He was placated, but not entirely. 'It really annoys me, you know. What if we were Americans, for instance, or *a fortiori* French? What would we think of London, paying what we just have for a meal like that?'

'If we were French,' said Gloria, 'we would take the view that our prejudices are confirmed. *Les rosbifs* know nothing about food.'

Rupert smiled wryly. 'Perhaps we should have ordered *le rosbif* rather than the Dublin Bay prawns.' He paused. 'When do you think those Dublin Bay prawns last saw Dublin Bay?'

'A long time ago. A month or two perhaps.'

Rupert nodded his agreement. 'Months in the freezer.'

They rose from their table. As they did so, a man sitting in the corner of the restaurant looked in their direction. Gloria noticed his stare, and returned it. How rude, she thought. But the man did not look away. After a moment, she averted her gaze.

'Rupert, that man,' she whispered. 'Over there.'

Rupert was struggling with his coat, a rather smart camel hair that he had bought in Jermyn Street. He was proud of this coat, with its velvet collar, which gave him, he thought, a rather raffish look. Prosperous and raffish. 'Mr Ten Per Cent,' Barbara Ragg had muttered when she had first seen him wearing it. He had seen her lips move but had not caught what she said.

'What?'

'I said, what a fetching coat.'

He had preened. 'Rather smart, isn't it. Camel hair, you know.'

'It makes you look . . . quite the man about town.'

Now, the coat having been donned, he glanced in the direction indicated by Gloria. At first he noticed nothing unusual, but then he intercepted the man's stare. Quickly he turned away.

'Do you know him?' whispered Gloria.

Rupert made a hurried gesture. 'Later,' he muttered. 'We can talk later.'

Outside the restaurant Rupert looked at his watch. 'The night is still young . . . Do you know, I've had a wonderful idea.'

Gloria took his arm. 'All your ideas are wonderful, Rupert.'

'Have you got those keys on you?'

'Which keys?'

'The ones I gave you. The keys to la Ragg's flat. Or rather, the keys to the flat that she occupies.' He gave Gloria a sideways look, and she understood the meaning immediately. This was a reference to his claim on Barbara's flat – a claim that might have had no substance in law (in the strictest sense) but had a moral backing which he felt only the deliberately perverse could deny. So he spoke about the flat in the same tones as an irredentist might speak about some ancient and painful territorial claim, or as they might speak in certain quarters about the Spratly Islands or some remote corners of South America – and with equal passion, too.

Gloria glanced in her handbag. 'They're there,' she said. 'But, look, that man back there. Did you know him?'

Rupert looked evasive. 'Perhaps.'

'What do you mean, perhaps? Either you knew him or you didn't. And he certainly seemed to know us – he was boring a hole in my back with his stare.'

'He's a chap called Ratty Mason,' muttered Rupert. 'I knew him at school.'

Gloria stopped in her tracks, almost causing Rupert to stumble into her. 'Ratty Mason? That's Ratty Mason?'

Rupert tugged at her arm, encouraging her to walk on. 'I think so. I could be wrong, though. It was dark in there.'

'Well, well,' exclaimed Gloria. 'At long last I've caught sight of Ratty Mason. How long is it since you saw him?'

'Ages,' said Rupert. 'Not since I was at Uppingham. A long time ago, as you know.'

Gloria was not going to let matters rest at that. She had tried before to get Rupert to talk about Ratty Mason, whose name had come up in some context that she did not recall. Rupert had refused, changing the subject rather quickly. She was determined to find out now, though, and she pressed him again. 'Why was he called Ratty?'

'He just was,' said Rupert. 'That's what we called him in those days. Everybody had a nickname.'

'Was he ratty?'

'Not especially. Sometimes the nicknames were chosen at random. There was a boy called Octopus Watkins. I have no idea how he got that name. He didn't have eight arms and legs, as I recall. Did you have nicknames at your school?'

Gloria could spot an attempt to change the subject. 'Ratty,' she persisted, 'suggests that he was, well, rat-like. Or that he turned people in to the authorities. One rats on people, doesn't one?'

'Maybe.'

She stopped him again. 'Come on, Rupert, you can't fool me. There's something fishy here. Why this reticence about Ratty Mason?'

He turned to her, his eyes narrowed. 'Just leave Ratty Mason out of it, will you? I don't want to talk about him. He's history.'

'Were you very friendly with him?'

Rupert snorted. 'Me? Friendly with Ratty Mason? Don't make me laugh.'

'So there *was* a problem then. What happened? Did he . . . betray you?'

At the mention of betrayal, Rupert sighed again. 'I really don't want to stand here in the middle of the pavement talking about somebody like Ratty Mason. I had a really very good idea and now you've gone and spoiled it.'

Gloria thought for a moment. Ratty Mason could wait; there would be another opportunity. 'All right, what's your idea?'

'We go to Barbara's flat and have a look round,' he said. 'You've got the keys.'

Rupert was holding Gloria's arm as he spoke, and he felt a jolt of excitement running through her.

'Rupert!'

'*Pourquoi non*? We have la Ragg's authority to go and let in those boiler people, so does it make any difference if we merely exercise that right of access a bit early? I don't think it does. Not in the slightest, if you ask me.'

'You make it sound so simple. But what would we do once we're in?'

'As I said, look around. We could see how she's using the place to which we are morally entitled. It'll be like a UN inspection. That sort of thing.'

Gloria looked about her, as if to see whether anybody might be capable of overhearing this dangerous suggestion. 'All right,' she said. 'I can just imagine what it'll be like.'

'So can I,' said Rupert, chuckling. 'Frightful taste, I bet. Flying ducks on the wall?'

'Undoubtedly,' said Gloria. 'We must brace ourselves.'

35. *Don't Go There*

Barbara Ragg's flat was on a street that ran off Kensington Park Road. It was not the most expensive part of Notting Hill – there were more fashionable and sought-after addresses – but it was, by any standards, comfortable and secure. From Barbara's point of view, it was ideal. The flat faced southwest and benefited from the late afternoon sun; the neighbours were quiet and inoffensive, but sufficiently attentive to any unusual occurrences to amount to an informal neighbourhood watch; the roof was in good order; and there were never any unseemly arguments with landlords or residents about the cost of painting the railings that gave onto the street or any of the other shared parts of the building. Barbara found it difficult to imagine herself living in any other area of London, and if she looked at the property pages of the newspapers it was only to reflect on her good fortune in being where she was, in having what she had.

The features of the flat which appealed to Barbara were, as it happened, exactly the same ones that gave rise to an intense and burning jealousy on the part of Rupert Porter. The flat he occupied with Gloria faced in the wrong direction and got very little light at any time of the day. It was also far pokier, having been built at a time when the Victorian confidence that inspired the architects of Barbara's flat had somehow flagged; perhaps there had been a defeat somewhere in that rambling empire, or a financial downturn, sufficient to make Rupert's windows and ceilings meaner, his public rooms less commodious.

Everyone knows, of course, that there are people who live in better accommodation than we do ourselves. Even the wealthy, in their well-appointed mansions, know that there are even wealthier people occupying even better appointed homes. At work, too, inequalities abound. Civil servants, as is well known, measure the size of their carpets to establish where they are in the pecking order; ministerial cars are carefully graded by engine capacity to suit the seniority of the person to whom they are allocated; in airports there are lounges for every grade of traveller, and for the lowest grade, no lounge at all. We all know this and accept that some people have things which we do not – unless we feel that they do not deserve what they have, in which case we look forward to their dispossession. Rupert generally did not resent the residential good fortune of others; he did not scowl as he walked past people standing on the doorsteps of houses that were clearly more desirable than his. That was not the issue. The issue was Barbara's occupancy of the flat that had once belonged to his father, Fatty Porter, and out of which he, Rupert, and any future Porters, had been *cheated*. Or so he believed; the fact that the flat had been quite properly sold to Barbara's father was not the point. Behind some contracts there is a hinterland of interpretation, and in Rupert's view the Raggs had quite simply *tricked* the Porters by ignoring what everybody involved plainly understood.

That was the history. And that was what Rupert was thinking about as he and Gloria made their way to the front door of Sydney Villa. There Rupert glanced quickly at the nameplate next to Barbara's doorbell – *Ragg*. He flushed with anger. *Porter*, it should have read.

'The keys,' he said, his voice lowered.

Gloria fished about in her bag. 'Here they are. Rupert, I wonder . . .'

'No,' said Rupert. 'We mustn't change our minds. Remember: we're *entitled* to this place. La Ragg is really not much more than a squatter.'

'But Watergate . . .'

'Nonsense!' He smiled. 'Notting Hillgate, if you must.'

There was an awkward moment as Rupert fitted the key into its keyhole. It was slightly stiff, and he had to withdraw it twice before it slotted into place. It occurred to him that his lack of familiarity with the key could alert any observer, but there was nobody watching, and he succeeded in opening the front door on the third attempt.

They moved through the common entrance hall and took the stairs up to Barbara's landing. They opened the door to the flat and went into Barbara's entrance hall. Rupert found a light switch and flicked it on. He pointed to a picture hanging on the far wall. 'Ghastly,' he said. 'She goes in for that sort of stuff in the office too. Look at it.'

'Pretty awful,' said Gloria. 'Let's look at her kitchen.'

Rupert was more interested in the drawing room, a room he had always particularly liked, but he wanted Gloria to have some fun too, so he followed her through to the kitchen.

'She's got one of those cheap blenders,' said Gloria. 'And look at this crockery. That's what happens when you put non-dishwasher-proof plates in the dishwasher. See here. And here. It takes off all the decoration.' She paused, examining a plate more closely. 'Mind you, some decoration is best removed, I suppose.'

'It's such a lovely flat, though,' said Rupert. 'If you threw out all this stuff you could make something really nice of it.'

'A criminal waste,' agreed Gloria.

'And Pa would have loved the thought of our living here,' continued Rupert. 'That's what he wanted. But he trusted Gregory – bad mistake.'

It was at this point that they heard the sound of a door opening somewhere in the flat. Rupert froze.

'She's in Scotland,' he whispered. 'I'm sure . . .'

He did not finish his sentence. A man had appeared in the kitchen doorway. He was wearing a blue dressing gown over a pair of extravagantly striped pyjamas.

'Teddy?' the man said. 'Barbara said that you two might be coming to stay while she was away.'

Rupert was a quick thinker. 'Yes. Sorry to have woken you up.'

The man smiled. 'No problem. I'm a light sleeper. Errol Greatorex, by the way. I'm one of Barbara's authors.'

Again Rupert thought quickly. 'The yeti man? *The Autobiography of a Yeti*?'

Errol Greatorex looked surprised. 'Barbara's told you about that?'

Rupert exchanged a quick glance with Gloria; he hoped that she would have worked out that this was their only option. He was Teddy and she was . . .

'She mentioned it,' he said.

'I'm almost done,' said Errol. 'Finishing touches. He's in London, you know.'

'Who?'

'The yeti. He's dictating the last chapter.'

Rupert was silent.

'Yes,' said Errol, gesturing behind him in the direction of the bedrooms. 'He'd sleep through an earthquake, though, so we won't have woken him up.'

This is absurd, thought Rupert. Utterly absurd. This man is completely deluded, and I'm stuck here, masquerading as somebody called Teddy, with Gloria, who doesn't even know what her name is meant to be. I shouldn't have done this. *Don't go there*, as the expression has it. Well, I did, and now I'm there.

36. *Our Obligations to Animals*

Freddie de la Hay – Pimlico Terrier, cohabitee of William French and now a temporary member of MI6's establishment – had been baffled when William suddenly handed him over to a completely unknown woman in St James's Park. Such a thing had never happened to him before, or at least not that he could remember. Dogs remember places and people, and scents; they have no sense of the sequence in which these are experienced, nor of the time that separates the present from the past. Heathrow Airport, where Freddie had once been employed as a sniffer dog, was there somewhere in his memory – a place of noise and movement and strange smells – but it was vague and unlocated, not much different from a half-remembered dream. Then there had been exile to his first domestic home in north London, a period of coldness and fear, as he was groomed for his role as an eco-dog: the carrot snacks rather than bones; the biodegradable dog blanket; the arbitrary, harshly enforced prohibition on chasing cats and squirrels. It had been rather like being Stalin's dog, not that Freddie would have made the analogy – or any analogy at all for that matter.

Since then, there was William, who had brought colour and fun back into Freddie's life, and had been rewarded with the dog's total and unconditional affection. But now William was abruptly no longer there, and already Freddie missed him as a Finnish sun-worshipper must miss the sun in winter; a warm presence had become a cold absence, and he did not understand why it should be so. Had he done something? Had he misbehaved in such a way as to merit this exclusion, this casting into darkness?

Freddie's relationship with William was, in traditional terms, that of dog and master. In traditional terms . . .

'You shouldn't call yourself Freddie's master, old man,' William's twenty-eight-year-old son Eddie had once remarked. 'Master is very yesterday.'

William stared. He wanted to tell Eddie that the term 'old man' was itself very yesterday, but he was not sure that it was. Pejorative names for parents were, he thought, very *today*. He had heard parents being described as wrinklies, olds and 'rents, all of which he thought unflattering at the very least.

'Owner?' he wondered.

Eddie shook a finger. 'Nope. Owner's very yesterday too. It implies that you own him.'

'Which I do,' William pointed out mildly.

Eddie laughed. 'You're not very switched on, Dad. Lots of people don't like that.'

William had been puzzled. Why could he not *own* a dog? If he could sell Freddie de la Hay (which of course he would never do, but it was possible) then surely he must own him. When he next took Freddie to the vet for injections, he had asked her about it.

'Can I call myself Freddie's owner?'

The vet sighed. 'It's a bit of a minefield,' she said. 'We get people coming in here who insist on being called their dog's companion. Sometimes they call themselves the animal's guardian or carer. There are quite a lot of dog carers in certain parts of London. Islington, for example. I don't mind, really. The idea is that the pet – oops, can't say that – that the animal has rights, has its own existence that humans shouldn't seek to control.' She paused, slipping the needle of the syringe under Freddie's skin. 'I have no problems with that. I think that we should respect an animal's right to have a decent life.'

'It used to be called kindness,' said William. He agreed with what the vet said; there was so much suffering in the world – a great sea of it – and it washed around the feet of animals as much as it did around humans. We should not add to it.

The vet withdrew the needle and patted Freddie on the head. 'Exactly. Everyone should be kind to animals. I can't disagree on that score. There you are, Freddie. That's you.'

As William walked back to Corduroy Mansions with Freddie de la Hay after the visit to the vet, he reflected on their conversation. He did not see why he should not call himself Freddie's owner, and would continue to use the term, whatever Eddie had to say on the subject. Eddie was not one to preach on this issue anyway; he had been prepared to involve Freddie in a dogfight of all things, and he had no experience of keeping an animal. And William was not so sure that those who described themselves as the companions of dogs were necessarily kinder towards their animals than those who described themselves as a dog's master.

A dog's master . . . What about cats? Of course nobody could tell a cat what to do, and so the term master was inappropriate. Cats have staff, as the saying went. Perhaps cats kept us, and it was they who should be described as the masters.

At home, over a cup of tea with Marcia, who had dropped in on her way back from an engagement serving sandwiches to the British Egyptian Board of Commerce, William raised the question of cats and ownership.

'Ha!' said Marcia. 'Have you been reading about that advice thingy?'

'What advice thingy?'

'I think they call it the *Code of Practice for Cat Owners*. The government brought it out recently.'

'Our government?' asked William incredulously.

'Yes, believe it or not. They said that all cat owners should follow the *Code*'s advice. It talks about providing your cat with intellectual stimulation and so on.'

At first William found it hard to believe, but Marcia didn't appear to be making the story up. 'I laughed and laughed,' she said. 'I actually read it because my aunt has cats and she was very worried about whether she was going to be prosecuted for something or other. So I agreed to read it.'

'And you reassured your aunt?'

'Yes,' said Marcia. 'But I kept something from her. She's ancient and rather vulnerable. So I didn't tell her this. It says at the beginning, "It is your responsibility to read the complete code of practice to fully understand your cat's welfare." Those are the exact words. So if you're a cat owner and you haven't read the *Code*, the government considers you to be in breach of your duty.'

William was silent. He was utterly appalled. This was not Stalin's Russia, this was England. And there was another thing. 'To fully understand your cat's welfare . . .' Not only were the people behind this *Code* breathtakingly interventionist and condescending, bossy indeed . . . they also split their infinitives.

37. *Philosophy for Dogs*

The darkness into which Freddie de la Hay found himself cast when taken from William in St James's Park proved to be metaphorical rather than real. Led away by the pretty woman with whom William had enjoyed a brief conversation, the Pimlico Terrier was bundled into a car that had been prowling along the edge of the park. Thereafter they took a drive to Notting Hill, to a small flat off Kensington Park Road. This flat was by no means dark; large windows in all four of its rooms admitted both morning and afternoon light, and on each of the window-ledges there stood a well-tended box of brightly coloured flowers – pansies, trailing aubretia, rare summer-flowering crocuses. The walls were painted a uniform white and the exposed timber floors stained a natural pine shade, and the overall effect was one of a pleasant lightness and airiness.

The woman who brought Freddie to this flat had not given William her name, which was Tilly Curtain, nor had she told him that she was a Senior Field Officer (Grade 2) in MI6, slightly – but only slightly – junior to Sebastian Duck, who was a Senior Field Officer (Grade 1) in the same branch of the service. Tilly had been at university, in her case the University of East Anglia in Norwich, where she spent three years studying for a joint degree in philosophy and French. She was the daughter of a male nurse from Nottingham, George Curtain, and his wife, Patricia, a dental hygienist. She had one brother, Tom, who was slightly older than her – she was now thirty-eight – and worked for a firm of civil engineers in Singapore.

George had spent a large part of his career in a psychiatric hospital, where he had been highly regarded for his exceptional skills at calming distressed patients. He had subsequently transferred to a community psychiatric team, where again he was much appreciated, to the extent of being nominated for and awarded an MBE. George had not tried to influence his daughter in her choice of career, but she had acquired from him a sense of public service that was eventually to lead her into the arms of MI6. Her first choice had been dental hygiene, her mother's calling, although once again there had been no deliberate parental influence in that direction. That is not to say that nothing was said in the home about her mother's profession – it was.

'I sometimes think of myself as bit of a missionary,' her mother used to say. 'A missionary for good dental hygiene. Floss. Proper brushing. If only people *knew*.'

Tilly knew. She flossed after every meal – *every meal* – and supported this with the use of a well-maintained electric toothbrush. The effects were evident; her teeth, in fact, were one of the most attractive features in an already appealing face, and although William was not aware of noticing her teeth during their brief meeting, subconsciously he had been taken by the brightness of her smile.

Tilly was similarly unaware of the power of her smile. It was the smile that had ensured that she was given every job she applied for during her gap year, that had secured her election (unopposed) to the students' representative council at university, and that had in due course resulted in her sweeping through every stage of selection for MI6.

'Tilly has such a wonderful smile,' George often observed to Patricia.

'Regular flossing,' Patricia would reply. 'It always shows.'

'It's going to get her far in life,' George continued. 'You know how people say that somebody's face is their fortune. In Tilly's case, it's her smile.'

Patricia agreed. 'So many people don't bother to smile. But they should try it. Add a smile to a request. Result: get what you want. Add a smile to a greeting. Result: a happier encounter.'

It was a particular mannerism of speech, one George did not notice because he had lived with it for so long: Patricia often used the word 'result', followed by a consequence. To her patients she said, 'Regular flossing. Result: no gum disease.' And to her husband, whom she sometimes had to urge to take more exercise, she said, 'A brisk walk each day. Result: cardiac health.'

As so many of us do, Tilly had fallen into her career. During her university days she would never have seen herself as in the type for security work, about which she knew nothing and in which she then had not the slightest interest. She had enjoyed her philosophy courses at Norwich. Less so the French part of her curriculum, largely because of an unpleasant experience in Montpellier, where she had been inconsiderately treated by a French student with whom she had become emotionally involved. His cavalier attitude to her feelings for him – which he dismissed as *vachement ennuyeux* – had led her to take against France in general, a ridiculous attitude, but very human and understandable. For that is what people do, even though they should not. If we meet one Eskimo whom we do not like, then of course we are going to take against the Arctic in general.

Philosophy was different. She had no particular enthusiasm for the aridities of some parts of the discipline, but she found herself responding warmly to the more engaged and accessible works of those philosophers who had something to say about the world in which ordinary, morally sensitive people lived. In particular, she read Iris Murdoch's *The Sovereignty of Good* with a curious sense of discovering afresh something that she had always known. Of course this was how one should approach the business of being human; of course it was.

But philosophy is a tiny trade, and, in spite of a good performance in her final examinations, her student career had not been stellar, and any opportunities to take philosophy further were effectively confined to those who were indeed stellar. So when a recruiter for MI6, a member of the academic staff, said that he knew of a job that might interest her, she had agreed to be interviewed.

This, then, was the person who took Freddie de la Hay into her flat in Notting Hill and introduced him to the place where he would be sleeping that night. After which she led him into the kitchen and gave him three large dog biscuits from a newly purchased box of Happy Dog Treats.

Freddie glanced down at the biscuits and then up at Tilly. Why was he here? What was going on? Where was God (William)? Why was the world so large, so strange, so filled with curious scents? (The sort of question that must have been posed by Iris Murdoch's dog.) There were cats somewhere about, somewhere not far off – he could smell them. Did they have something to do with this devastating alteration that had befallen him?

38. Sebastian Duck Collars Freddie de la Hay

With the sense that dogs have that enables them to distinguish between friend and foe – a sense that picks up *atmosphere* – Freddie knew from the beginning that Tilly was not hostile. Not having to worry about her as a threat meant that he could explore the flat in a leisurely way, pausing here and there to investigate enticing smells. There was something intriguing in the kitchen, for example, which he wanted to look into, and there were these troubling traces of cat – possibly safely historic – that would need to be interrogated more closely. There was also the question of food; Freddie, like any dog, was perpetually hungry, and the three dog biscuits that Tilly had obligingly placed before him would need to be eaten. He put his head down and took one of the snacks in his mouth. It had a delicious meaty odour, and was of just the right consistency. He made short work of it, and turned to wolf down the second, and then the third. Now there were only crumbs, and he licked those up off the floor. After that, it was time to explore.

It took Freddie no more than ten minutes to go into every room, sniff around and satisfy himself that all was in order. Then he returned to the kitchen to await further instructions. It had been a demanding day, and he felt agreeably sleepy. Heading to the comfortable mat at one end of the kitchen, he settled himself down and closed his eyes. Sleep followed quickly, a warm, comfortable sleep filled with the dreams that dogs have: of chasing and being chased, of running across wide spaces, of following new and irresistible scents. And, as in all dog dreams, at one's side at all times is one's human, one's god, the giver of meaning, the *reason*.

When he awoke it was because someone had entered the room, a man, whom Freddie had not heard come in, but who now stood beside the woman who appeared to be in charge; both of them stood there looking down on him. He opened first one eye and then the other before cautiously rising to his feet. Sleep, and its attendant dreams, had been pleasant, but now he had to be attentive.

'We meet again, old chap,' said Sebastian Duck. 'Everything all right? You seem happy enough.'

'He's a bright-looking dog, isn't he?' remarked Tilly. 'I gather that these Pimlico Terriers are meant to be very intelligent.'

'And friendly too. How are you feeling, Freddie, old bean?' Sebastian Duck reached down and let Freddie de la Hay sniff at the back of his hand. 'Remember me?'

Tilly smiled at the term 'old bean'. In most circles it was considered archaic, belonging to a Wodehousian world that had long disappeared, but this was not true of MI6, where it was still used extensively (a fact not widely known). It was almost a shibboleth, a password that identified one member of the service to another.

Sebastian Duck now withdrew his hand from Freddie's exploratory lick. He reached into his coat pocket and took out a collar. This collar was thicker and wider than the average dog collar and was punctuated at regular intervals by silver studs.

'These studs act as aerials,' he said, showing it to Tilly. 'The transmitter is here, in the middle. See? It's very cunningly concealed. And this part, here, this slightly thicker section, is the battery. It should last about ten days. Then you have to recharge the dog . . . or rather the battery.'

Tilly examined the collar. Taking it in her hands, she felt the weight of it. Poor Freddie de la Hay – he would certainly notice it. 'He's not a very big dog,' she said. 'It's going to be heavy for him.'

'The least of his worries,' said Sebastian Duck.

'What do you mean by that?'

Sebastian Duck looked down at Freddie, who was gazing up at him. 'Trusting little chap, isn't he?' He patted Freddie on the head. 'What do I mean? Well, you remember what happened to Rover Williams? Remember?'

Tilly shook her head. 'Before my time, I think.'

Sebastian Duck explained. 'He was one of the dogs sent down the tunnels in Berlin. We had a listening tunnel that went under the Russian sector. Rover Williams was sent in to plant a transmitter. He had been trained to detach the goods by biting at his collar.'

'And?'

'They got him.'

Tilly sighed. There were times when she wondered whether the service was quite right for her. Conflict. Risk. Duplicity. And, on top of it all, danger.

'Yes,' he continued. 'They got him. And then they turned him.'

Tilly showed her surprise. 'He worked for them?'

'Yes. We spotted him in the East once or twice thereafter. They used him as a listening post. You know the sort of thing – nobody suspects a dog, and so they would leave him lying around in a café or a bar. People talked, and it went straight through his transmitter. Very clever.'

Tilly closed her eyes for a moment and imagined the scene: a deserted street, one of those streets of the old East Berlin, with rain-slicked pavements and windows that were never more than half-lit. A drab state-run café on the corner, the smell of Trabi exhaust hanging in the air, a general atmosphere of fear and distrust. And there was Rover Williams lying patiently on the café floor, an unwitting pawn in the absurd human game of espionage.

'I suppose that dogs can't distinguish,' she mused. 'They can have no concept of loyalty.'

Sebastian disagreed. 'No, dogs are very loyal. It's just that their loyalty is to the leader of whatever pack they find themselves in. So Rover Williams would have thought he was doing his duty to his new masters. He was being loyal.'

Tilly mulled this over. She had difficulty with the concept of duty here. Did dogs actually think in those terms? Did a dog say to itself: I *have to* do this or that? Of course not. Dogs did not think in sentences. Then how did they think?

But there was no time for further discussion on the theme of loyalty. Sebastian Duck had taken the transmitter from her and was now removing Freddie de la Hay's old collar before replacing it with the new one. Freddie sat quite still as this took place. He was not sure what to think, but he was aware of a rather heavy weight being added to his neck. Something was happening to him, and he was not certain that he liked it.

Sebastian fastened the collar and straightened up. 'Right,' he said. 'Now let's go over what happens next. You wait a day or two. Let them see you with Freddie de la Hay. In particular let Podgornin – he's the chubby one – get to know Freddie. Watch for when he goes out to buy cigarettes – he's a sixty-a-day man, according to his file. Follow him and then let him meet Freddie. We know that he's very keen on these dogs. Then, on Tuesday, go and tell Podgornin that you've been called away. Sick relative. Can't take Freddie because she's allergic to dog hair. Could he possibly look after him?' He paused. 'Then we're in.'

Tilly nodded. 'It seems clear enough.' Then, after a moment's hesitation, 'But what if they find out about his collar?'

Sebastian Duck made a gesture of helplessness. 'He's a volunteer,' he said.

It struck Tilly as a callous remark, and she frowned and looked away. Freddie de la Hay was not a volunteer; no dog was. Every single one of them was a conscript, just as most of us were, ultimately, in many aspects of our lives. We were conscripts, she thought, in battles that very few of us actually chose. We worked and worked, often in jobs that we did not really like; we paid taxes, and yet more taxes; we shouldered the burdens of awkward relatives whom we did not choose, who were just there, issued to us at birth; we lived in places because that was simply where we found ourselves. Conscripts.

Freddie de la Hay looked up, first at Tilly and then at Sebastian Duck. More biscuits, he thought.

39. James Offers Risotto

James made the first move to patch things up with Caroline. 'That risotto,' he said over the telephone.

'What risotto?'

'The risotto I was going to make for you before . . .' Before what? He searched for the right word. 'Before our misunderstanding.'

Caroline was brisk. 'Oh,' she said, 'don't worry about that.

That's all over.' But not for Dee, she thought. She had yet to confront Dee about her duplicity in not confessing that she had gone out to dinner with James. But she would, she thought, when the time was right. On the other hand ... poor Dee, with all her vitamins and colonic irrigation and the rest of it; she was very rarely invited out by anybody to anything, and it seemed churlish to begrudge her a little treat with James. No, she would not confront her; she would, instead, forgive her, or, at the most, make a brief reference now and then to the Poule au Pot, just so that Dee would know that she knew all about it. Forgiveness was all very well, but one should not allow others to get away with *everything*.

'Are you listening, Caroline?'

'Yes, yes. My thoughts were just wandering a bit. You were saying something about a risotto.'

James sighed. Caroline lacked focus. Yet we all had our faults, and even he ... What were his faults? Indecision? Uncertainty about who he was? 'I'd rather like to come round and make it for you this evening. I'll get the shopping.'

Caroline hesitated. She was not sure whether she wanted to see James that evening. There were some times which seemed right for seeing James, and some which did not. This particular evening was of indeterminate status ... 'Oh, all right.' She realised that she sounded rude, and corrected herself. One should not be ungrateful for offers to cook risotto ...

James was punctual, and Caroline let him in. He had with him a green carrier bag bulging with risotto ingredients. From out of the top of the bag the neck of a wine bottle peeped.

Caroline leaned forward and planted a kiss on his cheek. She did it automatically, and then, realising what she had just done, for a moment afterwards was prepared for him to recoil. He did not.

James smiled. Extracting the bottle of wine from the bag, he held it up to show her. 'See this?' he said. 'This is not your average supermarket stuff. This is . . .' He looked at the label. 'Château Greysac 2005. And 2005, Caroline, was a very good year for Médoc. I read that. There's a chap called Will Lyons who writes about wines. He said that 2005 was an excellent year. He knows what he's talking about.'

Caroline laughed. 'What was I doing in 2005? Just started uni. Same for you.'

They moved through to the kitchen, where James started to unpack the rest of the contents of the bag. 'We were so *young*,' he said. 'Positively callow.'

Yes, thought Caroline, I was; and the things I wore . . .

James took a corkscrew from the cutlery drawer. 'I must buy you a new one of these,' he said. 'This one has had it. You have to be really strong to get the cork out.' He strained as he tugged at the cork, and Caroline found herself thinking: No, he's not all that strong. He's nice, but he's not strong. But then you did not necessarily expect physical strength in someone like James, and she was not sure that she wanted it anyway. He was nice exactly as he was, with that profile of his and those eyelashes . . . She looked away. She felt a sudden strong tug of desire, and she was not sure that it was right, that it would lead to a place where she wanted to be.

Having at last extracted the cork from the bottle, James poured wine into two glasses. 'We can taste this while I'm preparing dinner,' he said. 'I love cooking with wine.' He smiled at her and raised his glass. 'To you,' he said.

'And to you.'

She tasted the wine. There was an edge of tannin to it, something sharp, and she frowned. James noticed, and told her that this would go in seconds, once the air got to it. 'It'll be perfect,' he said.

And then he started to cry. At first Caroline said nothing, did nothing, such was her surprise, but then she put down her glass and went to him. She took his glass lest he spill the Château Greysac, and put it down on the table. She took him in her arms, embracing him, letting his head nestle against her shoulder.

'James,' she whispered. 'Don't cry, James. Don't cry.'

'I'm sorry,' he sobbed. 'I come for dinner at your house, and I start to cry.'

'Ssh!' She put a finger to his lips. She felt the moisture of his tears. 'What's wrong?'

She need not have asked the question; she knew, of course, what was wrong, and had known from the beginning, from virtually the first day when they had found themselves sitting next to one another in a lecture. She knew then, and she should have trusted her instinct. But she had not, because she felt that somewhere there must be a man who could be her soul mate, with whom she could talk about the things that really mattered to her, who would see the world in the same way. James was all of that – she could tell straight away – and, in her delight at finding him, she had ignored what should have been so very obvious. Now she had upset him, because she had encouraged him to be someone he was not.

She patted him gently on the back, a small gesture of reassurance, as one would comfort a child.

'It's my fault,' she said. 'I should never have let you think that it was possible. I was so selfish.'

She heard his muffled protest. 'No. It wasn't your fault. It's nobody's. It's just . . .'

'It is. I should have said from the beginning, we're just going to be friends. It would have been easy, but I was just thinking of myself – as usual.'

James drew away from her, although her arms were still around him. He looked at her. Again, she felt desire; she could not help herself. He is so beautiful, she thought. My own Botticelli. A Renaissance princeling incarnate, and in my arms, and . . .

'It's not what you think,' he said. 'You think that I . . . Well, it's not like that. The real truth is something different.'

Caroline waited for him to continue.

'I don't . . . I don't like boys. That's not it.'

She stared at him. 'You like girls then . . .'

He shook his head. 'Not in that way.'

'So . . .'

'Oh, Caroline, how can I explain it? I like neither. Can't you understand? I just want to be your friend. I just want us to be like this, well, indefinitely, and I know that it's terribly unfair on you because you're going to want a lover and all the

172

rest. And then there won't be any room for me in your life – how could there be?'

She released him from her embrace. 'I want us to be friends too, you know. I want that as well.'

'Yes, I know. But you're going to want more. You're going to want more than that, and Caroline, oh, it's so hard to know how to say this. But I suppose I should just come right out with it.' He hesitated. 'I'm just not into the physical side of things. I'm just not.'

40. Morphic Resonance

Terence Moongrove – mystic, dreamer, Porsche-owner – led his sister to her bedroom on the first floor of his Queen Anne house outside Cheltenham. 'I've put you in Uncle Eric's room,' he said. 'I know you like the view from that window. And I've asked Mrs Rivers to put some flowers in the vase that Uncle Eric once threw at that man who came to ask if we would vote for him. Do you remember? The man said something political to Uncle Eric, and he threw the vase. Just like that. Bang. It was a jolly dangerous thing to do, and Daddy was furious, really furious.'

Berthea did remember, and smiled at the recollection. 'Uncle Eric wasn't quite right. I think the man realised, and was very good about it. They get an awful lot of rudeness on the doorstep when they go canvassing.'

'I'm not surprised,' said Terence. 'You're eating your soup and some silly politician comes and rings the bell and asks if you'll give him your vote. Really! Do they seriously think that anything they can say in a few minutes on the doorstep is going to change the way you were going to vote?' They were now at the top of the stairs, and he paused. 'Do you think Oedipus does much canvassing?'

'I doubt it,' said Berthea. 'Oedipus doesn't exactly exert himself, as we well know.'

'I know he's your son,' said Terence. 'And I know he's my nephew. And I also know I shouldn't say things like this, but I'd hate to answer the door and find Oedipus standing there asking for my vote. I really would.'

'Yes,' said Berthea. 'Not an attractive thought. What would you do?'

Terence gave it a moment's consideration. 'I'd give him a jolly good push,' he said. 'I'd push him off the step and say, "I'm not voting for you, you Sam!"'

Berthea frowned. 'What's a Sam?'

'I'm not at all sure,' said Terence. 'But it fits Oedipus. And a lot of other politicians.'

'Maybe.'

They made their way to the end of the corridor where an open door led into an airy, square room. The curtains were pulled back and the late afternoon sun was streaming in. 'Lovely,' said Berthea. 'And Mrs Rivers has done those nice flowers there. I must thank her.'

'She likes you,' said Terence. 'She always has. And here, I've put out some magazines for you to read. This one is really interesting. There's an article in it about morphic resonance. Do you know what that is?'

Berthea glanced at the cover of the magazine. 'No, I don't, I'm afraid. I'm a bit hazy about these things, Terence. It's not really my—'

Her brother interrupted her. 'That's because you haven't bothered to find out. If you did, you'd learn an awful lot, Berthy, you really would.'

She sighed. 'Time, you know . . .'

'Well, I can tell you all about morphic resonance, as it happens,' said Terence. 'It's the idea that living things have a morphic field around them that determines how they will develop.'

Berthea rolled her eyes. Terence was always looking for something, and as a result seized upon any theory he encountered. Morphic fields. 'Have I got one?' she asked. 'Have I got a morphic field?'

Terence smiled. 'Of course you have, Berthy. Your morphic field is part of the human morphic field. All the experiences of mankind are . . .' He waved a hand in the air, in the direction of Cheltenham. 'All our experiences are out there in the vast morphic field made up of all our memories. You're part of that.'

'Sounds somewhat Jungian to me.'

Terence's eyes shone with enthusiasm. 'But of course it is! That's exactly what it is. Jung talked about the collective unconscious. That's the same thing, really, as what Rupert Sheldrake talks about.'

'Rupert Sheldrake?'

Terence paged through the magazine. Coming to a photograph, he showed it to Berthea. 'That's him. That's Rupert

Sheldrake. He wrote a jolly clever book, you know. *A New Science of Life*. He says that each species has a collective memory, and this collective memory influences how we behave.'

Berthea stared at her brother. She had often wondered at how little he was able to remember other than this sort of thing. 'Can you give me an example?' she asked.

'Yes, I can,' said Terence. 'And it's a really exciting example. You know that during the war—'

'Which war?' interrupted Berthea. 'We've had so many.'

'The big one,' said Terence. 'The Second World War. During the war, there was no aluminium for the tops of milk bottles. So they had to use a different system, and that was jolly bad news for the sparrows, who had got used to pecking off the tops of the bottles and having a sip at the cream on the milk.'

'Can't have made themselves very popular,' said Berthea.

Terence ignored this. 'Well, for six years or however long it was there were no foil caps like that. So all sparrows forgot how to do it because the sparrows that would have remembered those foil bottle tops were dead. There was a whole new generation of sparrows that knew nothing about how to get cream by pecking at the tops.'

Berthea's eyes glazed over.

'And then,' Terence continued, 'when the war was over, they brought back those foil bottle tops. And you know what, Berthy? You know what?'

She forced herself to concentrate. 'No. What?'

Terence paused for dramatic effect. Then, with the air of one revealing a resounding truth, he said, 'The sparrows immediately knew what to do! They pecked at the bottle tops straight away!'

'Their collective memory?'

'Of course,' said Terence. 'What else could it have been?'

'Smell,' suggested Berthea. 'They smelled the cream.'

'No,' said Terence abruptly. 'Impossible. It was morphic resonance. They picked it up from their collective morphic field. It's in Rupert Sheldrake's book. You read it for yourself.'

Berthea stared up at the ceiling. 'But if it's part of our collective memory,' she said, 'why would I have to look it up? I'd know it.'

Terence frowned. 'You're being very unhelpful, Berthy. You're just trying to wind me up. You're a naughty old psychologist!'

'Psychiatrist,' said Berthea.

'Same difference,' said Terence, pouting.

'No,' said Berthea, 'it isn't. The difference is MB, ChB, MRCPsych. That's the difference.'

41. May Contain Nuts

Terence left Berthea with a strict instruction to be in the drawing room by a quarter to seven at the latest, when he would serve pre-prandial martinis. The mention of martinis gave rise to an exchange of warning glances, but nothing was said; both remembered the last time Terence had mixed the cocktails, when the conversation had gone perhaps a little further than was wise, with fantasies on the theme of how best to dispose of Oedipus Snark. That would not recur, or at least not in the company of others, who might not understand the length and depth and breadth of the provocation offered by Oedipus over the years.

At about twenty to seven, Berthea was ready to go downstairs. She wanted to be punctual because she knew that Terence, who was otherwise vague in the extreme, nonetheless took punctuality very seriously, just as Auden had. Martinis, in Auden's household, were served on the dot of six, and woe betide any guests who were late. Berthea had often wondered about this: Auden was messy – his study filled with piles of paper, unwashed glasses, cigarette stubs – and yet out of such chaos came order, of thought, of metre and of cocktails. Perhaps it was something to do with notions of outer and inner cleanliness; Berthea had read that some travelling people – gypsies, as they used fondly to be known – liked the inside of their caravans to be spotless while the surrounds, the grass upon which they camped, would often be . . . well, less than spotless, bless them. And it was frequently the case, she knew from professional experience, that people whose lives were disordered in some respect had one or two areas of their existence where they were punctilious and highly observant. Such people might expect high standards from others and were capable of flying into a rage over some petty lapse by an official or a friend. Yet they could not see that they themselves were guilty of exactly the same lapses, and much worse.

Terence was not like that. As far as Berthea could tell, he had no passive-aggressive traits at all: he was not afraid of intimacy, he never lied, he was not given to sulking. Terence was a bit of an enigma for Berthea; he was certainly not *normal*, in the way in which most of us were normal – a very fuzzy concept, of course – but he was not *abnormal*, in the way Oedipus was. Oedipus was psychopathic *simpliciter*, or, in plain English, bad, and it was indicative of his condition that he had no insight at all into how bad he was. Which should not surprise us, thought Berthea – those most in need of help simply cannot see that need.

Plain English was useful, and she defended it, but had to accept that when it came to the human personality in all its complexity one had to resort to technical terms. Plain English terms did not allow for nuance: talk of 'madness' was very unhelpful, not because it disparaged those unfortunates who were afflicted by it, but because its brush was far too broad. One could not lump the psychotic together with the mildly neurotic; one could not put the mildly depressed alongside those suffering from vivid delusions. And yet Berthea some-times felt that the ordinary, vulgar terms for mental disorder expressed an essential truth, and were cathartic, too, for those who worked in the field. She had heard a colleague refer quite affectionately to a patient as 'completely bananas'. One would not find the term 'bananas' in that diagnostic *vade mecum*, the *DSM-IV*, but the psychiatrist who used it felt momentarily less oppressed by his calling simply because the word defused the tension and the sadness. Similarly, the term 'doolally', which people used for those who *lost their place*, seemed less clinical, less frightening than the conventional diagnostic sentence.

That same colleague, irreverent as he was – and therefore level-headed and popular – had once remarked, as he and

Berthea drove together past a psychiatric clinic, 'I think I should put a sign outside the place saying *May contain nuts*.' Berthea had laughed, and had woken up that night and laughed again at the recollection of his wonderful remark. Laughter, so rarely prescribed by any clinician, was surely the most therapeutic thing in the world. And now, she had read, there were studies to prove it – something the drug companies would not be happy about, since laughter was free, could be administered by anybody, and had no negative side-effects.

May contain nuts . . . The same might be said of Terence's house, with these odd friends of his. The last time she visited, there had been the sacred dance people and their Beings of Light; now there were these two resident gurus, Roger and Claire, who had insinuated themselves for the purpose of writing their magnum opus. And for the purpose of eating too, no doubt, and drinking Terence's martinis. Unless, of course, they did not indulge – shortly she would see whether it was carrot juice or gin they drank, and that would tell her a lot about whether they were genuine.

She left her room, and then, on impulse, went back in to collect her handbag. It contained her purse and her credit cards, and for some reason she felt uneasy about leaving them in her room. If Roger and Claire were capable of leeching off poor Terence then might they not be equally capable of removing a few banknotes or a card from a guest? The thought came to her quite powerfully, but she immediately felt guilty; how could she think such a thing about fellow guests whom she had not yet even met – apart from a brief sighting of Roger in the garden. I must not allow myself to be distrustful, she told herself firmly, but nevertheless she kept hold of her bag. It would not do to tempt Providence, at least not once Providence had been alerted to a possibility.

She made her way down the corridor. There was a door off to the left, to a room that she knew to be another spare bedroom; Uncle Edgar had stayed there when his wife had found it all too much to bear. She paused. The door was slightly ajar, just a tad, but enough for her to hear voices within – a man's voice and then a woman's. She was not one to eavesdrop, and the old adage that those who did heard ill of themselves was very true, as so many of those irritating old adages were. But she could not resist; she crept closer to the door.

A squeaky floorboard protested loudly. Berthea froze. The murmur of voices ceased, but then resumed. She breathed a sigh of relief, and strained to hear what was being said.

42. Behind the Arras

Polonius had an arras behind which to hide – not that it did him much good. Berthea Snark had no such cover as she stood on the first-floor landing of her brother Terence Moongrove's Queen Anne house. The unfortunate Polonius brought Hamlet's wrath upon him through an ill-timed call for help; Berthea would make no such mistake. She stood motionless, and unless she were to sneeze – which she had no plans to do – the only threat lay in the squeaky floorboard she had just trodden upon. That was silent now, and if the owners of the voices murmuring within the room off the landing had been momentarily disturbed, they were no longer on the alert as their conversation had resumed.

If there is one thing which one can always make out in an otherwise indistinctly heard conversation it is one's name. Being professionally interested in such phenomena, Berthea had been fascinated to read in the psychological literature of how people in certain stages of sleep may not react to stimulus but upon hearing their name being called may wake up quite quickly. She had experienced this herself while sleeping through a meeting of a committee of the Royal College of Psychiatrists; she had awoken at precisely the moment the chairman mentioned her name, and fortunately had been able to respond to his question quite satisfactorily. Sleeping in meetings, of course, was nothing to reproach oneself for, even though it could be occasionally embarrassing; many meetings were unnecessarily long, or indeed completely uncalled for, and if they provided an opportunity to catch up on much-needed sleep, that at least gave them some purpose. Berthea had once been at a meeting where everybody was asleep except her and the chairman, and the two of them alone had dispatched a great deal of business in a very efficient and appropriate manner. That same chairman, one of the great chairmen of his generation, was himself an accomplished napper, famous for being able to sleep through an entire meeting, only waking at the end, whereupon he would provide an excellent summary of everything that had happened during the meeting. Various explanations had been suggested, one being that he had a rare and useful ability to hear while he was asleep; another, more plausible explanation, was that he knew the members of the many committees very well, and knew that they were unlikely to come up with any novel remarks, and therefore he had no difficulty at all in imagining what they had said.

Berthea was aware that inside the bedroom off the landing, presumably preparing to go downstairs for their seven o'clock martinis mixed by Terence, were the two other guests in the house, Roger and Claire. She had seen Roger as she arrived at the house earlier that day, hanging about in the rhododendron bushes near the drive, and had on the spot identified him as a charlatan. What, she wondered, was he doing in the rhododendron bushes? But, more pertinently, what was he doing exploiting poor, innocent Terence's generosity by coming to stay for an indefinite period of time – possibly years, according to Terence – while writing some mystical magnum opus that was undoubtedly risible in the extreme. She was yet to see Claire, whose voice she now heard from within the room and who was, in fact, the one who was mentioning Berthea's name. Like a sleeper in stage three non-REM sleep, Berthea homed in on what was being said.

' . . . that woman. What's her name – Bertha?'

'Berthea. Berthea Snark, Terence said. His sister. She's the mother of that Lib Dem MP, Oedipus Snark. We've seen him on the box – going on about something or other.'

Claire laughed. 'They do go on, don't they?'

'Nice job,' said Roger. 'You get paid to go on and on about things. I've often thought I'd like to be an MP.'

Claire took a moment or two to reply to this. 'You? You must be joking. And your talents, Rog. Think of your talents. If you were an MP you couldn't set up the centre. All our plans . . .'

Berthea drew in her breath. Centre?

'True,' said Rog. 'Of course we can't treat anything as being in the bag. Not just yet.'

Claire appeared to agree. 'Naturally. What do they say? It's not over until the fat lady sings.'

'It's not over until Terence is kind enough to sign. Which he will.'

There now came from within the room the sound of a cupboard or drawer being closed. Berthea tensed. If Roger and Claire intended to be punctual for martinis then they might emerge at any moment. She would have to move.

She shifted her weight. Within the room, the voices resumed.

'Will she prove awkward – Berthea Stark or whatever she calls herself? I must say I didn't much like the look of her. I caught a glimpse when Terence drove her back from the station. Hostile-looking woman.'

'Well, if she's anything like him, she'll be no trouble.'

'Good. Oh, look at the time, shouldn't we . . .'

Berthea took a step backwards. The floorboard squeaked. Again she froze. It was difficult to decide what to do. She could not stay where she was, but if she took another step she could alert them to her presence right outside their door, and that would be hard to explain. She moved again, very slightly. The floorboard protested.

There was only one thing to do. She knocked loudly on the slightly ajar door.

Roger opened it. He was smartly dressed now, a handkerchief protruding from his blazer pocket in a rather jaunty way.

'Oh . . .'

'Sorry to give you a fright,' said Berthea. 'I wasn't sure if anybody was in. I was looking for . . .' She thought quickly. 'A hairdryer. There isn't one in my room, you see.' She was pleased with the line: saying that she was not sure that anybody was in indicated that she had not heard their conversation. Assuming Roger was listening to what she was saying, of course.

'A hairdryer?'

'Yes.'

He turned back into the room. 'Claire, is there a hairdryer in here?'

Claire appeared behind him, peering at Berthea. She was a rather plump woman, considerably shorter than Roger, and was, like him, somewhere in her forties. Berthea's eye was drawn to a prominent mole on her brow, and then to her carefully plucked eyebrows.

'Who needs a hairdryer?' she said, looking at Berthea. 'It doesn't look as if you've washed your hair. It isn't wet.'

Berthea's right hand went up to her hair in a spontaneous gesture of . . . guilt? Or dismay, perhaps, at having come up with a clever pretext that had such a fatal flaw.

'I'm planning to wash it later,' she said, trying to smile, but finding it rather difficult.

43. Terence Moongrove Entertains

Terence Moongrove was full of bonhomie. 'So you three have all introduced yourselves,' he said, beaming upon his guests.

'That's the nice thing about a house party. Everybody mucks in together. Such fun.'

Berthea gave him a sideways glance. She had known her brother to entertain on only very few occasions, and it was highly unlikely that he had ever held, or been invited to, a house party. He had once invited to dinner his *garagiste*, Lennie Marchbanks, and Lennie's wife, Chantalle, and had served them toad-in-the-hole and cold custard. Berthea had been visiting at the time, but she had been unable to persuade Terence to let her do the cooking.

'I'm a jolly competent cook, Berthy,' he had scolded her. 'You mustn't make sexist assumptions! Lots of men are jolly good cooks, and I think I'm one of them. Look at Ambrose Heath. Look at that chap with no clothes, the Naked Chef. Look at them. They're men, and they're jolly good at all sorts of dishes. That Delia person is not the only one who knows how to cook.'

It had not been an easy evening, as Lennie Marchbanks appeared to get into trouble with his false teeth: a piece of sausage, or perhaps it really was toad, became lodged between the roof of his mouth and the upper plate of his dentures, and it took him fifteen minutes to free it. Nor had the other occasion she had attended been much better, the evening on which Terence had held a dinner party for his neighbours Alfie and Moira Bismarck and their son, Monty. Monty Bismarck was fond enough of Terence, having known him all his life, but at twenty-six one has better things to do than listen to Terence talking about the internal politics of his sacred dance group, which was at the time in dispute with Cheltenham Public

Library over access to the dance space in one of its branches. Monty had frequently looked at his watch while Terence spoke, until Alfie Bismarck had told his son that if he knew of a better party to go to he should just go, rather than sit there like a cat on coals. Whereupon Monty had answered that there was indeed a better party just down the road at Celia Nutley-Palmer's place, and would Terence mind terribly if he went along there before all the action was over? Terence did not mind at all, it transpired, remarking that it was terribly good fun to be eighteen.

'Actually, I'm twenty-six these days, Mr Moongrove.'

Terence expressed surprise. 'Doesn't time fly, Monty? Perhaps we should call it Porsche time. Ha! What do you think of that?'

Now, standing in Terence's drawing room with Roger and Claire, Berthea noticed that Terence had already prepared a tray of drinks.

'Berthy and I have a soft spot for martinis,' Terence announced. 'You'll love these. I'm a jolly good mixer, aren't I, Berthy?'

Berthea made an effort to be polite. 'You have to watch him,' she said. 'His martinis are terribly good but he can be a little over-enthusiastic with the gin.'

'I read somewhere that Churchill just glanced in the direction of the vermouth bottle while he poured out the gin,' said Roger. 'He was a generous host, I believe. Just like you, Terence.'

Berthea looked over at Terence; he seemed pleased with the compliment.

'Well, let's not let these hang about,' he said, handing out the martinis. 'Here we are, Claire, and then you next, Berthy. Family hold back, as Uncle Edgar used to say.'

Berthea tried not to grimace.

'I'd rather hoped that you might consider us family by now,' said Roger suddenly.

Berthea spun round to face him. 'Oh?' she said. 'Have you and Terence known one another for a long time?'

Roger fixed his gaze on her. 'Not in the strictly chronological sense,' he said. 'But sometimes there are people whom you feel you've known all your life, even though you've just met them. You know about that, don't you, Terence?'

Terence smiled. 'Well, I think Roger's right. I do feel that with certain people.' He looked at Roger and Claire as he spoke, and Berthea realised that he was referring to them.

'Very strange,' she said. 'I must say I'm rather of the view that one shouldn't manufacture intimacy. It can be most unfortunate, I think, when one makes a snap decision about somebody and then finds that one has completely misjudged the situation.'

Berthea saw that Claire was staring at her with particular intensity. Terence, of course, was blissfully unaware of the tendrils of tension that were entwining his guests.

'It all depends on whether you're a trusting personality,' announced Claire, 'or a suspicious type. I prefer to trust others and let the karma assume a positive note. Of course, if there are people who are *blocked*, then . . .'

'That's an interesting term,' said Berthea, taking a deep sip of her martini. She had no need of Dutch courage, but it always helped. 'As a psychiatrist—'

'Berthy's a psychotherapist,' interrupted Terence. 'She helps an awful lot of people, don't you, Berthy?'

Berthea ignored her brother. 'As a psychiatrist,' she continued, 'I find it very interesting to hear *lay people* use these terms. What exactly is it to be *blocked*? It sounds more like a term for the gastroenterologist.'

Claire's martini glass was at her lips. She lowered it slowly. The mole on her brow, Berthea noticed, seemed to quiver slightly, as an antenna might be imagined to do when it transmits a particularly intense message. 'To be blocked is to have hostile feelings,' she said. 'When we are blocked, our hearts are closed to the life-enhancing powers and forces that are all about us – all about us, constantly circling, only waiting to be called.'

'Precisely,' said Terence. 'That is what is meant by being blocked.'

'I see,' said Berthea. 'How interesting. How remarkable it is that modern psychiatry, with its scientific understanding of human behaviour, built up through empirical observation over so many years, has no room for this concept.'

Roger suddenly entered the fray. 'Excuse me,' he said, 'but my understanding of Freudian theory is that that is what neurosis is in their terms. People are blocked, and neurotic behaviour is the result of their frustrated energies and instincts.'

'Exactly,' said Terence. 'That's what happens.'

Berthea looked at Roger through narrowed eyes. The gloves were off now – there was no doubt about that. The problem, though, was that there were two of them, and although one could probably discount Claire, Roger was evidently no fool.

She looked at her brother. She could not expect any support there; Terence had no idea that his guests were anything but happy to be standing with him in his drawing room, sipping at his strong martinis. And what he said next confirmed this.

'Isn't this fun?' he remarked. 'Four friends all enjoying themselves so much together. What a lovely house party.'

44. The Green Man

As the party of four filed into the dining room, Berthea felt her heart sink even further. There were several reasons for her feelings of dread. First and foremost, she was not looking forward to two or three hours in the company of Roger and Claire, to whom she had taken an overwhelming and quite unequivocal dislike. That aside, there was the meal itself to get through – Terence had boasted that three courses would be served, each one of them a treat in itself. 'They are entirely my own creations,' he announced as he relieved them of their martini glasses. 'I haven't referred to a single recipe book, not one! But I'm really sure that you'll love everything!'

'You're frightfully clever,' said Claire. 'So few men can cook . . . Mind you, quite a few women can't either.' She looked at Berthea as she delivered this remark.

'I can,' said Berthea loudly. 'I enjoy cooking a great deal. In fact, I've been on several residential cooking courses. You should try one.' She smiled at Claire as she spoke.

Claire was momentarily taken aback. *Love-fifteen*, thought Berthea. Your service.

'Claire doesn't need to go on courses,' said Roger. 'She's a very fine cook indeed. In fact, you've had several recipes published, haven't you, darling?' Fifteen-all.

'Parish magazine?' said Berthea brightly. 'I do love the amateur recipes one reads in such things. And they're such lovely little publications. You know, the local cub scouts' recipe book, that sort of thing – six pages, fifty pence. Vanilla sponge, upside-down-pudding, and so on. Absolutely charming. Not that one would care to attempt any of the recipes!' Fifteen-thirty.

Terence, who was unaware of the tension underlying this exchange, was busy with the placements. 'I'd like Claire to sit on my right,' he said. 'Here we are, Claire. Place of honour.'

Claire moved to her chair and sat down. She was rather overweight, and the chair creaked ominously.

'Terence, you are naughty,' said Berthea, with concern in her voice. 'You really should have given Claire a stronger chair.' Fifteen-forty. 'Let me take that one and I'll give her mine. I'll be fine on the weaker one.' Game, set and match.

Claire glowered. 'It's fine,' she muttered. 'This chair's perfectly adequate. Please don't bother.'

'It's Uncle Edgar's fault,' said Terence. 'He used to take that chair up to his room when he wanted to get something down from one of those high shelves of his. He stood right on the middle of the sitting-down bit. Mummy got jolly cross with him. She used to say, "Dining-room chairs are not ladders, Edgar." Do you remember her saying that, Berthy? Do you remember her ticking Uncle Edgar off?'

Berthea's eyes glazed over. 'Vaguely.'

'And he also used to drink in his room,' Terence went on. 'Nobody said anything, of course, but I remember seeing a large bottle of Scotch up there more than once. Mummy said that he had a weak chest and needed to take a drink for his breathing, but I think it went further than that. Don't you think, Berthy?'

Berthea unfolded her table napkin. 'I'm not sure,' she said, 'that Roger and Claire are all that interested in Uncle Edgar, Terence.'

'Oh, but we are,' said Roger. 'Family stories are always very interesting, and . . .' he paused and looked coyly at Terence. 'And, as Terence said, we think of ourselves as family now.'

Berthea's lip curled. 'Tell me,' she said, turning to Terence, 'what are you giving us this evening, Terence?'

'Pea soup, to start with,' he replied proudly. 'Followed by kedgeree. Then, to round off, we have Christmas pudding. Not that it's Christmas, of course, but I put the leftover pudding in the freezer and I came across it the other day.'

Claire clapped her hands together. 'What a lovely menu, Terence. It's a terrific balance of . . .'

'Yin and yang?' offered Berthea.

There was a silence, eventually broken by Terence, who announced that he would go to fetch the soup and the wine. 'We're having Sauternes with the soup,' he said. 'Then a very nice Rioja with the kedgeree. I saw it recommended in the paper. They said it was a jolly good bargain. Six pounds.'

'Terence, dear,' said Berthea, 'kedgeree is a fishy dish. I would have thought that it would be better to serve a white wine with fish. And Sauternes is really a pudding wine, don't you think?'

Roger looked up. 'There's no reason not to have red with fish and white with meat,' he said. 'I do it myself. A good choice, Terence, and I for one look forward to it.'

'There,' said Terence to Berthea. 'See?'

Terence went out of the room, and silence descended once again. Berthea occupied herself for a moment by rearranging her knife and fork; then she looked up and saw that both Roger and Claire were staring at her expectantly. 'I hear that you're writing a book,' she said to Roger. 'Do tell me about it.'

Roger nodded – pompously, she thought. 'It's about how we know the world,' he said.

'That's a very broad subject,' said Berthea. 'Epistemology?'

'In a way,' said Roger. 'But it's by no means a work of conventional epistemology. I'm not concerned with perception and understanding in the way in which modern philosophy is. I'm interested in how the old knowledge helps us to understand the world. I want to put people in touch with this deep wisdom. It's a cosmological work, really.'

Claire joined in. 'This wisdom is mainly to be found in myths and archetypes,' she said. 'The Green Man, for instance.'

Berthea smiled. 'The man who appears at morris dances? Wearing leaves – the tree?'

'That's only one of his guises,' said Roger. 'The Green Man appears in all sorts of iconographical contexts. You see him on churches and cathedrals, for instance.'

'Chartres cathedral,' said Claire. 'You generally see his face peeping through the leaves. He represents—'

Roger took over. 'He represents our connection with the life-giving earth. He is the forest. He is the growth principle.

He is what Hildegard of Bingen called *viriditas*, the green force.'

Terence returned with the pea soup. It was green, but with traces of brown where some sort of oil had separated from the rest of the mixture. Small lumps, of pea, or possibly ham, floated on the surface. *Viriditas*, thought Berthea. The green force.

Terence served the Sauternes. 'I hope this wine is sweet enough,' he said. 'If not, we can all add a tiny bit of sugar.' He raised his glass. 'But first, let me propose a toast to fellowship, friendship and . . . and what else, Berthy? Can you think of something beginning with an F?'

Fraud, thought Berthea, looking at Roger, but she did not say it, of course. Fat, she thought, looking at Claire, but did not say that either. 'Felicity,' she offered.

Terence thought this a completely suitable third element for his toast. 'To fellowship, friendship and felicity,' he said, with a flourish.

Glasses were raised. Claire did not look at Berthea; Berthea looked at neither Roger nor Claire; Terence looked at Claire, who returned his admiring gaze with a smile. Roger looked at his pea soup, perhaps divining on its oily surface the face of the Green Man himself.

Oh, Terence, thought Berthea. Oh, Terence, my dear, silly, but thoroughly kind brother. You are in dreadful danger, and you haven't an inkling of it, not an inkling.

45. A Question of Karma

Berthea had to save the little private word she intended to have with Terence until after Roger and Claire had gone to bed. It was a long wait, as the couple showed every sign of digging in and waiting until Berthea retired. But she would give them no quarter, and sat doggedly on until Roger started to nod off and Claire had no real alternative but to concede.

'I think we should all go off to Bedfordshire,' said Terence, looking at his watch.

'Not yet,' Berthea said quickly. 'Roger and Claire, you go up. Terence and I will have a little walk in the garden. It's such a nice evening. Just the two of us. Family chat, you know.'

The last sentence was accompanied by a warning look directed at Roger. *Real family*, it said, not ersatz family. Roger pretended not to notice. 'Such an enjoyable evening,' he said, stifling a yawn.

Once Roger and Claire had left, Berthea crossed the room and took her brother by the arm. He was reluctant. 'I'm terribly tired, Berthy,' he said. 'I really don't want to walk in the garden.'

'Come along,' she said briskly, and Terence, out of ancient habit, complied. His sister had told him to come along as a little boy, and he had meekly done as he was told. It was no different now.

They went out into the garden. 'Look,' said Terence. 'It's almost a full moon. It looks close enough to touch, doesn't it?'

'That's as may be,' said Berthea. 'But listen, Terence, what's all this about a centre? What have you been hatching with those . . . with those two back there?'

Terence looked petulant. 'How do you know about this? It's meant to be a secret.'

'Never you mind. The fact is that I know. So you may as well tell me exactly what's going on.'

Terence made a small sound of protest. 'You'll just ruin everything,' he said. 'You've always spoiled my fun. Even when we were young.'

Berthea was dismissive. 'Nonsense,' she said. 'What is it? A centre for what?'

Terence realised that resistance was futile; Berthea was such a *bully*, he thought. 'It's going to be a centre for cosmological studies,' he said. 'And self-discovery. People will come and discover themselves. We'll have courses in the old wisdom.'

'The Green Man and such stuff?'

'Exactly. The Green Man. And we'll have morris dancing too. Roger promised me that.'

Berthea drew in her breath. 'And this . . . this so-called centre will be run by them?' She nodded in the direction of the house. 'By Roger and Claire?'

'Yes,' replied Terence. 'I'm going to make the house over to a trust they run, and—'

She gripped his arm. 'Make the house over! Are you mad? Where will you live?'

'Oh, they promised me that I'll be able to live here the same as before. Only it'll be a centre as well.'

Berthea looked up at the moon. She was going to have to be very careful. 'Well, it all sounds such fun,' she said, forcing herself to utter the words.

'It will be,' Terence enthused. 'It'll be terrific fun, Berthy.

And you can come too. You can come and listen to some of the lectures and maybe give a talk yourself.'

'That'll be lovely,' said Berthea. 'But I wonder whether it might not be a better idea to hold on to the house. Don't make it over. You can let them run their centre here, but don't sign anything. You never know . . .'

Terence nodded sagely. 'I know what you mean. You have to be careful about these things. But I'm absolutely certain that Roger and Claire are trustworthy. You heard them – they said that they're almost family.'

'Yes,' said Berthea. 'That's lovely, Terence. But you know that you shouldn't give your house away – even to family. It's just not wise.'

'It's fine, Berthy. It really is. Roger's promised me that everything will be all right. Nothing will change.'

She decided to try a different tack. 'Don't do it, Terence,' she said. She searched for language that might get through to her brother. 'His karma, you see. It's a question of karma.'

'But his karma's fine,' said Terence. 'You're right to raise the issue, Berthy, but Roger's karma is absolutely positive. No, there's no problem there.'

She did not give up. 'It's just that I had this feeling about . . . about his aura. I felt that there was something negative there. I can't put my finger on it, but I think we should trust our intuitions.'

'You're right,' he said. 'We must trust our intuitions, and my intuitions all say that Roger is the right person to have a centre here. I just *know* it, Berthy. I'm convinced.' He paused. 'You know, I'm touched that you should take an interest in this. And I'm really pleased that you're getting on so well with Rog and Claire. It means a lot to me that the whole family should be happy with the space that everybody's in.'

Berthea gritted her teeth. 'So you haven't signed anything yet?'

Terence shook his head. 'Not yet. But Roger has had a deed of some sort drawn up and it's going to arrive next Wednesday. I'll sign it then.'

'Don't you think you should show it to Mr Worsfold?' Herbert Worsfold was the family solicitor; he might be able to stop this, thought Berthea. He had rescued Terence from a number of difficult situations before now, although none as potentially disastrous as this.

'Mr Worsfold's terribly busy,' said Terence. 'Lawyers always are – with all that law, you know. I don't want to bother him.'

'But you must!' pleaded Berthea. 'You really must, Terence. Mr Worsfold *loves* being bothered. He really does. It's . . . it's part of his karma.'

'No, Berthy. My mind is made up. If I start getting solicitors involved in all this, then the karma would certainly be wrong. This is a transaction based on love and respect, Berthy. Lawyers spoil all that with their notwithstandings and their hereins and all that nonsense. Not for me, Berthy. Not for me.'

Berthea looked back at the house. It meant a lot to her; she had spent her childhood there and it was rich in memories. She was perfectly content that it had been left to Terence rather than to her, as he was more vulnerable and would never have been able to find a place to live had he needed to. And with him living there, it felt for Berthea that it was still, in a way, her family home. She would not give it up without a fight. It did not matter if she had to resort to underhand techniques; she was prepared to do that. And she knew a thing or two about those, she reminded herself. After all, she was the mother of Oedipus Snark MP, which must make her in the eyes of some . . . well, not all that far removed from Lucrezia Borgia.

Very well, she thought. Gloves off. Roger and Claire: *you're toast*. She pondered the expression, alien in her mouth as it seemed. It was so vindictive, so primitive, so unforgiving. She should not use it, because she was neither vindictive nor primitive, and she was always willing to forgive. Except, perhaps, in the case of Oedipus. He would be toast too, she thought. In time. In time.

46. Blackmail

Freddie de la Hay had found a comfortable spot on the floor of the flat occupied by Tilly Curtain, a Senior Field Officer (Grade 2) in MI6. The salary of an MI6 field officer, though adequate, was not unduly generous and certainly not enough to stretch to a flat in that particular street in Notting Hill. Even C himself, who was paid at the level of a senior civil service mandarin – plus a twelve thousand pound annual danger allowance, and an automatic C ('C''s 'C'), leading, of course, to a K – would barely have managed the inflated monthly rental on this flat without feeling the pinch. The reason for the expensive rental was that the landlord had realised just how keen his prospective lessee was for this particular flat. He had suggested a number of other places to the young woman but she had not seemed in the slightest bit interested in those. That was when he understood that there was something about this flat in particular that she wanted. He could not see what it was, frankly, but people had their little ways, and if these idiosyncrasies enabled him to ask for twenty-five per cent more rent than he could normally expect to command for a short-term let, then so be it. And bless the little ways of tenants.

It had not occurred to the landlord that the attraction of this otherwise mediocre flat might be the neighbours. In the rental market, neighbours were usually a drawback rather than a positive feature, the one exception to this rule being celebrity neighbours, who by their mere presence could cause surrounding rentals to shoot skywards. To live next to a flamboyant and egocentric actor or actress should surely be counted a misfortune, but so great is the public fixation with the cult of celebrity that to many, such neighbours were a positive attraction rather than a drawback. The landlord, in fact, wondered whether this might explain the young woman's desire to secure the lease on the flat at all costs. He believed that an ill-mannered celebrity chef lived in the vicinity, as did a minor rock star. He quickly drew up the lease, with its exorbitant rental provisions, and the deal was struck.

He had no idea that it was the flat on the other side of the landing that was the draw. He had let that property six months ago to an East European company, which wanted it for its London employees. They paid the deposit immediately and appeared to be good tenants although they were reluctant to invite him over the threshold once they had moved in. 'There is no need for you to come in,' he had been told by a burly Russian who answered the door when he had called to see whether all was well. 'There is nothing wrong. Everything functions. We are very happy. Goodbye.'

The prosaically named firm seemed completely inoffensive; nobody would give such a business a second thought, and certainly not a second glance. It was obviously concerned with international trade, although not trade in anything interesting; it must deal in bearings, perhaps, or pork futures, or steel.

In reality, the firm was far from bland: it was entirely concerned with blackmail, which it used as a means of securing the sensitive trade secrets of major companies and government departments. These were then sold on to Russian companies who found themselves in competition with western counterparts. The resulting revenues were divided equally between a shady and virtually unknown Russian security agency – which provided the London staff – and the commercial backers, a syndicate of wealthy St Petersburg investors with no sense of commercial propriety, or indeed of any other form of honesty and fair dealing.

The techniques of blackmail used by this organisation differed in few particulars from the blackmail that had been so widely practised by certain agencies of the former Soviet Union. The most common form was sexual: a target would be identified – a middle-ranking official in an appealing company – and his appetites assessed. Thereafter there would be a sustained and carefully planned attempt to compromise him. (The victims were entirely men; women, it appeared, were considered less prone to temptation.) Once an indiscretion had been made, it was extraordinary how cooperative the victim became. Even in a permissive society, where there were few limits to what one could do, people were still sensitive to a light being shone upon their private affairs and indiscretions, and they would risk everything – including their careers – to avoid exposure.

These techniques paid off handsomely. It was in this way, for instance, that the firm obtained the formula for an improved fuel additive that could prolong the engine life of domestic cars by up to eighteen per cent. It was in this way that a radically more efficient refrigerator, which was upon the point of being granted European and American patent protection, suddenly popped up in an attractively priced Chinese version, having been licensed by a St Petersburg engineering company that had previously done no work at all on refrigerators, or indeed on any other kind of engineering. And when several British inventions in gun-sight optics were produced in Moscow before the release of the United Kingdom prototype, and the detailed designs for these devices were found on the laptop computer of the personnel officer of the firm developing them, MI6 became involved.

And now Freddie de la Hay too. His role was to spend time with the Russians suspected of being behind these dubious affairs, not so much with a view to arresting and punishing the Russians as to find out who was being targeted and get to them first, before they started doing their blackmailers' bidding.

In order to identify the targets, MI6 had to hear what the Russians were saying. Unfortunately, attempts to bug the flat had failed, an electronic sweep by the Russians having quickly discovered the tiny hidden microphones. After that, the occupants of the flat had started to have long and earnest conversations among themselves as they walked in Kensington Gardens. It was not easy to eavesdrop on what was said in the open, of course, but if they were to take a dog on their walks, and the dog had a transmitter in his collar, then everything could be heard loudly and clearly in a loitering surveillance van bearing the livery of the Royal Parks . . .

This was the mission upon which Freddie de la Hay now embarked. Wearing his new collar, in which a small transmitter had been expertly concealed, the obliging and urbane Pimlico Terrier was put on a lead and taken downstairs by Tilly Curtain. Freddie's new career had begun. He was now officially in the service of his country.

47. Freddie de la Hay Meets Mr Podgornin

For Freddie de la Hay it was just another walk, although he felt a bit strange wearing this new, rather heavier than usual collar. But it was not for him to argue with the choice of collar or lead: this, he recognised, was the domain of the humans in whose shadow he led his life. He had his views – which were strong enough, and sometimes vocal – on subjects such as biscuits, squirrels or smells, but when it came to the broader parameters of his life, as laid down by humans, Freddie understood that this was simply not his sphere. Had he possessed the words to express it, he would no doubt have said that this was part of the social contract that existed between man and dog, which had been negotiated a long time ago, presumably not long after the first dog had stood outside the early human cave, which was redolent of warmth and charred meat and comfort, and whined to be admitted. That was the moment that sealed the fate of both parties, but particularly of dogs. Man did not ask to join dog, dog asked man, and was therefore the supplicant to whom no concessions needed to be made.

Freddie missed William. Having no real sense of time, he had no idea how long William had been gone from his life. In human terms, it was less than a day; in dog terms, it could have been a month, a year, half a lifetime. He just knew that William was not there and might never be there again. But he did not dwell on what might or might not be; dogs do not see the point, they are concerned only with what is happening now, and with the possibilities of the present moment.

What was happening at that moment was that Freddie was in the park, constrained by a leash, at the other end of which was his temporary custodian, Tilly Curtain. There were intriguing smells at every turn, and Freddie applied his nose to the ground in quivering anticipation. Kensington Gardens was a mass of potential lines of enquiry, smells going in every direction: smells that ran straight along paths; smells that wound this way and that; smells that crossed flower beds and grass and path and then suddenly and inexplicably stopped at the base of a tree. It was enough to keep him busy for hours, for days perhaps, if this new person would only allow him the chance to investigate. But she was pulling on his collar, hauling him off in the direction of a thickset man who was standing on one of the paths, smoking a cigarette and looking pensive.

'Mr Podgornin,' said Tilly. 'What a fine day, isn't it? I love being out here on a day like this.'

Podgornin looked at the young woman standing before him; his neighbour, of course, the one who lived in the flat across the landing. And that dog of hers. It was a Pimlico Terrier, she had said something about that. What good dogs those were. I'm almost tempted to steal him! he thought. But no, she's a pleasant woman and one doesn't want to do anything to attract undue attention. The British are odd about that sort of thing. They become very excited if anybody does anything to a dog. Stupid people! Sentimentalists! No wonder they're finished, he said to himself.

'Good day, Miss . . . Miss . . .' What was she called? They had such ridiculous names, it was terribly hard to remember them. This young woman, for example, had a name that had something to do with furniture or construction or something like that.

'Tilly. Tilly Curtain.'

'Of course!' He took his cigarette out of his mouth with his left hand as he extended his right hand in greeting. Crude though he was, Podgornin knew how to behave gallantly to women. And they were always – always – impressed! They really were most predictable, he thought; like the whole country – utterly predictable.

'I think I may have mentioned to you that I was getting a dog,' said Tilly. 'A Pimlico Terrier.' She pointed to Freddie de la Hay, who looked up at Podgornin with mild interest, wagging his tail politely.

'Of course, you did,' said Podgornin, drawing again on his

cigarette. 'It's a breed I am particularly fond of. I had one myself a few years ago, when I first came to London. It was a very fine dog.' He paused, and bent down to pat Freddie on the head. Freddie smelled the tobacco tars on the approaching hand and struggled with the urge to turn his head away. He knew that this was not what was expected of him, and so he closed his eyes and let Podgornin's hand ruffle the fur around his collar. Now he had the smell of tobacco on his coat, an acrid, cloying smell that would make it difficult to distinguish the fascinating smells that he had been so happily investigating before this unwanted encounter. Who was this man? Was he a member of William's pack? Was he expected to accept him?

'I'm very pleased with him,' Tilly said. 'But . . .' She hesitated, and Podgornin, who had been staring at Freddie, looked at her quizzically. 'But, well, you may remember that I was concerned about what I would do if I had to go away and couldn't take him with me.'

Podgornin thought for a moment. 'Oh, yes, I remember. I said that I'd be very happy to look after him for you. Very happy. We Russians are very fond of dogs, you know. Woof, woof!'

Tilly looked relieved. 'Oh, thank you, Mr Podgornin. In fact, I'm facing a bit of a crisis right now.'

Podgornin frowned. He drew on his cigarette. 'Crisis?'

'Oh, nothing out of the ordinary really. It's just that I have this rather infirm relative – I think I spoke to you about her. She has a carer, but the carer needs respite from time to time. I have to go off tomorrow, actually, and look after things for a week or two.'

Podgornin smiled. 'I said I'd help you out, and of course I will. I'll be very happy to take this fine dog. You mustn't worry.'

'I'll get all his things together, his bowl, his food and so on. Would ten o'clock suit you?'

Podgornin nodded. He looked at his watch and then threw his cigarette butt on the ground. Freddie de la Hay looked with distaste at the small, smouldering object. He did not like Mr Podgornin. He did not like his smell. He did not like the way he looked at him. He was not dog-friendly in the way that this woman, or that other man in the park, or those people downstairs at Corduroy Mansions were. Corduroy Mansions . . . Where was it? Where was Pimlico? Where was William?

48. A Breakfast Exchange

On the morning after their impromptu inspection of Barbara Ragg's flat, Rupert Porter and his wife, Gloria, sat at their breakfast table, exchanging recriminatory glances. It was all Rupert's fault, thought Gloria, it had been his idea to go to the flat after dinner; it was true that she had agreed, but she would never have initiated such a visit herself. That was Rupert's trouble: he was so persuasive. And her trouble was that she allowed herself to be persuaded by him, often against her better judgement.

'You shouldn't have—' she began, breaking the increasingly frosty silence.

'Don't start!' he interrupted.

'I'm not starting anything, I'm simply observing that had

you not come up with the idea of going to Barbara's flat then we wouldn't have landed in that extremely – and I mean *extremely* – awkward situation. That's all I'm saying.'

Rupert pursed his lips. He would never – *never* – refer to that flat as Barbara's, just as no Argentinian – not even the most enthusiastic, polo-playing Anglophile – would refer to the Falkland Islands as the Falkland Islands. No, it was 'my father's flat' or 'Pa's flat'. But now was not the time to go into all of that.

'Well, we got out of it, didn't we?' he protested.

'Yes, but it could so easily have gone the other way. And it nearly did, Rupert – you can't deny that. What if the yeti had woken up?'

Rupert sighed. 'Don't be absurd, Gloria. There's no such thing as the yeti. It's all complete nonsense, encouraged, I might say, by la Ragg, who should know better but clearly doesn't. She's swallowed the whole story cooked up by that crackpot Greatorex. If ever there was a questionable piece of work, it's him.'

Gloria agreed with this assessment of Errol Greatorex, the yeti's biographer, but she was not yet quite prepared to let Rupert get away with last night's debacle. 'Do you really think he believed you?' she asked.

'Who?'

'Greatorex. When you came up with that perfectly farcical story about having forgotten that we were meant to stay with your mother rather than with Barbara. What a ridiculous excuse. Does anybody go to stay with somebody and suddenly remember they're in the wrong place?'

Rupert shrugged. 'I considered it was rather quick thinking on my part,' he said. 'And a fat lot of good you were. I had to do all the talking.'

'Well, I don't think he believed you. I saw his eyebrows go up. When a person's eyebrows go up, it's a sure sign that he's smelled a rat. And what's he going to say to Barbara when she comes back? What if the real Teddy, or whatever his name was, turns up at the flat? What then?' She paused. The mention of rats raised another issue that she needed to discuss with Rupert: Ratty Mason. Last night, just before the disastrous visit to Barbara's flat, Gloria had finally caught sight of Ratty Mason, dining alone in the restaurant in which they had eaten a rather unsatisfactory meal to celebrate her birthday. Ratty Mason had stared at them and when she had asked Rupert who the strange man was, he had revealed the name. But he had refused to tell her anything more.

'In any case, let's forget all about Errol Greatorex,' she said. 'And his yeti. What I want to know is this: who exactly is Ratty Mason? At least I've *seen* him now, but what else do I know about him? Virtually nothing. That he was at Uppingham with you, and that's it.' She fixed Rupert with a steely gaze. 'Rupert, what's all this with Ratty Mason? Why the secrecy?'

Rupert looked uncomfortable. He flushed. 'I've told you. I've told you more than once. Ratty Mason was a chap at school. I didn't know him all that well. In fact, hardly anybody knew him all that well, as it turned out . . .'

Gloria pounced. 'What do you mean, *as it turned out*? What turned out?'

Rupert looked flustered. 'It's just an expression. It doesn't mean anything.'

'Oh, yes it does. If you say "as it turned out", you are suggesting, I should have thought, that something happened. Well, what happened? What happened with Ratty Mason?'

Rupert rose from the table. 'I'm not going to sit here and be interrogated,' he said. 'Let's get this clear once and for all. I barely know Ratty Mason. I hardly knew him then. There's nothing more to be said about him.' He glared at Gloria. 'And now I'm going to the office. I've got work to do.'

He reached for his cup and took a final sip of his coffee, then banged the cup down, spilling the dregs on the table-cloth.

'Look what you've done,' said Gloria. But Rupert was not listening. He went into their bedroom, took his jacket from the wardrobe, and straightened his tie, ready to leave. Then he returned to the kitchen.

'I'm sorry,' he blurted out. 'I didn't mean to be rude. It's just that ... All this stress. Publishers are cutting advances across the board. Our authors are being terribly bolshy. La Ragg has swanned off to Scotland with her toyboy and ... and it's all a bit much for me. Sorry, my darling. So sorry.'

Gloria came to his side. 'Poor darling! I'm the one who should say sorry. I understand how things are. We should get away.'

'Where to?'

'Oh, anywhere. Amsterdam. Paris. What about somewhere in the UK? Aldeburgh. How about Aldeburgh? It's such a lovely place, and they've got a divine bookshop. Remember we met the booksellers, that nice couple the Jameses? We could potter about in there, and go to some funny little pub for lunch. And we could go and see the monument to Ben Britten, that amazing scallop shell, and watch the fishermen launch their boats from the stony beach. Just like Peter Grimes. It would be so therapeutic.'

Rupert looked wistful. 'I love that scallop shell,' he said. 'It's so much better than a statue. You can sit on it, and you can watch the sea from it, and listen. There are so few statues one can sit on.'

'I agree,' said Gloria. 'And yet it's recognisable. We know what it is. It's part of our world. Unlike anything that wins the Turner Prize. Not that *all* Turner Prize artists are useless. I know somebody who actually knows what she's talking about, and she says that some of them have been real artists.'

Rupert thought about this. 'Actually, the Turner Prize stuff *is* part of our world,' he said. 'That's the problem. Those installations are merely the banal replication of the ordinary, and nothing more.' He looked at his watch. 'We're so lucky, my darling.'

She looked at him enquiringly. Why were they lucky? Because they had one another? Because they could go off to Aldeburgh together, when lots of people had nobody to go to Aldeburgh with?

Rupert explained, 'We're lucky because we both think the same way about the Turner Prize. Imagine being married to somebody who actually thought all that pretentiousness had any actual merit. Imagine that!'

Gloria shook her head. 'Impossible,' she said.

Rupert looked at her fondly. 'Do you think we're reactionary?'

Again, Gloria shook her head. 'Not at all. Not us. Nobody really likes the jejune things those people create, Rupert. Nobody. But it's the Emperor's new clothes. Remember the story? Nobody will dare say: Look, can these artists actually sculpt, or paint, or make anything of beauty? Or – terrible, naive question – can they actually draw?'

'They can't,' he said. 'Or many of them can't. That's what David Hockney was complaining about when he talked about the art colleges . . .'

'He can draw,' said Gloria.

'He certainly can.' He looked at his watch. 'I really must get to the office, darling. *Tempus fugit.*'

'*Tempus* is so utterly predictable, darling. All he ever does is to *fugere.*'

Rupert shook a finger. 'Darling, you mustn't say "to *fugere*". That's like saying "to to fly". *Fugere* is the infinitive form, my little darling. Too many "to"s. No additional "to" required.'

She planted a kiss on his brow. 'Oh, darling, you're so clever.'

'Not as clever as you, my darling! *A bientôt!*'

49. In the Waiting Room

The offices of the Ragg Porter Literary Agency occupied one third of a comfortable-looking building overlooking a leafy square in Soho. It was convenient for both the agency's members of staff and for their clients, as it was a stone's throw or, as Rupert's father, Fatty Porter, used so wittily to put it, a manuscript's throw from Piccadilly Circus. He used the expression to describe to new authors how to find the offices, and they usually laughed, little realising that Fatty did, in fact, throw manuscripts out of the window if he considered them dull or they otherwise annoyed him. Behaviour was different in those days, and a literary agent who threw manuscripts out of the window was considered merely eccentric, or colourful, rather than an over-educated litter-lout. The sense of entitlement, now so deeply embedded in consumerism, that would regard such behaviour as insensitive and arrogant was then quite unheard of. In those days people took what they got from a literary agent, just as they did from doctors, teachers, policemen and virtually all other figures of authority. That this was grossly unfair – and intimidating – is surely beyond debate, especially in an age when the tables have been so completely reversed as to require doctors, teachers, policemen and other figures of authority to take what they get from members of the public, and to take it in a spirit of meekness and complete self-abasement.

The office occupied the top storey of the building, the two floors below having been let for as long as anyone could remember to a film-editing company and a dealer in Greco-Roman antiquities. The dealer in antiquities, Ernest Bartlett, was himself of great antiquity, and there was occasionally some debate as to whether he could technically still be alive. However lights still went on and off in his office, and sometimes on the stairs one might hear drifting from behind his door snatches of sound from the ancient device that Gregory Ragg had christened 'Bartlett's steam radio'. This radio was permanently tuned to a radio station of the sort everybody thought had stopped broadcasting. It played light classical music and big bands, but played them in a quiet, rather distant way, as if from a far corner of the ether. The effect was haunting.

Ernest Bartlett was always invited to the Ragg Porter Christmas party, and would normally attend. He would arrive wearing a very old silver-grey double-breasted suit and a Garrick Club tie, and bearing an armful of carefully wrapped gifts. In conversation with the staff, he would refer to Rupert as 'Fatty Porter's much-admired son', and to Barbara as 'Gregory Ragg's distinguished daughter'. He drank bitter lemon at these parties and rarely ate more than one or two small biscuits, which he described as 'egregiously Bacchanalian behaviour on my part'.

As Rupert made his way up the stairs that morning, he caught the faint sound of Ernest Bartlett's steam radio. Vera Lynn, he thought, and smiled. It was a good omen for a day that had not, he admitted to himself, had a brilliant beginning, what with that uncomfortable *froideur* from Gloria, now happily laid to rest with the paying of mutually satisfactory compliments.

He pressed the buzzer on the office door. He had a key somewhere, but he could see Andrea, the agency's receptionist, through the glass. She looked up at him, waved and triggered the mechanism to open the door.

'Nice and early this morning, Rupert.'

'Raring to go, Andrea. Unlike some.' It was a vague, slightly snide reference to Barbara, who was still away on her romantic trip to the Highlands. Andrea understood, but said nothing. She nodded her head in the direction of the small waiting room behind her. 'You have somebody waiting to see you,' she said.

Rupert frowned. He had been under the impression that his morning was free until at least eleven o'clock, when he was due to meet a publisher to discuss a manuscript that was four years late. He had already marshalled his arguments: the author had been busy; the topic was more complicated than he had at first assumed; he was a perfectionist, indeed he was a manuscript-retentive. There were so many reasons.

'An appointment?'

Andrea shook her head. 'No. Actually it's one of Barbara's authors. The American—'

She did not finish. The door of the waiting room swung open and Errol Greatorex appeared in the doorway.

Rupert did not move. He had been bending forward slightly to hear what Andrea had to say, and he stayed as he was, as if caught by a sudden attack of back pain. For his part, Errol Greatorex also froze, arrested by surprise rather than, as in Rupert's case, by mortifying embarrassment.

Errol Greatorex glanced briefly at Andrea. Then he looked at Rupert and frowned. 'Teddy?'

Rupert closed his eyes briefly. He drew himself up. 'What?'

It bought him time, but not much.

'Teddy? Last night.'

Rupert shook his head. Andrea watched. How could she make any sense of this? *Teddy. Last night.* How could one possibly interpret a situation where a man who is not called

Teddy is recognised as Teddy by another person who then says, 'last night'? To say 'last night' is potentially explosive, as it implies that last night . . . And to say it to somebody who must have been using a false name . . . And Teddy is so patently false. Well, what on earth was one to think?

'I beg your pardon?' said Rupert.

Americans do not mince their words – it is one of their great qualities, and indeed one of the great causes of misunderstanding between the United States and the United Kingdom, where words are regularly minced so finely as to be virtually unintelligible. So Errol Greatorex went straight to the point. 'But we met last night in Barbara's flat. Remember?'

Andrea looked at Rupert with interest. She knew that Barbara was in Scotland with her fiancé. What was Rupert doing in Barbara's flat with Errol Greatorex?

'I'm sorry,' said Rupert. 'I think you're mixing me up with somebody else.'

It sounded lame. He could hear it himself. But what else could he say?

'I don't think so,' said Errol. 'You were wearing the same tie, anyway. That stripy thing.'

Rupert looked down at his tie, as if seeing it for the first time. 'Oh, that! It's a very common tie, you know. Half the men in London wear this tie.'

Errol Greatorex looked confused. 'Strange,' he said. 'Very strange.'

'London is a large city,' said Rupert airily. 'One's bound to have a double. Several doubles, in fact. We are not unique – much as we might like to be.'

Errol was staring at him.

'You wanted to see me?' said Rupert. 'I'm Rupert Porter, by the way. Barbara's co-director.' He reached out to Errol Greatorex, who took his hand and gave it a perfunctory shake. His stare was still fixed on Rupert, and his tie.

'Strange,' he muttered again.

'Well, be that as it may,' said Rupert, now adopting a businesslike manner, 'if you'd care to come with me, we can have a chat over a cup of coffee. Andrea, would you be a real darling and make Mr Greatorex a cup of coffee? If he wants one, that is. We don't like to *force* our authors to do anything.' He gave a nervous laugh.

Errol Greatorex nodded to Andrea. 'No milk,' he said. 'But have you got any ghee? That's what the yeti drinks. Tea or coffee with ghee in it. Melted butter.'

50. The Yeti Goes Shopping

'Well, Mr Greatorex,' said Rupert, as they sat down in his office. 'This is an unexpected pleasure, I must say. Barbara has spoken to me many times about your manuscript. I find it most intriguing.'

Errol Greatorex fixed Rupert with an intense stare. 'Oh really? I was under the impression that her partners – and I assume she meant you – were sceptical.' He paused. 'To say the least.'

Rupert shifted uncomfortably in his seat. 'Oh, I should have thought that's a bit – how shall we put it? – extreme. There's all the difference in the world between a healthy degree of caution and undue scepticism. No, I have a completely open mind. Show me a yeti and I'll believe in him.'

He was rather pleased with this last statement. Show me a yeti and I'll believe in him. It had a resounding ring to it, and one might say it about so many things that were dubious or frankly non-existent. Show me a UFO and I'll believe in them. Exactly. Belief required proof, and what better proof than that provided by one's own eyes?

'I shall,' said Errol Greatorex.

Rupert was brought back from his contemplation of proof. 'Shall what?' he asked.

'I shall show you a yeti,' said Errol Greatorex. 'You asked me to show you a yeti. I said that I shall.'

Rupert smiled. 'Of course.' All this talk of the yeti was utterly ridiculous, and that was all it was – talk. The yeti was said to be in London – very well, let him be produced. There were plenty of radio shows for him to go on.

'Last night . . .' Rupert began, and then stopped himself just in time. He had been about to say 'Last night you said the yeti was sleeping in Barbara's flat.' But of course he – Rupert – supposedly had not been there and could not possibly have known about this.

Errol Greatorex pounced on his words. 'Last night what?'

'Last night I was thinking about these issues,' said Rupert quickly. 'Knowledge. Proof. That sort of thing.'

Errol Greatorex clearly did not believe him. 'The person who called at Barbara's flat last night could have seen the yeti,' he said. 'Had he stayed, of course, instead of rushing off.'

Rupert looked out of the window. He found the other man's stare singularly disconcerting. 'Oh yes?' He paused. 'I'm not sure where all this is leading, Mr Greatorex. Is there anything I can do for you while Barbara is away? I take it that work is proceeding on the manuscript. You said that the yeti was dictating the final chapters.'

Errol Greatorex's eyes narrowed. 'I said that, did I? When?' He had said it last night, in Barbara's flat, but of course Rupert had not been there.

Rupert saw that he had fallen into a trap – a trap entirely of his own creation. He squirmed. 'Barbara told me,' he said.

Errol Greatorex shrugged. 'OK. Yes, he's got to the part where his parents are killed in an avalanche. It's painful stuff.'

'I suppose that's a risk for abominable snowmen,' mused Rupert. 'Avalanches and so on. And global warming, too. I expect they're concerned when they read about it in the papers.' He paused. 'I assume yetis read the papers. Perhaps they don't.'

Errol Greatorex pursed his lips. 'You are very sceptical, Mr Porter. You clearly don't believe me, do you?'

'Please, Mr Greatorex – I've never said that. All I'm saying is that yetis are somewhat . . . somewhat *unproved*. And you can hardly blame me for thinking it, can you? Has anybody actually ever *seen* one, I ask myself?'

'I have.'

'Yes, but anybody else?'

Errol Greatorex still stared. 'You mean anybody reliable? Is that what you mean?'

Rupert did not answer, and so Errol Greatorex continued. 'There's a whole body of evidence,' he said. 'There have been numerous, perfectly well-documented sightings. They're all there in the literature.'

'And photographs?'

'Some.'

Rupert spread his hands on the table. 'Very well. Let's just say that this particular jury is still out. And now, is there anything I can do for you until Barbara returns?'

Errol Greatorex shook his head. 'No, I just wanted to bring in the latest chapters. She's been giving them to the commissioning editor at the publishers – passing them on personally.'

'You have them here?'

Errol Greatorex nodded, opening the briefcase he had brought with him. From this he extracted a folder and placed it on the desk in front of him. 'You can read them if you like,' he said.

Rupert took the folder. 'Thank you, I shall.' He began to rise to his feet to indicate that the meeting was over. Errol Greatorex took his cue, and rose to his feet as well. 'Do you want to meet him right now?' he asked.

'Who?'

'The yeti,' said Errol Greatorex. 'He's in the waiting room.'

Rupert struggled to remain calm. How should one behave in the presence of full-scale, florid delusions? Should one humour the person concerned, and then try to call, what, an ambulance? The police? Should one play along with the delusions, or did that draw one into a form of engagement with the sufferer which would merely exacerbate the problem? This was all Barbara's fault, he thought crossly. The rest of us are perfectly capable of identifying the lunatics when they send us their manuscripts. She has to go and get this man a contract of all things! Now he was a client, and one could therefore hardly slam the door in his face, or get him sectioned under the Mental Health Act. It would not be a good advertisement for the Ragg Porter Literary Agency were they to have their clients sectioned under the mental health legislation.

'Very well,' said Rupert. 'I'll see him.' He looked at his watch ostentatiously. 'I'm afraid I don't have a great deal of time, though.'

'Just a minute will do,' said Errol Greatorex. 'Just to shake hands with him.'

They left the office and walked down the short corridor to the reception area and waiting room.

'What's his name, by the way?' asked Rupert.

'His yeti name is fairly unpronounceable,' said Errol Greatorex. 'Most of the locals who get an education at the mission schools choose a saint's name. It makes things easier. There are a lot of Jameses and Johns, that sort of thing. A smattering of John-Pauls in recent years, for obvious reasons. But he's called Charles.'

Rupert did not know what to say, so he muttered, 'Mmmn. Charles.'

They reached the reception area. Andrea smiled at them. 'I gave your friend a cup of tea,' she said to Errol Greatorex. 'He drank it and then said he had to go out. He asked me to tell you that he'd meet you outside Fortnum & Mason at twelve.'

Errol Greatorex appeared to take this in his stride. 'He's got some shopping to do,' he explained to Rupert. 'Fortnum & Mason do a wonderful ghee. Another time.'

'Yes,' said Rupert. 'Another time.'

He showed Errol Greatorex out and then returned to face Andrea. 'You saw him?'

She looked blank. 'Who?'

'Greatorex's friend. The . . . er, man who was with him.'

She did not seem in the least perturbed. 'Yes. I made him tea – as I said.'

'Describe him,' said Rupert.

She shrugged. 'Tall. Very tall in fact. Wearing a sort of beige coat – Marks & Spencer's, I'd say.'

'And?'

'And a bit hairy, I suppose. Could have done with a shave.'

'Hairy?'

'Yes. Hairy. Some men are, Rupert, believe it or not. I don't go in for that sort of thing, not personally, but some people—'

'Yes, yes, I know all that. I wasn't born yesterday. But what did he sound like? What sort of accent?'

Andrea thought for a moment. 'Belgian, I'd say.'

51. A Painful Memory

William's sense that all was not well in his life, an incipient, nagging doubt, had now become a full-blown conviction. There were many reasons for this, but one of them – possibly the most important one – was simple loneliness. Just as Freddie de la Hay was missing him, so too was he experiencing that sense of incompleteness one feels when a familiar presence is suddenly no longer there. Such feelings can be profound and long-lived, as when we lose a close friend or a member of the family – at that level, we are in the presence of true grief – or they may be less substantial, more transient, as when a shop or coffee bar we have grown to like closes down, or a favourite office colleague is transferred. These may seem little things, but they constitute the anchor-points of our lives and are often more important than we imagine. If we lose enough of these small things, we risk finding ourselves adrift, as William now felt himself to be.

Nel mezzo del cammin di nostra vita mi ritrovai per una selva oscura . . . In the middle of the path through life I found myself in a dark wood. This was one of the scraps of William's education that had remained with him, and now, as it came to mind, he remembered the classroom in which the line had been explained to him by his English teacher, a chain-smoker with a nicotine-stained moustache and a wheezy voice. The middle of the path in Dante's days, the teacher had pointed out, was thirty-five – an impossibly distant age when you are sixteen, as William then was. Sixteen was not even quite the middle of the path to thirty-five, and now here he was, at forty-nine, or thereabouts, and thirty-five seemed distant from a quite different perspective. Life seeped away ever more quickly the further along Dante's path one went, he decided, just as water drained more quickly the emptier the bathtub became. When the plug was first pulled it all seemed so slow and then, towards the end, it rushed away in a tiny, feverish whirlpool.

These thoughts came to William as he closed up his wine shop for the night. It had not been a particularly busy day, and he had been able to use much of the morning to catch up on paperwork, which had kept his mind off his situation. But as the day progressed, he had increasingly dwelled on what he thought of as his *plight*. No dog, no wife nor girlfriend, no social life worthy of the name, and, to top it all, no letters after his name.

The letters he particularly wanted were MW. This stood for Master of Wine, a qualification awarded only after a gruelling examination that took four days, during which the candidate was subjected to searching theoretical and practical tests. William had sat the examination a few years ago and failed, a galling experience, heightened in its intensity by the sight of a whole cohort of younger people succeeding, some of whom were only *nel mezzo del cammin*, or not even that far. What did they know that he did not? How was it that they could write about wine with such authority when he, who had spent a lifetime in the business, had so manifestly failed to impress the examiners?

Of course he had nobody to blame but himself, and he recognised that. When he received his grade D he had felt humiliated, but he knew that a grade D was exactly what he deserved, particularly in the written part of the examination, where he had lost his self-control and made wild guesses at the provenance of the wines they were required to identify and write about. He had sat there with ten glasses set out in front of him, and panicked when he tasted the first. He thought that the wine was Portuguese, and was on the point of setting out the arguments to support this view when it had occurred to him that it might be Argentinian. From then on, his progress through the examination had gone downhill. Instead of using the small spittoon that each candidate had on his desk, William had drained the first glass dry. The second sample, a Côtes du Rhône, he found no difficulty in identifying. Encouraged by this success, he again swallowed the entire glass, and by the time he reached the sixth sample he was drunk. It was shameful and extremely unprofessional. The examiners had been tactful, quietly suggesting that he have a break. 'I'm very sorry, Mr French,' the chief invigilator had said, 'but you're disturbing the other candidates. It doesn't really help, you know, if one of the examinees is humming away.'

William had been unaware of the fact that he was humming 'I Am Sailing' under his breath. He stopped, but then, a few minutes later, was afflicted by a loud and persistent attack of hiccups, during which he spilled his two remaining samples, splashing the woman seated at the neighbouring table. This had resulted in his being asked to leave the examination room.

It had been a shameful performance and he smarted at the memory. But it was past now, and he had begun to wonder whether he should not sit the examination again. He knew as much as he ever had – possibly even more – and it would mean so much to be able to put MW after his name. Why not?

He took the decision there and then, as he closed up that evening. He would sort his life out: he would get Freddie de la Hay back; he would register for the next round of Master of Wine examinations; and he would get in touch with that woman he had met in the park.

Sebastian Duck had given him his card, which William had kept in his wallet. He extracted it now and dialled the mobile phone number given on it.

Sebastian Duck answered. 'Duck speaking.'

William had thought he might have to remind him who he was, but apparently that was not needed. 'Mr French.' Sebastian continued. 'I take it all is well.'

'That's what I'd like to find out,' said William.

Sebastian Duck understood. Freddie de la Hay, he explained, was now 'in the field'; William would be very welcome, if he liked, to telephone Tilly Curtain and get a first-hand report.

William's heart leaped. It was exactly what he had hoped for. He noted down the number that Sebastian gave him, engaged in a few pleasantries about the weather, and then rang off. Next he made the call to Tilly Curtain, who answered almost immediately. He explained who he was and there was a silence. Had something happened to Freddie? But then her voice came down the line, warm and encouraging: 'I'd hoped that you might phone.'

William closed his eyes in sheer ecstasy. 'Look, I know it's absolutely no notice at all, but would you by any chance be free for dinner tonight?' he asked.

Again there was a silence. And then, once again, came the words to boost any heart – even that of a middle-aged wine dealer, a failed Master of Wine, and a failed everything else – 'What a lovely idea! Yes, of course.'

52. *Dinner at Racine*

William chose Racine in the Brompton Road because he knew Henry Harris, the proprietor, and was sure that Henry would always find him a table, no matter how short the notice. And indeed a table was available at eight, and the staff said they looked forward to seeing him.

Now that he had invited Tilly, William found himself trying to remember what she looked like. It was almost like going on a blind date, he thought, something that previously he would never have dreamed of doing but he now found rather exciting. She was certainly attractive, he was sure of that, even if he had seen her only once, and for a very brief period. He had a memory of light brown hair, cut fairly short, pageboy-style perhaps, and he remembered, too, an appealing smile. Or was her hair more blond than brown, and was it maybe longer than he remembered? She was in her late thirties, he thought, or perhaps early forties. He could not be certain of that either, and even thinking about her age made him feel anxious. If she was in her early forties, then that would be fine, as he was in his very late forties, or had been last year, before his fiftieth birthday. If there were eight or even ten years between them, it would not matter; in fact, it would be ideal, at least from his point of view, and probably even from hers. William had always believed that women liked men to be a little bit older than they were, even if there were some women these days who went in for younger men. He was not so sure about that; he knew there was no reason at all why women should not have younger partners, given that men often did –

how many men in their fifties did he know who had girlfriends in their early thirties? Legions – practically *everyone*. Yet the thought that women might choose to do the same thing, to seek out younger men, secretly unsettled him. If more and more women chose younger men, then how many women would be left over for the likes of him?

More unsettling than this speculation about age was the realisation that he had no idea whether Tilly Curtain was single. He had not noticed a ring, but then he had not looked for one. Of course, if she were married she would never have accepted his invitation to dinner; she would have said something like 'Should I bring my husband?', which would have had the merit of directness and unambiguousness. Or she could simply have made an excuse about having other arrangements. It was possible that she was encumbered in some way by a boyfriend but was looking for a way out. That notion was equally unsettling; William did not wish to become involved in anything messy.

He put these ideas out of his mind and set about preparing for the evening. Going to his wardrobe, he surveyed the jackets hanging within. He had neglected his clothes for a long time and it showed, but at least there was a navy-blue blazer in reasonably good condition, and there was a time-lessness about blazers. He took it out and tried it on; the cut was good, and he had not put on weight since he last wore it. It would do, he thought. Trousers were more diffi-cult. Two pairs of the charcoal-black trousers he favoured were out of commission, one because of a broken zip and another because of bad fraying at the ends. Jeans? He remembered that there was some of Eddie's clothing still in the flat. He and Eddie were the same size, more or less, and when he lived with him his son had regularly borrowed William's clothing – admittedly, though, and insultingly, for fancy-dress and retro parties.

He went to the cupboard where he had stored Eddie's remaining possessions. There was, as he had remembered, a pair of jeans, and he took these out and unfolded them. They were distressed, but no more so than new jeans were these days, and they appeared to fit. William examined himself in the mirror; the jeans took off ten years, he thought, possibly more, and they were perfect with the blazer. This was the very essence of *casual smart*, he thought – that vague concept that allowed you to wear anything as long as you looked as if you had at least made some effort. He could hold up his head in any company in an outfit like this.

The hour between seven and eight was an ordeal. He tried to relax. He tried reading, but could not concentrate and put the book down; he tried listening to music, but found that he was not in the mood; he tried writing a letter, but found that he had nobody to write to, and put the pen and paper aside. At last it was time to go, and he made his way downstairs, conscious of the fact that his heart was beating faster in anticipation.

Tilly Curtain arrived at Racine a few minutes after William. They recognised one another immediately, and she came over to the table where he was waiting and shook his hand warmly. 'I hope I'm not late,' she said. 'You've probably been waiting for ages.'

He shook his head. He had been right about the smile – it was wonderful, transforming.

She sat down and William ordered drinks from the waiter who appeared at the table. They both took a gin and tonic. He looked at her and she smiled. It's the teeth, he said to himself, that's what I remember.

'I'm glad that you were free,' he said. 'I was at a loose end and I thought . . . Well, why not?'

'Why not indeed?' she said. 'No, I was glad that you phoned. I was going to phone you.'

'About Freddie de la Hay?'

The smile disappeared. She looked grave. 'Yes.'

William knew immediately that something was wrong. 'How's he doing?'

Tilly looked about her. Her voice, when she replied, was lowered. 'Well, it started pretty well. They took the bait, and we heard a certain amount. But then Freddie's transmitter suddenly went dead.'

He stared at her without saying anything.

'We tried to locate it,' she said. 'But there was no signal. None at all.' She paused, watching his reaction. 'We fear that they discovered it. They might have been suspicious of the weight of the collar or something like that. Anyway, we have to assume—'

He stopped her. 'Are you telling me my dog's disappeared? Is that what you're saying?'

She nodded. 'I'm very sorry. I really am. But that's what we have to conclude. It's a missing-in-action case. It happens.'

53. Meeting Sorley

The sleeper train carrying Barbara Ragg and Hugh Macpherson drew into Fort William station shortly before ten in the morning. The days of generous train breakfasts, served with copious quantities of – then – guiltless grease, eaten at table, and with cutlery too, had long gone, to be replaced by continental fare, conveniently healthier, served in sterilised plastic and cellophane, and eaten, of course, with one's fingers. Perched on the edge of Barbara's bunk, Hugh tackled just such a breakfast while both of them gazed out of the window of the train. They were making their way past the still waters of Loch Treig; like glass, Barbara thought; like glass reflecting the mountains and the sky in perfect inversion.

She had no appetite. To eat in the presence of such an inspiring landscape would be, she felt, like munching some pre-wrapped snack in front of a Botticelli in the Uffizi; the spiritual and the corporeal were not always appropriate bedfellows.

'You're not hungry?' asked Hugh, brushing from his fingers the last crumbs of a dried-up croissant.

She shook her head. 'Not here. Not in front of all this.' She gestured out of the window.

'It's very beguiling, isn't it?' he said. 'I never tire of it. Never. It's home, but it never seems to me to be anything but ... Well, just the way the world should be, if we hadn't messed it up. The perfect landscape. What heaven will look like, if we ever get there.'

She looked at him. She had always hoped to meet a man

who would react passionately to landscape; now she had. 'You must miss it.'

For a few moments he was silent. He continued to stare out of the window. 'I do. I miss Scotland every day. Every day.'

Barbara saw that the sky was reflected in his eyes – a tiny spot of light. Would she pine for England if she were ever to move away? Who spoke now of missing England, in the way in which Rupert Brooke had? To do so would be to invite a sneer from the sophisticates who thought it naive, even simple-minded, to love one's country. Of course a country had to be lovable, and if people lived amid ugliness and squalor, or if their country became a stranger to them, then perhaps they might be forgiven for not holding it in affection. It was easy enough to imagine what one might distil from a landscape such as this – a feeling of emptiness and space and sheer physical splendour – but what could one take from the litter-strewn streets of a city, from a forest of tower blocks? What niche in the heart could such a place occupy?

Of course Barbara loved London, as so many Londoners did, in spite of their occasional complaints. She loved it because it was her place, and anybody with any soul to speak of would love his or her own place. But it was more than that; she loved its little corners, its poky little shops run by shabby eccentrics, its oddly named pubs, its gardens, its sudden turns of architectural splendour. She loved its extraordinary tolerance, which felt like an old slipper, she thought – as uncomplaining and as pliant as such footgear is in the face of all sorts of pressures and provocations. In fact London was exactly that – an old slipper that had been home to countless feet and still welcomed and warmed the feet that came to it fresh. It was not a bad thing for a city to be, when one came to think of it, an old slipper. You could not call Paris an old slipper, nor Berlin, nor New York. Only London.

What if she had to leave London? She had never even entertained the idea – after all, where was there to go, after London? – but now the possibility crossed her mind that Hugh did not feel the same way. And if Hugh wanted to leave then she would have to face the prospect of moving on herself. Could she do it? She would lose her stake in the firm – and how that would please Rupert – and she would also have to find something else to do. It was a depressing thought, not one to be considered even for a few minutes. New Yorkers, Parisians, Londoners: you could hardly expect any of them to move, could you? Unless, of course, New Yorkers went to Paris, Londoners to New York, and Parisians to London. That made sense enough.

They passed the rest of the journey in silence, not because of any awkwardness, but because neither wished conversation to break the spell that the unfolding Highland landscape was weaving about them. And what remarks were needed here? If one listens to the talk of people looking at scenes of great natural beauty, their words are often revealing. 'Isn't it beautiful?' is what is most frequently said; to which the reply, 'Yes, beautiful,' adds little. What is happening, of course, is a sharing. We wish to share beauty as if it were a discovery; but one can share in silence, and perhaps the sharing is all the more powerful for it.

Hugh had said that his father would meet them and drive

them to the farm on Ardnamurchan. Now, as she peered out of the window of the slowing train, Barbara had no difficulty working out which of the small number of people waiting on the platform he was. 'That's him?' she asked Hugh, pointing at the tall man in a Barbour jacket.

Hugh nodded. 'His name is Sorley,' he said. 'Sorley Macfeargus Macpherson. Sorley to everybody except my mother, who calls him Somerled.'

'Somerled?'

'It's a complicated story,' said Hugh. 'Later.'

They got down from the train and made for the barrier. The air, Barbara noticed, smelled different; it was fresh and clear; air that had rain on its breath, and salt, and the sweetness of seaweed.

Sorley stepped forward and Hugh took the proffered hand. Then he leaned forward and the two men embraced, awkwardly, as men always embrace, but with clear affection – and perhaps even relief, thought Barbara. Had a stranger witnessed this scene, she told herself, he might have imagined that here was a son coming back from a long and dangerous trip and being greeted by a relieved parent. But Hugh had not really gone anywhere, other than London, which was only five hundred miles away and hardly dangerous. Yet perhaps that was the way it looked from this part of Scotland; in which case how would she appear to them? Would they think her some exotic metropolitan, some femme fatale who was keeping their son from his home and family? It was tempting to imagine that they might.

Sorley disengaged from the filial embrace and turned to

Barbara. 'So you are Barbara,' he said, leaning forward to embrace her too. 'My dear, you are so very welcome to our family.'

She felt his lips upon her cheek; the lightest of kisses. And then, looking into his face, she noticed that he had the same eyes as his son, and the same fine features. For a few moments she stared at him.

'I hope that I meet with your approval,' he said gently.

She laughed. There had been no barb in his comment. She could not tell him, though, what she had been thinking, which was that here before her was her future husband as he would be in twenty-five years' time. It was rather like looking at one of those pictures that forensic artists draw of the missing person as he would be now, after many years. With deft pencil strokes, the years are added, and there, before our eyes, the missing person, more weary, more worn, is suddenly revealed.

She looked at Sorley, and realised, more strongly and with greater conviction than ever before, that the planetary movements that had brought her and Hugh together in Rye could only be the result of divine blessing or sheer good fortune – on a cosmic scale.

54. Words of Welcome

Sorley led them to an ancient green Land Rover. Their cases loaded, he ushered Barbara into the front seat while Hugh prepared to climb in behind. 'I don't mind the back,' she said. 'Let Hugh . . .'

'Certainly not,' said Sorley. 'Hugh is perfectly accustomed to being back there – with the dogs, if we had any – aren't you, Hugh?'

'Of course.'

'And we would never expect a lady to sit in the back, would we, Hugh?'

'Certainly not.'

Sorley unfolded a tartan rug and laid it across Barbara's knees. They drove off. Hugh pointed to a mountain that rose almost sheer from the other side of the sea loch and named it. It was a name of liquid sounds, a Gaelic name she feared she would never be able to remember.

After ten minutes following a winding coastal road they came to the Corran ferry, a five-minute crossing of Loch Linnhe that would take them into the hills of Ardnamurchan. As they waited for the ferry to disgorge its last few cars and allow them to drive down the ramp, Sorley told a story.

'There was a doctor round these parts,' he said. 'He was a very popular figure. But he liked his whisky. Nobody minded that, of course, as everybody likes his whisky in Lochaber. Anyway, he drove onto the Corran ferry one day after he'd been up to the Fort to visit some friends. He'd had a few drams up there and decided to get out of the car to clear his head. When he got back in there was a terrible fuss and he called one of the ferrymen over to the car. "Somebody's stolen my steering wheel!" he complained. The ferryman had a look and said, "You're sitting in the back seat, doctor."'

Barbara laughed, and, glancing behind, she noticed that Hugh looked pleased that she had found the story amusing.

She would tell him later, she decided, that her own father, Gregory Ragg, used to tell stories too; substitute Soho for Argyll and the stories were the same.

The farm was a good distance down Loch Sunart, in the shadow of a towering hill that Hugh identified as the Holy Mountain. Sorley had become quiet; he had engaged Hugh in desultory conversation but this dried up as the journey continued. Then they were there, at a set of stone pillars between which an ordinary stock gate had been hung. An untarred road wound its way up through a stand of broad-leaved trees; beside it, down a bank that was covered with rioting whin, a burn, wide as a river in places, made its way seawards. Barbara looked up and saw that there was a long, wispy waterfall where this burn tumbled down the hillside. Hugh, following her gaze, reached forward from the back seat to touch her arm gently. 'I used to go up there every day when I was a boy,' he said.

'Can we?'

'Of course we can,' he said. 'There's a pool up there. Right under that high bit – see? – where the water falls about thirty feet. Look.'

He addressed his next remark to his father: 'The hydro scheme. How are things going?'

His father sighed. 'Where does one begin?'

'Not going well?'

'No.'

Barbara looked enquiringly at Sorley. 'A hydro scheme?'

'Hydroelectricity,' he said, pointing up at a far place on the mountain. 'Over there we have another body of water coming down the hill. Quite a decent volume of it. If we lay a pipe down the hill we get a terrific drop, which means that we can generate hydroelectricity down at the bottom.'

'For the house?'

Sorley shook his head. 'Far, far more than that. We can probably get eight hundred kilowatts. We could sell it to the electricity people. Pump it back into the grid.'

'It's very green,' said Hugh. 'It's far better than making electricity from coal or nuclear reactors.'

'Exactly,' said Sorley. 'And this part of the world is full of energy. Wind energy. Tidal energy. And so on.' He sighed again. 'That's the theory. But try getting any of this started and . . . Well, there are all sorts of difficulties and problems put in your way. And contractors too. Don't talk to me about contractors.'

The farm road veered sharply to the right and the house came into view. Barbara almost gasped, but stopped herself in time. She had expected something simple; they had passed a number of farmhouses on the way all of which had an air of solid, rural simplicity about them. This house, which was painted white, was considerably larger than the others she had seen, and considerably more beautiful.

'Is it Georgian?' she asked.

'Yes,' said Sorley. 'At least, in its inspiration. One of my forbears was a great devotee of Georgian architecture. He built this in the middle of the nineteenth century, when everybody else was building great piles like Glenborrodale Castle or Ardtornish. He went in for simplicity.'

They went inside. Hugh's mother had waved to them from a window and now appeared in the hall.

'Stephanie,' whispered Hugh.

Stephanie smiled at her son, but went first to Barbara. 'My dear,' she said, 'you are so very welcome to our family.'

The words were the exact ones used by Sorley, and Barbara had to make an effort not to register her surprise. Had they discussed in advance what they were going to say to her? If so, it disappointingly diminished in her mind the warmth of Sorley's welcome at Fort William station; rehearsed words always struck her as being so much less powerful than those that are spontaneous and unprepared. And yet there were many occasions when there were no alternatives to stock phrases that might mean little but nonetheless oiled the wheels of social life. 'Good morning' in one sense meant nothing, but in another meant everything. 'Have a nice day' in one sense meant nothing and in another . . . meant nothing too.

55. Martin Makes a Proposition

Early that week, Dee received a letter from Richard Eadeston, the venture capitalist. The letter arrived at the Pimlico Vitamin and Supplement Agency with the morning post, which was delivered while Dee and her assistant, Martin, were enjoying, during a slack period, a cup of redcurrant infusion. Their conversation had been wide-ranging and frank, comparing the merits of various products and even touching on a subject that they had not visited recently but Dee now felt sufficiently emboldened to raise.

'Have you given any further thought to the thing I spoke to you about a while ago?' she had asked Martin.

Her assistant looked blank. 'What thing? Echinacea?'

She took a sip of her redcurrant, looking at him over the rim of the cup. 'No. The other thing.'

She could be oblique, he thought, needlessly so. 'I really don't know what you're talking about. What other thing?'

'Colonic irrigation.'

Martin blushed. 'No,' he said bluntly. 'No, I haven't.'

'You really should,' said Dee. 'There's been another article on it in the mags. They're talking about making it available on the health service. About time too.'

Martin looked away. He said nothing.

'Not only should it be freely available,' Dee went on, 'they should make it compulsory. On health and safety grounds.'

Martin raised his eyebrows. 'Compulsory!'

'I'm only joking,' said Dee. 'Where's your sense of humour?'

'I don't think colonic irrigation is funny,' said Martin. 'And I wish you wouldn't go on and on about it.'

Dee defended herself. 'I don't go on and on, as you put it. All that I'm saying is that when I had a look at your eyes that time, what I saw made me think that you'd benefit from colonic irrigation. I was just thinking about your toxins – that's all.' She paused. 'But if you don't want me to care about your toxin levels, that's fine. Just don't blame me if you . . .'

'If I what?'

'Nothing. Just don't blame me.'

'Fine. I won't. So that's it. Don't talk to me about it again.'

She shrugged. 'You wouldn't have to pay. I'd do it for you. I've been trained.'

He said nothing, and it was at this point that the postman

entered the shop with the post, including the letter from Richard Eadeston. Dee opened it, and read it quickly.

She was clearly pleased. 'That's good news,' she said. 'Very good news.'

Martin was relieved to be talking about something other than colonic irrigation. 'What's good news?'

Dee told him about her meeting with the venture capitalist and his enthusiasm for her idea of marketing a Sudoku Remedy based on ginkgo biloba. 'He likes it,' she said. 'Listen, this is what he says: "I have discussed your proposal with my colleagues and they have agreed with me that this is a project that deserves backing. Obviously we shall need to see a proper business plan, but subject to that being put together satisfactorily, I think we shall be able to see our way to investing a small sum in your Sudoku Remedy. We are not prepared to fund the total cost, of course, and would want you, as a matter of principle, to put up a certain amount. What disposable assets do you currently have? If you can raise ten thousand pounds, we shall match that sum in the first instance, with the possibility of a further tranche of between fifteen and twenty thousand pounds later in the year. We would expect such a quantity of shares to be issued to us as would reflect our level of risk: I suggest that seventy-five per cent of the equity should be vested in us, with twenty-five per cent remaining with you. You should, of course, seek independent advice, but I would recommend the arrangement to you and I look forward to working with you in the near future."'

Martin's eyes narrowed. 'Twenty-five per cent? But the whole idea was yours. You deserve more than that.'

Dee told him that money was rarely a matter of desert. 'That's what happens,' she said. 'If you need to raise money, you always lose control of your business. Cash has a price tag, you know.'

'Well, it sounds unfair to me ... But then I don't know anything about it.' He looked at her enquiringly. 'Have you got ten thousand pounds, Dee?'

Dee was thoughtful. 'Not as such,' she said. 'No, I don't have ten thousand pounds as such. Not actual cash ... But I do have an asset worth a bit more than that. Twelve thousand, or thereabouts.'

'Shares?' asked Martin.

'No, not shares. It's an endowment policy I took out a few years ago. It's my pension – or the beginnings of it. I could surrender it.'

Martin drew in his breath sharply. 'You mustn't, Dee, you mustn't do that. Not your pension!'

'I won't need my pension for ages and ages,' said Dee. 'I'll have time to get another one sorted out. No, I'll cash this one in and use it to fund the Sudoku Remedy.'

Martin looked at her, the anxiety plain in his expression. 'I'd say that's very foolish. I really would. And anyway, can you trust this What's-his-name?'

'Richard Eadeston. Of course I can trust him.'

Martin was not sure. 'What if you give him the money and he just goes off with it. What then?'

She did not think this likely. Richard Eadeston was a graduate of the University of Sussex; he had frequented the same Brighton pub as she had, the Shaggy Dump. That was not the profile of somebody who might be suspected of fraud or other sharp practices. 'He's fine, Martin,' she reassured him. 'And I'm a big girl, I really am. I know how to look after myself.'

Martin realised that he was not going to persuade Dee to think again about using her pension fund in this way, so he moved on to more practical considerations. How would she market the Sudoku Remedy once she had it bottled? And who would bottle it?

'What I think I'll do,' said Dee, 'is a trial run. I'll get in some wholesale ginkgo tablets and then I'll get some labels printed. We – that's you and I – can stick these labels on to little bottles full of the ginkgo. And that's it – we'll put them in the window and see what happens.'

'You don't need ten thousand pounds to do that,' Martin pointed out. 'You could do that for a few hundred, surely.'

'Nice labels,' said Dee. 'And leaflets. We'll maybe even put an advertisement in one of the papers. You know those ads you see for booklets on how to talk to your cat – that sort of thing. Those companies do terribly well, you know. Everybody loves mail order.' She reached out and tickled Martin under the chin. 'We're going to be rich, Martin – or rather I'm going to be rich. But I'll pay you separately for the help you give me. Filling bottles and so on.'

'I wish you wouldn't tickle me,' he said. 'It's really annoying.' Tickling, and offers of colonic irrigation; it actually amounted to harassment, if one came to think of it. Dee should not assume she could treat him like that just because he was younger than she was, and her employee to boot. That kind of thing was no longer allowed, he believed, and Dee would have to learn that. How would she like to be tickled? How would she like it?

He sighed. My life is nothing, he thought. Nothing. Money – that was the answer. If you had money, then you could do something, and you would not have to put up with all this: being Dee's employee; being tickled under the chin in a condescending way; being threatened with colonic irrigation. What he needed to do was to make money so that he could be somebody at last, not just a complete nobody.

He had five thousand pounds. It had been given to him by his godfather, who had a minicab firm in Essex. He had done nothing with it, merely left it in a deposit account in the bank. What he needed to do was to put it to work, and perhaps this was his chance.

'Dee,' he said. 'This Sudoku Remedy of yours, will it really take off?'

Dee looked completely confident. 'Well, I think it will. And Richard thinks it will too.'

'Could I come in on it?' said Martin. 'I haven't got very much. Just five grand. But I could become a . . . a partner.'

Dee thought for a moment. Martin was so young. But . . . 'All right,' she said. 'As long as you're sure. I don't want to take your money unless you're sure.'

Martin swallowed. 'I'm sure,' he said. It was spoken with conviction – exactly that tone of conviction we use when we are profoundly unsure of what we are saying but hope that our words alone will make things work, will make everything all right.

56. Freddie de la Hay Goes Off Air

The event that Tilly Curtain described to William so cursorily at their meeting in the restaurant – the sudden fading into silence of Freddie de la Hay's transmitter – had only come about by pure chance. It was certainly not the result of anything that Freddie had done; he had behaved impeccably from the moment he had been brought by Tilly Curtain to the flat next door. He had been puzzled by what seemed now to be a fairly constant process of being passed from pillar to post, but he was not by nature a complainer, and he had accepted it.

Of course he did not like Anatoly Podgornin, the man to whom Tilly consigned him, but again he did not outwardly show this dislike – apart from a slight drawing back when the Russian bent down to pat him on the head. Nor did he like the smell of this new flat, which was heavily dominated by stale tobacco smoke. There were other disagreeable scents too: from the kitchen there came an odd, vinegary smell that made the inside of Freddie's sensitive nose prickle; there was a meaty odour there, too, which was more satisfactory, but he could tell that something had been done to the meat to make it rank in the canine olfactory spectrum.

On his arrival in Podgornin's flat, Freddie had been led into a sitting room. There was a woman there, and two other men, and they were engaged in some sort of meeting. When Podgornin entered with Freddie, one of the men gave a sarcastic cheer. 'Country gentleman, now, Anatoly Mikhailovich?' he called out mockingly. 'Going shooting? Off to the *dacha*?'

Podgornin cleared his throat. 'My house,' he said. 'If I want a dog, it's up to me. And it's just for a week. I'm looking after him for that charming young lady on the other side of the landing.'

'Fraternising with the locals?' asked the other man. 'Or only with the female locals?'

Podgornin watched as Freddie went to lie down on a rug. 'He's settling in. And as for this business about fraternising, how are we to make the necessary contacts unless we get out and meet people? Moscow made it clear: integrate, get on the inside track. You know that as well as I do.'

The woman was clearly irritated by this conversation and began to show her impatience. 'That's enough about dogs,' she said. 'Pointless creatures. I suggest we get back to the topic in hand, which is, if I may remind you, the issue of access to further information about energy acquisition strategy. I would like to know where you are with that young man in their liaison office. Coming along nicely?'

'Very,' said Podgornin. 'He is that very useful character – the incorrigible gambler. At the moment he has very little debt – he's been lucky – but I'm assured by our friend in the casino that it won't be long before we shall have him right where we want him. We shall very generously offer to pay his debts once they're large enough—'

'And pressing enough,' interjected the woman.

Podgornin laughed. 'Exactly. And then he's ours.' He hesitated. 'Although frankly I don't see what they'll get from him.'

The woman looked at him scornfully. 'You don't get it, do you? If we know the real position of our rivals in energy negotiations – how much they can really afford to pay, which officials they're bribing and so on – then we can . . . we can adjust our own offers . . . and inducements accordingly.'

'Oh, I know all that,' snapped Podgornin. 'What I was wondering was whether that particular man will have the information in his possession. I suspect we might be overestimating his importance in the office. The monkey doesn't always know what tune the organ grinder's going to play. That's all.'

'I shall be the judge of that,' said the woman coldly. 'And my sources tell me that he has access to the lot. Complete.'

Podgornin shrugged. 'We'll see.'

Freddie watched them from the rug. He did not like any of them, but he was developing a particular dislike for the woman. There was something about her that made the hairs on his back stand on end, and indeed that was now happening, giving him a slightly strange appearance, as if he had teased out his coat with hair gel.

The woman was looking at him intently. 'There's something odd about that dog,' she said. 'Look at him. He's ill at ease.'

'It's a new place,' said Podgornin. 'Dogs take a bit of time to get used to new surroundings. He'll settle.'

'I had a dog once who looked a bit like this one,' said one of the other men. 'Went mad. The police came in and shot him.'

'Did you need those rabies injections?' asked his colleague.

'Yes, but then they did the tests and they discovered that it wasn't rabies. He had just cracked. Stress, I suppose.'

'Oh.'

The woman was still staring at Freddie de la Hay, who returned her gaze cautiously, trying not to blink and thereby attract unwelcome attention. He felt distinctly uncomfortable now, and wondered how long his ordeal would last. Why was William letting this happen to him? Where was he? What had he done to bring about this rejection, this abandonment?

'Look at him,' said the woman. 'There's definitely something odd going on. Do you know this young woman who owns him, Anatoly?'

Pordgornin lit another cigarette. 'She lives next door. I already told you.'

'That means nothing,' said the woman. 'You can live next door to people for years and know nothing about them. What do you know about her? What does she do?'

Podgornin looked sulky. 'I don't know,' he spat out. 'In London you don't go round asking people what they do.'

The woman now began to move very slowly towards Freddie de la Hay. She was staring at his collar. He eyed her watchfully, his nose twitching very slightly, his whiskers erect and receptive.

She was now standing directly above Freddie, who whimpered, almost inaudibly. 'Nice dog,' she said, reaching down to stroke him. He tensed, but allowed her to try to smooth down the hair on his back. He could not see her hand; he just felt her touch. Now the hand moved forward and was about his neck. She was fumbling with something.

The woman gave a cry, and Freddie felt his collar being stripped roughly from his neck. 'What have we here?' she said triumphantly. And then turning to Podgornin, she waved the bulky collar in his direction, as if confronting a malefactor with the evidence.

She put a finger to her lips and mouthed the word 'silence'.

Podgornin looked flushed and confused. Freddie lay where he was. Nobody moved.

57. *Freddie de la Hay's Fate is Determined*

Nor spoke. Lying motionless on the rug, Freddie de la Hay noticed that all human eyes in the room were fixed on him – the worst of all possible situations for a dog. Embarrassed by this attention, he closed his eyes, hoping that when he opened them again, the unwelcome human interest would have passed. But it did not, and was still there when he opened them again.

At first, Podgornin said nothing as the woman flourished Freddie's collar at him. But then he raised a hand to quieten her and observed laconically that all dogs have collars – perhaps she did not know that.

'Yes, all dogs have collars,' she whispered. 'But do all dogs have collars as heavy as this one?'

He did not have time to answer the question before she reached for a letter opener on the table and started to unpick the stitching in the leather of the collar. Within a very short time, the first of the wires started to be exposed. This was the signal for the other two men to turn and stare accusingly at Podgornin. For his part, he stubbed out his cigarette in an overflowing ashtray and tried to snatch the collar from the woman. She resisted.

'It's probably just one of those behavioural devices,' he said, ignoring her gestures to silence him. 'They put them in collars so that the dogs can be given an electric shock if they bark too much. Surely you've heard of those things.'

She was still busy exposing the inner part of the collar. She found a battery, which she detached and waved in Podgornin's face, and then the transmitter itself, a small bundle of electronics that slipped out of its container and into the palm of her hand. Having detached the battery, she felt free to speak at normal volume.

'So, Anatoly, here is your behavioural device. Ha! And let's take a look at what this says.' She peered at an inscription on the casing of the transmitter: *Property of MI6*.

'MI6!' she exclaimed. 'What do you say to that, Anatoly? Our old friends – right here in the flat, courtesy of you. Well done!'

'Show it to me,' he said. 'You can't be sure . . .'

She passed the transmitter to him. 'See? There it is – clear as daylight.'

Podgornin examined the transmitter, and then looked reproachfully at Freddie de la Hay. 'MI6? Why would they put their name on it? No organisation would be so stupid as to do that. This is a joke, something from one of those novelty stores.'

'Don't underestimate the peculiarity of the British,' said one of the men. 'It's perfectly possible that their security people put their names on their transmitters. It's probably part of their perverse sense of fair play.'

The other man agreed. 'Yes. It's the same as using flies when you know that the real way to catch the fish is with a worm. Stupid people.'

Podgornin looked at the ceiling. 'Unless they *want* us to think they've been bugging us. That may be why they put "property of MI6" on the transmitter. They might have thought that we would discover it and then think that they—'

'Why?' snapped the woman. 'Why would they want us to *think* that they have been bugging us, when they have?'

One of the men had an idea. 'Perhaps they want us to think that they think that we think that they think that we think they're bugging us. That way we'll think that—'

'Quiet!' said the woman. 'I think that you think—'

'I don't think anything,' shouted Podgornin, interrupting her. 'Except this: this is the thing I think . . .'

He stopped, and they all stared at him, including Freddie de la Hay, who was relieved that attention seemed to have shifted from him.

'What do you think, Anatoly Mikhailovich?' asked one of the men.

Podgornin glared at the woman. 'I think this,' he began. 'I think that we have been listened to. So I think, therefore, that we are compromised. Our entire effort – all the work we've done – has been compromised.'

'And it's your fault,' said the woman, glaring at him angrily.

'I do not think fault comes into it,' said Podgornin. 'Every one of us in this room – and I mean everyone – has at some point or other compromised security. Yes, I mean it. You, too. Which of us can hold our hand up and say that he – or she – has not at some point in his career – or her career,' this accompanied by a glance in the woman's direction, 'committed some little act of carelessness that has compromised security? I cannot say that. Nor, I think, can any of you.'

There was complete silence. One of the men looked briefly

at the other, who averted his gaze. Each heart – such as it was – was laid bare by Podgornin's frank words.

'Very well,' said the woman. 'So what do we do now?'

'We disperse,' said Podgornin. 'We leave the country, as provided for in our dispersal plan. And we start now.'

One of the men got up from his chair and looked at his watch. 'There's a flight to Moscow ...'

Podgornin held up a hand. 'We go through France,' he said. 'It's all in the plan.'

The woman suddenly pointed at Freddie de la Hay. 'And him? What do we do about the dog.'

'Shoot him,' said one of the men. 'They won't like that.'

'Yes,' said the woman.

Podgornin looked at Freddie, who looked back up at him with dark, liquid eyes. 'He's innocent,' he said.

'Of course he's innocent,' said the woman impatiently. 'But that's not the point, is it? The point is to get the message back to them that if they use animals in this way, this will be the consequence. They won't like it. Dmitri is right – we need to show them.'

Podgornin looked again at Freddie de la Hay. 'I will deal with him,' he said. 'Leave it to me. I brought him here, and I shall deal with him.'

'How?' asked the woman. 'You tell us, Anatoly. How?' Her manner was entirely rude and aggressive, and, unlike the others, she did not address Podgornin by his patronymic.

'I shall give him something,' he said. 'I shall take him to a place where they will definitely find him and I shall administer something lethal. You leave it to me.'

The woman looked doubtful. 'The whole operation ruined by a dog,' she said.

'As in Shakespeare,' said one of the men.

'It was a horse,' said Podgornin. 'The king needed a horse, not a dog.'

'This is no time to discuss literature,' said the woman. 'It's time to act.'

'We are all actors,' mused Podgornin.

'What do you mean by that?'

He said nothing. He lifted up the now transmitter-less collar and approached Freddie de la Hay. Freddie watched him warily.

'Come along, my boy,' Podgornin said quietly. 'Come here. Come to your uncle Anatoly.'

58. Caroline Turns to Jo for Advice

For Caroline, it was a time of reappraisal. Her frank discussion with James, during which he had dashed such hopes as she had been harbouring for a romantic relationship, had been painful. She liked James, whose company she found both amusing and undemanding. They could talk together about anything and everything; he was considerate; he was understanding; they laughed at the same things. Now he had closed the door on anything more than a friendship between them, and she felt a curious emptiness that bordered on numbness.

It was not that James had gone away or refused to see her any more, as can happen when a romance comes to an end; it was not like that. He was still there, and he still wanted them to be friends. But after his declaration that their relationship had no chance of becoming a physical one, she felt that they were both on a path that led nowhere: a cul-de-sac.

She wanted to talk to somebody about this, but who? Many people have a friend at work whom they can confide in, but Caroline worked for Tim Something, the photographer, who employed nobody else. She wondered whether she could talk to Tim, but decided against it. One could not talk to a man about this, or not to most men; one could certainly talk to James about such questions, but then one could obviously not discuss this particular case with him. No, it would have to be a girlfriend, and there, Caroline had to admit, she had a problem.

Caroline was not one of those women who had difficulty in forming friendships with others of her sex. She had been reasonably gregarious at school and university, but since she came to London she found that she had not kept up with the friends she had made in those days. Her school friends had certainly drifted off – or she had drifted off from them – and although she occasionally saw members of her circle from university days, a number of them had become either engaged or even married, and this had resulted in another form of drifting apart. The world, she decided, was designed for couples; a discovery that the recently divorced or widowed also often reported. Couples might protest that this was not true, but it was something that Caroline was beginning to feel herself. And now she was in need of friends to discuss the very social isolation that came from not having friends.

Of course there were her flatmates in Corduroy Mansions,

and in normal circumstances who better to turn to than a group of female flatmates? But circumstances were not normal, because again Caroline felt that she had drifted away from the other three. She had never been particularly close to Dee, and recently, of course, Dee had lied to her about having dinner with James. This meant that she definitely could not discuss James with her. And even if she did, Dee was so obsessive that any discussion would probably end up being diverted into a conversation with a nutritional bent.

No, Dee would not do, which left Jo, her Australian flat-mate, whom she had barely seen for weeks, and Jenny, who had spent the last two months in Mexico with a software engineer from Sheffield. The software engineer was working on a contract in Cancun and Jenny had gone with him. They had received a few quite lengthy emails from her, saying that the two of them liked Mexico a great deal and were thinking of staying. George, the software engineer, had taken up scuba diving and Jenny was thinking of doing so too. They were both learning Spanish, and George was almost fluent, having previously done an A Level in the language at school. They had made numerous friends and George's hair had been bleached by the sun. 'I have a whole new life,' Jenny had written. 'When I think of what I put up with when I worked for Oedipus Snark, it makes me sick. I wasted all that time when I could have been here, learning to scuba dive and having my nails painted.'

'She never had her nails painted in London,' Dee had said at the time. 'She's changed, and that's not the letter of some-body who's coming back. She's finished with London.'

Caroline had agreed. Jenny had paid three months' rent in

advance before she left; in another month they could let her room again.

If she could talk neither to Dee nor Jenny, only Jo was left. Jo at least was approachable, and seemed the type to listen. So Caroline waited in the kitchen, flicking through a magazine, hoping that she would hear the sound of a key in the front door that would signify Jo's return from the gym.

She waited an hour or so before her flatmate returned. Jo came into the kitchen in a light blue tracksuit with a sweat band round her forehead.

'Hello Caroline. Haven't really seen you in a while. How are you doing?' Jo asked.

This was Caroline's opportunity. 'Not so well.'

Jo frowned. 'Not so well? What's the problem? Going down with something? There weren't many people at the gym, you know – I think there's a bug doing the rounds.'

Caroline shook her head. 'No. I'm not sick.'

'Well, you look a bit crook to me.' Jo used the Australian expression; Caroline had heard it before and knew what it meant to be crook. No, she was not crook – at least not in the physical sense; the emotional sense might be another matter.

'I don't think I'm crook,' she said. 'I'm just . . . Well, James and I are splitting up.'

Jo sat down opposite Caroline. She peeled the headband off her head. 'Oh. So that's it. Boyfriend trouble.'

Caroline nodded gloomily. It was so clichéd, this whole thing. Boyfriend trouble – what a cliché.

'Except I didn't think he was your boyfriend,' Jo said. 'You know what I mean?'

Caroline looked at her indignantly. 'I don't, actually.' She felt loyalty to James. What did Jo know about his inclinations? There were plenty of straight men who were artistic – a bit camp, even – and why should she not think that James was one of these? It was a blatant case of prejudice.

'Well, he doesn't strike me as the sort to have a girlfriend,' said Jo breezily. 'I thought that you and he were just friends. Know what I mean?'

Caroline could not constantly say no, she did not know what Jo meant. Of course she knew what the other woman meant.

'It's not like you think,' she said. 'He's not gay. He's . . . he's . . . Well, he's nothing in particular.'

Jo was silent for a few moments. Then she said, 'I see. So you and he are not . . . you know, actually sleeping together?'

Caroline shook her head. 'No. And he doesn't want to.' She paused. 'I'm so miserable, Jo, I really am. And I'm so confused. I love James. I love him, and he's not interested in me.'

She started to cry. Jo reached out and took Caroline's hand, and held it in silence. She caressed it, gently, and her touch was warm and reassuring.

'Oh,' she said. 'Oh. That's bad luck, Caroline. Rotten luck. But that's the problem with men. They're not really interested in us – not really. They use us. But that's all.'

Caroline sniffed. Jo handed her a tissue, which she used to blow her nose. 'I don't know if all of them do. Some, maybe. Not all.'

Jo shook her head. 'No,' she said. 'All of them, Caroline. All of them use us.'

'But how has he used me? I don't see how you can say James

257

has used me. If anybody's used anybody here, it's ... it's me. I've used him.'

'He's used you subtly,' said Jo. 'And that's often the worst way of being used. You don't know it, you see, and then you realise later that you've been used. And that hurts – it really hurts.'

59. The Reassurances of Home

'So what do I do?' Caroline asked. 'What do I say to him?'

Jo shrugged. 'I don't see that you need to say anything to him. I thought you had gone over that ground. He's told you what he feels – or doesn't feel, in his case. So now you both know and you can move on.'

'Move on?' People always talked about moving on, but Caroline wondered precisely what was involved in moving on. She assumed that you had to have somewhere to move to before you actually moved on; where did she have to move on to?

There was a faint smile on Jo's lips as she said, 'I take it that you're sure about yourself?'

Again, Caroline was puzzled. 'Look, I'm sorry, you must think me really stupid, but I'm not sure what you mean.'

'What I mean,' said Jo, 'is this: are you sure that men are where you're at?'

'That men are where I'm at?'

'Yes. Do you like men? Are you sure?'

Caroline looked at Jo. 'What about you?'

'This isn't about me,' said Jo quickly. 'It's about you. I've already moved on. You're the one who's to decide whether to move on or . . .'

'Or stay where I am?' Was that the alternative to moving on? she wondered.

'Yes, that's about it.' Jo paused. She was watching Caroline closely. 'There are alternatives, you know. You don't have to stay in the place you're at.'

Caroline thought quickly. No. Female solidarity was important, and sustained a lot of women – but she did not want to be too solid.

'I don't think so, Jo,' she said quietly. 'I know that for lots of people, that's . . . well, that's where they're at. But I don't think so. Not in my case.'

Jo looked down. 'Fair enough. In that case, just give it time. Move on, and wait.'

Caroline was intrigued. Moving on and waiting seemed to be a new option.

Jo explained. 'Be single. There's no pressure. Enjoy your life. Wait for somebody else to come along. He will. Eventually.' She paused. 'Does that make sense to you?'

Caroline nodded.

'And here's another bit of advice,' she said. 'You've got a home, haven't you?'

'You mean parents? All of that?'

'Yes, all of that. Your olds. People forget about them, but they're always there, aren't they? Go and chill with them.'

Caroline resisted an urge to laugh. The idea of chilling with her parents in Cheltenham . . . And yet, and yet . . .

'I'm not sure if they do chilling,' she said. The picture came to her of her mother, with her pearls and her county attitudes. And her poor father, with his utter certainties and his tendency to talk in platitudes. There was a vague sense of failure there, which was strange, as in many terms he had succeeded, certainly by the standards of those with whom he mixed. Neither of her parents had moved on, she decided. They were both still in the place they were at.

'It's hard for me to get back home,' said Jo. 'When I was at uni over in Melbourne and my folks were back in Perth, you couldn't go back for the weekend. But sometimes you could go for a week, maybe. I remember feeling really bad once. Something had happened. Something messy and I felt all raw inside. You know that feeling, when everything is just pointless and you feel that you're on the edge of a void – a void of meaninglessness? That feeling?'

Caroline nodded.

'I went and bought a cheap flight back to Perth. I didn't even tell my folks that I was coming back – I just got on the plane, and when I reached Perth I jumped in a taxi at the airport. Coming into Perth is fabulous, you know. Suddenly there are the hills – we've got these low hills just outside the city, you know – and there they were with all their trees, and there were the houses, with their large yards and gardens. And the smell of it. The eucalyptus. The dryness, which has a smell, you know. The taxi driver in his blue shorts. And I started to cry, there in the taxi, and he was really sympathetic, in the way that these guys some-times can be. Like a father. And I said that he shouldn't worry, that I was just pleased to be home, which of course was exactly how I felt.

'And then I went in and surprised my mother in the kitchen. She gave a shriek – a really loud shriek, a scream even. She was making scones – she makes these really good cheese scones for my old man – and her hands were sticky with the mixture. She screamed and ran to put her arms around me, flour and all that stuff, and it was all over my shoulders.

'And then my dad came in to find out what the fuss was. He was wearing shorts and a singlet. That's what he wears when it's hot – it was the hot season then. He looked at me and smiled and said, "Strewth!" That's all he said. He just smiled. I tell you, Caroline, it was all I could do to stop myself bawling my eyes out.

'Because, you see, that's what home's all about, isn't it? Scones and singlets and everything the same as it always was. And if you get a dose of that – of all that familiar stuff that you thought you never wanted to see again – then it sorts everything out, it really does.'

Jo had more to say. 'I went over the road. We have these neighbours who are really good friends, you see, and they were all in the house. They have a daughter who's my age and she was at uni in Perth. She was there with a friend of hers I knew a bit, and we sat and talked about people we all knew and hadn't seen for a while. And I asked them what was going on in Perth and they said nothing. So I laughed. Because that's what I wanted. I didn't want anything to have changed.'

She paused now, and looked enquiringly at Caroline. 'Can you go home for the weekend?'

Caroline said that she could. Cheltenham was a couple of hours in the train. Then, on impulse, she said, 'Come with me, Jo. Why don't you come home with me?'

Jo did not reply immediately. But then she accepted. She had nothing planned, she said – or nothing she could not cancel.

'There's nothing to do there,' warned Caroline.

'That's why you're going,' said Jo. 'Remember?'

'And I'm not sure what you'll make of my folks.'

'Or what they'll make of me?'

Caroline looked out of the window. 'They're not too bad,' she said. 'In their way.' Her father would not wear a singlet. And her mother bought her scones.

Jo looked at Caroline with concern. 'Feeling better?' she asked.

Caroline nodded. 'Yes. And thanks for . . . for helping. Thanks a lot.'

'It's what flatmates are for,' said Jo. 'That, and making dinner for their flatmate when she's feeling a bit low. Like now.'

'Really?'

'Yes, why not? I'm going to open a bottle of wine and pour us a glass. Then I'll make dinner.'

Caroline smiled appreciatively. 'Thanks. What'll you make?'

'Risotto, I think,' said Jo.

60. Outside Fortnum & Mason

Rupert Porter walked back down the corridor in the Ragg Porter Literary Agency in a state of mild astonishment. He was normally not one to allow another to have the last word, but he had found himself completely at a loss when Andrea, the agency's receptionist, had casually referred to her conversation with the person – if it was really a person – who had been sitting in the waiting room. It was a thoroughly ridiculous situation, and as he returned to his office, he went over in his mind each absurd development.

At the heart of it all was Errol Greatorex, Barbara Ragg's American author, who claimed – and it was an utterly risible claim – to be writing the biography of the yeti, the Abominable Snowman of the Himalayas. But Greatorex was no random crank; he had a significant body of publications behind him, including two travel books that had won awards in Canada and the United States, and had been published in London too, by a reputable publisher. He had also written for popular geographical magazines and the *Melbourne Age*, all of which amounted to a perfectly respectable set of credentials.

Greatorex's career suggested that he must have developed a healthy degree of intellectual caution. How, then, Rupert wondered, could somebody like him swallow the claim of some fakir that he was a yeti, of all things? Surely the whole point about yetis was that they were an intermediate primate – not quite *homo sapiens*, even if given to walking erect and leaving intriguing footprints in the snow. That was the legend, but, like all legends, it could hardly stand up to the investigative standards of our times. There were no mysteries left, none at all; not in an age of satellite photography, when the remotest corners of the globe were laid bare by unsleeping, all-seeing cameras. The Loch Ness monster, the yeti, Lord Lucan – all of these would have been *seen* if they really existed.

Yet many people were gullible, and when you combined this inherent gullibility with a wish to believe in things beyond the ordinary you ended up with a whole raft of myth. Errol Greatorex was either a charlatan, cynically prepared to exploit his credulous readers, or he was himself the victim of an even greater charlatan – this Himalayan type pretending to be the yeti. And it might not be all that difficult; one had only to be tall – yetis had always been thought to be on the tall side – and markedly hirsute. There were plenty of hairy people around, and one might expect that some of them were tall. So if a tall, hairy person, although *homo sapiens*, were to come up with a story of being taken from a remote valley and put in some mission school, there to be educated by . . . by Jesuits, perhaps, who had always claimed 'Give us the boy until the age of seven and we will give you the man', might not one say the same thing of a yeti? 'Give us the yeti until the age of seven . . .'

Rupert frowned. He was not sure whether the Jesuits ever actually said that. Perhaps it was one of those chance remarks, dropped as an aside, that were seized upon and magnified out of all proportion. Had Margaret Thatcher ever really said 'There's no such thing as society'? That statement had gone on to haunt her, although what she had in fact said – and Rupert had this on good authority, although very few people knew it – was 'There's no such thing as hockey'. It was a curious remark to make, and she certainly should not have made it, but it was not the same as saying that there was no such thing

264

as society. Had people heard her correctly and understood that she was talking about hockey, they might have been forewarned that she would go on to say a number of other very peculiar things.

He reached his office, and stopped. Thinking on these matters had made him momentarily forget about what Andrea had said to Errol Greatorex in the reception. She had said that the tall hairy person had gone off to do some shopping and would meet him in front of Fortnum & Mason at twelve. He looked at his watch. It was now ten o'clock, which meant that in two hours anybody who just happened to be walking along that particular section of Piccadilly would actually see this person who claimed to be the yeti. Even if there were other people waiting outside the shop – and there were many, he imagined, who met friends at midday outside Fortnum & Mason – it would not require a great deal of skill to identify a yeti, or a *soi-disant* yeti, among them.

Rupert smirked. If he went there himself, he could see this impostor. He could then tackle la Ragg when she came back from her jaunt to Scotland and reveal to her that he had investigated her so-called literary scoop and discovered it to be a squalid fraud – like so many much-vaunted publishing sensations.

Shortly after half past eleven, he left the office. As he walked past Andrea's desk, he stopped, on impulse, and told her where he was going.

'I'm just off to Fortnum & Mason,' he said. 'I might bump into that . . . person who was here with Errol Greatorex.'

Andrea nodded. 'All right.'

'If anything happens to me, Andrea,' he said quietly, 'you will remember what I said, won't you? Fortnum & Mason. Greatorex.'

Andrea nodded again. Why was he making such a fuss? What did he imagine could possibly happen to him at Fortnum & Mason? He's very peculiar, she thought. I won't be surprised if they cart him off one of these days – not in the least surprised.

61. In Fortnum & Mason

It did not take half an hour to walk from the Ragg Porter offices to Fortnum & Mason. In normal conditions, when the throngs of visitors milling about Piccadilly Circus were not too thick, it would take barely ten minutes to make the journey; when the streets were crowded, one might need a little longer. It depended, too, on how quickly one walked – Rupert was a quick walker, especially now, when he was keenly impatient to see whether there really would be a yeti outside the famous store. And understandably so: who would not find their pace quickening with the knowledge that there lay before them the chance of seeing that most elusive of creatures, the Abominable Snowman?

Of course Rupert knew full well – and reminded himself as he made his way – that whatever he was going to see outside Fortnum & Mason, it was *not* going to be a yeti. If a mysterious tall figure did indeed turn up, then that was all he would be – a mysterious tall figure. And if Rupert had the chance to see him at close quarters, and he intended to ensure exactly that, he was certain that his suspicions would be confirmed. Fraudsters and tricksters were usually rather banal types, he told himself, and this tall figure would probably be revealed as coming from Croydon, or Tooting, or somewhere like that. He would definitely not be Himalayan.

At a quarter to twelve, Rupert found himself opposite Fortnum & Mason. Ahead of him, hanging from the façade of the Royal Academy, were great banners, fluttering in the breeze, advertising the current show. Rupert was a member of the Friends of the Royal Academy and made a point of going to all the exhibitions. He had not seen this one and for a moment, forgetting his mission, he wondered whether he should wander in and see The Later Bonnard. But then he reminded himself why he was there, and looked back over the road to the stately grocery shop with its copper-green windows and elaborate chiming clock. His eye moved upwards to the warrant-holder's display of royal arms between the third and fourth floors. He could not make out any legend below the device: perhaps they provided fruitcake to the palace, or chocolate, or even something prosaic like butter. It would be something like that, he thought – something needed for the thousands of sandwiches that the palace served each year at the garden parties. Rupert had read that the official figure for sandwiches fed to guests each year was eighty thousand, with the same number of slices of cake being served. It was profoundly inspiring: eighty thousand sandwiches – what other country, he wondered, came even near that?

He looked at his watch. He could hardly loiter on the pavement for fifteen minutes; apart from anything else, he wanted to be inconspicuous so as to get a good look at the stranger. Yetis were notoriously shy creatures, and if one were to appear in front of Fortnum & Mason and see somebody loitering on the pavement opposite, he would be bound to take fright. But then this was not a yeti, Rupert reminded himself. Even so, he did not want to be spotted by Errol Greatorex, who he knew was also due to arrive there at midday, and accordingly he decided to cross the road and enter the shop. He could easily spend fifteen minutes looking at the displays of olive oil or some such; there was a lot to see in Fortnum & Mason. Then, when the time was ripe, he would sidle towards the front door to see whether Greatorex's mysterious companion had arrived.

Although the shop would be busy at lunchtime, when people from nearby offices took the opportunity to buy something in their lunch hour, it was still a little early for lunchtime crowds when Rupert went in, and there was no more than a handful of people walking along the aisles of the spacious food hall. He did not have a sweet tooth, and so the shelves of chocolates and sugared almonds held no charms for him. He was drawn instead to a display of china bowls of Patum Peperium; that was much more to his taste. These bowls, their lids decorated with Victorian hunting scenes, were considerably larger than the normal white plastic containers of the famous anchovy paste. Rupert picked one up to admire it and found that it was surprisingly heavy. He replaced it carefully, but as he did so his sleeve caught a neighbouring bowl and sent it crashing to the floor. The heavy china container shattered with an astonishingly loud report – rather like that of a gun being fired. Rupert gasped as he saw what he had inadvertently done.

In a very short time – not more than ten seconds – an assistant in a formal black suit appeared to investigate. The assistant glanced at the mess on the floor, and at Rupert.

'Are you all right, sir?'

Rupert nodded. 'I'm terribly sorry . . .' He gestured to the shattered bowl; large pieces of broken china stuck out of the exposed brown lump of anchovy paste.

The assistant seemed uninterested in the apology. 'The important point is that you are all right, sir. That's what matters.' He bent down and began to pick pieces of china out of the paste.

'Please let me help,' said Rupert, crouching down to join him. As he did so, he noticed a movement at the end of the aisle, behind the assistant. A tall man wearing a light olive-green overcoat had walked round the end of the line of shelves and was looking in his direction. Then, as quickly as he had arrived, he vanished.

Rupert stood up. The man he had seen was very tall, and although he had been unable to make out his face, he had had a distinct impression of facial hairiness.

The assistant straightened up too. 'We'll clear this up in no time,' he said. 'It's very easily done.' He paused. He had noticed that Rupert was staring down the next aisle, and appeared agitated.

'Have you seen something, sir?'

'I'm sorry,' said Rupert. 'I have to go.'

He stepped forward, unfortunately into the Patum Peperium.

It was soft underfoot, and it flowed out to cover the sole of his right shoe, creeping fishily up the sides.

'Do be careful, sir!'

Rupert looked down in dismay. His shoe was covered in thick anchovy paste.

The assistant looked concerned. 'Can I get you a cloth to clean up, sir?'

Rupert shook his head. 'No,' he said, craning his neck to get a better view of the tall figure disappearing out of the front door of the shop. 'I shall be fine.'

'Your shoe is very . . . messy, sir. I really think . . .'

Rupert brushed the assistant aside, and strode off, leaving anchovy-paste footprints behind him.

'Really, sir, if you wouldn't mind . . .'

He did not hear the objection. It was the yeti – he was sure of it. The yeti had been in Fortnum & Mason and was now leaving. Rupert pushed his way past the other shoppers. 'Sorry,' he muttered. 'I really must go. Excuse me.'

He would have to follow the yeti. He was not going to let him get away.

62. A la recherche d'un yeti perdu

The yeti walked at an unnaturally fast pace. It was only to be expected, thought Rupert, as he struggled to keep up with his quarry; years of loping across the snow plains of the Himalayas presumably gave him an advantage over others when it came to the firmer, less challenging pavements of

Piccadilly. But Rupert was determined that he would not let him out of his sight, and did not care if people stared as he broke into a run. Plenty of people ran in London; they ran for buses, they ran to keep out of squalls of rain, they ran for reasons known only to themselves. London, he thought, was used to everything, even to the sight of a suavely dressed man – Rupert had always been a natty dresser – pursuing a tall, lolloping figure out of the stately premises of Fortnum & Mason and into the crowds.

Fortnum & Mason. A thought suddenly occurred to Rupert as he pushed his way out of the front door of the shop – Ratty Mason. When they were at school together he had never asked Ratty Mason what his father did, but now he remembered a chance remark that the other boy had made: 'My old man's got a shop. Quite a big one actually.' He had said this when they were sitting together in Rupert's study eating toast made on the battered toaster that he kept, against the regulations, in a cupboard. And the toast, he now remembered, was spread with . . . Patum Peperium! The memory came unbidden, and was, like many such memories, richly evocative. Proust's hero's memory of Sunday mornings at Combray, when his aunt Léonie used to give him little pieces of madeleine cake dipped in her tea, had later been evoked by the taste of such a cake; for Rupert, perhaps the trigger was also a food, in this case Patum Peperium. He and Ratty Mason had eaten toast and anchovy paste; now here he was, all these years later, outside Fortnum & Mason, with anchovy paste on his shoe. It was all very powerful. And could the shop that Ratty Mason had referred to have been the centuries-old Fortnum & Mason? Was Ratty Mason's father a member of the same Mason family?

It was a complex line of thought. Such thoughts, though, are readily entertained by the human mind, so great is its capacity to wander off at a tangent. Now, as Rupert looked about him on the Piccadilly pavement to locate the vanishing figure of the yeti, he remembered something else that Ratty Mason had said. This time the remark had no association with Patum Peperium as they had not been eating toast but doing a compulsory cross-country run – he (Rupert), Billy Fairweather, Snark, Ratty Mason and Chris Walker-Volvo. The memory seemed so fresh: he could see them, all five of them, slowing down from their running pace as they went out of sight of the gym master, with the sun coming up over trees that were touched with soft rime – it was a clear day in winter – and their breath hanging in small clouds in the cold morning air. Five friends – as they then were – five boys on the cusp of sixteen, whose lives would turn out very differently, but who then thought that they would somehow be together for ever. And Billy Fairweather had made a chance observation about his father belonging to a club of some sort, and then Ratty had said, 'My dad's a mason.' Rupert had bent down to pick up a stick that was lying on the ground in front of him and had broken off a bit of this stick and thrown it across the field. 'Useless throw,' said Billy Fairweather, and Rupert turned to Ratty and said, 'Of course he's a mason, Mason.' Something had happened at that moment – something that distracted their attention – and they had started to run again, because they had to finish the course within a certain time or the gym master, a peppery figure who had been a fitness instructor in the Irish Guards, would make them do the run all over again.

Rupert spotted the yeti. The shambling figure had moved speedily in the direction of Piccadilly Circus and then, so quickly that had Rupert not been sharp-eyed he might not have noticed, he went through the front door of Hatchards book shop. The sight cheered Rupert: Hatchards, where he was a regular customer, was home ground. Rupert knew the staff there, as he would often accompany one of his authors to do a lunchtime signing. This meant that not only was he familiar with the layout of the shop – which would give him an advantage over the yeti, who presumably did not know the place – but also he knew that there was only one way out, for the customers at least. If he waited by the front door, just inside the shop, then the yeti would not be able to leave without walking past him. And that would be the moment when he would see his face for the first time, and would even be able to accost him and find out whether he really was a yeti – which he certainly would not be – or whether he was an impostor – which he certainly would be. That would put la Ragg's gas at a peep! 'Your so-called yeti,' he would say. 'I met him, you know. In Hatchards, no less. Himalayan section, of course, looking at the mountaineering books.' Ha! That would be funny. And la Ragg, who blushed easily, would look furtive, and Rupert would go on to say, 'You really need to be more careful, Barbara. Representing this autobiography stands to make us look very foolish indeed.'

And Barbara Ragg would be chastened, which is how Rupert liked her to feel. It was all very well getting possession of that

273

flat which had been intended for him, but where was the satisfaction in having a comfortable – although ill-gotten flat – when you were such a rotten failure at work, a soft touch for every crank and charlatan with a dubious manuscript about a yeti, of all things? Where was the satisfaction in that? Nowhere, though Rupert. Nowhere.

He went into Hatchards. Roger Katz, the legendary bibliophile, was standing just inside the door. He had just finished talking to a customer, and he smiled when he recognised Rupert. 'Ah, Rupert,' he said. 'I've got just the book for you.'

Rupert looked over Roger's shoulder into the shop beyond. Where had the yeti gone?

'Did you see anybody?' Rupert blurted out. 'A very tall chap. This tall.' He raised a hand to well above head height.

Roger nodded. 'Yes, I did, actually. He went upstairs, I think. Strange-looking fellow.'

'I have to find him,' said Rupert. 'Will you come with me?'

Roger shrugged. 'Yes, of course. One can usually locate a person quite easily.' He paused, and gave Rupert an enquiring look. 'Who is he? A friend?'

'It's complicated,' said Rupert. 'More complicated than you can imagine.'

63. Meeting Stephanie

Had Hugh's mother had a brood of other children, her relationship with Hugh might have been an easier one. But he was an only child and an only son, and for a mother in such a position it is not always easy to accept that another woman will eventually enter her son's life and, if all goes according to plan – the plan being that of the other woman – take him away. This common conflict, so understandable and so poignant, is played out time and time again, and almost always with the same painful result: mother loses. It is so, of course, if mother is overt in her attempt to put off the almost inevitable; if she is covert, then she stands a chance, admittedly a remote one, of introducing into her son's mind a germ of doubt that the woman he has chosen might not be the right one for him. That takes skill, and boundless patience, but it is a course fraught with dangers for the relationship between mother and future daughter-in-law, let alone for that between mother and son.

Stephanie, of course, adored Hugh – what mother could not? Her adoration was founded on precisely those qualities that Barbara had discerned in him and that had drawn her to him – his gentleness, his kindness, his masculine vulnerability. Stephanie knew that she should let go of him, should welcome other women into his life, but she found it almost impossible to do. If only she could *like* his girlfriends; but how, she wondered, do you like people whom you quite simply do *not* like?

She had been dreading this meeting with Barbara; on a number of earlier occasions Hugh had brought girlfriends home to whom she had found herself taking an almost imme-diate dislike – a dislike that she had great difficulty in concealing. This had been picked up on by her husband, as for all his apparent equanimity and farmerly appearance Sorley had an astute sense of atmosphere.

'You judge these poor girls too quickly,' he had said of one of them, a sound engineer from Glasgow. 'How can you tell? You really must give her a chance.'

'But she has a piercing in her nose,' Stephanie said. 'You must have noticed. And her tongue too. Did you see the stud right in the middle of it?'

Sorley shrugged. 'The world's changing,' he said. 'Aesthetic standards change. What's unattractive to us may be just the thing for Hugh and his generation – we have to remind ourselves of that, you know.'

'But her tongue,' Stephanie persisted. 'What's the point? And presumably it traps particles of food.' Or could trap her son, she thought – with horror. What if they were kissing and the stud got caught between a gap in Hugh's teeth? What then?

Again Sorley had urged her to be tolerant. 'But does it really matter if our son's girlfriend traps particles of food?' He smiled as he spoke. Who among us has never trapped particles of food? Indeed, that was part, surely, of being human; an inevitable concomitant of our imperfection.

At least Barbara Ragg had no piercings. That was noted with relief by Stephanie, who cast a quick glance at the other woman's tongue when she first spoke to her. Barbara noticed her future mother-in-law looking into her mouth and was momentarily concerned. What was this – a dental examination? Or was it the way country people, many of whom were incorrigibly horsey, looked at prospective members of the family, examining the mouth in the same way that they might look into the mouth of a horse being considered for purchase. Surely not?

She, in return, ran a quick eye over Stephanie. Hugh's mother was in her mid-fifties, she decided, but had weathered well. She was dressed more or less as Barbara would expect somebody like her to dress, sporting as she did an olive-green tweed skirt with a navy blue cashmere top – the sort of outfit worn by legions of country women in comfortable circumstances. Had she stepped out of a station at a point-to-point she would, Barbara thought, have raised no eyebrows. And yet there was something slightly exotic about her, a quality that Barbara perceived immediately, a hint of greater depths than such women usually showed.

This impression was strengthened as Stephanie showed Barbara to her room. 'We call this the Cadell room,' she said, pointing to a pair of pictures above the fireplace. 'My grandfather knew Bunty Cadell rather well. He gave him these paintings. They used to be in my parents' drawing room in Montevideo, when we were there.'

Barbara looked at the paintings. One was a small study of a woman in an extravagant hat; the other a picture of a yacht moored in a Mediterranean harbour.

'You lived in Uruguay?' said Barbara with interest. 'Hugh didn't tell me.'

Stephanie stared out of the window. 'Hugh doesn't speak much about South America. Ever since . . .'

She did not finish the sentence, but instead moved across the room to open the door of the wardrobe. 'I've cleared this out for you,' she said briskly. 'One gets so much clutter, and guests are a good reason to sort it out.' She smiled brightly at Barbara. Clearly there was to be no more discussion of South America.

Barbara found herself wondering about Stephanie's accent. She had assumed that she was Scottish, but there was something else there, a suggestion of French, perhaps; just a hint. Now she remembered something Hugh had said about his mother – a chance remark that she had not paid much attention to, but now came back. She had been educated in Switzerland, he had said. There had been a school outside Geneva.

But what had happened to Hugh in Colombia? Stephanie had said that he did not like to talk about it, but he had certainly talked to Barbara, although not at great length. She decided that there might not be another opportunity to raise the matter, and so she would ask.

'Did something bad happen to Hugh in Colombia? He once told me—'

Stephanie moved quickly to her side. 'Did he?' she asked with urgency. 'Did he tell you?'

'Well, he started to,' said Barbara. 'He began a story about being on that ranch near Barranquilla. But then . . .'

'What exactly did he say?' Stephanie was staring at her imploringly. Barbara noticed her eyes. They were a very faint green, like those of a Tonkinese cat. They were innocent eyes, and they now begged for information, their gaze as eloquent as any words.

'He didn't tell me much,' Barbara said.

Stephanie seemed relieved, and Barbara realised that her relief came from learning that Barbara did not know what had happened. That, she thought, suggested that Stephanie herself knew, but would not tell.

'You know, don't you?' she asked. 'Did he tell you?'

Stephanie turned away. 'You must excuse me,' she said distantly. 'I have to check on something in the kitchen. I should not like to serve burnt offerings on your very first day here.'

64. Inconclusive Conversation

Dinner was served at seven o'clock.

'We like to eat early in the summer months,' Stephanie said to Barbara. 'The evenings here are so lovely – so long drawn out. It gives us a chance to get things done after the meal.'

'Such as going for a walk,' said Hugh. He looked at Barbara invitingly. 'Would you like that?'

'Of course.'

He was accompanying her into the dining room, and took her arm as they went through the door. She nestled against him briefly, fondly, almost conspiratorially; she sensed that he was aware of her slight feeling of awkwardness – this was his family, his home, and she was the outsider. No matter how warm and welcoming a family may be, there is always a period of restraint, of mutual examination and testing, before a new member is taken to heart; no amount of social confidence could change that.

Barbara took her place at the dinner table under the stern gaze of a Highland ghillie, caught in paint, gaffing a salmon and, it seemed, looking directly at her as he did so. Was this Hugh's taste in art, she asked herself – wounded stags at bay, Perthshire hillsides with indolent Highland cattle, impossibly gloomy glens with mists descending? She realised that this was yet another thing she did not yet know about him. They had never discussed art, never been to a gallery together. You're marrying a stranger, she thought; and for a moment she wondered whether it would be wisest to call the whole thing off. Not immediately, of course; she would wait until the end of the weekend and see how she felt then. No, she could never do that. Never.

The hour or so at the table moved slowly. She was conscious that Hugh was watching her, as if he were trying to ascertain her reaction to his parents. When she caught his eye, he appeared to want to convey something to her – an unspoken apology, it seemed. Please understand, he said. Please understand that these are my parents, but none of us chooses our parents, and I am not the same as them. It was such a common message, one that almost everybody, at one time or another, sends to friends. And the response that comes back is usually one of sympathy and understanding. 'Yes, I see what you mean,' it says. 'But they're really not all that bad, and you should see mine!'

The conversation was mainly between Hugh and his father, with occasional interventions from Stephanie, who made an effort to include Barbara in their exchanges.

'I'm so interested to hear you're a literary agent,' she said. 'I've been writing—'

Hugh did not allow her to finish. 'Barbara is not that sort of agent, Mother,' he interjected. 'She deals with a very different sort of book.'

Stephanie tried again. 'But I thought that—'

Again, Hugh interrupted. 'For example, she has the most interesting autobiography at the moment. It seems that—'

Stephanie stared at her son. 'My own book—'

Sorley cleared his throat. 'I've been reading the most entertaining—'

And Hugh again: 'Please pass the salt.'

Barbara said, 'Does Ardnamurchan get a lot of rain?'

At the end of the meal Barbara and Hugh left for their walk. The sun was still quite high above the hills to the west; although it was shortly after eight, at these latitudes, and in high summer, it would be a good two hours before it sank below the Hebridean Sea. 'We've got time to get to the waterfall.' Hugh said. 'Would you like that?'

Barbara looked up at the hillside behind the house. There was a small expanse of cleared grazing and then, beyond that, rough land: heather, bracken, outcrops of granite.

'There's a path,' said Hugh, taking off his jersey and tying it around his waist. 'It's mild, isn't it?'

It was. Earlier in the evening there had been a breeze and this had now abated, leaving the air languid, warm on the skin. On impulse, Barbara moved to his side and kissed him lightly on the cheek. 'I'm so happy,' she said. And then, embarrassed at her sudden show of emotion, 'I just am. I normally don't go round telling people that I'm happy, like some Pollyanna, but I just am.'

'And I'm happy too,' said Hugh. But then he frowned. 'Why shouldn't you tell people you're happy? Why do people expect you to be miserable?'

'Do they?' she asked.

'Yes, I think they do.' He hesitated, but only briefly. 'Sometimes it seems as if people think that misery is the natural human condition. Misery and conflict.'

'For some it is,' said Barbara. 'For a lot of people, in fact.'

Hugh's expression was one of disappointment. 'You really feel that?'

Yes, she did; and she explained, 'I'm not saying that we *have to* feel miserable – obviously we don't. But we can't ignore the real misery of the world. We'd have to bury our heads in the sand, wouldn't we?'

Hugh defended his stance. He did not ignore the misery of the world, he said, but it did not dominate his thinking. Why should it? What was the point? 'You can know all about suffering,' he said, 'and you can still smile, and see the beauty of the world, and experience . . . experience joy, I suppose.'

She touched his forearm. 'Of course. Of course, you're right. And I'm not ashamed by happiness.' She paused. 'You've made me happy. It's you. Meeting you.' Which was true. Before she met Hugh she had been unhappy; she had been plain old Barbara Ragg – which was how she thought of herself – tagging after a man who had little time for her, living in fear of his rejection. And now everything was different. It was Hugh who had brought about this metamorphosis in her life.

All this at the start of the walk, before they set foot on the path that followed the course of the burn and then turned off into the fold of the hills; now Hugh took her arm and led her towards the path, matching his step to hers. 'Fine,' he said. 'That's fine, because I'm happier now than I've ever been. Ever. I'm not exaggerating.'

She began to say something, but he stopped her, placing a finger against her lips. 'We need to start,' he said. 'If we're going to swim, we need to get up there before the sun goes down.'

She shivered. They were going to swim under a waterfall. She looked up at the sky; it was a vast echoing vault of blue, empty apart from a sudden dart of swifts, dipping and swinging on some exultant mission of their own.

65. Under the Waterfall

They followed the path along the side of the burn, stepping cautiously over exposed rocks and the tangled roots of gorse. The tumbling water was the colour of whisky – from peat, explained Hugh. 'We could drink it if we wanted to,' he said. 'I always used to, when I was a boy. I lay down and drank it when I'd been walking across the hills. Lay down and drank like a . . .'

'Like a snake,' suggested Barbara.

He was surprised. 'Why? Why like a snake?'

'Because that's the image that springs to mind. From Lawrence's poem. You know, the one where a snake comes to his water trough and sips at the water. You lying on the ground makes me think of his snake.'

He recalled the poem, but only vaguely. 'I like Lawrence,' he said. 'I like the novels, although I must say that his characters seem to speak so formally.'

He smiled. 'Do you think that in real life people have the

sort of conversation we're having? Or do they only talk like this in books?'

She thought for a moment. 'No, this is real. This is really how people speak.' She looked at him and returned his smile. 'We're talking like this, aren't we?'

'We are.'

'Then there you are.'

The path now diverted from the course of the burn, climbing away to the west, crossing a steep stretch of hillside. The way was rougher there, not much more than a track scoured out by the hoofs of animals. 'Sheep use this?' asked Barbara.

'No. Deer. We don't have sheep any more. Just a few cattle. The deer are more important.'

She asked why, and Hugh explained that the ground was too rough to run even the hardy Scotch Blackface. 'They survive all right, but there's not much grazing, and you can't make much from sheep these days. People come to do deer-stalking in the autumn – that's much more valuable. It's the only money we make, I think.'

That was another thing they had never discussed – money. The house was well furnished enough, she had noticed, but everything was old and could have been bought a long time ago; perhaps there had been money once.

'Can't your father grow anything?' she asked.

Hugh pointed to the ground beneath their feet. 'The soil is very thin,' he said. 'Rock and peat. Sphagnum moss. Bog. No, you can't grow anything.' He looked at her with a playful expression. 'We're very poor,' he said.

Barbara was uncertain what to say. He had travelled; there

had been that school in Norfolk, which must have cost some-body something; there had been his year in South America. Poverty was relative.

He sensed her disbelief. 'No, it's true. It really is. There used to be a bit of money, but now it's all gone. We don't have anything.'

'Except this.' Barbara pointed to the hills around them.

Hugh laughed. 'Of course. But we can't sell this. We can't.'

She was not so urban as to be incapable of understanding what land meant to those who lived on it. 'No, of course not. I understand that.'

They walked on, making for a point where the path surmounted a spur. From there a view of the sea suddenly opened up, and Barbara stopped in her tracks, struck by what she saw. Hugh stopped too, watching her reaction. 'Yes,' he said simply. 'Yes.'

There was another hill between them and the sea, but it was lower than the one they had just climbed, and they could easily see over it. There was an expanse of blue, silver at some points, almost white at others, and that was the sea; there was an island beyond, and yet others further out, strips of land laid down upon the horizon of water. 'Coll,' said Hugh, pointing. 'And that's Tiree.'

Coll and Tiree. She had heard the names in the radio weather shipping forecasts; amid all the gales and the squalls and the zones of low pressure that the radio warned about, there had been Coll and Tiree, reassuring guardians against the Atlantic.

Hugh said to her that they should continue. If they followed the path a bit further, he explained, she would see how it swung back to where the waterfall was. And then they could swim – if she wanted to. 'It's cold for the first few minutes,' he said. 'And then you don't notice it.'

She heard the waterfall before she saw it: a soft, thudding sound, not unlike that of some distant engine. And when they came to the point on the path where it revealed itself to them, again she stopped, and stood quite still in wonderment, her gaze travelling up the wispy column of water that fell, so effortlessly, like the tail of some supernatural white mare. At the foot of the waterfall, a pool had been hollowed out in rock from which all superficial accretion had been washed away; the pristine water was clear enough to show that the pool was deep in parts, deep enough to swim in, as Hugh had promised.

She looked at him as they stood at the edge of the pool. The sun felt warm, even this late, even at this height, and his brow was damp from the exertion of the climb, as was hers too. She half turned to find out whether they had lost sight of the sea, which must be behind them now. They had not; the field of blue was still there, and she saw a boat ploughing a tiny white furrow through it, halfway to the island of Mull.

She glanced over at Hugh, who took off his shirt and tossed it down upon a rock. She turned away, involuntarily, and looked again at the sea in the distance.

'I know that boat,' he said from behind her. 'It belongs to some divers from Tobermory. They dive for scallops.'

The remark – made as a casual aside – made it easier for her to turn round. She saw him standing on the edge of the water, his clothes abandoned on the rock. He said, 'Am I brave enough?'

She wanted to freeze the moment. 'Yes, of course you are.' She paused, her hand upon the buttons of her blouse. 'And I'll try to be brave too.'

It was cold, cold to the bone, as he had said it would be, but they became accustomed to the temperature within minutes, again as he had said they would. She swam beside him, letting her hair float about her on the surface; he held her hand lightly, under the water. The spray from the waterfall was delicate upon her face; touched it, and disappeared.

He said, 'I love this place so much.'

'I know. And I can see why.'

He swept his hair back, a wet slick across his forehead. 'I want to live here, you know. I have to.'

She spoke without hesitation. 'I know that too.'

'My father's got only one chance of staying here – staying on the farm – and that's if I help him with the hydro scheme. He can't do it himself.'

'Then you must do it.'

'And you?'

'I want to be where you are. That's all.'

How easy, she thought; how easy it was to change a life, to give up everything. A few words could do it.

He pressed her hand. She felt his leg touch hers. He was holding her, cradling her, so that she need not swim. 'There's an old place, a cottage that was used by the shepherd. It's been empty for years. We could do it up – we could take our time, and do a little bit each year, as we can afford it.'

She looked up at the sky. Under which I shall live, she thought; and her decision was made. 'We can do it right away.

I can sell my flat in London and we can use the money to do up the cottage and live on the rest for ... well, for ages, I expect.'

'If you find a buyer. It can take some time, can't it?'

'I have a buyer.' She would sell it to Rupert. He had always wanted it, and now she would give it to him. She did not want to leave London to begin her new life in anything but a state of grace, which was what this place, this holy place, now asked of her, and would be given.

66. Eddie Upbraids William over Freddie

William French's son, Eddie, had been an utter disappointment to his father, and to his late mother, his teachers, his scout leader and most of his friends – except, of course, the loyal, uncritical Steve. His failure to achieve anything had begun early – at nursery school, in fact – and had continued throughout his brief period of tertiary education, when he had been given a last-minute place on an under-subscribed course at a struggling university in a remote part of the city. The course in film studies was not unduly onerous, requiring not much more than the watching of a certain number of films each week, but even that proved a strain on Eddie's staying power, and he had dropped out. After that he had taken to spending the morning in bed in the flat he shared with his father in Corduroy Mansions.

Eddie had ignored his father's frequent hints that he should find a place of his own. These had become more and more direct, and had eventually included offers to help with a mortgage. But why move? If one had a comfortable, reasonably central flat with porterage (father) and all meals provided (father), then why rough it in a shared flat where cooking would have to be done (Eddie) and contributions made to electricity (Eddie), gas (Eddie) and telephone (Eddie) bills? No, in common with many contemporary twenty-something-year-olds, Eddie saw no reason to leave the entirely comfortable nest that his father so thoughtfully provided.

Eventually the worm had turned, and Eddie had been driven out of Corduroy Mansions by William's friend, Marcia, who had stood up to him in a way his father had singularly failed to do. Smarting, Eddie had moved into a flat with his friend, Steve, a move that would eventually have resulted in trouble over unpaid bills had it not been for a singular stroke of luck in meeting Merle. She was ten years his senior, but endowed with an overwhelming advantage that would cancel out any drawback in age: she had a beach house in the Windward Islands, where she owned a thriving marina and yacht chandlery. Eddie liked Merle, and she for some inexplicable reason reciprocated his affection. They set up home together, spending six months each year in the Windward Islands and six months in London. Eddie thought the arrangement ideal. He took to wearing an ex-Greek merchant navy captain's cap, and spending his mornings at the marina telling the staff what to do.

'Sure thing, Captain Eddie,' they replied. But they never did what he asked them to do, and Eddie never noticed. So everybody was content.

Eddie and Merle were now back in London, and Eddie had

decided to visit his father, whom he had not seen since his return. William had hoped that Eddie would bring Merle – he had never met her – but apparently she had business to do in Southampton and was unable to come.

'Next time, Dad,' said Eddie. 'Merle's not going anywhere.'

William thought this remark applied very aptly to Eddie, but did not say so. Instead he said, 'I look forward to meeting her. She sounds very . . . very nice.' The trite praise was lame, but he wondered what else he could say about a person whom he had never met. She would probably be blowsy, he thought, a bit like a younger version of Marcia . . . He stopped himself. That was a disloyal thought. Marcia was not blowsy, or perhaps only a little bit. It was disloyal to think such things about a woman who had offered him nothing but friendship, and brought round to the house all those marvellous surplus snacks from the diplomatic receptions for which she catered.

'So, what are you up to, Dad?' asked Eddie cheerfully. 'Same old, same old, I suppose.'

William drew a deep breath. He would not allow his son to condescend to him. He should point out that at least he worked, whereas Eddie did the same old, same old *nothing*. But he did not say it; he simply replied, 'The usual. You know how it is.'

'Yes,' said Eddie. 'It must be pretty boring.' He paused, looking around the room. 'Where's the dog? Where's Freddie de la Hay?'

William looked out of the window. 'He's . . .'

He broke off. What could he tell Eddie?

Eddie looked suspicious. 'Yeah? He's what? Has he kicked the bucket?'

'No, he hasn't.' William glared at his son. 'He's serving his country!'

'Come again?' said Eddie. 'A dog? Serving his country?'

'I've lent him to MI6,' said William softly. 'They asked whether he might help them with surveillance duties. They put a transmitter in his collar and he was passed on to a group of Russians—'

He did not finish. Eddie leaped to his feet. 'You lent him to MI6? Have you gone off your rocker? What happens if . . .'

It had already happened, and William confessed to Eddie that Freddie de la Hay had been exposed and gone missing as a result. Eddie listened with growing horror.

'You hear this, Old Man,' he said. 'You go and get that dog back, you hear? You go and rescue Freddie de la Hay.'

'I don't know—' began William.

'You just go,' shouted Eddie. 'You should be ashamed of yourself! You're not fit to own a dog, you know!'

William said nothing. He feared that Eddie was right. He was not fit, and he felt miserable about it.

67. *In Farmer Brown's*

Eddie stormed out, leaving his father profoundly shaken. For a few minutes after his son's departure, Eddie's final words of condemnation ringing in his ears, William stood quite still in the middle of his entrance hall, staring at the pattern on the rug beneath his feet. He had never expected that Eddie, his feckless and inconsiderate son, would berate him in quite such a way – and with such clear justification. Eddie was in general in no position to criticise anybody, but on this occasion William had to acknowledge that he was absolutely right. Yes, he had behaved with complete disregard for Freddie de la Hay's feelings; yes, he had let the trusting dog down. He had handed him over without any enquiry as to provisions for his welfare, taking instead the vaguest of assurances as to how he would be looked after. And all the time his head had simply been turned by two female agents of MI6. What a fool he had been! Of course they would use women to deal with him – they must have known his susceptibility. And Tilly Curtain, who had seemed so attractive and interested in him, was probably laughing behind his back all along, thinking how easy it was for her to trap this middle-aged wine dealer (well, only just fifty, late forties really) into a harebrained scheme to listen in to the gossip of Russian gangsters in Notting Hill.

William turned round and went back into his sitting room. Eddie had brought a newspaper with him and had left it lying on the floor – even as a visitor, thought William, he leaves the place untidy. He picked up the paper, and grimaced; it was just the sort of paper that Eddie would read – a salacious, hectoring mixture of indignation and populist diatribe. He glanced at a headline: *Espionage Boss Found in River*. He read the few lines beneath the heading: the unfortunate espionage boss in question was French and had nothing to do with MI6, but still the story filled him with alarm. Was this the fate awaiting Freddie de la Hay, or was it the fate that had by now been doled out to him? Was Freddie already floating in the Thames somewhere, or possibly lying in the mud on the river bottom, a block of concrete tied to his collar? William closed his eyes. He could not bear the thought that it was he who was responsible for this. It was his fault.

He reached into his pocket, taking out the piece of paper on which he had jotted Tilly Curtain's telephone number. They had parted on frosty terms, having barely managed to complete their dinner together. There had been no mention of a further meeting, and all the MI6 agent had promised to do was to telephone William if there was any news of Freddie de la Hay. Well, that was not good enough, he thought. If this is my fault – which it is – then I am going to be the one to do something about it.

He picked up the telephone and dialled the number. 'I want to see you,' he said when she answered.

There was a brief silence at the other end of the line. 'I'm afraid I've got no further news.'

'That's neither here nor there,' said William. 'I want to see you. I insist.'

Tilly agreed – reluctantly – and suggested that they see one another at Farmer Brown's, a café on a small street off St Martin's Lane. William knew the place; he had occasionally dropped in for a cup of coffee or for lunch. They agreed to meet in forty minutes and rang off.

She was already there when he arrived. Although her manner on the telephone had been distant, it struck William as he sat down at the table with her that there was something different now – a sympathy, perhaps, that he had not witnessed at their last meeting.

'I'm very sorry about . . . about what happened at dinner,' she said. 'And I've been thinking about it.'

William made a non-committal gesture. He was waiting to see what she would say.

'I was acting on instructions, you see,' she said, her voice lowered. 'I was told that I was not to say anything to you. Or at least not to say anything significant.'

He leaned forward. 'Oh?'

Tilly lowered her voice further, although there was nobody who could overhear them. The café was virtually empty, apart from a couple of stage designers from a nearby theatre sketching something out on a paper napkin.

'Yes,' said Tilly. 'What I was not allowed to tell you is this: Freddie de la Hay is alive. And we know where he is.'

William's heart gave a great leap. Instinctively he reached out and took her hand, clutching it tightly. 'Oh, that's marvellous, marvellous news. Where is he? And when will he be coming back?'

Tilly frowned. 'Well, I don't actually know. When I said *we know* I meant that the service knows. Ducky does – I'm sure of that. But I don't know personally.' She paused. 'And I shouldn't really be telling you any of this.'

William looked puzzled. Ever since he had started having dealings with MI6, he had felt that he had wandered into a maze of some sort – a garden of twisting paths and passages, with no signs to show one the way and nobody to ask for directions. He was pleased that Freddie de la Hay was alive, but he wondered whether this was the same thing as being safe. One could be alive and yet at the same time very unsafe, and perhaps that was the position that Freddie was now in.

'All right,' Tilly went on, her voice now barely a whisper. 'Listen to me, William. Freddie de la Hay has been set up. They knew all along that the transmitter in his collar would be discovered. They knew it.'

William stared at her. 'Why . . .'

He did not finish. She raised a finger to silence him. 'Ducky wanted to find out where their other place was. He knew that they had somewhere else in London, but we could never find it. He thought that if they discovered Freddie was working for us, they would take him there. And so he fitted a small locating transmitter under Freddie's skin. It's been sending out homing signals loud and clear.'

William sat back in his chair, stunned by this disclosure. 'We've got to find him,' he said weakly.

Tilly looked down at her cup of coffee. She's ashamed, thought William. She's every bit as ashamed as I am.

'You could try speaking to Ducky,' she said. 'You could appeal to him. Try to get through to his better nature. Ask him to tell you where Freddie is and how to get him out of the cold.' She sighed. 'I don't think he will, of course. But you could try.'

68. Going Home

'This is such fun,' said Jo, as she and Caroline settled themselves into their seats on the train from Paddington.

Caroline looked about her. She was so used to this train, which she thought of simply as the train home, that she never really took much notice of it. For most of the passengers, who were commuters, she imagined that it would hardly be fun either: it would be a journey to be endured, something that one did, Monday to Friday, in a state not far off suspended animation.

Or it could be, she thought, that Jo was referring to the fact that they were going to Cheltenham to spend a weekend with Caroline's parents. Again, she would not have described that as fun, although Jo, of course, had yet to meet her host and hostess. Not that they were particularly bad, as parents went; it was just that, well, they were her parents, with all that this entailed. Parents were very rarely just right, no matter how fond one might be of them. For instance, her father, Rufus Jarvis, was extremely conservative in his outlook; she only hoped that the conversation would not stray on to politics. What would Jo think? Or was she used to it? After all, she had parents back in Western Australia, and they no doubt had views of their own.

'Yes,' she said, in delayed answer to Jo's observation, 'it is going to be fun.'

'It's good of you to invite me,' Jo said, as the train began to pull out of the station. She looked at Caroline quizzically. 'Did you ever take James back to meet them?'

Caroline winced. 'Not a success.'

Jo smiled at this. It was what she had expected. 'Maybe James is not ideal material to take home,' she said.

Caroline said nothing. James was her friend. Kind, amusing,

stimulating James was still her friend. And that was all, she thought ruefully. Jo was right: it was time for her to abandon her expectations for that relationship. It was to be friendship, and nothing more.

'What about you?' she asked. 'Did you take anybody home?'

She realised immediately after asking the question that she might be venturing into awkward territory for Jo. Her flat-mate had never been explicit about her private life and Caroline was as a result uncertain about where Jo's real interests lay. She had talked in the past about a boyfriend, but Caroline had not been sure whether she meant a boyfriend in the sense in which she herself sometimes talked about girlfriends: a friend who was a boy. James was a boyfriend, but not her *boyfriend* . . .

And now, as she looked at Jo in the seat facing her, she thought: it's the clothing that makes one speculate; the rather masculine-looking jacket. And the short hair. And the boots. But one should not jump to conclusions, she reminded herself, and it could be something to do with coming from a rather sporty family in Perth.

'Oh yes,' said Jo. 'I took boys back. Quite a few, actually.'

Well, thought Caroline, that settles that.

'Not that I wanted to marry any of them, of course,' Jo went on.

And that unsettles that, Caroline decided.

The journey passed quickly. Jo dropped off to sleep, and Caroline read, and looked out of the window, and reflected on her life. Now that she had let go of the idea of James, it seemed to her that everything had become much less complicated. She had a job; she had somewhere to live; she had a home to go back to if London became too much – which it was unlikely to do. She could meet somebody now, somebody who would suit her rather better than James – poor James – did. Where was the problem? There was none. That was the answer. There was nothing holding her back.

They took a taxi from the station to the house. Rufus answered the door and embraced Caroline warmly. He smelled so familiar; he put bay rum on his face after shaving, and it lingered. It was one of the smells of childhood that she loved. He smelled of bay rum and newspapers, and sometimes of smoke, when he had been making bonfires in the garden, which he liked to do.

He shook hands with Jo. She saw his eyes flicker and move quickly to hers but she did not meet his glance. Then Frances, her mother, arrived, dusting her hands as she came out of the kitchen. Frances looked at Jo before she turned to her daughter, and then the same thing happened – a quick exchange of glances. Did Jo notice this, Caroline wondered. She guessed not; Jo was patting Patrick, the aged dog, who had come to sniff arthritically at her boots.

They went upstairs to put their bags in their rooms. The guest room had been prepared for Jo, and there were flowers in a vase near the window. A small tin of biscuits had been placed on the bedside table, and a bottle of mineral water. The comforts of home, thought Caroline. These little touches.

Jo turned to her and said, 'It makes me want to cry.'

Caroline was alarmed. So she had noticed. She had seen the

expressions on her parents' faces, and she had been wounded. Of course she would be; this was what people had to put up with, day in, day out. If they did not conform, if they were different, they had to put up with these glances, these expressions, this unspoken passing of judgement.

'I'm sorry,' she said. 'This is England . . .' It was all she could think of to say, and it was not very well put.

'Of course it's England,' said Jo. 'That's what makes it so nice.'

Caroline realised that she had misunderstood. 'I thought . . .'

'The flowers and the biscuits,' said Jo. 'And look at the towels laid out at the end of the bed. It's home, Caroline, it's home. That's what makes me want to cry.'

And she did, and Caroline instinctively went up to her and put her arms around her. 'Dear Jo. Dear Jo.'

She knew why her friend was crying. She was crying because she was far from home, and who among us has never wanted to do that? There need be no other reason; just that. We cry for home, and for flowers on tables, and biscuits in little tins, and for mother; and we feel embarrassed, and foolish too, that we should be crying for such things; but we should not feel that way because all of us, in a sense, have strayed from home, and wish to return.

69. Preparing Canapés with Frances

Caroline's mother, Frances, was preparing canapés in the kitchen. Caroline was helping her but only desultorily, as she was more interested in paging through a large recipe book that she had found lying on the kitchen table.

'I'm so pleased that you managed to come down this weekend rather than next,' said Frances. 'We've been meaning to hold this drinks party for ages and it's lovely to have you with us.' She paused. 'And your friend, Jo, of course.'

Caroline turned a page of the cookery book. 'Delia,' she said. 'The blessed Delia. You call her that, don't you? And everybody uses her book. Everybody, as far as I can see. How does she do it?'

'She's a real cook,' said Frances. 'She actually knows how to do it. And she rescued English cooking more or less single-handed. Back when she was training everybody used French recipes. Delia went into the British Library one day and looked through the seventeenth-century cookbooks – English cookbooks – wrote out the recipes and published her own versions.'

'Nice.'

'Yes, and then she went on and showed everybody how to cook proper roast potatoes. And the whole nation started to eat crispy roast potatoes after that.' She clicked her fingers. 'Pass me the pepper please, Caroline. It's over there.'

Caroline handed the pepper grinder to her mother.

'Are you unhappy, darling?' her mother said rather absent-mindedly, as she sprinkled pepper on a small side of smoked salmon.

Caroline stared at the recipe book. 'A bit.'

Frances started to cut the salmon into squares. 'You'll get over it,' she said. 'I remember being unhappy at your age. The whole world seems so complicated. Nobody seems to understand you. And so on. Then things sort themselves out. You don't believe it now, but they'll sort themselves out.'

She turned and looked at her daughter. 'You do know, darling, that Daddy and I will always be behind you. You know that, don't you? No matter what you choose to do, we'll always be there to support you. And I do like Jo – or what I've seen of her. You mustn't worry . . .'

'About what? Worry about what?'

'About . . . about . . . You know what I'm talking about.'

Caroline shook her head. 'Actually, I don't.'

Her mother sighed. 'Well, darling, let me let you in on a little secret. You know that I married Daddy because, well, I supposed it was the thing to do. I'm sure you must have gathered that. And sometimes when you do that you don't actually know what you're doing, or what you're really about. Daddy is a lovely man, as I'm sure you'll agree. But he's not exactly the most romantic figure in the county, is he?'

Caroline shrugged. It had never occurred to her to wonder how her father rated in romantic terms. 'Daddy's quite good-looking,' she said. 'I imagine that . . .'

It was as if Frances had not heard her. 'So if you're wondering what I think about Jo, then let me assure you that I understand.'

Caroline was now beginning to see where the conversation was going. She realised that she would need to correct her mother, but before she had the opportunity to do so, Frances went on, 'So many of us are, well, a little bit that way, including me. I had a tremendous passion for somebody, you know. Not that I had the chance to do anything about it. She was—'

Caroline's jaw sagged. 'Mummy! Please!'

Frances looked at her, smiling. 'But darling, I only want you to know that if you're wondering where it comes from, obviously it comes from me!'

Caroline put her hand to her mouth. 'Oh Mummy, I wish you hadn't started to talk about all this. There's nothing between Jo and me. And I don't think Jo would want it anyway. So she wears boots. She's Australian. From Perth. You *need* boots there. She's just my flatmate – that's all.'

Frances collected herself quickly. 'Mummy's little joke,' she said. 'Not at all serious. I was just having a little fun.'

'Of course.'

'So, let's get on with the canapés,' Frances went on briskly. 'Tell me what Delia says I have to do after I've cut the puff pastry.'

They began to work in silence, each remembering and reconstructing the conversation that had gone before. When they were finished, they each went to change and get ready for the arrival of the guests. Caroline thought: Our parents are not always what we think they are. And Frances could have had the same thought about her daughter, but had decided not to think about it at all. She had her duty as hostess before her, and she always attended first to her duty, no matter what.

The guests arrived. They were mostly neighbours or Rufus's colleagues. But a newly arrived retired couple was there – people who had recently moved to Cheltenham from Ely – and they had with them their son, Anthony. He was a year or two older than Caroline, and he was brought across the room by Frances to be introduced.

Caroline looked at him as he spoke to her. He had grey eyes, she noticed, and a pearl-grey jersey. He matched. She looked down at his shoes: he was wearing ankle boots. They somehow matched his trousers. His hair was blonde and swept back to reveal a strong forehead. His hair seemed just right too. He asked her where she lived in London. His voice matched . . . Matched him.

'I live in Pimlico,' she said. 'In a block of flats called Corduroy Mansions.'

He laughed. His laugh matched his voice. 'Hey, I know that place,' he said. 'I live quite close by. Three streets away, in fact.'

She could think of nothing to say but, 'Oh.' There was so much else she could say; so much else that she wanted to tell him.

'Would you like to have dinner?' he asked. 'After this? After this party?'

She did not hesitate for a moment. Why hesitate when you were so sure, so utterly sure? 'Of course. That would be great.' Jo would entertain herself; she was good at that.

'Italian?'

'Perfect.'

Anything would have been perfect. Italian, French, Indian, Chinese, Thai. Anything. She remembered Delia. Even English.

70. A Developing Crisis

Terence Moongrove was only very vaguely known to Rufus and Frances Jarvis, as he moved in different circles from them. He had his sacred dance association, peopled by sundry adherents of the Bulgarian mystic, Peter Deunov; Rufus and Frances had their golf club. Between the sacred dance association and the golf club there was very little, indeed no shared ground, even if the members might recognise one another in the street, as happened when Rufus and Frances had seen Terence Moongrove in the supermarket car park, bundling his shopping into the rear seat of his Porsche.

'What an extraordinary sight,' Rufus had said. 'That Moonshine character seems to have acquired the tart cart that used to belong to Alfie Bismarck's boy. Look at that!'

'Moonwater,' corrected Frances. 'Is it really his? Mind you, he's getting into the driving seat, so it must be. My goodness. Whatever next!'

'I'll be keeping well out of Moonwater's way,' said Rufus. 'He'll be lethal in that machine. Why is it that middle-aged men buy themselves these totally unsuitable cars?'

'Precisely because they're middle-aged men,' said Frances. 'A car like that compensates for a lot, you know.'

'Poor Moonwater,' said Rufus.

'Indeed.'

This slight acquaintanceship – if one could call it that – meant that it was very unlikely that Terence would be one of the guests at the Jarvises' drinks party. And indeed while the Jarvises were shopping that day for their evening entertainment, Terence was sitting in his conservatory, meditating, while his sister, Berthea, rifled through his papers in his chaotically untidy study. Berthea had a very specific objective – to find the telephone number of Lennie Marchbanks, the *garagiste* who had sold Terence the Porsche. She had looked for the number in the telephone directory and failed to find it because unbeknown to her Lennie Marchbanks traded not under his name but that of Stellar Motors. At last, however, she found a receipt bearing the garage name and his signature – a crumpled, slightly greasy document – and was able to dial his number.

'Mr Marchbanks?'

'Yes. Lennie speaking.' There was a curious clicking sound as he spoke, and she remembered that he had an ill-fitting pair of false teeth that often protruded awkwardly.

She gave him her name and asked whether she could possibly see him on a matter of great urgency. It was, she explained, in connection with Terence, who was in the gravest danger.

'Lordie!' exclaimed Lennie Marchbanks. 'Has he had an accident or something? The Porsche? I've told him a hundred times not to drive fast.' *Click.* 'I told him, so I did.'

Berthea assured him that it was nothing to do with the Porsche. 'Financial danger,' she said.

Click. Click.

'Yes. But it's difficult to explain over the phone. Can you please meet me in the lane outside the house in half an hour? I can tell you all about it then.'

Lennie agreed. He was fond of Terence, and had always recognised his vulnerability. He would be there, he said, and he would do whatever he could to help. And he was as good

305

as his word, arriving exactly thirty minutes later in the appointed spot, where he found Berthea waiting for him.

The two had met before and Berthea did not bother with preliminaries. She told Lennie about Roger and Claire, and explained their plan to divest Terence of his house and, she suspected, his money too. Lennie Marchbanks listened, wide-eyed. 'He's not the most worldly of men,' he said in a concerned tone. 'In fact, I must say I've always regarded your brother as an accident waiting to happen. Sorry to have to say it, but that's what I think.'

Berthea shook her head. 'You don't have to apologise for thinking that,' she said. 'I've thought as much for years. Ever since he was a little boy. But he's a good man, at heart, even if he is a little bit . . .'

'Weak in the head,' supplied Lennie Marchbanks helpfully.

'Yes. Perhaps.'

'But, as you say, he's a kind man and we need to protect him.' Lennie Marchbanks paused. 'Do you want me to say something to these people? Do you want me to tell them to clear off?'

This would not work, said Berthea. She explained that Terence had a tendency to become very determined when told not to do something, and the only way of dealing with the situation, in her view, was to get him to come to the realisation himself that Roger and Claire were a threat.

'And how do we do that?' asked Lennie Marchbanks. *Click*.

Berthea found her eyes drawn inexorably to the mechanic's false teeth, the top row of which had slipped forward over the bottom set. He sucked them back into place as she answered his question.

'Terence believes in all sorts of things,' she said. 'And at the moment he seems to be interested in the Green Man. Have you heard of—'

'There's a pub down the way called that,' said Lennie Marchbanks. 'The Green Man. Does a nice pint of mild.'

Berthea nodded. 'I'm sure it does. There are an awful lot of pubs of that name, of course. The Green Man is a mythical figure who still occurs in the collective imagination. He pops up in all sorts of places . . . In fact, if he were to pop up in the rhododendron bushes in Terence's garden and issue some sort of warning to my brother . . .'

Lennie Marchbanks was not a slow man, and it took him very little time to guess what Berthea was asking of him. 'I see,' he said. 'Now that's an interesting idea.'

'Yes,' said Berthea. 'You dress up as the Green Man. We can stick leaves all over your face – you'll have seen drawings and carvings of him. Then I get Terence to go for a walk in the garden – the rest is over to you.'

'I jump out of the bushes and say, "Beware Roger and Claire," or something like that? Then I vanish?'

'More or less. But I think you should say something like, "There are people in the house who are planning to harm you." Something like that. He's quite capable of putting two and two together – sometimes.'

Lennie Marchbanks rubbed his hands together. 'That'll sort them.'

'But then there's part two of the plan,' said Berthea. 'Let me tell you about that . . .'

307

71. *The Green Man Cometh*

Berthea rather enjoyed covering Lennie Marchbanks with foliage. They did this on a piece of vacant land behind the house, using leaves from nearby laurel bushes.

'The last time I dressed somebody up like this was when I was a child and we were making Guy Fawkes,' she said. 'Terence and I used to have tremendous fun dressing him up in one of our father's old shirts.'

'I think these leaves suit me,' said Lennie, from behind the greenery. 'Careful. Not too much glue.'

'Such an interesting figure,' said Berthea, applying a splash of glue to Lennie's chin before sticking a large laurel leaf on it. 'We had all sorts of pagan gods in this country, you know. Not that the Green Man was a god – more of a spirit, I suppose. A bit like Pan.'

Lennie was now largely bedecked with leaves, and Berthea stood back to admire her handiwork.

'Convincing?' asked Lennie.

Berthea stroked her chin. 'I think so. Say something in your Green Man voice.'

Lennie lapsed into an exaggerated West Country burr. 'Green Man here,' he said. 'I come from the forests.' *Click.*

'Very nice, very nice,' said Berthea warmly. Then she hesitated. 'Except . . .' She was not sure how to put it. People with mannerisms often did not know that they were doing whatever they did, and she thought it unlikely that Lennie Marchbanks ever noticed the unscheduled movement of his false teeth. Yet if Terence heard the familiar clicking sound he would almost immediately realise who was hidden behind the leafy disguise.

'Do you think . . .' she began. 'Do you think . . . I've had an idea, Mr Marchbanks. If you were to remove your teeth, then your voice would be even more disguised. I hope you don't mind my suggesting that.'

Lennie did not mind at all. Reaching into his mouth, he extracted his teeth and handed them to Berthea. 'Good idea,' he mumbled. 'Here.'

Berthea tried not to show her distaste as she took hold of the false teeth. They were of course moist, and she quickly popped them into a pocket of her coat before wiping her hands discreetly. 'There you are,' she said. 'You already sound much more like a real Green Man.'

Lennie was pleased with the compliment. 'I'll tell the morris dancers,' he said. 'I used to dance a bit with them in my younger days. Maybe they need a Green Man.'

Berthea thought it highly likely that they did. Even as she expressed her agreement, she was mulling over in her mind the possibility of a paper for the *International Journal of Psychoanalysis*. It would be an exploration of our need for Pan-like figures – a need that seemed to survive our loss of Arcadia – and an explanation of the role such figures play. The Green Man, she thought, was a reminder of our suppressed knowledge that ultimately we all relied on the growth of plants; no matter how assiduously we covered our world with concrete, we knew at heart that without grass and leaves we would simply not survive. The Green Man, then, was a figure of reassurance: we might have made his life difficult by destroying his habitat but he was still there, lurking in the inmost recesses of our consciousness.

She looked at Lennie Marchbanks. Here was a man whose life was one of machinery, and yet he had reverted so quickly and easily to a man of the woods and hedgerows. The entire Age of Machines had been rendered as naught by the simple application of dabs of glue and a few laurel leaves.

Berthea brought herself back to the business in hand. 'Right,' she said. 'Now, if you wouldn't mind, you go and hang about in the rhododendron bushes, and I shall bring Terence out for a walk.'

'Will do,' mumbled Lennie. 'Do we need to synchronise our watches?'

Berthea laughed. 'I don't think that'll be necessary, Mr Marchbanks. But please remember one thing: I won't see you. So don't look at me, and I won't look at you. Just look at Terence.'

Lennie Marchbanks nodded, causing a leaf to fall off the end of his nose. Berthea retrieved it from the ground and stuck it back on. 'Premature autumn,' she remarked. 'A well-known hazard for green men.'

They made their way back to the garden. While Lennie Marchbanks burrowed into the thick foliage of the rhododendrons, Berthea returned to the house, where she found Terence still meditating in the conservatory.

'Terence,' she said. 'It's lovely outside. I think we should have a little walk together.'

'Perhaps later, Berthy,' said Terence. 'I've just reached a jolly high level of inner calm.'

'An ideal state in which to commune with nature,' she said briskly, taking his arm in encouragement.

They went outside. 'Let's look at those beds first,' said Berthea. 'What lovely pinks. And freesias, too. I've always loved freesias. Such a delicate smell, and such beautiful colours too. And look at those lilies over there, Terence.'

'Lilies are so contented,' said Terence. 'They neither spin, nor do they toil, yet Solomon in all his glory . . .'

'Indeed,' said Berthea. 'Mind you, I've always imagined that Solomon wore rather dull clothes. I'm not surprised the lilies eclipsed him. But enough of flowers, let's go down there, Terence. Over by the rhodies.'

Berthea glanced at the large mass of greenery that was the cluster of rhododendrons. She thought she detected a movement, but was not sure.

'Berthy,' Terence said suddenly. 'I think I can see something in the rhodies.'

'Really? I can't.'

They moved closer. At that moment Lennie Marchbanks's leaf-covered face emerged from within the green embrace of the bushes.

'Beware!' he called.

Terence grabbed his sister's arm. 'Berthy! Look! Look! The Green Man!'

'Oh, don't be so ridiculous, Terence. There's nothing there.'

'Beware!' Lennie Marchbanks called again. 'Beware of a person within your house, O mortal!'

Berthea was impressed with Lennie's acting, but could not show it of course.

311

'Why are you shaking like that, Terence?' she asked. 'Are you cold?'

There was a further movement in the bushes and Lennie Marchbanks disappeared.

'Let's go back to the house, Terence,' said Berthea, leading her brother away. 'You've obviously been meditating far too hard and it's gone to your head. A cup of tea will bring you back, no doubt. It always does.'

72. A Meeting with MI6

There are few harsh words that have greater effect than those spoken by child to parent. A home truth delivered by our offspring is for most of us far less easily ignored than one emanating from a colleague or a friend. *Et tu, Brute* is bad enough; *et tu, fili* tends to be uttered with real reproach.

William had been shocked by the upbraiding that he had received from his son, Eddie. Part of this reaction was attributable to astonishment on his part that Eddie, who had shown fecklessness since early childhood, should believe himself to be in a position to criticise anybody, let alone his father. If there is high moral ground – usually claimed by politicians – then there must also be a middle moral ground – normally claimed by most of the rest of us – and, of course, a low moral ground. This low terrain, susceptible to moral flooding, was that occupied by Eddie and his friends, and it was ground from which one might not expect much moral advice to be issued. But Eddie had given such advice in clear and unequivocal terms:

William should never have let Freddie de la Hay be used by MI6; to do so was to ignore the moral obligation that people owed to their animal charges, and in this case it made William unfit to own a dog.

The shock had spurred William into action. He had demanded a meeting with Tilly Curtain, at which she had told him that Freddie de la Hay was still alive and, most importantly, that her colleague Sebastian Duck knew where he was. Now, back in Corduroy Mansions, William dialled Sebastian Duck's number, determined to confront him over Freddie's whereabouts.

'Mr Duck?'

'Yes, Duck here. And that's you, Mr French?'

Once again, William could not help experiencing a moment's surprise at being recognised, but then if MI6 did not know who was phoning them, who would?

William came straight to the point. He wanted to see Sebastian Duck, and he wanted to see him immediately.

'By immediately, do you mean—'

'Immediately.'

Sebastian Duck was surprisingly obliging, and they arranged to meet in a coffee bar on Brook Street. When William arrived, the other man was already there and beckoned him over.

'I know you like latte,' Sebastian Duck said. 'I've taken the liberty of ordering for you.'

William frowned. How did he know that he liked latte?

Sebastian Duck seemed to have anticipated the question. 'You'll remember that we told you we'd been watching you,' he said quietly. 'In a friendly way, of course.'

William felt his irritation grow. How dare these people *spy* on others. And then he thought, well, they are spies . . . But that did not excuse it in his case.

'I want my dog back,' he said bluntly. 'I agreed to *lend* him to you, not to give him. So, if you don't mind, I'd like him back right now.'

Sebastian Duck stared into his coffee cup. 'Would that the world was as we wanted it to be, Mr French. But it isn't, is it?'

William glared at him. 'That's a somewhat opaque thing to say. And I don't see what it's got to do with my dog.'

Sebastian Duck looked up. 'Oh really? It has everything to do with your dog, I'm afraid, Mr French. You would like your dog back, and I'm telling you that there are some requests that are frankly impossible to meet. Your dog, I'm very sorry to say, is lost.'

William tried to remain calm. 'Lost in what sense?'

Sebastian Duck shrugged. 'The word "lost" has many meanings in our world. In a sense we're all lost, aren't we? We imagine—'

William cut him short. 'Is he dead?'

'I'm sorry. Yes, he is.'

William sat back in his chair. 'I believe you're lying.'

Sebastian Duck raised an eyebrow. 'You're distraught, Mr French.'

'I've heard that you know where he is.'

Sebastian Duck's expression was impassive. 'Oh? And who told you?'

William realised he could not reveal that it was Tilly Curtain. He had promised her he would not say anything about their meeting, and yet he had to say something. He thought of the terms espionage figures used in novels and one came to him. 'A mole,' he said.

The word caused an immediate reaction in Sebastian Duck. 'A mole?' he asked sharply. 'A mole by the name of Tilly Curtain?'

William was no actor, and his face must have given away the secret. 'Well . . .' he began.

Sebastian Duck leaned forward. 'Let me tell you something, Mr French. We know about her. Do you know that? We know.'

'Know what?'

Sebastian Duck lowered his voice even further. 'We know that she's not quite what she seems to be.'

William hesitated. 'I don't know what you're talking about. I really don't.'

'Well, let me tell you then. Your friend Miss Curtain is paid by HMG but is also in the pay of . . .' Sebastian Duck reached for a tiny packet of sugar, tore it open neatly, and poured it into his half-empty coffee cup. 'Of the Belgians.'

William sat quite still. 'The Belgians? Why?'

Sebastian Duck shrugged. 'What interest do you think the Belgians have in the growth of the influence of Brussels?' He did not wait for an answer. 'Exactly.'

'That is ridiculous,' said William. 'Utterly absurd.'

'In that case, I'll take my leave,' said Sebastian Duck, rising from the table. 'Goodbye.'

William remained where he was. After a minute or two, he took his mobile phone out of his pocket and dialled Tilly Curtain's number.

'Thank heavens you called,' she said. 'I've found out.'

'Found out what?'

'Where Freddie de la Hay is.'

73. Chipping Campden

Everything was now in place for the second stage of Berthea's plan. Once inside the house, Terence, still pale from the shock of seeing the Green Man in the rhododendrons, sat himself down in the kitchen. 'I swear I saw him, Berthy,' he said breathlessly. 'You know me – I don't make things up.'

Berthea knew him as well as any sister might be expected to know a brother, and she knew there were no discernible limits to Terence's gullibility and imaginative capability. 'Of course not,' she said. 'The eye tricks us very easily. I quite understand how one might imagine that one has seen the Green Man when there are all those leaves moving about.'

Terence shook his head vigorously, becoming quite agitated. 'It's not a trick of the eye,' he said. 'The Green Man was right there – in the flesh. I promise you, Berthy – cross my heart – he was standing right there, as real as anything. I promise you.'

Berthea spoke calmingly, 'Well, we'll see, won't we? If the Green Man is frequenting your garden, then I'm sure we'll see him again some time.'

Terence appeared mollified. 'I hope so. I really enjoyed our conversation. He gave me a warning, you know.'

Berthea, pouring boiling water into the teapot, affected nonchalance. 'Oh, did he? About what?'

Terence looked at her sideways. 'About somebody in the house who was a danger to me. A traitor, I assume.'

Berthea glanced at him out of the corner of her eye and saw that he was staring at her. His manner, it seemed, was suspicious. *He thinks it's me*, she thought with horror. *He's got the wrong end of things again.*

She quickly served her brother his tea and left the room. In the drawing room she telephoned Lennie Marchbanks and told him to come round again, immediately. 'Remember,' she said. 'Crop circles.'

About ten minutes later, while Terence was still drinking his tea in the kitchen – pondering the Green Man, Berthea imagined – Lennie Marchbanks drove up to the house in his ancient silver Volvo. Terence noticed his arrival. 'I must tell Lennie about the Green Man,' he said, rising to his feet. 'He's very interested in these things.'

Lennie came to the door and was admitted to the kitchen. 'Great news, Mr Moongrove,' he said. 'More crop circles!'

In the excitement of this news, the Green Man was quite forgotten. Terence listened entranced as Lennie explained that two new crop circles had been spotted in a field about five miles away. 'I wanted to take you to see them,' he said. 'Sometimes the crops spring up before you have the chance to appreciate them.'

Terence required no persuasion. 'You're very kind, Mr Marchbanks.'

Lennie glanced at Berthea. 'We'll go in my Volvo,' he said. 'I know the way.'

Berthea watched them drive away before going up to the

room occupied by Roger and Claire. They had installed desks in the room and she supposed that they would be sitting there reading or working on Roger's magnum opus, which proved to be the case.

'I'm terribly sorry to disturb you,' she said. 'But Terence has had to go off with a friend. He asked me to ask you, though, whether you could possibly meet him for lunch at the Cotswold House Hotel in Chipping Campden.'

Roger looked at her suspiciously. 'Chipping Campden? Why?'

'He mentioned something about wanting to sign some papers,' said Berthea vaguely. 'He hoped that you could all do it over lunch.'

Roger turned and looked at Claire. The mention of signing papers had animated him. 'Of course,' he said. 'We'll be very happy to do that, won't we, Claire?' He turned back to Berthea. 'But how will we get out there?'

'He said that you should take his car,' Berthea answered. 'His Porsche. The keys are in the kitchen. He said go out there and wait for him. He hasn't booked a table but he thinks it will be all right.'

Roger and Claire got up from their seats and began to prepare for their departure, ignoring Berthea's presence. Berthea went downstairs and looked at her watch. She had asked Lennie Marchbanks to make sure that he was away a good half hour. That would give Roger and Claire time to get ready and then drive off in the Porsche.

They left twenty minutes later, and precisely ten minutes after that Lennie Marchbanks' silver Volvo drew up outside the house.

'We were too late,' said Terence as he came into the kitchen with the *garagiste*. 'The stalks of the oats or whatever had all sprung up again. So disappointing.'

'The spacecraft must have nipped in and out,' said Lennie.

Berthea noticed that his voice was slurred, and she suddenly remembered that his teeth were still in the pocket of her coat, which was hanging on the back of the kitchen door. She signalled to the mechanic, who frowned as he tried to make out what she meant. Then he realised. 'My teeth!' he exclaimed. 'You've still got them, haven't you?'

Terence looked astonished. 'Why have you got Mr Marchbanks' teeth, Berthy?' he asked. 'Did he drop them?'

'Yes,' said Berthea. And Lennie Marchbanks at the same time answered, 'No.'

Terence looked at Mr Marchbanks. 'What happened to your teeth, Mr Marchbanks?'

'Your sister cleaned them for me.'

'He dropped them and I cleaned them,' said Berthea.

Terence seemed satisfied with this explanation and returned to the topic of crop circles. 'I wonder what shape they were,' he said. 'Roger and Claire have a book which has some of the main patterns.'

Berthea took her cue. 'I wonder where they are . . . ?' She paused. 'I've just remembered something, Terence. I heard the sound of your car about fifteen minutes ago. I thought nothing of it because I'd forgotten that you had gone out with Mr Marchbanks.'

'My Porsche?'

'Yes.'

'Did you tell them they could take it?' asked Lennie Marchbanks.

'Certainly not,' said Terence.

'Then they must have stolen it,' said Lennie. 'Just think.'

Terence was silent. 'The Green Man said . . .' he began.

'Green Man?' asked Lennie Marchbanks.

'It's rather complicated,' Terence explained. 'I was given a warning, you see, and . . .'

Berthea stopped him. 'Where would they have gone, do you think, Mr Marchbanks?' she asked.

Lennie Marchbanks, who had fitted the false teeth now returned to him by Berthea, answered quickly, 'Chipping Campden, I expect. There's a well-known car fence near there. That's where all the stolen cars end up.'

'Then we should go there,' said Berthea. 'We might still catch up with them.'

'It's really bad of them to steal my Porsche,' said Terence. 'And if we catch up with them, I'm jolly well going to tell them that.'

'Steal your Porsche?' muttered Berthea. 'Not only that. They want to steal your house. The Green Man was right, you know.'

She spoke quietly, but Terence heard.

74. *What Did the Green Man Say?*

Terence Moongrove was largely silent on the trip to Chipping Campden. Sitting in the back of Lennie Marchbanks' silver

Volvo, he looked out of the window in a thoughtful, slightly injured way. From the front passenger seat, Berthea half turned to check up on her brother. Poor Terence, she thought. The shattering of an illusion is never easy, even if one's life is filled with illusions.

Lennie Marchbanks, sensitive to the atmosphere, tried to make conversation. 'I drove along here the other day with Alfie Bismarck,' he remarked. 'We were going to see a horse that Alfie's got up there. Nice horse that he bought from Christopher Catherwood last year. Christopher had some success with him on the flat races over in Newmarket, but wanted to concentrate on something else.'

'Oh yes?' said Berthea. 'That's interesting, isn't it, Terence?'

'Jolly interesting,' he mumbled.

'Alfie's got the touch all right,' continued Lennie. 'He turned round a really useless horse that had done the rounds. Ireland. France. Back to Ireland. Then Alfie started working on him and he began to romp home. I said, "Alfie, you're giving that horse something in his oats," and Alfie got all shirty and said I shouldn't talk like that. I said it was only a joke, but he said there are some things you shouldn't joke about.

'Alfie's honest, though. I'd trust him with my shirt, more or less, as long as I had a spare one, ha! And that boy of his, Monty, I've heard what people say about him but it isn't true, you know. He's a chip off the old block, that boy. He won two grand last week at some small meeting up north. Came home with his pockets full. I said, "Monty, you should invest that, you know. Buy some shares in something solid, like futures in helium." He looked at me like I'd suggested that he should fly to the moon. So I said, "How do you think your old man made his money?" I was referring to Alfie's eye for a good investment, but young Monty says, "Gambling, Mr Marchbanks. That's how he did it."'

The conversation continued in this vein until just outside Chipping Campden, when Lennie told them all to start looking out for Terence's Porsche. 'We'll just cruise through,' he said. 'Then if we don't find it, we can start looking along some side roads I know. Good places for stolen vehicles, those side roads.'

They drove slowly. There was a Porsche parked outside a newsagent's premises, but it was the wrong colour. Then, as they made their way into the main square, Lennie gave a low whistle. 'See over there?' he said. 'See?'

'My car,' said Terence. 'What a nerve.'

'They're in that hotel,' said Lennie. 'Probably having lunch. Stuffing their faces.'

'Shall we call the police?' asked Terence.

Berthea shook her head. 'The police will complicate matters. All those forms. The police have bad karma, Terence.'

Terence nodded. 'I just want to give Rog and Claire a piece of my mind. That'll be worse for them than being arrested. I can get jolly cross, you know.'

'You're right,' said Berthea. 'That'll teach them.'

Lennie Marchbanks parked his car and they went into the hotel. Roger and Claire were seated in the dining room, perusing the menu. They looked up, and were surprised when they saw that Terence was accompanied.

'We thought it was just us,' said Roger, rising to his feet.

'Well, you thought wrong!' snapped Terence. 'You Sam!'

Roger frowned. 'What?'

'You Sam!' repeated Terence. 'You great Sam!'

Roger looked angry. 'You're calling me a Sam? What have I done to deserve that?'

'You stole my Porsche,' spluttered Terence. 'We saw it outside.'

'Yes,' crowed Lennie Marchbanks. 'Fine pair of car thieves, parking the car in broad daylight.'

Roger looked at Lennie in astonishment and then turned to Berthea. 'But you told me to take it,' he said. 'You said that Terence had said . . .'

'Delusions,' said Berthea.

Roger let out a cry. 'Delusions? You told us! Claire heard, didn't you? You told us that Terence wanted to meet us here.'

'A likely story,' interjected Lennie Marchbanks.

Roger spun round and glared irately at Lennie. 'You shut your face! You Sam!' he shouted.

'You calling me a Sam?' *Click.* Lennie's voice was filled with anger, and his teeth, dropping forward, made the familiar clicking sound. *Click.*

'It's jolly rude to tell somebody to shut his face,' said Terence. 'You shouldn't say things like that in public. You shouldn't.' He turned to Berthea. 'Did you tell them that, Berthy? Did you tell them to take my car?'

Berthea swallowed. 'Of course not, Terence. Have I ever lied to you? Ever? Once? And have I ever let you down? Ever? Even when Uncle Edgar accused you of eating those sponge finger biscuits of his when you were eight. Remember? And I said that you hadn't, although I knew you had because I'd seen you.' She paused, adding under her breath, 'And what did the Green Man say?'

'I didn't eat all of them,' said Terence. 'The dog had four.'

'For heaven's sake,' snapped Claire. 'This has got nothing to do with biscuits.'

'Indeed it hasn't,' said Berthea coldly. 'But it has everything to do with the theft of a Porsche. Give me the keys, please.'

'No,' said Roger.

'Then I shall call the police.'

Roger hesitated, and then handed over the keys to the Porsche.

'Now we can go home,' said Lennie Marchbanks. 'And these two can make use of public transport to get back to Cheltenham.'

Berthea looked at the dejected fraudsters. 'You'll find your cases with all your possessions at the front gate,' she said. 'You may remove them without entering the property.'

They left. Terence drove back with Berthea in the Porsche.

'I'm really grateful to you, Berthy,' he said. 'There was something about that couple that I didn't quite trust. I saw it all along, you know.'

Berthea nodded. The delusions of which the human mind is capable are manifold and varied, she thought. We are imperfect creatures in every respect, and it was her job to lend wholeness to those who were shattered and unhappy. Not every mission ended quite as well as this one, but that did not mean that one should not try. Every day we should try, she said to herself; we should try to make life better for those around us, and for ourselves. We should try to be kinder. We should try to control our impatience with people like Terence – and others.

'Dear Terence,' she said fondly. 'Now you have your car back.'

'Thanks to you,' said Terence. 'Dearest Berthy.'

75. Dee and Martin Do the Business

If it is the case, and it undoubtedly is, that all business start-ups are fraught with fret and worry, then the bottling and marketing of Dee's Sudoku Remedy was very atypical.

The task of designing the packaging for the remedy had been referred to a client whom Dee knew to be a graphic designer. He had produced a label within a matter of days and had also been able to find a sympathetic and cheap printer. After that had been done, all that was required was to purchase a large quantity of ginkgo biloba in pill form and have these pills put in bottles to which the label had been affixed. Again Dee had a contact who was able to arrange for this to be done on very favourable terms, and quickly too.

'Simple, isn't it?' Dee remarked to Martin. 'Now we do a bit of advertising.' She paused. 'Your five thousand pounds, Martin . . .'

Martin had been impressed by the speed with which the project had progressed. 'No problem,' he said. 'It's ready.' He looked away. It was his entire capital, and he was not sure how, if the money were to be lost, he would explain this to his godfather, who had given it to him. His godfather was short-tempered and, in Martin's view, rather too close to certain criminal elements in Romford. He imagined that his godfather might, as he occasionally put it, 'wish to have a fireside chat' with him if Dee's scheme did not work out.

But now there was no going back. An advertisement was booked in a puzzle magazine and in a daily newspaper. *Want to improve your sudoku performance?* it asked. *The Sudoku Remedy, an entirely herbal product, increases the supply of blood to the brain, thereby enhancing your skill at solving even the most complex sudokus. Also contains anti-oxidants.*

'I hope it works,' said Martin.

'Hope what works?' asked Dee. 'The product or the advertisement?'

'Both,' said Martin. 'But especially the product.'

'Of course it'll work,' said Dee. 'We all know that ginkgo biloba increases the supply of blood to the brain and improves mental performance. If it does that, then you'll be able to do a sudoku better. Stands to reason.'

Martin still looked concerned, and Dee tried to cheer him up. 'Come on, Martin,' she said. 'You have to have confidence in business. If you just sit on the sidelines and worry, then nothing ever gets done. This is our big chance.'

'Maybe,' said Martin. 'It's just that . . .'

'Just that nothing,' said Dee. 'This is going to work, Martin. You'll see.'

The product was launched on a Monday. The advertisement in the newspaper had listed the telephone number of the shop for orders and had also given a website address. By nine-thirty in the morning, when Dee and Martin turned on their computer in the shop, there were already over four thousand email orders.

'Maybe it's a mistake,' said Martin, looking over Dee's shoulder as she scrolled down the list of emails. 'Maybe it's a virus.'

'No,' said Dee, her voice cracking with excitement. 'This is for real, Martin. And look, more are coming in.'

Then the telephone began to ring, and more orders were taken. For the entire day Martin remained glued to the telephone, writing down the address of each customer and noting down how many bottles were wanted. Many took two; several took more than that, intending to send the remedy out to sudoku-addicted friends abroad.

At the end of the day, in a state of utter exhaustion, the two of them switched off the computer and disconnected the telephone.

'That's that,' said Dee. 'Now we have some breathing space we must get more staff.'

Over the following week, Dee and Martin took on four people full-time. A further advertisement was booked in the newspaper, and this time the response was even larger. Then, at the end of the week, Richard Eadeston, the venture capitalist who had invested in the project, came to see them.

'Fantastic trading,' he said. 'Stellar performance. Well done!'

Dee was almost too tired to talk. 'Not bad,' she said.

'Not bad?' mocked Richard Eadeston. 'Seriously good. Grade One fab.'

'Thank you,' said Dee.

'And here's the really good news,' said Richard Eadeston.

'We've been approached by somebody who wants to put an offer to you. I don't think that you'll be able to turn it down, frankly.'

'Try me,' said Dee.

'If you are prepared to sell the business,' said Richard, 'I'm authorised to offer you four and a half million pounds for it. That includes the intellectual rights to the product.'

Dee closed her eyes. *Four and a half million pounds.* Three quarters for Richard Eadeston and his company, and a quarter split between her and Martin. Martin had not invested as much as she had, and therefore would not get as much return; but it would still be a lot.

She opened her eyes and looked at Martin. 'What shall we do?'

Martin shrugged. 'Maybe we should sell,' he said. 'But then again, maybe we shouldn't.'

'Should I flip a coin?' asked Dee.

'Why not?' replied Martin. 'I'll go along with that.'

Dee took a pound coin out of her pocket. 'Heads we sell,' she said. 'Tails we keep the company.'

The coin spun up in the air and was caught by Martin, who slapped it down on the top of his wrist, shielding it from view with his left hand. Then he exposed the coin.

'Sell,' he said.

Dee nodded. 'We'll sell the product,' she said. 'Lock, stock and barrel.'

'Very wise,' said Richard. 'Well done.'

Martin did not think that he deserved congratulation. He had produced virtually nothing in any physical sense and yet here he was being offered a great deal of money. So this, he thought, is capitalism. It was a strange feeling.

'That's a lot you'll be getting,' she whispered.

Martin looked at her, his eyes fixed on hers. 'A hundred thousand?'

'Yes, at least. Like it?'

Martin did not know what to say. He felt disconnected, and empty. He was not sure he wanted so much. It seemed such an impossibly large sum of money.

'Be grateful,' said Dee. 'Your life is about to change.'

Martin thought she was right. His life *was* about to become different, although just how different he did not yet know, and would not know for another few months.

Dee, by contrast, knew exactly how her life would change. She would buy a flat now and get out of Corduroy Mansions, would go to live in her own place. It was all very well living with a whole lot of others when one was young and impecunious; now things were different. My own place, she thought, with deep pleasure. *All I want is a flat somewhere . . . Wouldn't that be loverly . . . loverlee!*

76. With One Leap . . .

Tilly Curtain told William to stay exactly where he was, in the coffee bar on Brook Street.

'Has Ducky gone?' she asked.

'Yes.'

'Are you sure?' she asked. 'Sometimes he pretends to go, but still hangs around.'

William looked around the coffee bar, then rose to peer out of the window. There were a few people on the street outside, but none of them, as far as he could see, was Sebastian Duck.

'The coast seems quite clear,' he said.

Tilly Curtain arrived fifteen minutes later. Without taking off her coat, she sat down opposite him at the table. 'All right,' she said. 'Listen carefully. We know Freddie de la Hay is alive. Our ops people are monitoring the signal from the transmitter under his skin. He's fine.'

William reached out impulsively and took her hand. 'I'm so relieved,' he said.

'Yes. So am I. I'm . . . well, I'm fed up with all the lies, all the compromises. I've had it.'

William watched her. He was not sure whether to raise the issue of her working for the Belgians. Perhaps he could hint that he knew and see if she took it up.

'Everybody tells lies,' he said. 'States operate on the basis of lies. They claim to be above it all, but there are tawdry lies underpinning everything, aren't there? Even the Belgians . . .'

She stared at him. 'Did he say that? Did he say that I was a Belgian double agent?'

William lowered his eyes. 'He did.'

Tilly sighed. 'He's made the accusation before. He's told people I'm a Belgian mole. There's just no truth in it, William. And you know why he says it? It's because *he himself is a Belgian agent!* I'm sure of it.'

William made a gesture of helplessness. 'A world of mirrors reflecting mirrors,' he said.

'Exactly,' said Tilly. 'But enough of that. Let's go and get Freddie de la Hay.'

They left the coffee bar and travelled by taxi to a street on the edge of St John's Wood. 'He's in a mews house down there,' said Tilly. 'I've already done a quick recce. It has a garden gate at the back. We can enter unobserved that way.'

William followed her. There had been light rain, but it had stopped and London seemed bathed in a curious misty white light. He had got into the taxi without thinking; now he asked himself whether it was all about to end for him too. Had Duck been right? Was this woman he hardly knew working for the Belgians? In a shifting, confusing world, anything could be true; anything could be false.

They made their way into a garden. There was a pergola; a bench; a child's ball that had dropped in from a neighbouring garden and remained unretrieved. Fear makes us leave things where they are, thought William; makes us leave them the *way* they are.

Tilly was ahead of him, crouching behind a bushy wisteria. She made a sign for him to join her. 'Look,' she whispered. 'Look up there.'

William studied the back of the mews house, his gaze travelling up. There was a small dormer window in the roof, an afterthought child's bedroom, perhaps. He squinted. There was a movement behind the glass, but it could just have been the sun, which had come from out of the clouds, breaking through that misty light and glinting off the glass. The sun upon glass can be like sun on the water – a movement, a liquid dash of gold, of silver.

331

'Freddie de la Hay,' whispered Tilly.

William looked again. His heart was thumping hard within him, as hard as a hammer. He felt as he had felt when he was about to be beaten as a boy. They had beaten him. Beaten him. That awful, horrid history master.

Freddie de la Hay. It was Freddie de la Hay, his nose pressed up against the glass. And even though no sound could reach him, William knew that Freddie had seen him.

'We must get him out,' William said. 'Is that door locked?'

'Locked and alarmed,' said Tilly. 'But are you prepared to climb up on the roof? Its pretty low, if I give you a hike up you could break the window and get him out. Could you do that?'

William did not hesitate. 'Of course.'

They crept forward. When they came to the back wall of the house, Tilly Curtain bent down and invited William to step on her back. 'I can take it,' she muttered. 'Go ahead.'

He climbed carefully on top of her. It was a long time since I've climbed on somebody's back, he thought. Here I am, very late forties, MW (failed), and I'm climbing on a woman's back. But he put such thoughts out of his mind as he clambered up on to the roof. There above him was the window, and there was guttering to give him purchase. He climbed further up, and in less than a minute he was just below the window at which he had seen Freddie de la Hay.

He peered in, and Freddie de la Hay looked back at him. Neither moved for a few moments. Then William called out, 'Sit, Freddie! Sit!' He did not want Freddie to be right in front of the glass when he broke it.

Freddie de la Hay sat, and that gave William his chance. Taking from his pocket the stone he had picked up in the garden, he brought it down sharply on the glass pane. From within, Freddie gave a yelp of surprise. William wondered whether he had been hit by shattering glass, but it was too late to stop. He quickly cleared the window frame of the last few vicious shards. Then he called to Freddie. 'Come here, Freddie! Quick, Freddie! Good boy, Freddie de la Hay!'

The dog responded immediately. Leaping up, he hurled himself out of the window, straight into the arms of his owner.

'Oh, Freddie,' William shouted with joy. He did not care who heard him. He did not care what happened now. Freddie de la Hay was free. Freddie de la Hay was coming home.

In the taxi, which they hailed at the end of the street, William examined Freddie for injury. The dog seemed in good shape, he thought, apart from a small cut that he had received from a piece of glass still in the window frame. There were a few drops of blood – bright, canine blood – and William thought as he dabbed his handkerchief on the tiny wound, *Freddie de la Hay has shed this blood for his country. It is blood no different from that which other animal heroes have shed.* He remembered the monument to animals in war, that strange, unexpected monument on the edge of Hyde Park, where people left small, movingly inscribed wreaths; where the words said that they had no choice . . .

'We'd normally take him to a safe kennel in these circumstances,' said Tilly. 'But I think that, given everything that's happened, he should go right home with you.'

'I think so too,' said William. He looked at her. 'And thank you, Tilly. Thank you.'

She seemed embarrassed by his words of appreciation, and glanced away. He wondered for a moment whether he should invite her for dinner that night, but then he decided, no. She came from a different world; she still inhabited a world of deceit and deception. There was no place for him, he thought, in that shadowy landscape.

They would go home together, he and Freddie de la Hay – back to Corduroy Mansions.

77. *A Kind and Generous Soul*

In Hatchards on Piccadilly, Rupert Porter stood, Patum Peperium on his shoes, wondering what to do. He had told Roger Katz that he was looking for a tall man of somewhat hirsute appearance, and Roger had confirmed that such a person had recently gone upstairs. So now, at long last, he was within grasping distance of the yeti, if that was what he was pursuing. In reality, of course, there was no yeti – he was sure of that. What he was therefore pursuing was a person who *looked like* a yeti, a person of sufficient cunning not only to have given him the slip in Fortnum & Mason but also to have persuaded the time-served travel writer Errol Greatorex that he was a genuine abominable – or perhaps a genuinely abominable – snowman.

For the first time in this pursuit, Rupert Porter felt fear. He had not been frightened in Fortnum & Mason, and he had not been the least bit concerned while tearing down Piccadilly. But now, in the narrower confines of Hatchards, he felt a frisson of anxiety that was not far, he realised, from fear. He wondered why he should be afraid. The yeti was presumably unarmed, and it was highly unlikely that he would set upon anybody in broad daylight, in the middle of London. Yetis had no record of harming anybody; in fact, the yeti was meant to be a shy and elusive character, given to loping off into the snowy wastes should anybody get too close. There was no reason to believe, then, that this yeti – if he was a yeti, which of course he was not – would behave any differently.

And yet Rupert could not get out of his mind that terrifying scene in Daphne du Maurier's *Don't Look Now* where the art historian pursues a tiny red-coated figure through the streets of Venice, and, in a petrifying denouement, is suddenly confronted by a malign knife-bearing dwarf. What a harrowing story that was, and how tragic the outcome. What if he were to confront the yeti and, to the strains of Mahler or whatever it was, have his throat slit from side to side with a sweep of a blade? He would slip to the floor and see the blood ebb out, the flow matching the last beats of the heart, a pumping that would diminish and stop as the last chords of Mahler played out. Or was that Visconti? It was, he remembered, and the outcome there had not been very good either.

Roger Katz was suddenly called away and could no longer attend him. 'You should find your friend upstairs,' he said. 'I'll see you later on.'

On his own now, Rupert began to make his way up the spiralling staircase that led to the first floor. As he reached the landing, he looked along the gallery ahead of him. There were one or two people browsing – an elderly woman, a young man. There was no sign of the yeti.

Rupert approached the archway that led off to his left. The trouble with Hatchards, he thought, is that it has so many rooms. Unlike many modern bookshops, which could double as aircraft hangars should the need arise, Hatchards was a rabbit-warren of charming rooms. But the very quality that made it such a fine bookshop also made it a difficult place to pursue somebody who was determined to elude you. The yeti might have left the staircase at the first floor, or he might have gone up to the second floor, or beyond. It was impossible to tell.

Rupert had to make a choice, though, and he chose to look on the first floor. Walking very slowly, he made his way into the further reaches of the first floor. He stopped. There were three people in the first gallery – two women standing together, paging through a book they had extracted from a shelf, and one man. He was a tall man, and he was wearing exactly the colour of coat that Rupert had seen in Fortnum & Mason. It was the yeti; he was sure of it.

Rupert advanced very slowly. The yeti was facing away from him, apparently absorbed in a book. Rupert took a deep breath. There was a strong fishy smell rising from his shoes, and he hoped that the two women, whom he was now passing, would not notice it. They did not.

He was now only a couple of yards from the yeti. He noticed odd details: the hem of the green coat had been inexpertly stitched and was hanging down; the yeti's shoes were brogues, but in need of a clean, and his hair, which was dark in colour, almost pitch black, was neatly combed in what seemed, from the back, to be a centre-parting.

Rupert cleared his throat. 'Mr . . .' he began. 'Mr Yeti?'

The effect of his words was electric. Without turning round, the yeti dropped the book he was reading and launched himself towards a door at the back of the gallery.

'Excuse me!' shouted Rupert. 'I only want to have a word . . .'

The yeti did not slow down. Ignoring the shouts of his pursuer, he pushed open the door and slipped through it. Not once did Rupert see his face.

Rupert reached the door and tried the handle. It was now locked from the other side. For a moment he wondered whether he should run up to the floor above and try the equivalent door there, assuming it led onto another staircase, but he suddenly felt very weary. The yeti had eluded him – again – and there was no point. He was not a yeti anyway; he was a deluded charlatan who was spinning some ridiculous story to a gullible author and agent. There was no reason to waste any more time on him.

Rupert went downstairs. He noticed, as he did so, that he had left a trail of anchovy paste on the carpet. *It's not my fault*, he thought. None of it has been my fault. It's la Ragg. She's the one who has caused all this. She's the one.

He returned to the office, where he wiped his shoes clean. There was still the smell of the Patum Peperium, but it was not so strong now. By the time he went home perhaps the last vestiges of anchovy paste would have dried completely.

He listened to his voicemail. There was only one message.

'Rupert. Barbara here. We're having a lovely time up in Argyll, and I need to talk to you. Essentially it's this: I want to move up here for three weeks out of four. One week in London and the rest up here.'

Rupert pressed the pause button. No, he said to himself. La Ragg is not going to have her cake and eat it. Never.

He pressed play and allowed the message to continue. 'I can work perfectly well in Scotland, you know. So it shouldn't make any difference. Of course, I won't need the flat in London as I can stay with a friend who has a spare room. Would you like to buy my flat? You've always liked it, I believe, and I'll be very happy to let you have it at a very favourable price. Talk to you later.'

Rupert sat quite still. You kind, good woman, he thought. You generous soul.

78. No Man is so Lonely

William stood by the window of his flat in Corduroy Mansions, the washed-out London sky before him. He could hardly believe that he had done all this – got himself mixed up with MI6, climbed onto the roof of a mews house, broken a window and freed Freddie de la Hay. It was not that he regretted any of it: in retrospect the whole thing had been the most extraordinary adventure, and he was at the stage of life where any adventure was welcome. But he was pleased that it was over, and that he – and Freddie de la Hay – had emerged more or less unscathed. Once was enough, he decided, and if MI6 were ever to come to him again and ask for his cooperation he would simply say 'no, thank you'; as far as he and Freddie de la Hay were concerned, from now on they were civilians, unambiguously so. The tides of history might wash about them, but not carry them off.

To celebrate the safe return of Freddie de la Hay, William had decided to hold a spontaneous party. He had issued the invitations in the form of a short note, urging his neighbours to join him for a glass of wine and 'such food as may be available'. The shortness of the notice had precluded more than a handful of acceptances, but that was exactly what William hoped for: he did not like parties at which crowds prevented anything but shouted conversation, if that. So the guest list in the end was Marcia, Caroline and Jo from the flat below (with Caroline bringing a friend), Basil Wickramsinghe, and Berthea Snark, whom William knew slightly and whom he had encountered by chance in the street a few hours earlier. Eddie had been invited, but had a prior engagement he could not cancel. He had been pleased to be invited, though, and had congratulated his father on getting Freddie de la Hay back. 'Don't do it again, though, Dad,' he said. 'You're far too old for that sort of thing, know what I mean? Take up bowling or something.'

Marcia was the first to arrive, bearing food – the surplus from a finger supper she had catered at the Australian High Commission. 'Such generous hosts,' she said, gesturing to several large trays she had brought with her. 'They always have masses of leftovers.'

William took plates from the cupboard and Marcia began

to arrange the food on them. He watched her, thinking how a man would be so perfectly and comfortably looked after by Marcia; but how would such a man feel? What would they talk about in the darkness at night? What communion of souls could there be between him and her? No, it could not be. Nor had any of those MI6 women been more suitable; he had been foolish in allowing his feelings for them to develop. Tilly Curtain was too young and lived in too different a world; that would never work either. He must find somebody more suitable, and he would. He had a very good feeling about it; he would find somebody.

Shortly after Marcia had finished setting out the Australian leftovers, Caroline arrived with Anthony. They were holding hands, William noticed as he opened the door to them, and he felt a momentary pang. Young love; he remembered what it was like – vaguely. He glanced at Caroline as she introduced Anthony to him; he saw her expression of pride. Later he said to her, 'What happened to James?' And she replied, 'He's busy being James, and doing it rather well.'

William reflected on that. We should all busy ourselves in being who we are, although many of us do not and spend so much time and energy being something else. We try to be what others want us to be, or what we ourselves want to be. And then we suddenly realise that our lives have shot past and we have not got round to being who we really are.

He reflected on this, and then noticed that at the end of the room Marcia was engaged in deep conversation with Basil Wickramsinghe. They appeared to be getting on rather well, as they had the last time they met, and William thought, why not? Basil seemed to be such a lonely man, and so thin too. Marcia would fatten him up. He smiled at the idea, but then he saw her passing Basil a chicken drumstick and realised that his intuition had been right.

And he looked down at Freddie de la Hay, who was lying in a corner, one eye open, watching the human comedy, or that small part of it that was playing out in the room. Dear Freddie, loyal Freddie; for whom there were no great existential questions because he knew at all times, and in all places, what he had to do – which was to do William's bidding and make him happy. That was Freddie's world-view, his *Weltanschauung*, and it was as good as any world-view, thought William. We had to love somebody, and we had to want the best for that person. Freddie knew as much because it was in his nature so to do.

William moved away from his guests. He went back to the window at which he had been standing before the guests arrived. He knew the view so well because he had lived with it so long; it was London, and it was his place. For all its difficulties and its drawbacks, for all its frustrations and failings, it was his place, his beloved place.

We create, he said to himself, *in the places where we live,*
A nest of meaning. And how big or small it is,
Is neither here nor there; a banker
May live in a mansion, a tramp in a cardboard box,
Each is as much a human home, each equally valuable
To its owner; I know a man who sleeps beneath a bridge,
But at night it is his bridge, it is his alone.

341

No man is so poor that he can have no home,
No man so lonely that there is none at all
To love him, to listen to his heart,
To hold him, cherish him, and make him whole.

CORDUROY MANSIONS

Alexander McCall Smith

Welcome to Corduroy Mansions in Pimlico:
comfortably and genteelly weathered, it is home to
a delightfully eccentric cast of Londoners.

At the top lives William, with a faithful ex-vegetarian
dog named Freddie de la Hay and an indolent son who he
hopes will soon fly the nest. Four young women share the first-
floor flat, including twinset-and-pearls Caroline, Dee, vitamin
addict and avid subscriber to *Anti-oxidant News*, and Jenny, a
put-upon PA. And round the corner resides Oedipus Snark MP,
possibly the world's only loathsome Lib Dem, who has
succeeded in offending everyone he knows, and many others
besides. But what dark revenge is being plotted by his mother,
Berthea Snark, and by his girlfriend, Barbara Ragg . . . ?

Abacus
978-0-349-12239-7

THE IMPORTANCE OF BEING SEVEN

A 44 SCOTLAND STREET NOVEL

Alexander McCall Smith

Despite inhabiting a great city renowned for its impeccable restraint, the extended family of 44 Scotland Street is trembling on the brink of reckless self-indulgence. Matthew and Elspeth receive startling – and expensive – news on a visit to the Infirmary, Angus and Domenica are contemplating an Italian *ménage à trois*, and even Big Lou is overheard discussing cosmetic surgery. But when Bertie Pollock – six years old and impatient to be seven – mislays his meddling mother Irene one afternoon, a valuable lesson is learned: that wish-fulfilment is a dangerous business.

Warm-hearted, wise and very funny, *The Importance of Being Seven* brings us fresh and delightful insights into philosophy and fraternity among Edinburgh's most lovable residents.

'A joyous, charming portrait of city life and human foibles, which moves beyond its setting to deal with deep moral issues and love, desire and friendship' *Sunday Express*

Abacus
978-0-349-12316-5

Now you can order superb titles directly from Abacus

☐ Corduroy Mansions	Alexander McCall Smith	£7.99
☐ 44 Scotland Street	Alexander McCall Smith	£7.99
☐ Espresso Tales	Alexander McCall Smith	£7.99
☐ Love Over Scotland	Alexander McCall Smith	£7.99
☐ The World According to Bertie	Alexander McCall Smith	£7.99
☐ The Unbearable Lightness of Scones	Alexander McCall Smith	£7.99

The prices shown above are correct at time of going to press. However, the publishers reserve the right to increase prices on covers from those previously advertised, without further notice.

⸺⸺⸺⸺⸺ ⟨ABACUS⟩ ⸺⸺⸺⸺⸺

Please allow for postage and packing: **Free UK delivery.**
Europe; add 25% of retail price; Rest of World; 45% of retail price.

To order any of the above or any other Abacus titles, please call our credit card orderline or fill in this coupon and send/fax it to:

Abacus, P.O. Box 121, Kettering, Northants NN14 4ZQ
Fax: 01832 733076   Tel: 01832 737526
Email: aspenhouse@FSBDial.co.uk

☐ I enclose a UK bank cheque made payable to Abacus for £ . . . .
☐ Please charge £ . . . . . . to my Visa, Delta, Maestro.

Expiry Date ☐☐☐☐   Maestro Issue No.   ☐☐

NAME (BLOCK LETTERS please) . . . .

ADDRESS . . . .

. . . .

. . . .

Postcode . . . . Telephone . . . .

Signature . . . .

Please allow 28 days for delivery within the UK. Offer subject to price and availability.